PRAISE F

INSTANT #1

"[An] irresistible placement of a complicated family in a bewitching place."
—*The New York Times*

"*The Paper Palace* . . . is a tense, evocative tale of guilt and forgiveness."
—*The Guardian* (London)

"Even the writing seems to drip with secrets and longing. . . . you can't help [but] be just drawn in." —NPR

"An assured debut. A sultry tale of Waspish New England that captures the spirit of Updike and Cheever." —*The Times* (London)

"Beguiling."—*Vogue*

"Nail-biting." —*Town & Country*

"This one's filled with secrets, love, lies and a summer beach house. What more could you ask?"—*Parade*

"[A] page-turner filled with longing and lost love, humor and heartbreak."
—*E! Online*

"The gorgeous scenery of Back Woods (a stand-in for Wellfleet, Mass.) provides an atmospheric backdrop to Elle's ruminations and revelatory flashbacks."
—*Los Angeles Times*

"Ensconced in her family's rustic compound on Cape Cod for an annual summer trip, Elle Bishop is at a crossroads, forced to choose between the two great loves of her life. Should she run off with the longtime bestie she's secretly been in love with since they endured a ghastly childhood trauma together? Or stay with her cherished husband, a dashing Brit who's the father of her kids?" —*People*

"A deeply emotional love story . . . the unraveling of secrets, lies, and a very complex love triangle." —Reese Witherspoon (Reese's Book Club July '21 Pick)

"Tightly woven and immediate, *The Paper Palace* takes us deep into a vivid summer landscape, a family, and a private, longstanding love story, and holds us there from start to finish."

—Meg Wolitzer, *New York Times* bestselling author of *The Interestings* and *The Female Persuasion*

"*The Paper Palace* turned out to be the very page-turner I needed. If you want to learn something about love over a long time—how it can hurt, how it can soar—read this book."

—Mary Beth Keane, *New York Times* bestselling author of *Ask Again, Yes*

"Miranda Cowley Heller has written a magnificent page-turner, a love story that shimmers with desire, intelligence, and humor. Lush and gorgeously written, *The Paper Palace* is as intoxicating as a summer night by the sea. I didn't want it to end."

—Cynthia D'Aprix Sweeney, *New York Times* bestselling author of *Good Company*

"It's been ages since I was so absorbed in a contemporary novel. I loved it."

—Nick Hornby, *New York Times* bestselling author of *Just Like You*

"Set in the physical and psychic landscape of Cape Cod, *The Paper Palace* is a fever dream of a novel, luminous with love and shot through with humor and heartbreak. It is a book that explores the indelibility of childhood, what it means to be shaped by place, and all that is unpredictable about the human heart. I couldn't put it down."

—Adrienne Brodeur, author of *Wild Game*

"A beautifully constructed, wonderfully intelligent, and beguiling novel, rich with a multitude of pleasures." —William Boyd, author of *Any Human Heart*

"It's glorious and gorgeous. I was absolutely immersed and gripped and I'm devastated to have finished it." —Marian Keyes, author of *Lucy Sullivan Is Getting Married*

"In rich and sensuous prose, Cowley Heller cracks open the human heart and exposes her character's choices: the paths not taken and the devastating consequences. I smelled the old cabins and the backwoods, felt the pond water lapping around my ankles, experienced the love and loss of family. A perceptive and powerful story that will stay with me for a long time." —Claire Fuller, author of *Unsettled Ground*

"I can't think of a more brilliant debut than *The Paper Palace*. Enticing, assured, and multilayered, it introduces a major new voice in American fiction . . . A marvel."

—Cressida Connolly, author of *The Happiest Days*

"Absolutely phenomenal novel—dazzling writing and utterly addictive. Read it."
—Rosamund Lupton, *New York Times* bestselling author of *Sister*

"It felt as if I read *The Paper Palace* in one go. It was completely immersive, and shocking, and utterly alive. I loved it." —Nina Stibbe, author of *Love, Nina*

"Beautifully written, richly compelling, *The Paper Palace* is as dark and uncompromising as it is tender and lyrical. Here is a love triangle that keeps you turning the pages, a vivid evocation of place, and an exploration of the one of the most unsettling of secrets." —Rachel Joyce, author of *The Unlikely Pilgrimage of Harold Fry*

"Captivating debut . . . full of lush atmospheric details. This will keep the reader guessing all the way to the end." —*Publishers Weekly*

"The moody and atmospheric setting of the shadowy paths and ponds of the Back Woods is described in lush detail that makes a sharp contrast to the colder, sharper elements of Elle's story. . . . From the first pages of her debut novel, Heller pulls no punches. Some of them just sneak up on you later on." —*Kirkus Reviews*

"A dark, moody, propulsive story, a love triangle decades in the making, with far-reaching implications for every character in the book." —*Booklist*

"A tightly woven and intoxicating exploration of the small decisions that lead to momentous choices . . . Heller has a distinctive ability to ply you with crisp, vivid details and then summarize them in breathtaking, lyrical turns of phrase that make you feel as if you alone have been invited to something special. . . Vivid, luscious, and soaring."
—*Bookreporter*

THE PAPER PALACE

◆

Miranda
Cowley Heller

RIVERHEAD BOOKS · NEW YORK

RIVERHEAD BOOKS
An imprint of Penguin Random House LLC
penguinrandomhouse.com

The Library of Congress has catalogued the Riverhead hardcover edition as follows:

Names: Cowley Heller, Miranda, author.
Title: The paper palace / Miranda Cowley Heller.
Description: New York : Riverhead Books, 2021. |
Identifiers: LCCN 2020045754 (print) | LCCN 2020045755 (ebook) |
ISBN 9780593329825 (hardcover) | ISBN 9780593329849 (ebook)
Subjects: GSAFD: Love stories.
Classification: LCC PS3603.O88945 .P37 2021 (print) |
LCC PS3603.O88945 (ebook) | DDC 813/.6—dc23
LC record available at https://lccn.loc.gov/2020045754
LC ebook record available at https://lccn.loc.gov/2020045755

First Riverhead hardcover edition: July 2021
First Riverhead trade paperback edition: April 2022
Riverhead trade paperback ISBN: 9780593329832
International edition ISBN: 9780593541814

Printed in the United States of America
1 3 5 7 9 10 8 6 4 2

BOOK DESIGN BY LUCIA BERNARD

For Lukas and Felix, my own two loves

And for my grandmother Muriel Maurer Cowley

whose fierce love never wavered

We look before and after,
And pine for what is not:
Our sincerest laughter
With some pain is fraught;
Our sweetest songs are those that tell of saddest thought.

—Percy Bysshe Shelley, "To a Skylark"

Book One

ELLE

1

Today. August 1, the Back Woods.

6:30 A.M.

Things come from nowhere. The mind is empty and then, inside the frame, a pear. Perfect, green, the stem atilt, a single leaf. It sits in a white ironstone bowl, nestled among the limes, in the center of a weathered picnic table, on an old screen porch, at the edge of a pond, deep in the woods, beside the sea. Next to the bowl is a brass candlestick covered in drips of cold wax and the ingrained dust of a long winter left on an open shelf. Half-eaten plates of pasta, an unfolded linen napkin, dregs of claret in a wine bottle, a breadboard, handmade, rough-hewn, the bread torn not sliced. A mildewed book of poetry lies open on the table. "To a Skylark," soaring into the blue—painful, thrilling—replays in my mind as I stare at the still life of last night's dinner. "*The world should listen then, as I am listening now.*" He read it so beautifully. "For Anna." And we all sat there, spellbound, remembering her. I could look at him and nothing else for eternity and be happy. I could listen to him, my eyes closed, feel his breath and his words wash over me, time and time and time again. It is all I want.

Beyond the edge of the table, the light dims as it passes through the screens before brightening over the dappled trees, the pure blue of the pond, the deep-black shadows of the tupelos at the water's edge where the reach of the sun falters this early in the day. I ponder a quarter-inch of thick, stale espresso in a dirty cup and consider drinking it. The air is raw. I shiver under the faded lavender bathrobe—my mother's—that I put on every summer when we return to the camp. It smells of her, and of dormancy tinged with mouse droppings. This is my favorite hour in the Back Woods. Early morning on the pond before anyone else is awake. The sunlight clear, flinty, the water bracing, the whippoorwills finally quiet.

Outside the porch door, on the small wooden deck, sand has built up between the slats—it needs to be swept. A broom leans against the screen, indenting it, but I ignore it and head down the little path that leads to our beach. Behind me, the door hinges shriek in resistance.

I drop my bathrobe to the ground and stand naked at the water's edge. On the far side of the pond, beyond the break of pine and shrub oak, the ocean is furious, roaring. It must be carrying a storm in its belly from somewhere out at sea. But here, at the edge of the pond, the air is honey-still. I wait, watch, listen . . . the chirping, buzzing of tiny insects, a wind that stirs the trees too gently. Then I wade in up to my knees and dive headlong into the freezing water. I swim out into the deep, past the water lilies, pushed forward by exhilaration, freedom, and an adrenaline rush of nameless panic. I have a shadow-fear of snapping turtles coming up from the depths to bite my heavy breasts. Or perhaps they will be drawn by the smell of sex as I open and close my legs. I'm suddenly overwhelmed by the need to get back to the safety of the shallows, where I can see the sandy bottom. I wish I were braver. But I also love the fear, the catch of breath in my throat, my thrumming heartbeat as I step out of the water.

I wring as much as I can from my long hair, grab a threadbare towel from the clothesline my mother has strung between two scraggly pines, lie down on the warm sand. An electric-blue dragonfly lands on my nipple and perches there before moving on. An ant crawls over the Saharan dunes my body has just created in its path.

Last night I finally fucked him. After all these years of imagining it, never knowing if he still wanted me. And then the moment I knew it would happen: all the wine, Jonas's beautiful voice in ode, my husband Peter lying on the sofa in a grappa haze, my three children asleep in their cabin, my mother already at the sink washing dishes in her bright yellow rubber gloves, ignoring her dinner guests. Our eyes lingered one beat too long. I got up from the noisy table, took my underpants off in the pantry, and hid them behind the breadbox. Then I went out the back door into the night. I waited in the shadows, listening to the sounds of plate, water, glass, silver clunking together beneath the suds. Waited. Hoped. And then he was there, pushing me up against the wall of the house, reaching under my dress. "I love you," he whispered. I gasped as he shoved himself into me. And I thought: now there is no turning back. No more regrets for what I haven't done. Now only regrets for what I have done. I love him, I hate myself; I love myself, I hate him. This is the end of a long story.

1966. December, New York City.

I am screaming. I scream and gasp until, at last, my mother realizes something is wrong. She races with me to the doctor's office, imagining herself Miss Clavel as she runs up Park Avenue, terrified, clutching her three-month-old baby. My father is racing, too, briefcase in hand, up

Madison Avenue from the Fred F. French Building. Thoughts stammering, afraid of his own impotence, now, as in everything he does. The doctor tells them there's no time—if they wait, the baby will die—and rips me from my mother's arms. On the operating table, he slices me open across the belly like a ripe watermelon. A tumor has snaked itself around my intestines, and a toxicity of shit has built up behind its iron grasp, pushing poison into my tiny body. The shit always builds up, and surviving it is the key, but this I will not learn for many years.

While the doctor is inside me, he cuts off an ovary, careless, rushing to carve the death out of life. This, too, I will not learn for many years. When I do, my mother cries for me for the second time. "I'm so sorry," she says. "I should have made him be more careful . . ."—as if she'd had the power to change my fate, but chosen not to use it.

Later I lie in a hospital cot, arms tied down at my sides. I scream, cry, alive, livid with rage at this injustice. They will not let my mother feed me. Her milk dries up. Almost a week passes before they free my hands from their shackles. "You were always such a happy baby," my father says. "Afterward," my mother says, "you never stopped screaming."

7:30 A.M.

I roll over onto my stomach, rest my head on my forearms. I love the salty-sweet way my skin smells when I've been lying in the sun—a nut-gold, musky smell, as if I'm being cured. Down the path that leads from the main house to the bedroom cabins I hear a quiet slam. Someone is up. Feet crunch on dry leaves. The outdoor shower is turned on. Pipes groan awake for the day. I sigh, grab my bathrobe from the beach, and head back up to the house.

Our camp has one main building—the Big House—and four one-bedroom cabins along a pine-needled path that hugs the shoreline of the pond. Small clapboard huts, each with a roof pitched to keep the snow off, a single skylight, long clerestory windows on either side. Old-fashioned, rustic, no frills. Exactly what a New England cabin should be. Between the path and the pond is a thin windbreak of trees—flowering clethra, bay and wild blueberry bushes—that protects us from the prying eyes of fishermen and the overenthusiastic swimmers who manage to make it across to our side of the pond from the small public access beach on the far shore. They aren't allowed to come aground, but sometimes they will tread water five feet away, directly in front of our tree line, oblivious to the fact that they are trespassing on our lives.

Down a separate path, behind the cabins, is the old bathhouse. Peeling paint, a rusted enamel sink covered in the beige flecks of dead moths drawn to the overhead light at night; an ancient claw-foot tub that has been there since my grandfather built the camp; an outdoor shower—hot and cold pipes attached to a tupelo tree, water pooling straight into the ground, runneling the sandy path.

The Big House is one large room—living room and kitchen, with a separate pantry—built of cinder blocks and tar paper. Wide-board floors, heavy beams, a massive stone fireplace. On rainy days, we close up the doors and windows and sit inside, listen to the crackle of the fire, force ourselves to play Monopoly. But where we *really* live—where we read, and eat, and argue, and grow old together—is on the screen porch, as wide as the house itself, which faces out to the pond. Our camp isn't winterized. There would be no point. By late September, when the weather turns chilly and all the summer houses have been shut down for the season, the Back Woods is a lonely place—still beautiful in the starker light, but solemn and sepulchral. No one wants to be here once the leaves fall. But when summer breaks again, and the woods are dense, and the blue herons come back to nest and wade in the bright pond, there is no better place on earth than this.

The moment I step back inside, onto the porch, I'm hit by a wave of longing, a quicksilver running through my solar plexus like homesickness. I know I should clear the table before the others come in for breakfast, but I want to memorize the shape of it—re-live last night crumb by crumb, plate by plate, etch it with an acid bath onto my brain. I run my fingers over a purple wine stain on the white linen tablecloth, put Jonas's glass to my lips and try to taste him there. I close my eyes, remembering the slight pressure of his thigh against mine under the table. Before I was sure he wanted me. Wondering, breathless, whether it was accident or intention.

In the main room, everything is exactly as it has always been: pots hanging on the wall above the stove, spatulas on cup hooks, a mason jar of wooden spoons, a faded list of telephone numbers thumbtacked to a bookshelf, two director's chairs pulled up to the fireplace. Everything is the same, and yet, as I cross the kitchen to the pantry, I feel as though I am walking through a different room, more in focus, as if the air itself has just awakened from a deep sleep. I let myself out through the pantry door, stare at the cinder-block wall. Nothing shows. No traces, no evidence. But it was here, we were here, embedding ourselves in each other forever. Grinding, silent, desperate. I suddenly remember my underpants hidden behind the breadbox and am just pulling them on under my bathrobe when my mother appears.

"You're up early, Elle. Is there coffee?" An accusation.

"I was just about to make it."

"Not too strong. I don't like that espresso stuff you use. I know—you think it's better . . ." she says, in a false, humoring voice that drives me insane.

"Fine." I don't feel like arguing this morning.

My mother settles herself in on the porch sofa. It is just a hard horsehair mattress covered in old gray cloth, but it's the coveted place in the house. From here you can look out at the pond, drink your coffee, read your book leaning against the ancient pillows, their cotton covers specked with rust. Who knew that even cloth could grow rusty with time?

It is so typical of her to usurp the good spot.

My mother's hair, straw-blond, now streaked with gray, is twisted up in an absent-minded, messy bun. Her old gingham nightgown is frayed. Yet she still manages to look imposing—like a figurehead on the prow of an eighteenth-century New England schooner, beautiful and stern, wreathed in laurels and pearls, pointing the way.

"I'm just going to have my coffee, and then I'll clear the table," I say.

"If you clear the table, I'll do the rest of the dishes. *Mmmm,*" she says, "thank you," as I hand her a cup of coffee. "How was the water?"

"Perfect. Cold."

The best lesson my mother ever taught me: there are two things in life you never regret—a baby and a swim. Even on the coldest days of early June, as I stand looking out at the brackish Atlantic, resenting the seals that now rear their hideous misshapen heads and draw great whites into these waters, I hear her voice in my head, urging me to plunge in.

"I hope you hung your towel on the line. I don't want to see another pile of wet towels today. Tell the kids."

"It's on the line."

"Because if you don't yell at them, I will."

"I got it."

"And they need to sweep out their cabin. It's a disaster. And don't you do it, Elle. Those children are completely spoilt. They are old enough to . . ."

A bag of garbage in one hand, my coffee cup in the other, I walk out the back door, letting her litany drift off into the wind.

Her worst advice: *Think Botticelli*. Be like Venus rising on a half shell, lips demurely closed, even her nakedness modest. My mother's words of advice when I moved in with Peter. The message arrived on a faded postcard she'd picked up years before in the Uffizi gift shop: *Dear Eleanor, I like your Peter very much. Please make an effort not to be so difficult all the time. Keep your mouth closed and look mysterious. Think Botticelli. Love, Mummy.*

I dump the garbage in the can, slam the lid shut, and stretch the bungee cord tight across it to keep out the raccoons. They are clever creatures with their long dexterous fingers. Little humanoid bears, smarter and nastier than they look. We've been waging war against each other for years.

"Did you remember to put the bungee cord back on, Elle?" My mother says.

"Of course." I smile demurely and start clearing plates.

1969. New York City.

Soon my father will appear. I'm hiding—crouched behind the built-in modular bar that separates our living room from the front hall foyer. The bar is divided into squares. One houses liquor, another the phonograph, another my father's record collection, a few oversize art books, martini glasses, a silver shaker. The section that holds the liquor bottles is open through to both sides like a window. I peer through the bottles, mesmerized by the blur of topaz—the scotch, the bourbon, the rum. I am three years old. Next to me are my father's precious LPs and 78s. I run my finger along their spines, liking the sound I make, breathe in their worn cardboard smell, wait for the doorbell to ring. Finally my father arrives and I don't have the patience to stay hidden. It has been weeks. I hurtle down the hallway, throw myself into his bear-like embrace.

The divorce is not final, but almost. They will have to cross the border into Juárez to do that. The end will come as my older sister Anna and I sit patiently on the edge of an octagonal Mexican-tiled fountain in a hotel lobby, transfixed by the goldfish swimming around an island of dark-leaved tropical plants in its center. Many years later, my mother tells me she called my father that morning, divorce papers in hand, and said, "I've changed my mind. Let's not do this." And though the divorce had been entirely her choice, and though his heart was broken, he said, "No. We've come this far—we might as well finish it, Wallace." *Might as well*: three syllables that changed the course of everything. But in that moment, as I sat feeding the goldfish crumbs from my English muffin, kicking my heels against the Mexican tile, I had no idea a sword hung over my head by a hair. That it could have gone a different way.

But Mexico hasn't happened yet. For now my father is falsely jolly and still in love with my mother.

"Eleanor!" He sweeps me up in his arms. "How's my rabbit?"

I laugh and cling to him with something approaching desperation, my loose blond curls blinding him as I press my face to his.

"Daddy!" Anna comes running now like a bull, angry that I got there first, shoves me out of his arms. She is two years older than me and has more right. He doesn't seem to notice. All he cares about is his own need to be loved. I nudge my way back in.

My mother calls out from somewhere in our sallow prewar apartment, "Henry? Do you want a drink? I'm making pork chops."

"Love one," he booms back, as if nothing between them has changed. But his eyes are sad.

8:15 A.M.

"So, I thought that was a success last night," my mother says from behind a battered novel by Dumas.

"Definitely."

"Jonas was looking well."

My hands tense around the pile of plates I'm holding.

"Jonas is always looking well, Mum." Thick black hair you can grasp in your fists, pale green eyes, skin burnished by sap and pine, a wild creature, the most beautiful man on earth.

My mother yawns. It's her "tell"—she always does this before she says something unpleasant. "He's fine, I just can't stand his mother. So self-righteous."

"She is."

"As if she's the only woman on earth who has ever recycled. And Gina. Even after all these years, I still can't imagine what he was thinking when he married her."

"She's young, she's gorgeous? They're both artists?"

"She *was* young," my mother says. "And the way she flaunts her cleavage. Always prancing around as if she thinks she's the cat's pajamas. Clearly no one ever told her to hide her light under a bushel."

"It's bizarre," I say, going into the kitchen to dump the plates. "Self-esteem. She must have had supportive parents."

"Well, I find it very unattractive," Mum says. "Is there orange juice?"

I take a clean glass from the dish drain, go to the fridge. "As a matter of fact," I call out, "that's probably the reason Jonas fell in love with her.

She must have seemed so exotic to him after the neurotic women he grew up with. Like a peacock in the woods."

"She's from Delaware," my mother says, as if this closes the subject. "No one is from Delaware."

"Exactly," I say, handing her a glass of juice. "She's exotic." But the truth is, I've never been able to look at Gina without thinking: *That's* who he chose? *That's* what he wanted? I picture Gina: her petite, perfect little bee-sting of a body; curated dark roots growing into peroxide blond. Evidently, stonewashed is back.

My mother yawns again. "Well, you have to admit she's not the sharpest knife in the drawer."

"Was there anyone at dinner you *did* like?"

"I'm just being honest."

"Well, don't be. Gina is family."

"Only because you have no choice. She's married to your best friend. You've been oil and water from the day you met."

"That's completely untrue. I've always liked Gina. We might not have a ton in common, but I respect her. And Jonas loves her."

"Have it your way," my mother says with a smug little smile.

"Oh my god." I may have to kill her.

"Didn't you once throw a glass of red wine in her face?"

"No, Mum. I did *not* throw a glass of wine in her face. I tripped at a party and spilled my wine on her."

"You and Jonas were talking the whole night. What were you talking about?"

"I don't know. Stuff."

"He had such a crush on you when you were growing up. I think you broke his heart when you married Peter."

"Don't be ridiculous. He was practically a kid."

"Oh, I think it was more than that. Poor creature." She says this idly as she returns to her book. It's good she isn't looking at me because, in this moment, I know my face is transparent.

Out on the pond the water is absolutely still. A fish jumps and, in its wake, leaves a trail of concentric circles. I watch them bleed out around the edges until they are reabsorbed, as if nothing ever happened.

2

8:45 A.M.

When the table is empty, dishes piled by the sink, I wait for my mother to take her cue to get up and go for her morning swim—leave me alone for ten minutes. I need to sort things out. I need clarity. Peter will be awake soon. The kids will be awake. I am greedy for time. But she holds out her coffee cup.

"Be a saint, will you? Just half a cup."

Her nightgown has ridden up, and from here, I can see everything. My mother believes that wearing underpants to bed is bad for your health. "You need to let yourself air out at night," she told us when we were little. Anna and I, of course, ignored her. The whole idea seemed embarrassing, dirty. The very thought that she had a vagina repulsed us, and, even worse, that it was out there in the open at night.

"He should leave her," my mother says.

"Who?"

"Gina. She's a bore. I almost fell asleep at the table listening to her blather on. She 'makes' art. Really? Why would we care?" She yawns before saying, "They don't have any kids yet—it's not like it's even a real marriage. He might as well get out when he can."

"That's ridiculous. They're completely married," I snap. But even as I'm speaking, I'm thinking: Is she reading my mind?

"I don't know why you're getting so defensive, Elle. He's not *your* husband."

"It's just an idiotic thing to say." I open the icebox door and slam it, slosh milk into my coffee. 'No kids make it not a marriage?' Who *are* you?"

"I'm entitled to my opinion," she says in a calm voice designed to wind me up.

"Lots of married couples never have children."

"Mmhmm."

"Jesus. Your sister-in-law had a radical mastectomy. Does that make her *not a woman*?"

My mother gives me a blank stare. "Have you gone mad?" She heaves herself off the sofa. "I'm going to take my swim. You should go back to bed and start your day over."

I feel like smacking her, but instead I say, "They wanted kids."

"God knows why." She lets the screen door slam behind her.

1970. October, New York.

My mother has sent us next door to her lover's apartment to play with his children while his wife babysits us. They are trying to decide whether or not he should leave his wife. I am older now—not old enough to understand any of this, but old enough to think it odd when I look across the interior courtyard from his apartment into ours and see Mr. Dancy holding my mother in his arms.

In the railroad kitchen, the Dancys' two-year-old son is in his high chair, playing with Tupperware. Mrs. Dancy stares at a pregnant water bug that has rolled onto its back on the doorjamb between the galley kitchen and the dining room. Tiny little roaches are pouring out of it, quickly disappearing into the cracks of the parquet floor. Anna emerges from a back bedroom with Blythe, the Dancys' daughter. Anna is crying. Blythe has cut off all of her bangs with a pair of craft scissors. The top of Anna's forehead is now fringed by a high, uneven crescent of dark brown hair. Blythe's smug, triumphant smile makes me think of mayonnaise sandwiches. Her mother doesn't seem to notice anything. She stares at the exploding bug, a tear rolling down her cheek.

8:50 A.M.

I sit down on the sofa, settle into the warm spot my mother has left in her wake. Already I can see a few figures gathering on the little beach at the far side of the pond. Usually they are renters—tourists who have somehow found their way deep into the woods, and love that they have discovered a secret idyll. *Trespassers,* I think, annoyed.

When we were young, everyone in the Back Woods knew each other. The cocktail party moved from house to house: barefoot women in muumuus, handsome men in white duck trousers rolled up at the ankle, gin and tonics, cheap crackers, Kraft cheddar, mosquitoes swarming, and Cutter—finally, a bug spray that worked. The sandy dirt roads that ran through the woods were stippled with sun filtered through scrub pine and hemlock. As we walked to the beach, fine red-clay dust kicked up, filled with the smell of summer: dry, baked, everlasting, sweet. In the middle of the road, tall beach grasses and poison ivy grew. But we knew what to avoid. When cars passed, they slowed, offered us a ride on the running board or the front hood. It never occurred to anyone that we might fall off, fall under the car. No one worried their children might be sucked into the ocean's rough undertow. We ran around unleashed, swimming in the freshwater kettle ponds that dotted the Back Woods. We called them ponds, but they were actually lakes—some deep and wide, others shallow and clear-bottomed—ancient relics formed at the end of the Ice Age when the glaciers retreated, leaving behind them massive blocks of melting ice heavy enough to dent the earth's crust—hollow deep bowls into the landscape, kettles filled with the purest water. There were nine ponds in our woods. We swam in all of them, crossing other people's property lines to reach small sandy coves, clamber out over the water on the trunks of fallen trees. Cannonball in. No one minded us. Everyone believed in the ancient rights of way: small shaded paths that led to the back doors of old Cape houses, built when the first dirt roads were carved, still standing in sober clearings preserved by snow and sea air and hot summers. And watercress pulled from a stream—someone else's stream, someone else's watercress.

On the bay side, the Cape was pastoral, more civilized. Cranberry bushes, beach plums, and laurels rolled out on the low-lying hills. But here, on the ocean side, it was wild. Violent with crashing surf, and dunes so tall you could run down from a great height, see the ground racing to meet you before you threw yourself into the warm sand. Back then, none of my mother's friends carped, as they do now, accusing children of eroding the dunes just by playing on them—as if their small footprints could possibly compete with the rough winter storms that eat away the land in greedy bites.

Sitting around a beach bonfire at night, grown-ups and children ate sand-crunchy hamburgers covered in ketchup and relish, set up on driftwood tables. Our parents drank gin from jelly jars and disappeared in the darkness beyond the fire's glow to kiss their lovers in the tall beach grass.

Over time, doors began to close. PRIVATE PROPERTY signs came out. The children of the original settlers—the artists and architects and intellectuals who had colonized this place—began to fight each other for time on the Cape. Feuds began over noise on the ponds, over who had more right than whom to love this place. Dogs awoke in the manger. These days even the beaches have been taken over with KEEP OUT signs: huge areas cordoned off to protect nesting shorebirds. Piping plovers are the only creatures left with a right of way. But it is still my woods, my pond. The place I have come to for fifty years—every summer of my life. The place where Jonas and I first met.

From the porch sofa, I watch my mother swimming the mile-long stretch across the pond. Her even strokes, arms slicing the water, an almost mechanical perfection. My mother never looks up when she swims. It's as if she has a sixth sense for where she is going, a migrating whale following an ancient tread. I wonder now, as I often have, whether her sonar picks up more than whale songs. *He should leave her.* Is that what I want? Gina and Jonas are our oldest friends. We have spent almost every summer of our adult lives together: shucked oysters and drank them live from their shells; watched the full moon rising over the sea, while listening to Gina complain that the moon was making her period cramps worse; prayed the local fishermen would start culling the harbor seals; overcooked Thanksgiving turkeys; argued about Woody Allen. Gina is my daughter Maddy's godmother, for fuck's sake. What if Jonas did leave Gina? Could I betray her that way? And yet I already have. I fucked her husband last night. And the thought makes me want to do it again. The mercury-shimmer of it shudders through me.

"Hey, wife." Peter kisses the back of my neck.

"Hey, yourself." I start, struggle for normal.

"You looked deep in thought," he says.

"There's coffee."

"Excellent." He roots around in his shirt pocket and pulls out his cigarettes. Lights one. Sits down on the sofa beside me. I love the way his long legs look poking out from his faded surf shorts. Boyish. "I can't believe you let me fall asleep on the sofa last night."

"You were exhausted."

"It must have been the jet lag."

"I totally get it," I say, rolling my eyes at him. "That one-hour time difference between here and Memphis nearly killed me."

"It's true. I could barely wake up this morning. The clock said nine a.m., but I swear it felt like eight."

"Funny."

"I drank too much."

"Understatement."

"Did I do anything stupid?"

"Other than refuse to read the Shelley poem for Anna and pick a fight about Quakers?"

"Well, everyone agrees they're basically fascists," he says. "Such a violent people."

"You're an ass." I kiss him on his lovely scruffy cheek. "You need to shave."

He shoves his glasses up his nose, runs his hand through his curly dark blond hair, now graying at the temples, trying to make some order out of it. My husband is a handsome man. Not beautiful, but handsome in an old-fashioned movie star way. Tall. Elegant. British. A respected journalist. The kind of man who looks sexy in a suit. An Atticus. Patient, but formidable when angered. He can keep a secret. He rarely misses a beat. He's looking at me now as if he can smell the sex on me.

"Where are the kids?" Peter grabs one of the large white sea-clam shells that line the screen-window ledge, turns it bowl side up, crushes out his cigarette.

"I let them sleep in. My mother hates it when you do that." I take the shell from him, carry it into the kitchen, dump the butt into the trash, rinse it. My mother has almost reached the far shore.

"Jesus, that woman can swim," Peter says.

The only person I've ever known who could beat my mother in a race was Anna. Anna didn't swim across the pond—she flew. Left everyone behind her. I follow an osprey as it wings its way through the sky, chased by a small black bird. Wind ruffles the lily pads on the pond's surface. They sigh, exhale.

9:15 A.M.

Peter is in the kitchen scrambling eggs. From the porch, I smell onions frying. A pile of thick applewood-smoked bacon drains its grease into a fold of paper towels on the counter. There's nothing better than bacon and eggs for a hangover. Actually, there's nothing better than bacon. Food of the gods. Like arugula and unfiltered olive oil and Patak's Brinjal pickle. My desert island-disc foods. That, and pasta. I've often fantasized about surviving alone on a desert island. How I would live on fish; build a tree house high off the ground, so that no wild animals could get to me; become really fit. In my fantasy, there's always a *Complete Works of Shakespeare* that has somehow washed up on the beach, and with nothing else to do to pass the days, I read (and care about) every single line. I am forced by circumstance to at last become my best self—that supposed potential self. My other fantasies were prison or the army: someplace where I had no choice, where every second of my day was proscribed, where I was too afraid to fail. Self-education and a hundred push-ups and nibbled portions of dry biscuits with fresh water—these were my childhood dreams. Jonas didn't come into the picture until later.

I wander into the kitchen and reach for a piece of bacon. Peter slaps my hand away.

"No picking." He stirs shredded cheese into the eggs, grinds fresh pepper.

"Why are you using the deep saucepan?" I hate the way British people cook eggs. It's obvious: a nonstick frying pan and lots of butter. This stupid, soupy, slow-cooking method leaves me a pan that is completely impossible to wash. I'll have to soak it for two days. "*Grr.*" I poke him with a spatula.

Peter's shirt is covered in splatters of grease. "Fuck off, gorgeous. I'm making the eggs." He walks over to the breadbox, grabs a loaf of sliced bread. "Toast this, please."

I feel my face redden, the sudden flush of heat as I picture my underpants crumpled behind the breadbox, a heap of black lace, the nakedness under my skirt, the way his finger traced a line up my thigh.

"Hello? Earth to Elle."

My mother's toaster holds two slices at a time. It burns the bread on one side, leaves it raw on the other. I turn the oven on to Broil and start lining up bread on a cookie sheet. I pick up a stick of butter, not quite sure whether to butter first or later.

"What's our timing?"

"Eight minutes," Peter says. "Twelve most. Go get the kids up."

"We should wait for Mum."

"The eggs will get tough."

I look out at the pond. "She's halfway back."

"You swim, you lose."

"K. You deal with the fallout." When my mother feels slighted, she makes very sure everyone else in the vicinity feels equally afflicted. But Peter doesn't give a shit about her shit. He just laughs at her, tells her to stop being such a loon, and for whatever reason, she takes it.

1952. New York City.

My mother was eight years old when *her* mother, Nanette Saltonstall, married for the second time. Nanette was a New York socialite—selfish and beautiful, famous for her lush, cruel lips. As a child, my grandmother Nanette had been wealthy—pampered by her banker father. But the Crash changed everything. Her family moved from their Fifth Avenue townhouse into a dark railroad apartment in Yorkville, where the one luxury my great-grandfather George Saltonstall still indulged in was his six p.m. vodka martini stirred with a long sterling silver spoon in a crystal shaker. Their eldest daughter's beauty was the only currency they had left: Nanette would marry a rich man and save the family. That was the plan. Instead she went to a fashion design school in Paris and fell in love with my grandfather, Amory Cushing, a Boston Brahmin but penniless sculptor, whose sole collateral was a rambling old Cape house on the shores of a remote freshwater kettle pond in the Massachusetts woods. He had inherited the house *and* the pond from a distant uncle.

Grandfather Amory built *our* camp during the short time he and my grandmother were in love. He chose a long narrow stretch of shoreline, hidden from his own house by a sharp curve in the land. He had an idea to rent the cabins out in summer for extra money to support his glamorous young wife and two small children. On the outside, the cabins are solid—watertight saltboxes that have withstood endless harsh winters, nor'easters, and generations of squabbling families. But my grandfather was running low on funds, so he built the interior walls and ceilings out of pressed paperboard, Homasote, cheap and utilitarian, and nicknamed the camp the Paper Palace. What he didn't count on was that my grandmother would leave him before he had finished building it. Or that Homasote is delicious to mice, who chew holes through the walls each winter and feed the regurgitated paper, like a breakfast of muesli, to the minuscule babies they birth inside the bureau drawers. Every summer, the person who opens the camp has the job of emptying mouse nests into the woods. You can't really begrudge the mice: Cape winters are hard, as the Pilgrims discovered. But mouse piss has a warm stink, and I have always hated the terrified squeaks of dismay as they fall from the wooden drawers into the scrub.

After she divorced my grandfather, Granny Nanette spent a few months swanning around Europe, sunning herself topless in Cadaqués, drinking cold sherry with married men, while Mum and her little brother Austin waited in hotel lobbies. When her money ran out, Nanette decided it was time to go home and do what her parents had wanted her to do in the first place. So she married a banker. Jim. He was a decent sort of fellow. Andover and Princeton. He bought Nanette an apartment overlooking Central Park and a long-haired Siamese cat. Mum and Austin were sent to fancy Manhattan private schools where first-grade boys were required to wear a jacket and tie, and Mum learned to speak French and make Baked Alaska.

The week before her ninth birthday, my mother performed her first blow job. First, she watched as little Austin, his tiny six-year-old hands shaking, held their stepfather's penis until it got hard. Jim told them it was all very natural, and didn't they want to make him happy? The worst part, my mother said, when she finally told me this story, was the sticky white ejaculate. The rest she could, perhaps, have dealt with. That, and she hated the warmth of his penis, the slight urine smell of it. Jim threatened them with violence if they ever told their mother. They told her anyway, but she accused them of lying. Nanette had nowhere else to go, no money of her own. When she found her husband in the maid's room off the kitchen screwing the nanny, she told him not to be vulgar and shut the door.

One Saturday, Nanette came home early from lunch at the Club. Her friend Maude had a headache and my grandmother didn't feel like going to the Frick on her own. The apartment was empty—just the cat, who curled around her ankles at the front door, arching his back seductively. She dumped her fur coat on the bench, took off her high heels, and headed down the hallway to her bedroom. Jim was sitting in a wingback chair, pants around his ankles. My mother was on her knees in front of him. My grandmother strode over to them and slapped my mother hard across the face.

My mother told me this story when I was seventeen. I was in a rage because she had given Anna money to buy a new lip gloss at Gimbels, while I stayed home and did chores. "Oh, for heaven's sake, Elle," she said as I stood at the kitchen sink, fuming over a pile of dishes. "You have to wash a plate . . . you don't get a lipstick. I had to give my stepfather blow jobs. All Austin had to do was masturbate him. What can I tell you? Life's not fair."

9:20 A.M.

The odd thing is, I think now as I walk down the path toward the kids' cabin, my mother lost her respect for women but not for men. Her stepfather's perversion was a hard truth, but it was her mother's weak-willed betrayal that made her go cold. In my mother's world, the men are given the respect. She believes in the glass ceiling. Peter can do no wrong. "If you want to make Peter happy when he comes home from work," Mum advised me years ago, "put on a fresh blouse, put in your diaphragm, and smile."

Think Botticelli.

3

1971. April, New York.

Mr. Dancy stares into a small square tub in the maid's-room bath off the sunless kitchen of our apartment. Mrs. Dancy has moved out of the building. Mr. Dancy visits us often, his shirt-sleeves rolled up to reveal his muscular arms. The enamel faucets he closes now have letters on them, H and C. The old brass drain shines from underneath the cool water. A tiny alligator is swimming around the tub. Mr. Dancy bought it in Chinatown for his children as a pet. He was told it was a species of alligator that would never grow more than a foot long. Now he has learned he was conned. The alligator is just a baby alligator. Soon it will grow to be dangerous. Even here in this little tub it has a menacing light in its eyes. I lower a wooden chopstick into the water and watch it snap angrily in frightened, futile little grabs.

"Give me the stick," Anna says, leaning perilously close to the water. "Give it!" Her long black braid trails the top of the water like a lure.

I hand it over to her and she jabs at the creature. Mr. Dancy watches, strokes his thick butterscotch mustache. After a while, he lifts the baby alligator from the water by its nubbly tail and holds it over the toilet bowl. It writhes in the air, snapping at his wrist. I watch in fascination as he drops it in the toilet and flushes it down.

"We couldn't keep it," he says. "It would have grown into a monster."

"Carl," my mother calls from somewhere in the apartment, "do you want a drink? Supper is almost ready."

1971. June, New York.

Anna's and my first week in our father's new apartment. It is a grubby walk-up on Astor Place, but he makes it seem exotic and adventurous. The air is heavy, hot, no air conditioning—the wiring is too old for that—but he has gotten us our own rotating fan. And he promises, as soon as he gets his next paycheck, he will buy us each an International Doll. I want Holland. He promises us many wonderful things that we will eventually learn not to expect. "From here on out, it's just me and my girls." We jump up and down on our new trundle bed, dance to the Monkees, and eat Dannon blueberry yogurts. If you keep stirring the fruit up from the bottom the yogurt becomes darker and darker, he tells us when he turns on the evening news.

On Monday morning, our father dresses himself with precision in a blue pinstripe Brooks Brothers suit and brown wing tips that he shines to a high gloss with a chamois. He smells of Old Spice and shaving foam. He looks at himself in the hall mirror, parts his hair with a small tortoiseshell comb, adjusts his tie so it sits exactly right between his starched collars, pulls his cuffs, centers his gold cuff links. "Your father was famously handsome when he was young," our mother tells us. "They called him the Belle of the Ball when he played football at Yale. That silly game ruined his knees."

I hold on to the edge of his suit jacket as we go down the dark creaking staircase. My hair is a tangled mess. No one has reminded me to brush it. I have a nervous feeling in my stomach. Today is our first day at Triumph Day Camp. Anna and I are taking the bus alone. We are both wearing our camp uniforms: navy blue shorts and white T-shirts that say *TRIUMPH* on the front. On the back, they say *All Girls Are Champions*.

"There are very few girls in the world who are lucky enough to wear a shirt like that," our father tells us. On the way to the bus, he stops at Chock full o'Nuts and buys us cream cheese and date-nut bread sandwiches for our lunch. I don't want him to be mad at me, but the tears come on their own, betraying me. I hate cream cheese, I say, when he asks me what's wrong. He tells me he's sure I will like it, and hands me the paper bag. I can see he's annoyed and it worries me. When he loads us onto the camp bus, I beg him not to make me go. He can't be in two places at once, he says. He has to earn a living. Book reviews to write. Time-Life is waiting. But he'll be right here waiting for us when the bus comes back. And I will love camp, he promises.

As the bus pulls into Sixth Avenue traffic, I watch him getting smaller and smaller. I tear a piece of paper off the edge of my lunch bag and chew it into a ball. What will I do if I need to pee? How will I know where to go? I want a swim badge, but I'm not allowed in over my head. Anna chats to the little girl next to her, ignoring me, and eats half her sandwich before the bus reaches Westchester.

Triumph Day Camp is on a lake. We drive in past baseball diamonds, a field covered in big dart boards, a giant teepee. The driver pulls in behind a long line of yellow buses. The parking lot is a sea of girls. All of them wearing the same Triumph T-shirts.

My counselors introduce themselves as June and Pia. They both wear Triumph shirts, but theirs are bright red.

"Welcome, *five-to-sevens*! For those of you who are new: if you need to find us, look for our red shirts," June says. "Raise your hand if you were at Triumph last year."

Most of the girls in my group raise their hands.

"Then you are *already* champions!! First things first. Let's head over to your cubbies to put away our lunches. We're in Little Arrow." She lines us up behind her, leads us to a big brown building. Pia walks at the back of the line. "To make sure there are no stragglers. Rule number one: Never, *ever* leave your group. But if you ever do get separated, don't move. Sit down right where you are and wait. One of us will come back for you," Pia tells us.

On the edge of each cubby is a piece of masking tape with our names and birthday written in marker. *Eleanor Bishop, September 17, 1966.* I bite my finger. Now they will all know I haven't even turned five yet and they won't want to play with me. Barbara Duffy has the cubby next to mine. She is seven and has a Beatles lunch box.

"Grab your knapsacks!" June calls out. We'll have a potty break and then change into our bathing suits. Who here knows how to tread water? That's the art studio." She points as we pass a room that smells of construction paper and paste.

The changing room is lined with little curtained stalls. I go into a stall and pull the curtain shut. I'm in my underpants before I realize my father has forgotten to pack me a bathing suit. By the time I get dressed again, everyone has already gone to the lake. I sit down on a wooden bench.

June and Pia don't notice I'm missing until snack time, when they do the after-swim head count. From the changing room, I hear them calling my name again and again. A whistle blows, shrill and panicky. "Everyone out of the water," I hear a lifeguard scream. "Now!"

I sit quietly, waiting for someone to come back for me.

9:22 A.M.

The cabin steps—three old pine planks attached by struts that have been on the verge of rusting-through since before I was born—bow under my weight. I bang on the kids' door. It is one of those metal-framed doors with screens and glass windows that can be raised or lowered and, with a satisfying click, slot into place. My three children are tucked safely into their beds, the brightly painted yellow floor covered in wet towels and bathing suits. My mother is right. They really are pigs.

"*Oi!* Breakfast!" I pound on the door. "Up and out."

Jack, my eldest, turns in his bed, gives me a look of cold disdain, and pulls his scratchy wool blanket over his head. He is being forced to bunk in with the little kids for a few nights while my mother fumigates his cabin for carpenter ants. Seventeen is a vile age.

The younger two emerge, bleary-eyed, from their cocoons, blinking in the morning light.

"Five more minutes," Maddy groans. "I'm not even hungry." Madeline is ten years old. Astonishingly beautiful, like my mother. But unlike most of the women in our family, she is small-boned and delicate, with pale English rose skin, Peter's gray eyes, and Anna's thick, dark hair. Every time I look at her I wonder how this creature came out of me.

Finn climbs out of bed in his sweet saggy underpants, rubs the sand out of his eyes. God, I love him. His cheeks have tiny sleep wrinkles on them from the pillowcase. He's only nine—still on the verge of being a small boy. But soon he, too, will come to treat me with utter contempt.

When Jack was born, I looked at the tiny baby in my arms, suckling, pig-perfect, kissed his eyelids and said, "I love you so much, and someday, no matter what I do, you will hate me. At least for a little while." It's a fact of life.

"Okay, my lovelies. Come, don't come. But your father is making eggs, and you know what that means."

"A total nightmare and a huge fucking mess," Jack says.

"Correct." I bang down the stairs. "Language," I call over my shoulder as I head down the pine-needled path.

I wait until my cabin door slams shut behind me before allowing myself to take the breath I've been holding since Peter startled me on the porch. The normalcy of everything in our room seems impossible: clothes hung on ancient metal hangers along a makeshift wooden pole. Our oak dresser with a bottom drawer that sticks when it rains. The bed where Peter and I have slept for so many years, curled together like fiddleheads, entwined in sweat and sex and kisses, his sweet-sour smell. He has left the bed unmade.

I hang my bathrobe on a rusty nail that serves as a hook. Next to it is a cloudy full-length mirror aged by half a century of moisture and frost. I have always been grateful for its dim reflection, its pockmarks. I can look at myself through a mottled scrim of silver that hides my bumps and imperfections: the jagged scar on my chin that has been there since the night Peter and I were burglarized; the long thin scar that splits me across my belly, still visible after fifty years; the small white scar beneath it.

Jack came right away. But after Jack, nothing. No matter how hard we tried, what position, legs up, legs down, relaxed or tense, bottom or top. Nothing. At first I thought it was Jack. Maybe something had torn during my labor. Or maybe I loved him too much to allow myself to share him. In the end, the doctor made a small cut above my pubic bone and put a camera inside me, plumbing for answers.

"Well, young lady," he said when I came out of anesthesia, "someone made quite a mess in there when you were a baby. It's like a Spaghetti Western with all that scar tissue. What's worse, the surgeon managed to chop off your left ovary in the process. But there's some good news," he said as I started to cry. "Your healthy tube had a kink—got tacked to a bit of scar tissue. Eggs were piling up behind it. I've cut it free."

Maddy was born a year later. And Finn eleven months after that.

"Congratulations," the doctor said to me and Peter as I lay on the exam table. "You're having Irish twins."

"*Irish* twins?" Peter said. "That's not possible."

"Of course it is," the doctor said.

"Well," Peter said. "If you're right, I'm going to find the drunken Irishman who fucked my wife and throw him off the highest cliff in Kilkenny straight into the sea."

"Kilkenny is landlocked," the doctor said. "I was there for a golf tournament a few years back."

I position myself in the largest remaining patch of mirror and stare at my naked body, assessing it, looking for something on the outside that might give away the truth, the panic inside me, the hunger, the regret, the breathless desire for more. But all I can see is the lie.

"Breakfast!" Peter shouts from the Big House. "Chop-chop."

I pull on my bathing suit, grab a sarong, and sprint down the path, banging on the kid's door. As I near the Big House I check myself, slow to a walk. It's unlike me to snap to attention, as Peter well knows. I push through a thicket of bushes onto the damp shoreline, dig my toes into the wet sand. Out on the pond, my mother's steady scissors kicks leave a white trail behind her. The water is blue-ing up. Soon even the transparent brown-greens of the shallows will be mirrored over. For those few hours at least, the minnows and largemouth bass hovering over their sandy crop-circle nests will be invisible. What lies beneath will be hidden from us.

1972. June, the Back Woods.

I am running through the woods in my cotton nightgown along the narrow path that connects our camp to my grandfather Amory's house. The path follows the shape of the land uphill and down around the pond's ragged shoreline. My father cut it between our two properties when he and my mother were first together. Granddaddy Amory calls it the "Intellectual's Path" because, he says, it wanders around and around without ever getting to the point. Where the path approaches my grandfather's house there is a steep downhill run. I race along it, careful not to stub my bare toes on the stumps of the bushes my father cut down. Those nasty little stumps are my father's only other legacy to this place.

I tiptoe past my grandfather's bedroom window, careful not to disturb him, then sprint to the end of his wooden dock. I sit down, dangle my feet in the water, scratch my itchy stomach, try my best to sit perfectly still. Microscopic bubbles cover my feet in a carbonated sheath. Soon they will come. Hold still. Don't move. Let your feet be lures. Then the swift dart from the shadows. Their courage gets the best of their fear, and at last I feel a little sucking feeling. One by one the sunfish are kissing my feet, sucking off little bits of dead skin and the crumbs of forest floor that have attached themselves to me. I love the sunfish. They are the color of pond water, with dappled backs and sweet, pursed lips. Every morning I bring them this breakfast of fresh feet.

My mother and Mr. Dancy are still in bed when I get home. Their cabin has a plate-glass window overlooking the pond. I run into their room without knocking, jump up and down on their bouncy mattress with my wet, sandy feet. My nightgown rises into the air every time I come back to earth.

"Out," Mr. Dancy growls in a half sleep. "Wallace, Jesus Christ."

Through the window I see Anna and her best summer-friend Peggy in the water, splashing each other. Peggy has orange hair and freckles.

"What are those?" My mother points at my belly. "Hold still!"

I stop jumping, pull up my nightgown, and let her examine my stomach. It is covered in red spots.

"Oh, for god's sake," she says. "Chicken pox. How did this happen? I'd better go check Anna."

"They itch," I say and flip off the bed.

"Stay here," my mother orders. "I'll get the calamine lotion."

"I want to go swimming."

"Stay in this room. I don't need you infecting Peggy."

I push past her and make a run for the door.

Mr. Dancy snatches my arm, hard. "You heard your mother."

I try to pull away, but his grip tightens.

"Carl, stop. You're hurting her," my mother says.

"She needs to be controlled."

"Please," Mum says. "She's five."

"Don't tell me how to do my job."

"Of course not," Mum says, placating.

He throws off the covers and starts pulling on his clothes. "If I want to deal with spoiled brats, I'll go spend time with my own kids."

"What are you doing?" My mother's voice sounds tight, high-pitched.

"I'll see you back in the city. This place makes me antsy."

"Please, Carl."

The door slams behind him.

"Do. Not. Move," Mum says. "If I find you out of this room there will be hell to pay." And races out to stop him.

I sit down on the bed, watch Anna putting on a mask and snorkel. She squats down at the water's edge, her back to the pond, dips her mask in the pond, empties it, spits in it. Behind her, Peggy wades out into deeper water. With every step, a few more inches of her disappear. A car engine starts up. I hear my mother shouting, her voice getting fainter and fainter as she runs up the driveway, chasing Mr. Dancy's car. I watch as the bottom of Peggy's red pigtail disappears. Now only her head is above water, floating, disembodied. Now only the top of her head, like a turtle's back. Now Peggy is a trail of bubbles. I imagine the suckerfish, giving her their soft kisses. The bubbles stop. I wait for her to reappear. I bang on the glass, trying to get Anna's attention. I know she can hear me, but she doesn't bother to look up. I bang again, harder now. Anna sticks her tongue out at me, sits down on the beach to pull on her yellow flippers.

4

10:00 A.M.

There are already five cigarette butts in the ashtray next to Peter. A Camel Light dangles from his mouth. He drinks his coffee through it, unaware. No hands. Like a carny trick. A thin trail of smoke drifts from his lower lip as he swallows. He reaches into his shirt pocket and takes out an orange Bic lighter, worries it over and over in his hand like a string of prayer beads, turns the newspaper page, gropes blindly for a piece of bacon. If it were possible to smoke in his sleep, he would. When we were first together, I hounded him, begged him to stop. But it was like asking a chicken to fly. I want to save his life, God knows, but he's the only one who can do that.

The kids have sprawled themselves over the couch, glued to their screens, white chargers in every outlet, their dirty plates still on the table, my mother's tattered novel kicked to the floor. All of the bacon and most of the eggs have been eaten. I watch my mother wade out of the pond, shake the water off. Bright droplets arc through the sky. She lets her hair down out of its chignon, squeezes it, then quickly twists it right back up again, clips it into place with a barrette. She reaches for an old mint-green towel she's hung on the branch of a tree and wraps it around herself. I take a bite of my toast. At seventy-three, she is still beautiful.

The morning Peggy drowned, I stood almost where I am now, watching her evaporate into the water. And then my mother was there, still in her negligee, screaming at Anna, splashing into the pond, diving under. When she came up, she had Peggy by the hair. Peggy was pale blue. My mother dragged her back to shore by her pigtail, banged on her chest, and kissed air into her mouth until Peggy gulped and gasped and vomited back to life. Mum had been a lifeguard when she was a girl and she knew a secret: that some drowning victims can come back from the dead. I watched. While my mother played God. While Mr. Dancy drove out of our lives forever. While Anna poked a branch at Peggy's feet, trying to wake her.

Now I watch my mother lift her face into the warm breeze. The backs of her arms have age spots. Spider veins break the surface of the skin behind her knees and thighs. She looks around blankly, then gives a little shrug that I recognize as "Aha!" and picks up her prescription sunglasses from the end of the canoe where she left them. I've seen all this a hundred times before, but this morning she seems different. Older. And it makes me sad. There is something eternal about my mother. She's a pain in the ass, but she has great dignity. She reminds me of Margaret Dumont from the Marx Brothers movies. She doesn't take on airs, she has them naturally. We should have waited for her for breakfast.

"Can you pass the toast, or have the locusts finished that as well?" Mum says, coming onto the porch and pulling up a chair.

Peter peers over his newspaper. "Good swim, Wallace?"

"Hardly. The bladderwort is back. It's those damned fishermen. They drag it in on the bottoms of their boats from God knows where."

"Nevertheless, you're looking radiant this morning."

"Pish," Mum says, reaching for a piece of toast. "Flattery will get you nowhere. And it certainly won't bring the bacon back."

"Then I shall get up and make you some."

"Your husband's in an unusually good mood today," Mum says to me.

"I am indeed," Peter says.

"You must be the only person in the world who's ever been *improved* by a trip to Memphis."

"I do so adore you, Wallace." Peter laughs.

I get up from the table. "I'll make more bacon. And eggs. Those are cold."

"God, no!" Mum says. "And create an even bigger pile of dishes? Is there a single pot you didn't use?"

"Scrambled or soft-boiled?" I'm hating her again already. "Jack, clear those plates off the table and bring your grandmother the marmalade."

"Maddy, go get Wallace the marmalade," Jack says to his sister without looking up. My mother has always insisted that the kids call her by her first name. "I'm not ready to be a grandmother," she said before Jack had even started to talk. "And I certainly hope you aren't expecting me to babysit."

Maddy ignores Jack.

"Guys? Hello?" I actually put my hands on my hips.

"You're already up," Jack says to me. "You get it."

I hold my breath for ten seconds, trying not to explode. I am underwater, watching the fish through murky green. I close my eyes. I am Peggy. I choose the quiet of the reeds.

Peter lights another cigarette. "Jack, do what your mother says. Stop acting the fool."

"Yes, Jack," Mum agrees. "You're behaving like an asshole. That sort of behavior is unbecoming."

1956. Guatemala.

My grandmother Nanette moved to Central America after her third husband left her. She had divorced the monstrous Jim at last, but she had no way of surviving in the world without a man to support her. Vince Corcoran was her way out—a millionaire, which in those days meant something. Vince had made his fortune in import/export—fruit and coffee. He wasn't handsome, but he was a genuinely good man—bighearted, kind to the children, madly in love with their mother. She had married him for his money. She couldn't stand the way his breath smelled, and when they had sex, big drops of sweat would fall on her face from his brow. It disgusted her. She was mortified that she had stooped to marrying a banana salesman, but she had a townhouse in Gramercy Park and a cabernet Rolls-Royce. Vince divorced her after reading this in her journal, or so the story goes. All Granny Nanette got in the settlement was the car, a small monthly stipend, and a massive villa in Guatemala she had never even seen. Vince had won it from a colleague several years back in a poker game. So Nanette, a single woman, barely thirty-three years old, three times divorced, left her New York socialite life behind: sold her furs, packed up her leather trunks, piled Wallace and Austin, aged twelve and ten, into the Rolls-Royce, and drove all the way to a remote valley on the outskirts of Antigua, a small and beautiful Spanish colonial city that sat in the shade of volcanoes.

Casa Naranjal was a crumbling, iguana-infested estate. Its lands were filled with orange, lime, and avocado orchards. Jacarandas burst into lavender fireworks in the spring. Clusters of bananas hung heavy under rattling fronds. In the rainy season the river swelled, then broke its banks. The estate was walled off from the prying eyes of the local villagers. Don Ezequiel, a toothless old man, guarded its massive wooden gates. Most days, he sat in the shade of an adobe hut eating frijoles on the blade of a knife. My mother loved to sit beside him on the hard earthen floor and watch him eating.

Along with the estate, Granny Nanette had inherited a small staff of servants, a private cook, and three horses that roamed the property untethered. A handsome dark-haired gardener, dressed only in white, picked mangosteens for their breakfast, chased armadillos off the lawns, and fished large worms out of the black-bottomed pool. My grandmother spent her days locked away in her bedroom, terrified of the strange world that had saved her, unable to communicate with anyone but her two children. Her bedroom was on the upper floor of an octagonal tower covered in purple bougainvillea. Directly underneath was a grand living room with soaring ceilings and massive doors that opened onto the landscape. The closest the kids ever got to their mother during the day was the sound of her pacing back and forth above them on the Saltillo floor.

A colonnaded terrace connected the living room to the kitchen, where every morning the cook prepared the masa for tortillas and crushed green tomatoes into salsa verde. Gilded birdcages filled with brilliant-colored parrots and cockatiels were strung between the terraced arches. Wallace and Austin would eat alone at the long dining table, feeding the birds bits of their fried plantains while the parrots chattered to them in Spanish. Mum has always claimed this was how she learned to speak Spanish. Her first words were "*Huevos revueltos? Huevos revueltos?*"

For three months, the children never went to school. Granny Nanette had no idea how to arrange it. (My mother loves to tell me this any time I express worry over my children's education. "Don't be so ordinary, Elle," she says. "It doesn't become you. Slide rules are for the meager." An attitude largely informed by the fact that she can barely add, as I like to point out.)

Austin was afraid to leave the grounds, so Mum wandered around on her own with an old Leica her father had given her, taking photographs of white bulls in the empty fields; wild horses in dry riverbeds, their rib cages swollen from hunger; scorpions hiding in the shade of the woodpile; her brother drinking Limonada by the pool. Her favorite place was the graveyard outside the village. She loved the caged madonnas, the spicy marigolds brought in armfuls by the villagers, the pink-stucco tombstones that looked like dollhouse cathedrals, the paper flowers draped over painted crypts—turquoise, tangerine, lemon-yellow—whatever was the favorite color of the deceased. She would go to the cemetery to read, curled up in the shade of a tomb, comforted by the souls of the dead.

Most afternoons, my mother rode her favorite horse across the valley and over a steep hill into Antigua. She would tie her horse to a post and wander the cobbled streets, explore the ruins of the ancient churches and monasteries, long ago destroyed by earthquakes, still scattered throughout the city. She loved the milagros that the old women sold in the main square to hang on silver chains—tiny charms: amputated legs and arms, eyes, a pair of lungs, a bird, a heart. Afterward, she would go into the cathedral and burn incense, praying for nothing.

One evening, as she was riding home to the valley down a steep trail that narrowed between two boulders, a man stepped out from behind the rocks, blocking her way. He took the reins of her horse and told her to get down. He put his hand on his machete, stroked his crotch. She sat there, cowlike, mute. *Enough of this,* she thought. She kicked her horse hard in the gut and ran straight over the man. She says she still remembers hearing the crack of his leg bone, the squelch of the horse's hooves in his stomach. That night at dinner, over a bowl of turkey soup, she told her mother what she had done.

"I hope you killed him," Granny Nanette said, dipping a tortilla into her soup. "But Wallace, dear," she added, "that sort of behavior is unbecoming in a girl."

10:15 A.M.

The shock of being called an asshole by his grandmother has gotten Jack up off the sofa. I should try it, but it would only devolve into a hideous shouting match that would leave me in tears and Jack in adolescent triumph. I don't have my mother's haughty gravitas.

My cell phone buzzes. Peter reaches across the table and picks it up before I can get to it. "Jonas is texting you." He clicks on the message.

Fuck, fuck, fuck, fuck. My heart stops beating.

"They want to meet us at Higgins Hollow. They're saying eleven. They'll bring sandwiches."

Thank you, God.

"I have a horrible feeling I made a plan with Gina last night before I passed out," Peter says.

"Do we really want to spend hours on the beach? I'd rather lie in the hammock in a heap."

"I don't want to be rude. Gina can get a bit chippy."

"She won't care. We're all nursing hangovers." But I sound disingenuous even to myself.

Peter drains his coffee. "It has forever amazed me. Jonas is a brilliant painter. Successful. Looks like a bloody screen idol. He could have married Sophia-fucking-Loren. I think he hooked up with Gina just to irritate his mother."

"Well, that was a worthy cause, anyway," my mother says.

Peter laughs. He loves it when my mother is bitchy.

"The *two* of you," I say. "Enough."

"So, chickadees? You up for the beach?" Peter says.

"When's low tide?" Maddy asks.

Peter turns the local paper over and runs his finger down the tide chart. "1:23."

"Can we bring the boogie boards?" Finn asks.

"*May* we," my mother corrects him.

"I'm not coming," Jack says. "I'm meeting Sam at the Racing Club."

"How are you planning to get there?" I ask.

"I'll take your car."

"Not happening. You'll have to take your bike."

"Are you kidding me? It's, like, fifteen miles."

"Last time you drove my car you forgot to fill it and I almost ran out of gas. I *limped* to the Texaco station."

"We already made the plan. He'll be waiting."

"Text him. Tell him the plan's changed."

"*Mom.*"

"End of subject." My cell phone buzzes again. This time I get there first. "Yes to beach?" Jonas is asking. I can feel him there at the other end holding his phone, touching me through it, feel his fingers typing, each word a hidden message to me. "I need to text Jonas back, Pete. What time should I say?"

"Tell them eleven thirty."

Jack walks into the living room and picks my purse up from the table. I watch as he digs around, pulls out my car keys.

"What exactly are you doing?" I ask.

"I'll bring it back with a full tank. I promise."

"Give me those," I hold out my hand for the keys. "Either you come to the beach with us or you bike to the Racing Club. *Basta*."

"Why are you doing this? You are literally going out of your way to make problems for me." Jack throws my car keys on the floor and slams out the porch door. "How can you stand being married to such a bitch," he shouts over his shoulder as he storms off to his cabin.

"You make a great point," Peter calls back, laughing.

"Are you kidding me, Pete?"

"Relax. He's a teenager. He's supposed to be rude to his mother. It's all part of the separation process."

My entire being bristles. There is nothing that makes me *more* tense than being told to relax. "Rude? He called me a *bitch*. And your laughing only encourages him."

"So, this is my fault?" Peter raises an eyebrow.

"Of course not," I say, exasperated. "But he takes his cues from you."

Peter stands up. "I'm going into town to get cigarettes."

"We're in the middle of a conversation."

"Is there anything else we need?" His voice is cold as stones.

"For fuck's sake, Pete."

Maddy and Finn have gone completely still, like small animals at a watering hole watching as a Komodo dragon slithers toward a water buffalo. It is unusual for them to see their father angry. Peter rarely loses his cool. He much prefers to laugh things off. But he is looking at me now narrow-eyed, as if he can feel the molecules around me vibrating at a different wavelength—as if he has caught me in the act, but doesn't know the act of *what*.

"Can you pick up some half-and-half?" Mum calls from the kitchen, where she's pretending to reheat coffee, listening in. I can hear her voice inside my head saying, *Think Botticelli*. The sane part of me knows she's right: I need to back down. I fucked my oldest friend in the bushes last night. All Peter did was laugh when our teenage son disrespected me, which is a daily occurrence. But it's the tone of warning in Peter's voice that makes me rise to the bait.

"Don't make this about you, Pete."

"About *me*? Are you sure you want to go there, Eleanor?"

Breakfast rises in my throat. A sudden panic. I glance over at Maddy and Finn on the sofa, their small nervous expressions. Their sweetness. Their worry. What I did last night. A terrible mistake I can never take back.

"I'm sorry," I say. Then I hold my breath and wait for whatever happens next.

5

1972. August, Connecticut.

Rural Connecticut is an oppressive place in late summer. By eight in the morning the air is already thick with landlocked humidity and the suffocating greenness of everything. After lunch, I like to hide in the shade of my grandfather's cornfield, run from one end to the other, the lazy husks pattering against me; lie on a dark stripe of plowed earth between the rows, secret and safe, listen to the quiet rustle; watch soldier ants carrying their heavy loads across the ruts and furrows. In the late afternoon, clouds of gnats appear from nowhere and swarm us, forcing us to run inside for cover until they disappear back into the shadows of the sour plum tree.

Every evening at our grandparents' farm, we wait for the air to cool before taking our after-dinner walk. In the heat of the day, the road's blacktop oozes and blisters. But later, it is lovely to walk on, the tar still soft but not sticky, like walking on marshmallows, the sweet smell of lava rising. Granddaddy William, my father's father, carries his hickory walking stick, pipe and packet of tobacco shoved in his trouser pocket. We walk together past the cornfield, past the old cemetery across the street from their farmhouse, past the little white church with its darkened windows, the minister's small clapboard house, reading lights on, his lace curtains drawn. We walk up the hill, where sheep bells tinkle in the dusky hollows of the neighbor's farm.

Anna and I carry sugar cubes in our pockets and run ahead to feed the Straights' piebald horse from the palms of our hands. He waits for us at the edge of the field, waist-high in stinging nettles, his warm, snuffling nostrils picking up our scent. Anna scratches him between the eyes and he harrumphs and stomps his foot. When we get home, Granny Myrtle always has cider and homemade sugar cookies waiting. She says she wishes we could stay here with her all the time—divorce is never good for the children. "I've always admired your mother," she says. "Wallace is a very handsome woman."

The church has a small playground for Sunday school—swings and a jungle gym—but Anna and I prefer to play in the cemetery, with its big shade trees and clipped green lawns. The rows and rows of gravestones are perfect for hide-and-seek. Our favorite place is the suicide grave. It is all by itself, halfway up the hill. People who kill themselves aren't allowed near the other graves because they have sinned, Granny Myrtle tells us. The suicide grave has a tall stone marker, much taller than me, with a cyprus tree on either side. His widow planted them, Granny says. "At first they were only shrubs. But that was long ago now. Your grandfather helped her dig the holes. She moved to New Haven after that." When Anna asks her how the man died, Granny Myrtle replies, "Your grandfather cut him down."

On the back side of the grave is a wide marble step. It's meant to be for flowers, Granny tells us, but as far as she knows, no one has ever visited. On very hot days, Anna and I like to sit there, hidden from the road, in the cool shade of the tombstone. We've started making paper dolls. We draw them on paper and cut them out. Anna always does the faces and hairstyles: ponytails, Afros, Pippi Longstocking braids, pageboys. We make teensy clothes with square tabs that fold around the dolls—striped purple bell-bottoms and hip-huggers, kitchen aprons, leather jackets, crayon-white go-go boots, maxiskirts, neckties. Bikinis. "Every doll has to have its own wardrobe," Anna says, carefully cutting out a microscopic handbag.

We are sitting on the grave step when we hear a car turn into our gravel drive across the road.

"He's here!" Anna says.

Our father is coming for a whole week. We haven't seen him in ages—he's been traveling for work. He misses his bunny girls he tells us when Granny lets us speak to him on the phone. He cannot wait to see us. He's taking us to the Danbury Fair and swimming at Candlewood Lake. He is bringing a surprise. We may not recognize him, he says. He has grown a moustache.

We pack up our paper dolls and race down the hill, calling his name, excited for our surprise. He gets out of his car at the top of the driveway. Then the passenger door opens.

11:00 A.M.

In the wake of my argument with Peter, his car engine gunning away up the driveway, Finn and Maddy have settled back into their books and machines like seabirds after a swell.

"Mind if I squeeze in, chublets?" They make room for me without bothering to look up. "One more squidge."

"Mom!" Maddy says, annoyed at another disruption.

I lean back between them, close my eyes, grateful for my children's familiar smell, their eggy breath, a momentary reprieve. Jack is still in his cabin, sulking, single-minded, refusing to come out. Which is typical. Jack was stubborn when he was still in my womb. No matter how many liters of cod-liver oil I drank, he refused to leave his safe watery nest. He finally agreed to emerge two weeks late, after an agonizing and interminable labor. I remember being certain, at one point, that I was going to die in childbirth. By the next morning, I was convinced my baby was dead inside me, though the doctor had seventeen monitors attached to me all pinging Jack's solid heartbeat. It was the terror of losing the thing I loved most in the world, without ever being allowed to love him. But out he came, pink and squalling, long frog feet, pleated and wrinkled, fish-eyed, blinking. A creature of water. Primordial. Wiped off and swaddled in blue. Handed to me. A softness wrapped in softness wrapped in my arms, inside of me and outside at the same time.

When the nurses took Jack away to let me rest, I sent Peter home. We had both been awake for so many hours. I woke in dimness. I could hear Jack's snuffling breath, tiny squeaks of dreams, just there, beside my head. The nurses had wheeled him back to me while I slept. I cradled him out of his bassinet, tried to latch him to my breast, no idea what I was doing, feeling like an impostor pretending to be a real mother. Wept as we struggled to connect. Happiest and saddest. Inside and out.

There was a knock on the hospital-room door. The nurse, I thought, relieved. But it was Jonas who came through the door. Jonas, whom I had not seen or spoken to in four years. Who had walked out of my life in anger and hurt when I married Peter. Who was married to Gina now. Jonas, my oldest friend, who stood in the doorway with a massive bunch of white peonies wrapped in brown paper, watching me sob onto my baby.

He came to the edge of the bed, lifted Jack from my arms, gently, not asking permission, knowing he had it. Pulled the blue baby blanket away from Jack's soft cheek, kissed him on the nose, and said, "Is it me, or does she look a little bit masculine?"

"Fuck off," I smiled. "Don't make me laugh. It hurts."

"Is it your perineum?" he asked, concerned.

"Oh my god." And I laughed through the weeping. Happiness and loss.

I picture Jack now, lying on his bed, hands crossed behind his head, earphones cutting out the world, trying to decide whether or not he should forgive me—wondering whether I will forgive *him*. "Yes, and yes," I want to shout to him, down the path. There is no such thing as *unforgivable* between people who love each other. But even as I'm thinking it, I know it's not really true.

A fly has gotten itself trapped inside the porch. It buzzes against the screen, wings and legs rasping the metal filaments. Every so often it stops to rethink and the porch goes silent, only the sound of pages turning, Finn's spit bubble popping with a faint plip as he concentrates on his game. Across the pond, on the small public-access beach, people are already staking out their patch of sand for the day, unpacking picnics onto cotton tablecloths to prevent anyone else from impinging. I should never have let Peter convince me to meet Jonas and Gina at the beach. The thought of facing Jonas in the stark light of day, eating Gina's tuna sandwiches and rehashing last night's dinner party; the lie in my smile. There's no reason I have to go. Peter made the plan. He can take the kids. No one will care. Except me. Because then they will get to be near Jonas and I won't. They will get to lay their towels next to his in the hot sand. And the thought of not seeing him fills me with an agonized tangy ache to touch him, brush his hand under the surf, a hunger. An addiction. A siren. *A siren with a penis*, I think, and laugh out loud.

"What's so funny?" Maddy asks.

"Nothing." I catch myself. "Nothing's funny."

"That's kind of weird, Mom," she says, going back to her book. "Laughing for no reason. It's like a creepy clown." She scratches a mosquito bite on her ankle.

"The more you scratch, the more it itches." The kids are still in their pajamas. A drip of candle wax has hardened on Finn's sleeve, there from last night, when they came in to say good night to the drunken grown-ups.

"We heard you singing before," Finn had said, coming in through the screen door with a mischievous "I know I'm supposed to be in bed, but here I am" expression.

"Oh, for heaven's sake. You were meant to be asleep hours ago," I said.

"You people are making too much noise," Maddy said. "Jack's asleep. He passed out."

"Climb on," I said, pulling Finn onto my lap. "But only five minutes."

He leaned forward to peel a wax stalactite off the side of a candlestick. A few drops of wax dripped onto his sleeve. "Can I blow out the candles?"

"No, you may not."

"Will you walk us back to bed? I heard something in the bushes. I think it might be a wolf."

"There's no wolves here, dummy," Maddy said. "I'm getting a glass of milk."

Finn climbed off my lap and went over to curl up on the sofa next to Peter, who carried on talking to Gina, stroking Finn's back as if he were a cat. Across the table from me, Anna's godfather John Dixon and my step-grandmother Pamela were arguing with Jonas's mother about the nesting shorebirds.

"It's our beach," Pamela was saying. "What right does the Park Service have to cordon it off?"

"I couldn't agree more. It's for the birds," Dixon said, laughing too loud at his own pun.

"The beach belongs to Mother Nature," Jonas's mother said. "Do you honestly care more about where you put your towel down than the possible extinction of a species?"

"Can someone open the screen door for me?" Maddy came out of the pantry, balancing two glasses of milk.

Peter stood up, a bit unsteady on his feet, opened the porch door, mushed the top of her hair.

"Daddy! I'll spill." Maddy laughed, spilling a puddle of milk.

Finn got down on all fours and slurped the milk off the floor. "I'm a cat," he said.

"Gross." Maddy blew me a kiss. "Night, Mama. I love you. Night, everyone."

"Night, sugarplums," Peter said, lying back down on the sofa. "And not another peep."

I watched Jonas peel wax dripping off a candle as Finn had just done. He molded the wax between his fingers absent-mindedly. First into a ball, then a swan, then a turtle, a cube, a heart—if his fingers were exposing his thoughts in Claymation. And it occurred to me that the first time I met Jonas he was about Finn's age. A sweet little boy. Impossible to imagine that my small, tufty child could ever become a hurricane in someone's life. Jonas glanced up, saw me looking at him.

"You spoil those children," my mother said after they'd disappeared down the path into the darkness. "In my day, children were supposed to be seen and not heard."

"If only that rule *still* applied to you, Wallace," Peter called over.

"Your husband is terrible," Mum said, pleased. "I don't know how you've put up with him all these years."

"Love is blind, thank god. Or at least my wife is." Peter laughed. "That's the secret to my happiness."

"In my day, we simply divorced and remarried," Mum said. "So much simpler. Refreshing, even. Like buying a new suit of clothes."

"Huh," I said. "That's not quite how I remember it. And if Anna were here, I can guarantee she'd agree."

"Oh, please," Mum dismissed me. "You turned out just fine. If your father and I had stayed married, who knows what you might have been. You might have become some happy, namby-pamby twit. You might have become a hotel manager. Divorce is good for children." She stood up and began clearing away a few lingering dinner forks. "Unhappy people are always more interesting."

I could feel the familiar fight rising inside me, but Jonas leaned over and whispered, "Ignore her. She says things she doesn't mean when she drinks. You know that."

I nodded, poured myself a glass of grappa, handed the bottle to him. Our fingers touched as he took it from me and poured one for himself.

"A toast." He held up his glass.

"What are we toasting?" I asked, clinking glasses.

"Blind love." His eyes never left mine.

I waited a few minutes before getting up from the table.

Mum was at the sink, her back to me. "I could use some help with these dishes, Eleanor. The hot water's refusing to get hot again."

"In a minute. I'm going to the bathroom."

"Pee in the bushes. That's what I always do."

I slipped out the back door, waited in the shadows wondering if I had read him correctly, wondering how I would feel if I was wrong, left standing here like some pathetic sixteen-year-old. The porch door opened and footsteps came down the sandy path. Jonas stopped, looked around into the darkness, found me. We stood there, a rustle of wind off the pond, bullfrogs lowing.

"Are you waiting here for me, Elle?"

"Shhh." I put my fingers to his lips. Inside, the dim lull of voices. Something on the record player.

"Turn around," he whispered, lifting my skirt. "Put your hands against the wall."

"Are you arresting me?"

"Yes," he said.

"Hurry."

"*Mom!*" Tugging at my shirt. "Mom! Are you even listening?" Maddy is saying. "Can we go snorkeling, or not?"

"We found a fish nest yesterday," Finn says. "There could be eggs."

"So? Can we go?" Maddy asks. "Mom!"

I shake my head clear, try to rehinge myself. "The masks and flippers are in the first cabin," I manage to say. I feel filthy, contaminated, desperate to scour my insides. And heartbroken. Because I know the radiation has already gotten through the tear in my body's hazmat, and I don't know whether I will survive it.

1973. May, Briarcliff, New York.

A beautiful late spring morning. My father's wedding day. I'm wearing a lace dress, patent leather shoes, white opaque knee socks. I am six.

My father is marrying his girlfriend Joanne. Joanne is a bestselling novelist—"a catch," our father tells us the first time we meet her. "Nothing more attractive than a strong woman," he says. Her hair smells of Herbal Essence.

"Your father just likes being bossed around," Joanne laughs. And they kiss right in front of us.

Joanne is only twenty-five. "We could practically be sisters!" she says to Anna. She is pretty and stocky and has a sheepskin coat. It worries me that the sheep has to live without its skin. They have moved out to the suburbs. My father commutes into the city for work every day, but we rarely see him anymore when he is there.

Joanne drives a new red Mustang. My mother says red is tacky, I tell her, the first time I see the car. You should have gotten blue. And she fakes a laugh. Blue is tasteful, I say. You don't even know what that means, Anna says, pinching me hard on the arm.

Joanne likes Anna, but she and I "simply aren't a good fit," she tells Anna, who repeats it to me. Sometimes Joanne comes into the city and takes Anna for special "girl days": window-shopping at FAO Schwarz, lunch at Schrafft's, ice-skating at Wollman Rink. She buys Anna a fuchsia-and-orange bag at Marimekko with shiny silver buttons that look like dimes. She loves Anna's thick, dark chestnut hair and teaches her how to brush it for ten minutes a day to make it shine.

Every night at exactly six o'clock Joanne has her scotch and soda while my father makes dinner and opens the wine so it can breathe. He likes to cook with shallots, and lets me sit on a tall stool in the kitchen so I can help him peel the carrots. He cooks in a big black cast-iron pan that he has to wipe out with oil instead of soap and water. That would ruin the pan, he says. He says the oil cures it, and I ask him, "Cures it of what?"

Joanne bitterly resents that my father has to pay child support. On Sunday evenings when she drives us back to the train station she hands us a folded piece of paper—a list of things she has deducted from my mother's "pay": *8 slices bread, 4 tbsp. peanut butter, six yogurts, two frozen chicken pot pies, Swanson Salisbury Steak. . . .*

Now I watch my father walk down the aisle. Next to me, in the pew, Granny Myrtle sits up straight, her pillbox hat askew, lips tight. She doesn't like Joanne, either. The last time Joanne and my father dropped us off at our grandparents' house, our suitcases were filled with dirty laundry. "The woman is a slob," my grandmother had said. "And lazy as a cat in the sun. Your father may have graduated summa cum laude from Yale, but he doesn't have a brain below the waist. How he could have chosen her. I'll have to check you for bird mites."

I look down at the folds of white lace in my lap, pick at a scab on my knee. My legs are covered in impetigo scars and scabs from falling onto the rough concrete under the jungle gym in the playground. Granny Myrtle reaches over and takes my hand, gives me a reassuring squeeze. I like the way her worn silver wedding band feels against my knuckles. She rests our hands together on my lap. I trace the thin blue veins on the back of her hand. I love her so much.

Anna is wearing navy. She has gotten chunky and Joanne thought the color would be becoming. I tap the floor nervously with my shoe. Anna kicks me in the shin. I have been told not to fidget. A beam of red light crosses the altar in front of the church. I trace it back to a high stained-glass window. It is the blood of Christ, trailing from his open wounds. My father walks past me now, toward the priest. I run into the aisle and throw myself at his feet, grab his pant leg and hold on. He tries to get free of me, still smiling at the wedding guests, but I won't let go. I am a fury of white lace, snot, and tears. He inches forward, pretending to ignore the small child latched onto his ankles. I am a suckerfish.

My father and I have reached the altar. The organist begins the

"Wedding March." The guests get to their feet, a bit unsure. Now Joanne is steaming toward us down the aisle, a big pouffy veil hiding her rage. She has chosen a satin minidress, and her thick legs poke out from under it. They look like sausages stuffed into tiny shoes. She steps over me, takes my father's hands, nods at the priest. I am lying on the ground, curled around his ankles as they take their vows. *Why isn't she wearing underpants?* I'm thinking when they say the words "I do."

1973. November, Tarrytown, New York.

One of our father's "weekends." He's meant to have us every other weekend, but this is the first time we've seen him in over a month. They've had endless engagements. Joanne has too many friends and they all want to meet her old man, he tells us. "Who is the old man?" I ask. "Have *we* met him?"

The house is brown. In the yard, ropes hang from a bare tree where a swing used to be. Beyond it, a rocky ridge leads down to a small, muddy pond. Not swimmable, my father says, but in winter it will freeze and we can ice-skate. The living room is long and narrow with a huge plate-glass window overlooking "the lake," as Joanne calls it. "Waterfront property is impossible to find," she says. The only room in the house without wall-to-wall shag carpeting is the kitchen.

Saturday afternoon. Anna and I are sitting on the kitchen floor playing jacks. Outside, rain slashes the windows, a relentless gloom. I've gotten to tensies and I'm about to flip when Joanne comes in brandishing her hairbrush. She pulls a few strands of hair out of it, waves them at me.

"You used my hairbrush, Eleanor. After I specifically told you not to."

"I didn't," I say, though I did.

"There was an outbreak of lice at your fancy new school. I'll have to boil it." She is furious. "If this brush gets ruined, I'm sending the bill to your mother. These are boar bristles."

"It wasn't me!"

"The hairs are blond. I will not stand for lying in this house." She reaches down and sweeps our jacks up off the floor.

"Give them back!" I shout.

My father wanders in from the garage. "C'mon, you two. No fighting, no biting."

"Don't speak to me as though I'm a child, Henry," Joanne says.

"She took our jacks for no reason, and she won't give them back," I say.

"Elle used Joanne's hairbrush without asking," Anna says.

"That's not true!" I say.

"It's just a hairbrush," Dad says. "I'm sure Joanne doesn't mind. Did I ever tell you your grandmother was jacks champion of her school?" He opens the freezer and looks inside. "How does chicken pot pie sound for dinner? Jo and I are out tonight."

"I don't want you to go out," I say. "You always go out."

"We'll be right next door. And we found a great local girl to babysit."

"Can we watch TV?" Anna says.

"Anything you want."

"I don't like it here," I say. "This house is ugly. I want to go home."

"Shut up," Anna says. "Stop ruining everything."

I run from the room in tears.

Behind me I hear Joanne say, through her own angry tears, "I can't take this anymore, Henry. I didn't sign up to be a mother."

I throw myself on my bed, bury my face in my pillow. "I hate her, I hate her, I hate her," I chant, like a prayer. When my father comes to comfort me, I turn away, curl myself into a pill bug.

He lifts me onto his lap and strokes my hair until my sobs subside. "I won't go anywhere tonight, rabbit. It's okay. It's okay."

"She's mean."

"She doesn't mean to be. This is hard for both of you. Joanne is a good woman. Please give her a chance. For me."

I snuggle deeper into his arms and nod, knowing it's a lie.

"Good girl."

"For god's sake, Henry," Joanne says when he tells her he's staying home with us. "We made this plan with the Streeps weeks ago."

"You'll be fine. The Streeps are more your friends, anyway. And Sheila will have cooked something delicious. I haven't seen my girls in weeks."

"It's Saturday night. I'm not going out on my own."

"Even better. Stay home with me and the girls. We'll watch a movie, make popcorn."

"The babysitter is already on her way. We can't cancel her now." She turns her back to him and looks in the hall mirror, putting in her large gold-hoop earrings. She smooths her eyebrows and gives each of her cheeks a hard pinch.

"We'll pay her for her travel time. She'll understand."

I stare at Joanne's reflection in the mirror, watching, fascinated, as her nostrils get bigger and smaller and bigger and smaller. Her mouth is a furious slash. When she catches me watching her, I smile in triumph.

But in the end, she wins. Every weekend after that, when our father meets us at the train station, he loads us into his car and drops us with Joanne's parents, half an hour away. There is always some new excuse: Joanne has the curse and is feeling sick; the house is being treated for wood rot; they've been invited to a house party in Roxbury and Joanne thinks we'll be bored, but next weekend we will stay with him, he promises. When he waves goodbye to us from the car he always looks sad, and I know it's my fault.

Joanne's father, Dwight Burke, is a famous poet. He has a lovely scratchy voice and wears a three-piece suit to breakfast. He carries a glass of bourbon with him when he goes up to his study in the morning. His wife Nancy is a big, warm woman. A Catholic. She carries a rosary in her apron pocket and asks me if I believe in God. She bakes round loaves of buttery bread, and calls lunch "luncheon." Her hair is always done. They are the sorts of parents I have only ever read about in books. Tweedy and kind. I can't understand how they raised such a horrible cow.

Joanne's younger brother Frank still lives at home. He is fifteen. Frank was a surprise. "A blessing," Nancy tells us when Anna asks why Frank is so much younger than Joanne. "She means a mistake," Frank says. He has a blond military crew cut and acne. When he bends over in his chinos, we can see the crack of his behind.

The Burkes live in a three-story white brick house surrounded by delphiniums and banks of sweet pachysandra, overlooking the ribbon of the Hudson River. The house is filled with chocolate Labradors with names like Cora and Blue, and the constant smell of rising yeast. On Sunday mornings, we go to church.

Anna and I have our own room on a little half-story behind the kitchen. A hidden staircase leads from a broom-closet door in the pantry up to our room. "The maid's," Nancy calls it. No one else uses this section of the house. Our diamond windowpanes look out on steep gray bedrock that weeps chill water from somewhere deep inside it.

Anna and I are friends again. We play Red Light, Green Light in the garden, sit on the wooden stairs making paper dolls, or read our books curled up in bed. No one bothers us. No one shouts. When it's time for luncheon, Nancy rings a cowbell and we run downstairs to the dining room, where a fire is always lit, even in early summer. Nancy loves having us here, she tells us. She smothers us in hugs and kisses and unpacks our weekend suitcases into hickory bureau drawers.

Frank has a rec room in the back of the house, where he raises mice, hamsters, and gerbils in fish tanks. They stare across the room at Waldo, the boa constrictor who lives in a larger glass cage in their midst. At night, after dinner, Frank forces us to watch as he feeds teensy baby mice to his snake. Pinkies. I beg to be let out of the room, but he blocks the door. The room smells of cedar sawdust and fear.

"Are you kids having fun in there?" Nancy calls from the kitchen where she is finishing up the dishes.

"We're feeding Waldo," Frank yells. "Here. Take this." He shoves a squirming pinky into Anna's hand.

"I don't want to." She tries to hand the mouse back to him, but he sticks his hands in his pockets.

"If you don't feed Waldo he'll be hungry tonight. He might try to escape. Did you know that even a young boa constrictor can strangle a human to death in seconds?"

Anna opens the top of the snake cage, closes her eyes, and releases the baby mouse. I watch it fall into a soft pile of aspen shavings. For five long seconds, it blinks and looks around, relieved to be alive. Waldo slithers forward, then strikes. The mouse is gone. All that is left is a small bump the size of a marble in Waldo's throat. We watch as the muscles move it down toward his stomach—a gagging, sinuous movement.

Frank loves his snake, but he loves his hamsters even more. He breeds them and sells them for pocket money. They are his most prized possessions. One weekend Goldie, his favorite hamster, escapes. Frank is frantic. He races up and down stairs, looking under sofas, pulling books off the shelves calling for her. He is certain one of the dogs has eaten her and kicks the oldest Lab, Mabel, in the shin. Mabel yelps and limps away.

"Is everything okay?" Nancy calls out from the kitchen, where beef stew is cooking.

Frank turns on me now. Accuses me of having fed Goldie to Waldo. "I know you think I'm ugly," he says. "I heard you say it." He pins me against the staircase wall. His breath smells of Chee-tos and milk. I stare at the neon-orange dust that has built up around his lips as I swear to him that I did not.

That night, when Nancy pulls up Anna's blanket to tuck her in, Goldie's limp body shakes out onto the bed. She has been squashed flat between the bed and the wall. Nancy fetches a broom and dustpan, opens the window, and tosses Goldie into the hydrangea bushes.

Frank is watching from the doorway. A high-pitched gurgling sound comes from his throat. His face twists and pinches, his acne bulges dark red. I'm certain that he is choking. I watch, transfixed, wondering if he will die. Instead, he lets out a strangled sob. Anna and I look at each other, horrified, and then burst out laughing. Frank runs away, shamefaced. I listen to the thump of his feet on our wooden staircase, hear the faraway slam of a door. Nancy stares out into the darkness, her back to us.

The next weekend, when we arrive at the train station, our father tells us we will be spending the weekend with him and Joanne. Dwight and Nancy feel it would be best.

6

11:30 A.M.

In my mother's family, divorce is just a seven-letter word. Letters that could easily be replaced with *I'm bored* or *bad luck*. Both of her parents married three times. My grandfather Amory, who built the Paper Palace, lived in his house on the pond until the day he died, chopping wood in his hiking boots, fishing, canoeing, watching the changing ecosystem of the pond. He tracked the water lilies, the great blue herons, counted painted turtles basking on the tree trunks that rotted and grayed in the shallows. Wives moved in and out, but the pond remained his. He had found it, stumbled out of the deep woods with his hunting rifle at the age of eighteen, found the pure fresh water, its white sandy bottom, and drunk from it. When he died, Grandfather Amory left his house to Pamela, his third and final wife. She alone had proved herself worthy of it, understood its powerful hold, its soul—the religion of the Pond. The Paper Palace he left to Mum. Her brother Austin, who had never left Guatemala, wanted nothing to do with it. But to Mum, it was everything.

On the wall of my office at NYU there's a black-and-white photograph of my mother as a young girl in Guatemala. My office is a hoarder's paradise—books falling off the shelves, desk piled high with graduate theses, pencil stubs, Comp Lit papers to be graded, a depressing, old-womanish avocado plant I am forced to keep because Maddy "made" it for my birthday when she was six. The only clean spaces are the white walls, entirely bare except for that single photograph. In the photo, my mother is sitting astride a palomino horse. She has long braids and wears an embroidered peasant blouse, blue jeans rolled up at the cuff, leather huaraches. She is fifteen. Behind her, a young boy dressed in white walks down the dusty road pushing a wooden wheelbarrow; open fields stretch toward lava cliffs in the rugged foothills of a shrouded volcano. In one hand, my mother holds the burnished horn of her Western saddle. In the other, a single ear of corn. She is smiling at the camera, relaxed, happy—a looseness and freedom I have never seen on her face. Her teeth are white and straight.

She told me the photo was taken by the handsome gardener, that the little boy was his son; that seconds after the picture was taken, the boy nicked the horse with his cart and the horse bolted, galloped across the field and threw her, breaking her arm and two ribs. She never got back on a horse. The following fall, my mother left Guatemala for a posh New England boarding school, where she played in tennis whites and had chapel every morning. She never looked back.

I have always loved that photo. It reminds me of Michelangelo's *David*: a split second carved in eternal time, the instant before the throw—right before everything changes; the randomness of the things that lead us to turn left, or right, or simply sit down on a dusty road and never move forward again. That boy, that cart, that horse, that fall, my mother's choice to leave Guatemala, come back to the woods—gave me the pond.

From the porch, I watch Finn and Maddy flopping about in the shallows. Maddy points to something moving near the lily pads. Finn takes a step backward, but Maddy takes his hand, maternal. "It's okay. Water snakes are harmless," I hear her say. They watch its little black head making its ticktack S curves through the reeds. "Look! Minnows," Finn says, and they disappear under the water together. The bright yellow tips of their snorkels plow figure eights on the surface.

"Has anyone seen my dark glasses?" My mother wanders out to the porch from the kitchen. "I know I left them on the bookshelf. Someone must have moved them."

"They're right here. On the table," I say. "Exactly where you left them."

"I'm going next door. I promised Pamela I'd bring over a jar of milk and two eggs."

"You should have asked Peter to pick up groceries for her."

"Hardly. Anyone with sense knows to avoid your husband like the plague when smoke starts coming out of his ears. But you, Eleanor, insist on wading in with a match and setting everyone's hair on fire. I am removing myself, with my jar of milk and my parcel of eggs. I'll be back when you and your husband have stopped acting like infants in front of your children. You should try not to be so impossible, dear. He's a good man. A reasonable man. You're lucky to have him."

"I know."

"And take something for that hangover," Mum says. "You're positively green around the gills. There's ginger ale in the icebox."

My mother has always had a mini-crush on Peter. She's not wrong. He's a wonderful man. A towering hickory. Gentle but never weak. The strength of rivers. Opinionated, thoughtful, thought-provoking. A sexy

English accent. He makes us laugh. He adores me. He adores his children. And I adore him right back, with a love as deep and strong as tree roots. There are times when I want to tear him limb from limb, but that's probably the definition of marriage. Toilet paper can lead to World War III.

My mother disappears into the trees at the far end of our beach, egg basket in one hand, jar of milk in the other. Three minutes later, I can hear her calling "*Yoo-hoo!*" as she emerges from the woods onto my grandfather's property. He has been dead for many years, but it will always be *his* house. A screen door opens, shuts, a garbled laugh, Pamela saying, "Oh my!" Although Pamela is a decade older, she and my mother are close friends. "She's practically the only person I can bear in these woods anymore," Mum says. "Though it would be restful if she ever wore a color other than purple. And you'd think she invented botulism, the way she cooks. I found a piece of blue cheese in her icebox that turned out to be butter. Everyone says Daddy died from old age, but I suspect she may have poisoned him by mistake."

There's the sound of gravel and sand, Peter's car pulling in. I brace myself for whatever is coming. Everything? Nothing? Something in between? This powerless moment. Not knowing what to expect. I hear him walking down the path toward me and my stomach does a slight free fall. I turn my back to the screen door, settle my body into a neutral position on the sofa, and pick up my book so he won't be able to read me, either. It's all judo. But he heads past the porch and walks down toward the cabins.

"Jack, open up!" He bangs on the cabin door. "Out. Now."

I turn around and try to read Peter's face from where I'm sitting. Jack emerges and sits down beside his father on the steps. I can't hear them, but I see Peter talking emphatically, Jack listening with a sullen glare, then bursting into laughter. My entire body unclenches in relief.

My husband and my tall, lanky son get up and walk toward me. They are both smiling.

"Have you calmed down a bit, missus?" Peter reaches into his pocket for his cigarettes, pats down his pockets for a lighter. "I've brought you your sheepish son. He understands that he behaved like a little shit and must never, ever speak to his mother that way again. Apologize to your mother." He ruffles Jack's hair.

"Sorry, Mom."

"And . . ." Peter prompts.

"And I will never, ever speak to you like that again," Jack says.

Peter takes me by both hands and pulls me up off the sofa. "Cheer up, grumpy. See? Your son loves you. Now—beach-ward?" He goes to the porch door and yells to Maddy and Finn. "*Oi!* Out of the pond. We're leaving in five minutes."

They splash each other and duck under the water, ignoring him.

"So, can I take the car?" Jack asks.

"In your dreams, mate."

"Then can you *at least* drop me off at Sam's house?"

Two seconds, and already Jack has reverted to entitled teenager being unfairly denied his rights. It should rile me. But in this moment, when my heart is spinning off its axis, his utter predictability is a life preserver. I turn my cheek toward him. "Kiss, please, you pill."

He gives me a reluctant peck, but I know he loves me.

Peter looks at his watch. "Crap. We're incredibly late. Round up your kittens, Elle. I'll load the car. Jack, call Sam and tell him to pick you up at the end of the road in ten minutes."

I yell to Finn and Maddy and head down the path to the bathroom. The gummed-up ziplock bag with all our sun block in it has mysteriously vanished. I know I left it in the pantry yesterday. I yank open the wide bottom drawer of the built-in linen closet where my mother shoves anything she finds lying around the house that she deems unsightly. It is there, of course, along with a pair of Maddy's flip-flops I've been looking for and a damp bathing suit of Peter's that now has that forgotten-in-the-washing-machine-for-three-days stench of mildew. Buried at the bottom of the drawer is a large red-plaid thermos my mother has had since I was younger than Maddy. Once upon a time, it had a chic, beige plastic coffee cup that fit snugly onto the top. I unscrew the stopper and give the thermos a sniff. It has probably been twenty years since my mother used it, yet the faintest smell of stale coffee still lingers in its hard-plastic walls. I rinse it out, fill it from the bathtub tap, take a sip. The water has the slightly metallic taste of pipes. I need ice.

At the end of the path I stop for a moment, watching my lovely husband rounding the corner with three boogie boards on his head, a pile of towels under his arm, the children nipping at his heels. I do not deserve him.

"Peter," I call out.

"Yes?"

"I love you."

"Of course you do, you silly git."

7

1974. May, New York.

Cherry blossom season. The hill behind the Metropolitan Museum is a sea of pink. I would eat it if I could. I climb up into the low-hanging boughs of a tree and hide myself in a canopy of flowers. Through the blooms I can see the ancient hieroglyphics on Cleopatra's Needle.

Below me, my mother spreads a checkered cloth on the dappled slope, takes a paper plate from her basket, and dumps out a baggie of peeled hard-boiled eggs. She unfolds a square of tinfoil filled with a mixture of salt and pepper, dips in the pointy end of her egg, and takes a bite.

"Yum," she says out loud to herself. She fishes her red-plaid thermos from the basket, unscrews the plastic cup from the top, and pours herself some milky coffee.

"Eleanor, come down from there. We don't have all day."

I make my way carefully. I'm wearing my new leotard and tights under my jumper and I don't want to snag them. We are going straight from the park to my first ballet lesson.

"Here." My mother hands me a brown paper bag and a little box of milk. "There's peanut butter and butter, or liverwurst."

It's Saturday, and the park is crowded, but no one else bothers to climb up over the rocks and down into this hidden grove. I find a dry spot in the grass, lay my cardigan on it, and sit beside Mum. She's deep in a novel, so we eat our lunch in silence. Above us, the sky is the crispest blue. I hear the distant crack of a baseball, a sudden happy cheering. The rocks smell sweet and clean. It's the first real day of spring, and they are airing themselves in the sun after a long winter hibernating under banks of snow and dog shit.

"I brought Pecan Sandies," Mum says. "Do you want the last hard-boiled egg?"

"I need to pee."

"Well, go behind that rock."

"I can't."

"Don't be prissy, Eleanor. You're seven years old. Who on earth will care?"

"I'm wearing my leotard and tights."

"Well then, you'll just have to hold it until you get there." She dog-ears her page, shoves the book in her bag, and starts packing away our picnic. "Help me pack this up."

The ballet lessons were a present from my father—one I do not want. I wanted gymnastics, like every girl in my grade. Front hand-springs and bridges. Anna says I'm way too big-boned for ballet. Worst of all, I missed the first lesson, so all the other girls will be ahead of me.

Mum looks at her watch. "It's 2:45. We need to race or we'll be late."

By the time we get to Madame Rechkina's studio, the other girls are already lined up in front of the mirrored wall, their perfect little buns in black nets. I'm out of breath, my tights covered with smudges of dirt.

"Mum, we're too late."

"Nonsense."

"I need to go to the bathroom."

"You'll be fine." She opens the studio door and gives me a little shove. "See you in an hour."

Madame Rechkina gives me a tight-lipped smile and gestures for the girls to make a space for me in the center of the room. I take my place. Put my feet in first position. The pianist begins a minuet.

"Plié, mesdemoiselles." Madame walks through the room, making corrections.

"Plié encore! Graceful arms, please!"

I watch the girl in front of me and try to copy her.

"*À la seconde*," Madame calls out.

I place my feet wider apart and bend my knees. And then it happens. A large puddle forms on the glossy wooden floor beneath me, spreads out quickly, soaking the edges of my pink ballet slippers. Behind me, I hear a shriek. The music stops. I run from the room in tears, leaving a trail of wet footprints on the pristine floor, and lock myself in the bathroom.

"Miss Josephine!" I hear Madame call out to her assistant, "A mop, *s'il vous plaît. Vite, vite!*"

The next weekend, my mother makes me go back. "Eleanor," she says sternly, "we are not a family of cowards. You have to face your fears head on. Otherwise you've lost the battle before it's begun."

I plead with her to let me stay home with Anna, but she waves me off.

"Don't be ridiculous. You think those little girls have never peed before?"

"Not on the floor," Anna says, laughing so hard that she has to hold her stomach.

12:30 P.M.

The beach parking lot is broiling. I climb out of the car onto the sandy blacktop and let out a yelp.

"Jesus fuckery." I leap back into the Saab. "I think I scalded the skin off the bottom of my feet." I feel around the floorboards in front of me for my flip-flops, find them wedged under the passenger seat.

"Both of you should put on socks. The sand will be scorching." I hand Finn a pair of white sweat socks from my bag. "Maddy?"

"I'm fine. I'm wearing sandals," she says.

"The sides of your feet will get burned."

"Mom." Maddy gives me a pained look. "I'm not going to wear socks and sandals. Gross."

"What's wrong with socks and sandals?" Peter gets out and starts unloading gear from the trunk. "It's the Englishman's uniform abroad."

I wait until everyone is out of the car before pulling down the visor to check my face in the mirror. I run my fingers through my hair, pinch my cheeks, re-tie my sarong lower around my hips. I can see Jonas's beat-up truck parked farther up ahead.

Peter opens my car door. "Here." He takes my hand and pulls me up and out.

I grab a pile of towels and the thermos of ice water from the backseat.

"And be nice to Gina when she points out that we're an hour late. No bitchy Eleanor. Just nice Eleanor."

"I'm always nice." I give him a kick in the butt as he walks past me, but he manages to dodge it.

As we crest the dune, a hundred umbrellas come into sight. Solids. Stripes. Red, white, and blue. The water is clear turquoise, an even break. No red tide, no mung. A perfect beach day. A *Jaws* day. Kids playing Frisbee, making castles and digging deep moats around them that fill with water from a wellspring underneath the sand. Gorgeous young things strut self-consciously in bikinis, pretending not to know they're being watched. I scan for Jonas. He always walks to the left.

Peter sees them first. They've set up a yellow-and-white-striped beach tent. It looks like a circus pavilion, enclosed on three sides but open to the sea. Gina stands next to it waving a fuchsia towel, signaling us. Maddy and Finn race down the dune toward her, Peter following behind. I hang back, girding myself for whatever happens. What if Peter senses something different between me and Jonas? What if Gina noticed we were both gone? I try to visualize the room just before I went out the back door. Jonas at the table, leaning back in his chair, outside the fall of the candlelight. Peter lying on the sofa, Gina laughing at some comment Dixon had made, my mother pouring grappa into espresso cups, clearing plates, washing glasses in the sink. I'm pretty sure Gina's back was to me. Jonas is sitting on the sand, staring out to sea. I take a deep breath. We are not a family of cowards.

1976. July, the Back Woods.

I am floating on a blue rubber raft. My eyes are closed, face to the sun. Black motes dance around under my eyelids in the opaque red. I drift, listen to the sound of my breath going in and out, let the salt wind carry me to the middle of the pond. There is nothing but me. No one here but me. A perfect moment. I dangle my arm over the edge of the raft, open my fingers, feel the resistance of the water as it passes through them. I imagine I'm a duck. Any moment now a snapping turtle will swim up from the cold bottom and grab my sharp yellow feet, drag me to the deep. In the distance, I hear the clatter of wooden paddles being dumped in the bottom of a canoe. Anna and her friend Peggy have paddled over to the far side of the pond. It's only a short walk to the beach from there. When I open my eyes, I can just make out the tiny flames of their bright orange life vests as they pull the boat up onto shore and disappear into the tree line.

Mum and her boyfriend Leo have gone into town to collect his kids from the Greyhound bus stop. They are coming to stay with us for ten days. Leo is a jazz musician from Louisiana. Saxophone. He has a thick black beard and laughs a lot. He believes exercise is for the weak. His favorite food is shrimp. Anna isn't sure about him, but I think he's nice.

Leo's kids, Rosemary and Conrad, live with their mother in Memphis. They have heavy southern accents and say *y'all.* Rosemary is seven. Mousy. "Irrelevant," Anna says. "And she smells weird." Conrad is eleven, one year older than me. He is short and squat, with Coke-bottle glasses and bulging eyes. He stands too close. We've only met them once before, at a luncheonette, when they came to New York to visit their father. Rosemary ordered a rare steak and talked about original sin.

"His ex-wife wants him dead," my mother says to a friend over the kitchen phone. "If it were up to her, Leo would never see his children again." She lowers her voice. "Frankly, I'm with her, but don't you dare repeat that. They aren't very likable children. Though I suppose very few people actually *like* other people's children. Leo says the boy hates to get in the water, so being on the pond with him in this infernal heat is bound to be an absolute nightmare. Let's just hope he bathes."

She has told us to be on our best behavior.

In the center of the pond where the water is deepest, forests of bladderwort grow up from the bottom. The fish like to hide here. I flip onto my stomach and peer over the edge of the raft. The patch of shade I cast creates a lens that allows me to see everything beneath me in focus. A school of minnows moves through lily pad stems and rotting grasses with swift, jerky motions. A painted turtle swims slowly through the dull green toward the surface. Far below it, a sunfish guards its nest with a vigilant, lazy waft. I lean forward and put my face into the water, open my eyes. The world becomes a soft blur. I lie like this for as long as my lungs can take it, listening to the sounds of the air. If I could breathe underwater, I would stay here forever.

Across the pond, I hear the slam of a car door, Leo's booming laughter. They are here.

12:35 P.M.

Jonas is leaning back on his elbows, his black hair slicked like an oily duck. A thin white cotton shirt clings to his shoulders. A spark of sunlight glints off his wedding ring. He doesn't turn as we approach. I wonder if it's because he can't face me now, face what we have done. Or maybe wanting me all those years was the point, and now I'm just someone he fucked and has to deal with. Or maybe he, too, wants to avoid this moment of acknowledgment—keep his old life alive for one moment longer, before everything changes. Because, either way, it will.

Peter sits down right next to him, points to something on the horizon. Jonas leans in to answer. Dizzying ripples of heat rise off the sand.

"Hey!" Gina shouts, eyes narrowed, and starts coming at me across the sand. I stare at her pierced belly button as it comes in and out of sight beneath her tankini top. Finn and Maddy have spread out their towels nearby and are spraying each other with sun block.

Jonas hasn't turned, but I think I see his forearms tense ever so slightly.

I glance over at the kids; a rising dread.

"Seriously, Elle?" Gina says, squaring off with me.

"Mom," Finn calls out, "I need you to tighten my goggles."

I open my mouth to speak, but nothing comes out. *Whatever you have to say,* I think, *please say it quietly.*

"We've been waiting for you for over an hour. The sandwiches are gonna be totally soggy."

I will my voice to keep its cool, stay level, sure my face is betraying me. Under the pile of towels I'm carrying, my hands are shaking. "I'm so sorry. We should have called. I had a stupid fight with Jack this morning and it spiraled. Let me just put these towels down. I'll run to the market and get fresh sandwiches."

Gina looks at me as though I've gone nuts. "Um, earth to Elle? I'm kidding! I can't believe you honestly thought I'd be pissed off about the sandwiches." She laughs, but for a millisecond a strange expression flashes across her face, and I wonder if she has felt my intestines unfurling.

"Of course not." I force a laugh. "I'm losing it. It's either the Ambien or perimenopause."

Gina puts her arm through mine, drags me over to the others. "I'm just glad you got here. Jonas is refusing to come into the water. Is this the most beauteous day, or what?"

"It's too hot."

"I swear to Christ, I will never understand you Back Woods people. You have the perfect life in the most gorgeous place on the planet and all you can say is 'It's too hot.' Jonas was like pulling teeth this morning. Swim time," Gina calls out to Finn and Maddy. "Last one in, cutie pies. It's time to boogie." She gives a little booty shake. Maddy looks over at me with an expression of pure horror, but they follow her down to the water, racing to dive in headfirst.

"Hey, missus," Peter calls over to me. "Toss me that water jug, will you? I'm dying of thirst over here."

I take aim and throw the thermos at him. It slaloms through the air and lands perfectly upright at his feet.

"Nice," Peter says.

Jonas turns then. Looks directly at me. He stands up and brushes the sand off his palms, walks toward me, arms outstretched, grabs the stack of towels I'm carrying, leans in to kiss me on the cheek. "I missed you," he whispers in my ear.

"Hi," I say softly. I can't bear it. It is too much to bear. "I missed you, too."

He runs the tip of his finger down my arm and I shudder.

"Who's going in?" Peter calls over to us. "It's bloody broiling."

1977. February, New York.

Fifth grade. A snow day. Anna and I are staying with her godfather Dixon for the week. Dad and Joanne are living in London—he has been transferred for work—and Mum and Leo have gone to Detroit for a gig. They are getting married in May. Dixon is Mum's "cool" friend. Everyone loves Dixon. He has long dirty-blond hair in a ponytail and drives a pickup truck. He knows Carly Simon. Mum says he doesn't need to work.

They've been best friends since they were two years old; otherwise I don't think he would even speak to her. They went to preschool together and spent summers together in the Back Woods, skinny-dipping and digging for quahogs and littlenecks in the muck when the tide was out. "Even though I hated shellfish," Mum says. "But Dixon has a way of making you do things." A long time ago, Anna asked Mum why she hadn't married Dixon. "Because he's a rake," Mum had said. And I thought of leaves.

The Dixons live in a rambling apartment on East Ninety-fourth right off the park. Dixon's daughter Becky is my best friend. Anna and Becky's older sister Julia are the same age, but they've never really clicked. Julia is a gymnast. Two years ago, their mother left them to join a commune. Becky and I spend most of our time unsupervised, playing cat's cradle, going into Central Park on roller skates, coming up with disgusting recipes we force each other to eat. This morning we made shakes in the blender out of brewers' yeast and instant strawberry pudding mix. Dixon says he doesn't give a shit, as long as we eat. The last time Mum left us at Dixon's he took us to see *Deliverance* at the Trans Lux. We ran around the rest of the weekend screaming, "Squeal like a pig." Mum had a fit, but Dixon told her to stop being so narrow-minded and puritanical. He's the only person who gets to talk to her like that.

A strange quiet has come over the city. Out the window there is nothing but a blinding flurry of white. I listen to the clanging of hot steam in the pipes as they expand and contract. The apartment is claustrophobic with dry heat, and the metal radiator cover burns the fronts of my legs as I lean forward, using all my weight to inch open the heavy window, but it refuses to budge.

"Can someone please help me? I need air." But no one moves. We are playing Monopoly, and Anna has just landed on Marvin Gardens. She needs to think.

Dixon and his new wife Andrea have been in their room all morning with the door shut. "They have a water bed," Becky says, as if this explains everything. Andrea and Dixon met at a sweat lodge in New Mexico. Andrea is six months pregnant. They're pretty sure it's his.

"I don't mind her," Becky says when Mum asks what she thinks of her new stepmother.

"I think she's nice," I say.

"Nice?" My mother looks as though she's just swallowed an olive pit.

"Why is that bad?" I ask.

"Nice is the enemy of interesting."

"She talks to us like we're grown-ups, which is pretty cool," Becky says.

"Well, you're not. You're eleven," Mum says to Becky.

"The other night at dinner she asked me whether I was excited to begin menstruating," Becky says.

It's the first time I've ever seen my mother at a loss for words.

"Elle," Anna calls out now, "it's your turn." I sit down next to her on the living room floor and roll the dice. The wood floors smell good to me. The same butcher's wax my mother uses.

I'm looking down the long hallway that leads to the bedrooms, trying to decide whether I should use my Get Out of Jail Free card, when a door opens. Dixon steps into the hall, naked. He scratches his balls absent-mindedly. Behind him, Andrea emerges. She arches her back like a cat, stretches her arms up in the air. "We just had such a good fuck," she says. The light is dim, but we can see everything—her massive red bush, her frizzy Janis Joplin hair, her satisfied smile.

Dixon walks past us across the living room, squats down next to the turntable, and places the needle on an album. I can see dark hair in the crack of his behind.

"Listen to the backing vocals on this track," he says. "Clapton is a genius."

I stare at the miniature silver wheelbarrow in my hand, wishing I could disappear into the floor.

Becky shoves me, just a bit too hard. "Are you going or not?"

8

12:45 P.M.

"Coming in?" Peter asks.

"Five minutes. I need to recover after crossing the fucking Sahara." I grab the cooler from him and drink from the spout.

"That's attractive," Peter says. "My wife was raised by wolves."

Jonas laughs. "I know. I was one of them."

Peter hands me the SPF 50 sun block. "Can you do my back?"

I kneel behind him and squeeze sun block into my hand. Somehow he has already managed to get sand on the tube, and I'm irritated by the feeling of grit as I rub the cream onto his shoulders. Jonas watches as I stroke Peter's skin.

"There." I give Peter's back a pat for good measure. "You are officially blocked." I wipe my hands off on a towel and crawl into the shade of the tent. "Better," I say.

Peter gets to his feet and grabs a boogie board. "Don't be long. I don't want to go pruney waiting for you."

The moment Peter leaves, I wish I'd gone with him, because now Jonas and I are alone, and I have never felt more uncomfortable in my life. We've been together on this beach a thousand times since we were kids, walked the tide line looking for sea urchins and toenail shells, spied on creepy naked Germans from up in the dunes, wondered what it would be like to drown at sea. But right now, right here, huddled in the shade of his tent, I feel like I'm with a complete stranger.

There's a small mesh window in the side panel of the tent. I watch Jonas through it, sitting inches away from me but completely separate. He's concentrating—drawing something in the sand with the edge of a shell. I can't make out what it is from this angle.

"Where's young Jack?" he asks without looking up.

"Protesting."

"Protesting what?"

"I wouldn't give him my car."

"Why not?"

"He was being a complete asshole," I say, and he laughs. Gina waves to us from the break, beckoning. Jonas waves back. He leans in to the mesh window. "Can I come in?"

"No."

"Then will you hear my confession?"

"I'm not sure three Hail Marys are going to help much," I say.

He presses the palm of his hand against the mesh. "Elle—"

"Don't," I say. But I put my hand up against his. We sit like this, silent, unmoving, palm to palm through the fine mesh.

"I've been in love with you since I was eight."

"That's a lie," I say.

1977. August, the Back Woods.

In the tree cover above me, there's a window. I lie on the mossy banks of a stream, gazing up at the almost perfectly-square patch of sky. One minute it's solid blue, the next a cloud floats past like a painting on the ceiling of a church. A sea gull swings into frame. I can hear its searching, mournful cries long after it disappears from view. I reach into my pocket and grab a Tootsie Roll. This is where I come almost every day now. Occasionally my mother asks me where I've been and I say, "Around," and she seems fine with that. I could be hitchhiking into town with a serial killer and she wouldn't notice. It's all Leo and Anna, all the time. They argue about everything. It's been like this since Leo and Mum got married. I dread sitting down at the table for dinner. It starts out okay—Leo lecturing us about China or why the Pentagon Papers are still relevant. But pretty soon he starts in on Anna. He doesn't approve of her friend Lindsay: she dresses like a hooker; she's overdeveloped and under-intelligent; she thought the Khmer Rouge was a lipstick color; her parents voted for Gerald Ford. Why did Anna get a C+ in math? How can she sit there without helping while her mother serves us? Her skirt is too short. "Why are you looking, creep?" Anna says, and when he gets up out of his chair, she runs to her room and locks the door.

"It's just hormones," my mother tells Leo, trying to smooth things over between them. "All teenagers are a nightmare. And girls are worse. Wait until Rosemary hits puberty." He has promised to make an effort. But it's been worse since we got to the woods. Leo has decided to "put his foot down." He sends Anna to our cabin if she back-talks, and Mum refuses to interfere. "I'm sorry, but I can't be constantly refereeing," she says to Anna. Anna lies on her bed refusing to cry, and yells at me if I try to come in. One morning in July, Anna and Leo were having such a humongous fight at breakfast that Mum threw an egg at the kitchen wall. "I honestly cannot take another minute of this. I'm going next door to see my father and Pamela." She handed me a banana. "I recommend you find somewhere else to be for the day if you don't want to go deaf."

I was walking to the ocean, thinking about how I was going to poison Leo—how I'd have to be the one to save Anna since Mum wouldn't—when I tripped on a root and tore my flip-flop apart. I sat down on the path to shove the Y back into the buttonhole. Under the low-hanging branches of the trees was a faint trail—probably a deer path. I crawled into the woods and followed the trail until it dwindled and dead-ended in a thicket of catbrier. I was turning back when I noticed the sound of running water. Which made no sense, because everyone knows there's no running water in this part of the woods. That's why the Pilgrims kept going to Plymouth after they landed on the Cape. I pulled the brambles aside bunch by bunch with my towel, stepped through the tangle, trying not to scratch my legs too badly, and emerged from the overgrowth into a small clearing. In the center was a freshwater spring, burbling out of the ground into a narrow stream. The looming trees had backed away, leaving a carpet of velvet moss below. I lay down on the bank and closed my eyes. *Poison might be too obvious*, I thought. Maybe Anna and I should run away from home, move here. We could build a tree house with a platform and a roof made out of branches. We'd have fresh water; we could catch fish on the beach—early, before anyone else was awake; collect cranberries and wild blueberries so we wouldn't get scurvy. I started to make a list in my head of the supplies we'd need: empty Medaglia d'Oro cans with plastic lids for watertight storage, wooden matches, candles, fishhooks and line, a hammer and nails, a cake of soap, two forks, a change of underwear, sleeping bags, bug spray. Mum was going to be sorry she let Leo punish Anna and never took Anna's side. Maybe not right away, but eventually she would miss us.

But it's almost Labor Day now, and the only survival supplies I have managed to collect are two rusty coffee cans, an old pair of pliers and a few candle stubs. High above me, a flock of birds write a V for victory, like a fleeting thought winging its way away across the chipped blue sky. A shadow falls across my face. I freeze. Try to make myself invisible.

"Hello." A small boy—maybe seven or eight—is looking down at me, his approach so silent I never heard him coming. He has thick black hair that reaches his shoulders. Pale green eyes. He's barefoot. "I'm Jonas," he says. "I'm lost." He doesn't seem upset or scared.

"Elle," I say. I've seen his family on the beach. His mother is a frizzy-haired woman who yells at us if we leave our apple cores in the sand. They live somewhere in the Back Woods.

"I was following the osprey," he says, as if that explains everything. He sits down next to me on the mossy bank and looks up at the sky. For a long time, neither of us speaks. I listen to the bristling woods, springwater clipping over rocks. I know Jonas is there, but somehow he makes himself a shadow.

"It's a window," he says after a while.

"I know." I stand up and wipe crumbs of soil off the butt of my jean shorts. "We should get back."

"Yes," he says, with a small, serious expression. "My mother will be frantic."

I want to laugh, but instead I take his hand, walk him down the path, and return him to his mother, who thanks me with what feels like reproach.

12:50 P.M.

"It's not a lie."

Finn, Maddy, and Gina have waded out beyond the shoals to the edge of the sandbar, the abrupt drop of the ocean floor. Behind them, Peter splashes forward, dragging his boogie board over the crests. I want to cry.

"Yes. It is. That night at the beach picnic, the very first time I met Gina? You made a huge point of telling me you had fallen in love with Gina and were 'thankfully' one hundred percent over me. And that was probably twenty years ago. So."

"I only said that to hurt you."

"I remember exactly where I was standing. Which, oddly, was on this beach. I even remember what I was wearing. I remember what *you* were wearing. I felt as though my body had suddenly been hollowed out—the way your stomach drops on a roller coaster."

"You were wearing jeans," Jonas says softly. "The cuffs were wet."

Maddy catches a wave, surfs it all the way to shore. When she hits sand, she stands, does a triumphant little dance before racing back into the sea.

"Fuck. Fuck. Fuck. What have we done?" I am choked with dismay. For then. For now. For all of it.

"What we should have done a long long time ago."

"No," I say.

"Last night was the best night of my life. The first night."

I shake my head, my entire body a sob. "It was already too late for this years ago."

He pulls his hand away from mine. I feel as though I've been slapped—desperate now to have him back. Then something brushes my leg. Jonas has tunneled his hand under the bottom of the tent. He runs his hand up my leg, finds the inside of my thigh. "I like this part of you," he says.

"Stop that." I swat his hand away.

"Soft, baby skin." His fingers tug at my bathing suit.

"I'm serious, Jonas. They're right there. I can see the kids."

"They're a hundred yards out. Lie down. Close your eyes. I'll keep watch."

"No," I say. But I drape my towel over my hips, lie back on the sand. Footsteps crunch past the nylon tent behind my head. I listen to a loose Velcro flap scratch-scratching across the sand. The back-and-forth thwack of a rubber ball hitting wooden paddles. A drifting smell of coconut oil.

Jonas pulls my bathing suit bottom aside, traces the rim of me, presses just the tip of his finger inside me.

"Gina's right there," I whisper. "Peter."

"Shhh . . ." he says. "Way, way out. Beyond the break. I'm staring at your husband right now." He plunges his finger inside me, draws it out so slowly I can barely breathe, opens me up with his fingertips. I moan, pray the wind has carried away the sound. He finger-fucks me then, hard and fast. I move my hips, shoving myself up and down on his fingers, wanting his whole hand inside me. I am on a crowded beach. My children are playing in the waves. And the thought of Gina and Peter a skipping stone's throw away makes me more turned on than I have ever been in my life.

"Gina's getting out of the water," Jonas whispers. He pinches my clitoris hard between his fingers. I come in a hundred shudders, swallowing a scream as she walks up the beach toward us.

"It's not too late," he says. He wipes his hand in the sand, gets up, and goes to join his wife.

9

1978. September, New York.

The doldrums between the end of summer and the beginning of school. It's a day to buy new shoes at Stride Rite—get a free salted pretzel and a comic. No thunderstorms and lightning, no hail or brimstone—just a still, overcast day. But today Anna is being sent away to boarding school in New Hampshire for high school. Her bus leaves at noon from the corner of Seventy-ninth and Lex. The week we got back to the city, Leo was coming home from a gig when he saw Anna and her friend Lindsay standing on our corner begging for change. They were telling a man in a suit they had been mugged and needed money to get a bus home. The man fished a ten out of his pocket and told the girls to take a taxi. Leo waited until the man was gone before stepping out of the shadows.

"Anna," he asked benignly, "what are you doing out here? It's late. Shouldn't you be upstairs?"

"I was walking Lindsay to the bus stop," Anna said.

"I don't think so."

"That's because you don't think," Anna said.

"I saw what you were doing."

"Oh, really? What?"

"Lying. Stealing. Acting like a couple of cheap hookers on Fourteenth Street."

"You're such a pervert," Anna said.

He put out his hand. "Give me the money. Now. Your mother and I will discuss what to do with you."

"He thinks he can tell me what to do," Anna said to Lindsay, sneering. "But he's not my father. Thank god. Let's get out of here."

"Your father is gone," Leo said.

"He's not gone. He's living in London."

"If he wanted to see you, he would."

"Fuck you," Anna said. "Oh, wait, that's what you want to do anyway, isn't it?"

Leo says he doesn't remember raising his hand to slap her across the face, but Lindsay told me he had this look, like he wanted to hurt her. Now every time Leo sees her, he says he feels like a monster. One of them has to go. So, it will be Anna. I'm okay she's leaving. Last week she caught me trying on one of her bras and she ripped my summer reading assignment in half. But I'm sad for her, too. Because I know she's scared and homesick, even before she's left. And I know she wishes our mother had chosen her.

I sit on the edge of her bed and watch while she packs the last few things into her suitcase. I pick up a pair of click-clacks from her doorknob.

"Don't touch my stuff." She grabs them from me and throws them into the back of her closet. "And if you wear any of my clothes, I'll kill you."

"Can I have this?" I pull an old issue of *Tiger Beat* out of her wastebasket. Donny Osmond stares at me.

"Fine." Anna sits down on top of her suitcase and tugs the zipper closed, then looks around the room, concerned, like she's forgotten something. There's a small bottle of Love's Fresh Lemon on her bureau. She walks over to it. "Here," she hands it to me. "Since I won't be around for your birthday."

She has taken her posters down, but there are still thumbtacks everywhere and dark smudgy rectangles that look like shadow frames. A small ripped corner of glossy paper is trapped behind a tack. It's all that is left of Anna's stuff: a puzzle piece of Sweet Baby James, the rest of him crumpled in the trash.

"Why can't I have your room?" I ask. "Why does he get it?"

Anna bursts into tears. "I hate you," she says.

The worst thing of all is that Anna is being replaced. Conrad's mother has decided she can't handle a thirteen-year-old boy. She will keep weird Rosemary and her creepy obsession with Gregorian chants and original sin, and we will get Conrad. Horrible, staring Conrad with his short, thick wrestler's body. Anna says it's because his mother caught him jerking off into the toilet. We are picking him up at the airport after we put Anna on the boarding school bus. Anna is scared of traveling alone, and Mum knows it, but Leo insisted Mum be there to welcome his son into the family, so she can't drive Anna to New Hampshire. "I can't be two places at once," she told Anna.

"You should go live with Dad," I say now.

Anna goes to her desk, opens the bottom drawer and pulls out a blue airmail envelope. "I wrote to him this summer. I told him about how bad everything was with me and Leo. I asked if I could come live with him in London." She hands me the envelope.

Dad's letter is short. He says he wishes Anna could come live with him but they can't afford a larger apartment right now. Things are tight and Joanne needs privacy to write. If it were up to me, he says, of course you could live with us. He's sure things will get better. Leo is a good man. It is signed: *Love, Dad.*

"He didn't want me," Anna says.

"He says if it was up to him," I say.

"It *is* up to him, moron," Anna says.

When it's time to go, Anna locks herself in the bathroom. She turns the faucet on full blast, but I can hear her crying. Leo is out running last-minute errands, so there are no angry goodbyes. The ride downstairs in the elevator is silent. We watch the landing of each floor slip upward until the elevator man stops the brass handle with a lurch and pulls open the cage door.

"Bon voyage," our wiry doorman Gio says as we file through the lobby, keeping our eyes on the black-and-white marble floor. "Come home soon, Anna. We'll miss you."

Anna manages a smile. "Apparently you're the only one." She gives my mother an icy glare.

"You girls need a taxi?"

"No, thank you, Gio," my mother says. "We'll manage. If my husband comes home, please tell him we've taken Anna to the bus. Eleanor, help your sister with that suitcase."

We trudge down Lexington Avenue, past Lamston's, past the drugstore, past the coffee shop that makes root beer floats, down the hill to the corner, where the boarding school bus is waiting.

"Maybe it'll be like camp," I say to Anna. "You always wanted to go to sleepaway camp."

"Maybe," Anna says. She grabs my arm and puts it through hers. "I wish you were coming with me," she says. It is the nicest thing she has ever said to me.

"I'm sorry," I say.

We shove her suitcase under the bus and stand there together. "Don't let him win," she says. And without a single word to our mother, she gets on the bus and doesn't look back.

1:15 P.M.

I stand knee-high in the sea. Each time a wave crashes on me I steady my leg muscles, turn my body to the side, grip the sand beneath my toes. I don't want to get pulled under.

Peter and the kids are still far out, floating on their boogie boards. I scan the water around them, looking for fins. Looking for shadows. It's been a long time since I swam here innocently. Every time we come to the beach, I imagine a shark approaching. I'm the first one to see it. I imagine my cries of warning, the frantic splashing as they half run, half swim toward me, toward safety, toward shore. I imagine screaming for help, and then, with no one else in sight, my own frenzied plunge toward danger. Pulling them from the shark's grip, risking my own life to save my children. And every time, the other thought comes: If it was just Peter in the water, would I swim out to save him?

Peter waves to me now.

"Lunchtime!" I yell, gesturing for him to bring the kids in.

He looks over his shoulder at a big wave approaching and starts paddling with all his might. He catches the wave at its crest and rides it past me. His face is pure joy.

Gina has set up the picnic in the shade of the tent. I can see the indentation of my body in the sand, next to a pile of tuna sandwiches on a paper plate.

"Jonas went to find a bathroom." Gina passes out cups of lemonade. "Look," she says. "He's so sweet." She points to Jonas's drawing in the sand. The one I couldn't see from the tent. It's a heart. In it he has written: *I love only you.*

Gina hands the kids a bag of mini carrots. "Can you imagine having such a romantic husband?" she asks Maddy.

"You're so lucky, Gina" Maddy says.

"She *is,*" I say.

"What am I, chopped liver?" Peter says.

"Kind of," Maddy says. "But nice chopped liver."

"I hate liver," Finn says. "Never make me eat liver. Because I hate it."

I watch Jonas coming back over the dune from the bathrooms.

"Hey, man," Peter calls to him. "You missed some excellent surf out there. It was a perfect break."

"I was too busy flirting with your wife." Jonas lies down beside me on the sand, hands crossed behind his head. I can feel the warmth of his skin next to mine. The small space between us is dense. Not air, but water. Our illicit proximity thrills through me.

"She's yours for a price." Peter laughs. "I've been waiting for the right buyer." He stuffs the last bite of his sandwich into his mouth.

"I'll have my people talk to your people," Jonas says to Peter, letting his arm brush mine. I allow myself to breathe him in for a second, before sitting up and shifting away.

"Ha-ha," I say.

There's a smudge of mayo on Peter's cheek. "You have a thing there." I wet the corner of my towel with a bit of saliva and wipe it off.

"Eww," Finn says.

"It's just spit, goose. And, Peter? Don't ever say, 'Hey, man,' again. Ever."

Gina is busy putting rocks and bits of brittle black seaweed around the outline of the heart Jonas drew for me in the sand. Maddy is helping collect pebbles and shells for her. She runs up with a sand dollar in her hand.

"Look!" She sounds as if she has found the treasure of the Sierra Madre.

"It's perfect," Gina says, and puts it in the middle of the word *love*.

I can't look at Jonas.

"We should go soon," I say to Peter.

"I want to stay longer," Finn whines.

"No whining," I say.

"Me too," Maddy says.

"I'm getting burnt to a crisp."

Peter looks at his watch. "The kids are having a good time. We can stay another half an hour."

He's right. The kids are happy. It's not their fault I fucked Jonas.

"Leave them with us," Gina says. "We can drop them off later."

"That works," Peter says before I have a chance to say no. "You can have a swim in the pond. Rinse the salt off."

"Perfect," Gina says.

I look at Jonas, willing him to come up with an excuse. He smiles, amused.

Peter starts collecting our stuff. "Three-ish?"

"Sounds good," Jonas says to everyone, but he's looking at me. "If you wait for me to take your afternoon swim, I'll swim across the pond with you, Elle."

"I'll be making margaritas," Peter says.

"Salt me a glass," Gina says.

In the car, Peter puts his hand on my thigh. "Alone at last, gorgeous."

"No thanks to you. I was trying to get rid of them. They'll come back to the camp and hang around 'til dinnertime."

"But now we have a few free hours. I thought we could have a swim at Black Pond."

He leans over, nuzzles my neck. "A naked swim," he says in his "suggestive" voice. "That bathing suit makes me horny."

"My ratty old black bathing suit makes you horny?"

"My ratty old white wife does, actually."

I laugh. This is the thing about Peter.

"C'mon, it'll be fun." He reaches between my legs, strokes my thigh where my sarong has fallen open. "When was the last time you had sex in a public place?"

My leg flinches. The memory of Jonas's hand. "You know what? That's a great idea," I say, trying to cover it. "We haven't been down there in ages."

"Excellent," he says, but he takes his hand away.

10

1979. June, Connecticut.

Through the large plate-glass window in my grandparents' dining room, where I'm setting the table for dinner, I can see all the way across the low hills to the neighboring farm. Up against a barbed-wire fence, their cows chew the cud. The last bronzing light of the summer day flashes the tops of the trees beyond. My father and Joanne are getting divorced. He tells us it's because he missed his girls too much and Joanne refused to move back to the States. He chose *us*. We are spending June together.

In the living room, where they are watching the six o'clock evening news, my father and Granny Myrtle are arguing in low voices. I tiptoe around the dining table, placing a silver fork on each napkin, silver knife to the right, trying to listen-in, careful not to make a sound.

"What hogwash," I hear Granny Myrtle saying to him. "That insufferable woman cuckolded you. And I'd call it a blessing in disguise." She turns the volume on the television up a notch. "I must be going deaf in my old age."

"You're wrong, Mother," my father says. "I missed the girls." But there's a limpness in his voice that makes me think of empty rooms.

"Those two girls are the only good thing you've managed to accomplish," she says.

I hear my father get up and go to the bar, hear the sound of ice cubes landing in his bourbon glass.

Anna lies on her twin bed in our room off the kitchen, staring at the ceiling. "I have to get out of here," she says when I come in.

We've only been here two days, but already she wants to leave. Her boarding school roommate Lily has invited Anna to spend three weeks at the family's summer "cottage" in Newport. "They belong to the country club. Her brother Leander is a pro in the tennis shop."

"You don't even know how to play tennis," I say.

"God, you're annoying."

"If you leave, I'll have nothing to do."

"I have no interest in being stuck here for a month, just because Dad decided to come home." She stands up and fishes a magazine out of her bag, flops back down.

I watch her read.

"Stop looking at me," she says.

"Do you want to go swimming tomorrow?"

"No."

"Do you want to go for a bike ride?"

She ignores me.

I sit on the edge of my bed, looking around the room. "If you had to choose between Tab and Fresca for the rest of your life—if you could only have one—which would you choose?"

"I don't have to choose."

"I know, but hypothetically."

"Hypothetically, I may hit you if you don't shut up."

"Dad will be sad if you leave."

"Please," she says. "He has zero right to put us on some big guilt trip. He deserted us. And now that he's back, we're supposed to be *grateful*?"

There's a soft knock on the door. Dad pokes his head in. "There're my girls," he says brightly. "Dinner's almost ready. Mother made a pot roast."

"I'm not hungry," Anna says.

He sits down on the bed next to her. "What are you reading, kiddo?"

"A magazine." She doesn't bother to look up.

"You girls must have grown a head taller since I saw you at Easter. How was spring term?" he asks Anna. "Your mother tells me you got an A in French. *Mademoiselle, tu es vraiment magnifique!*"

His terrible accent hangs in the air.

Anna looks at him with contempt.

"Well," he says. "Both of you wash your hands. Supper is ready."

"Shut the door behind you," Anna says.

It must be early. Thin rulers of gray light stripe my bedspread through the slats of the Venetian blinds. A mourning dove is calling for its mate. I lie in bed listening to its sad, hollow song. Anna is asleep. Low voices are coming from the kitchen. I climb out of bed and walk quietly across the linoleum floor. Our door is ajar. My father is at the kitchen table with his head in his hands. Granny Myrtle stands at the kitchen counter making a piecrust, her back to him. I watch her cutting butter into flour, trickling ice water in.

"There's an eleven twenty bus on Friday morning. I looked up the schedule. It connects in New Haven." She opens a cupboard and takes out a bag of sugar.

"Anna's so angry with me."

"Well, what on earth do you expect, Henry? She's a fifteen-year-old girl who barely knows her own father. She'll need a tennis skirt. We can drive into Danbury tomorrow."

"Mother, tell me how to fix this."

"There's nothing to tell. You made your bed. Now you'll just have to figure out how to *un*-make it."

Through my bedroom window I watch my grandfather, already down the hill in the vegetable patch, kneeling in the moist earth. He is weeding the rhubarb, a full basket of sugar peas next to him. A screen door slams shut. My father walks across the lawn toward him. Granny Myrtle pulls a wooden rolling pin out of a lower drawer.

I pull on my jean shorts and a T-shirt and go in to breakfast. There's half a grapefruit laid out for me on the table, its pink triangles carefully cut away from the skin, a sprinkling of brown sugar forming a sweet crust. Next to it is a silver spoon on a linen napkin. I kiss my grandmother on her soft duck-fuzz cheek, sit down at the table.

"I thought I would take you and Anna for a swim in the Wesselmans' pool later." She kisses the top of my head. "You need to wear a hat, Eleanor. Your hair is so bleached by the sun, it's almost as white as mine."

"Hats make my forehead itch."

"Afterward we can take out some new books at the library. I'm making lamb chops for dinner. And you can help me pick asparagus from the patch."

"I don't want Anna to leave," I say.

"Asparagus isn't easy to grow, you know. Your grandfather was worried the deer and the rabbits would eat all the shoots this spring."

"I won't have anyone to be with."

"There's no reason your sister should have her summer ruined simply because your father chose to marry that god-awful woman." My grandmother hands me a pile of buttered white toast and a mason jar of homemade crabapple jam. "Your father is a good man, but he lacks backbone." She sits down beside me. "Now you, Eleanor, you have backbone. Anna is tough as a bull's hide, heaven knows, but *you* are a stoic." She pours herself a glass of buttermilk. "I blame myself for your father's weakness. I pampered him."

Behind us a floorboard creaks. My father stands there. Above the stove, a wall clock ticks the seconds. I stare down at my toast, mortified for him, wishing I could disappear, save him from his embarrassment.

"Elle and I were just talking about a swim," my grandmother says to him, as if nothing has happened. "I've put in a call to the Wesselmans. Joy tells me their blueberry bushes are positively groaning."

"I'd like to take the girls for a swim at the quarry today," my father says.

"I've already made a pie crust." She gets up, opens and closes a few cupboard doors. "I know I put those plastic berry buckets in here somewhere."

I wait for my father to push back, but he stares out the kitchen window, hands in his pockets. "The black walnut Father and I planted last year has really taken off," he says.

"Actually, Gran, I'd rather go to the quarry with Dad. We can pick blueberries for you after."

My father stands up straighter, turns to me, his face smiling so broadly I feel stricken.

"Well, of course, dear," my grandmother says to me. "If that's what you would like, then I think it's a perfect plan."

The quarry is hidden in the fold of two hills that rise up behind the Straights' farm. I've convinced Anna to come with us. Now that she knows she's leaving on Friday, her mood has lifted. The three of us climb the slope, towels in hand, following a cow path toward a wide swath of pasture. At the flat top of the hill, black-and-white cows graze, tails flicking flies from their hinds, udders drooping with grassy milk. Everywhere the field is dotted with cow pies—some dry enough to burn, others steaming wet. Across the field, shaded in a copse of trees, is the quarry: a deep, clear watering hole, its granite sides slippery with moss and drip, its roughhewn ledges perfect for leaps into the bracing cold. But first we have to make it past the cow-pies.

My father takes off his loafers and lines them up side by side in military formation. "Race you across," he says, grinning at us, and starts hopscotching his way expertly across the field. He's been coming here since he was a kid. "Last one in is a rotten egg," he shouts over his shoulder. He looks so happy, carefree, and it makes me happy. Anna kicks off her sneakers and races out into the field behind him, competing for the far side. I follow behind her, laughing, wind in my face, towel streaming out behind me like a banner. The cows move and munch around us, their swayed backs gently rocking, oblivious to the young girls rocketing past.

2:00 P.M.

The road to Black Pond is almost invisible, the center strip overgrown with wild grasses so high that as we drive, they brush the underbelly of our car, a sound like wind across a prairie. Ahead of us the road turns, forks, forks again, and again, before dead-ending at a broken split rail fence. Beyond the fence is a faint trail. I climb out of the car and follow behind Peter sharply downhill, dodging piles of coyote scat, gray with rabbit fur and thistle, to a little sand beach. Black Pond is the smallest kettle pond in the woods—a place only "Woods People" know about.

Our pond is wide and clear. Its beauty is in its size, its mile-long expanse of pristine blue, the sweep of sky. This pond is older, wiser, wizened, as if it holds too many secrets. A bottomless watering hole surrounded by dense forest, that lives half of its day in shadow.

The beach is undisturbed, thick with pine needles. No one has been here in a while. When I was a child, this was a place to bring picnics. A place for a special outing. And each time we came, we had to remind ourselves which branch of the road to take, which fork. It was easy to get lost on the way. Once when I came here with Anna, there was a naked couple on the beach having sex. The woman was lying on her back, enormous thighs spread wide, the man rutting on top of her. There was something obscene about it. Not the sex, which frightened and fascinated me, but the way her body squished out on the hard ground like uncooked dough, and the way she didn't seem to care if we saw them. We had backed away, racing for home, giggling in shame and delight.

Peter and I sit down on the bank. He fishes a cigarette out of his pocket. Lights it. "Do you remember the first time you brought me here?"

"Our very first summer."

"I still think it may have been the most romantic moment of my life."

"Well, that doesn't say much for the rest of our life together."

Peter laughs, but what I'm saying is true. I had brought him here for a late-afternoon swim. Later, when we made love on the beach, I suddenly remembered the naked couple, the woman's legs wide open, the fleshiness of it all, and I'd moaned loud enough to make the pond echo. Peter had come then. I have always known there was something bad in me, a secret perversion I have tried to hide from Peter. That I hope he will never see.

"Look," he says, taking my hand, "I owe you an apology."

"For what?"

"For this morning. For last night. I know you were upset that I didn't read Anna's poem."

"I was upset in the moment. But Jonas read it beautifully. And reading it for her every year is all that really matters."

"Still, I'm sorry. I acted like a boor, and I regret it."

"We'd all had too much to drink. You have nothing to apologize for. I promise." *Nothing.*

"Just now in the car when I put my hand on your thigh, you flinched."

"I didn't flinch," I say, hating myself for the lie. "In fact, I wish you would do that more often."

He stubs his cigarette out in the sand, looks at me with skepticism, as if making sure I'm telling him the truth. "Well then, good." He leans in, kisses me. His lips taste of smoke and salt. A few feet away from us, a box turtle slides off a log into the shallows.

I stand up, start stripping off my bathing suit. "What about that swim?" I cannot have sex with him now. Not after what I have just done with Jonas. I cannot wrong him this way, too, humiliate him. He grabs at me, but I dash away—dash for the water that I hope will purify me. Peter chases me, naked, flapping. I swim, breathless, toward the shadowy side of the pond, trying to stay ten strokes ahead. But he is faster, stronger, catches me from behind, pleased.

"Got you." He presses his erection against my rubbery back.

"Rain check," I say, wriggling out of his hold. "We really do need to get home."

"Five minutes won't make a difference," Peter says.

"Exactly." I laugh. "I need at least ten." Then I dive away from him, swim for the beach, for my clothes, for what feels like my soul.

1979. July, Vermont.

Row upon row. A sea of quivering green. I have never seen so much corn. William Whitman's cornfields are endless, formidable. They move up and over the hills toward his farm like an enemy battalion. Whitman is Leo's oldest friend. They've been best friends since elementary school. Sunday is Whitman's birthday, and we've been invited to spend the weekend on his three-hundred-acre farm in northern Vermont.

"Whit moved up here from Philadelphia a few years back, after his wife died," Leo says now as we drive the long dirt road that will, Leo promises my mother, eventually arrive at the farmhouse. She is certain we have made a wrong turn. "Left everything behind him in the rear-view mirror—fancy law firm, beautiful home in Chestnut Hill."

"I think we were meant to take that last left fork," Mum says.

"What did she die of?" I ask. Conrad and I are squashed up against opposing windows in the back seat to make room for a large, dinged-up guitar case in the middle seat.

"Well now, that's a terrible story," Leo says. "Whit and his son Tyson were away on a father-and-son bonding weekend. Ty must've been around ten at the time."

"Bonding weekend?" Mum says, trying to read a road map in the fading light. "That sounds unpleasant. Possibly a bit profane."

Leo laughs. "Hardly. Indian Guides. Big Owl, Little Owl . . . Mighty Wolf, Mighty Cub. Sit around the campfire. Bead. Whittle arrowheads."

My mother looks at him blankly, as if she can't even absorb the concept.

"Like Cub Scouts," Leo explains. "At any rate. They got home from their camping trip on Sunday night. Louisa was lying in the foyer, stabbed so many times her dress had turned red. Whit said young Tyson stood there, silent. Not a sound. Not a tear. Then he lay down on the marble floor, curled up close against his mother's body, nose to nose, searching her dead, open eyes. Like he was trying to find her soul, Whit said."

"That's so sad," I say.

"Boy never recovered. Barely speaks."

"He's a retard," Conrad says without looking up from his *Mad* magazine.

"*Conrad*." Leo keeps his voice controlled, but the warning is unmistakable.

"He's totally retarded," Conrad says to me in a stage whisper. "I met him."

Leo's hands tighten on the steering wheel. Since Conrad moved in with us last year, Leo has been making an effort to avoid any conflict. It's important to him that Conrad isn't unhappy living with us. But no matter how nice Leo is, it's pretty obvious Conrad wishes he were back home in Memphis and that, like Anna, he wishes his mother had chosen him. Most of the time, he stays in his room—Anna's old room—with the door shut, listening to ABBA and Meat Loaf, lifting weights or watching *M*A*S*H* on his rabbit-eared TV. His room stinks of feet: nauseating, moist, and sour.

We reach the farmhouse at dusk. Whitman and Tyson are waiting for us in the driveway, three dogs jumping at their heels.

"We heard that old clunker of yours coming down the road from a mile away. Could have walked out to meet it." Whitman gives Leo a bear hug. "And you, Wallace. Still looking good enough to eat."

"Been too long, man," Leo says, slapping him on the back.

Tyson is surprisingly handsome. Tall, in worn overalls, with a gentle face.

"I'm Elle," I say, putting out my hand.

But he looks away, bone-shy. Kicks at the ground.

"Tyson must be about your age, Conrad." Whitman picks up our bags, and we follow him inside. "Grab those other bags, Ty. Put them up in the loft."

Whitman is the polar opposite of his son. Small, jaunty, talking nonstop—so fast I don't know how he manages to take a breath. He reminds me of a cartoon rooster, his bantam-crackly laugh, southern accent, the swift, jilty way he moves. I like him.

Inside the old farmhouse he has laid out dinner. "Fresh rabbit stew and succotash. I've become quite the homesteader since we left Philly," he says proudly. "Baked the bread myself this morning. All the food on this table comes from our garden. Even the rabbits."

"You grow rabbits?" Conrad says, poking at his stew.

Whitman laughs. "We *catch* rabbits. They're a menace. Pests. We have to put traps out if we want a single vegetable to survive. But around here, we eat what we kill. Though we don't get to eat rabbit as often as I'd like. Ty goes around tripping the traps when I'm not looking. He can't stand the screaming."

His son sits at the end of the long oak table, eyes down, eating his rabbit stew.

Whitman turns to me. "Ever hear a rabbit scream?"

I shake my head no.

"Not pretty. Can't blame my boy." Whitman tips back in his chair. "Talking of pests, the deer are worse this year than ever." He turns to Conrad. "You know what that means, don't you, young man?"

Conrad shakes his head.

"Tomorrow night, venison."

Conrad looks horrified. Whitman bellows.

"Conrad's not exactly the adventurous-food type," Leo says, tearing off another piece of bread. His beard is a nest of crumbs. "If it was up to him, he would live on fish sticks and Whoppers."

I take a big bite of my stew. "You should try it, Conrad."

"I did," Conrad says. "It's really good."

"No, you didn't. You've just been pushing it around on your plate."

"Tattletale," Conrad spits.

"Liar," I spit back.

"Jerk-off."

Tyson has gone completely still, as if he is trying to hide in plain sight.

"Not to worry." Whitman breaks the tension. "I ate nothing but baked eggs in cream until I was twelve. I'm making spaghetti and meatballs tomorrow. And no, young man, I didn't go out and shoot a cow. Which reminds me, if any of you want to take a walk in the woods, be sure to wear something bright red. I've been having a problem with deer hunters trespassing on my land off-season."

"I hate hunters," I say.

"Well now, I don't have a problem with them if they're trying to put dinner on the table," Whitman says. "But these hunters are shooting for sport. No moral compass. Leave the damn animals lying there to bleed out. Not even a shot to the head. Shameful. My dogs find them in the woods. Come home with their mouths all crusted in blood."

"I think I'm gonna puke," Conrad says.

"*Conrad*." Leo looks as if he's about to boil over.

"We had a dog when I lived in Guatemala as a girl," Mum says. "It would get into the henhouse and bite the heads off the chickens. The gardener shot it."

"Guatemala?" Whitman raises an eyebrow, refills her glass.

"My mother moved us there when I was twelve."

"Why Guatemala?"

"An unfortunate divorce. And the help was cheap. In those days, you could have a private cook for eight cents an hour. Nanette was used to the finer things. But she hated Guatemala with a passion. She was convinced she was going to be attacked by a villager with a machete."

"Does she still live there?"

"She died a few years back. *Not* a machete. My brother Austin never left. Married a local girl. Hates the States. Thinks we're all a bunch of savages." She laughs, downs her glass. "He's an ornithologist. A parrot specialist, of all pointless things."

"I love parrots," Tyson says quietly.

After dinner, Whitman leads us up an almost vertical staircase to a loft-like attic, high ceilings open all the way to the rafters. Three mattresses are made up on the floor.

"I'll leave the bathroom light on downstairs," he says. "Don't want any of you tripping in the dark. Hope no one has a problem with bats."

"What the heck, Dad," Conrad says after Whitman has gone. "We're all sleeping in the same room?"

"It'll be fun. Like camping," Mum says, though she, too, looks doubtful.

Sometime in the night I am woken by whispers in the dark. Low raspy voices. It takes a moment for my ears to adjust. Mum and Leo are arguing. My mother sounds unhappy.

"Stop it, Wallace. Enough." I hear the rustled pull of sheets as Leo moves away from her.

"We haven't made love in weeks."

"Goddammit!" Leo hisses. "Not in front of the kids."

"I'll be quiet. I promise."

I have to pee, but if I get up now, she'll know I've heard them. She'll be mortified. And I can't bear that for her.

"You're drunk." Leo's voice is cold.

"Please, Leo," she begs.

I cover my ears, pull my blanket over my head so I won't hear her pleading. She sounds so pitiful—panicked, desperate. Maybe this is what it sounds like when a rabbit screams.

It must be early when I wake again. The whole house is asleep. The ashen light of dawn seeps in through a small dormered window. Conrad is on top of his covers, fully dressed. He hasn't even taken off his shoes. Leo and my mother lie with their backs to each other. I hope that, when they wake, Leo will tell her how much he loves her.

I tiptoe down the stairs, anxious for fresh air. Outside, the morning still holds its chill. I haven't seen the farm in daylight, and it is beautiful. Brambles of wild roses climb up and over split rail fences. In the kitchen garden, rows and rows of zucchini blossoms, sugar snap peas on stilts, a tangle of orange nasturtiums licking at their ankles. Three rabbits are feeding in the lettuces.

Past the garden, the cornfields stretch all the way to the base of the hills, where dark forests pitch toward a pinking sky. I pull my sweater on and head out through a potato field that borders the corn—its musky-sweet smell rises, hovers a few feet above the ground.

I follow a wide tractor path that slices through the center of the fields, parting the sea of corn. Cornstalks like hedgerows flank me on either side. I listen to their swish, their whispers. I wish I could *un*hear my mother.

I've been walking for almost an hour when I come around a sharp bend and stop short. Ten yards ahead of me, an enormous buck stands in the middle of the track. A Bambi's-father buck, his proud, towering antlers like bare trees in winter. He looks directly at me and I look back, willing him not to spring away. And then the crack of a gunshot. His eyes open wide in surprise, and he falls. Blood pours from a hole in his neck. He lies there in soft, sad silence. There's a movement in the corn, the barrel of a gun. I step back into the thick green, hidden from the hunters. Tyson emerges onto the track. He wipes his mouth with the back of his hand. His eyes are blank, dull, the eyes of a sleepwalker. He lowers himself to the ground and lies down beside the dying animal. He looks so small next to it, childlike. He stares into the buck's eyes, watches, unblinking, until its life slips away to nothingness. He gets to his knees and in a gesture somehow both beautiful and sickening, he leans down and kisses the dead deer gently on its mouth. Tyson hears my sharp intake of breath. He leaps to his feet, gun cocked.

"Tyson, wait!" I step out onto the track.

He looks at me for a moment and then, before I can say another word, he is gone. I watch the tops of the corn snaking behind him in his path.

When I get back to the farm, Conrad is in the vegetable garden with Whitman. He stirs a water bucket as Whitman pours dark brown powder into it. Tyson stands nearby, a small bloodstain on the tip of his boot.

"Morning, Elle," Whitman calls out when he sees me. "We wondered where you'd gotten to."

"I walked out through the cornfields."

Tyson watches me intently. The entire walk home, I've tried to process what I witnessed, to understand why he would do such a cruel thing. I imagine the kind of agony he must still feel, the rage at his mother's killer still out there, unpunished. And yet what I saw seemed more an act of love than of misplaced revenge.

Whitman hands me a bucket. "Come on and give us a hand spreading this."

"It stinks," I say. "What is it?"

"Dried cow blood. Keeps the deer and the rabbits away. They can't stand the smell, either. Just a trickle around each plant. It doesn't take much. Hope you kids are hungry. There's a whole load of bacon in the oven. Eggs from the henhouse were still warm to the touch when I collected them."

Conrad and I help Whitman pour blood on his crops while Tyson watches us from the sidelines of baby lettuces and cucumbers. By the time we have finished, all the life in Whitman's garden smells like death to me.

11

4:00 P.M.

“Drink?” Peter squeezes a lime around the cobalt blue edge of a Mexican glass, then dips it rim side down onto a plate of kosher salt.

“Are we legal yet?” My mother wanders in, looking at her watch.

“Definitely not.” Peter pours a hefty slug of tequila into a martini shaker.

“Well, in that case, I can’t resist.”

God, it annoys me—the banter of WASPs around alcohol. “Where on earth are they?” I say. Jonas and Gina still haven’t appeared with the kids, and with every minute that passes, I’m becoming more agitated. Since Peter and I got back from Black Pond, I’ve spent the entire time waiting for Jonas to appear. Not playing backgammon with Jack, not giving myself a much-needed manicure, but rereading an old issue of *The New Yorker*, biting my fingernails. It hasn’t even been twenty-four hours and already, when I’m not with him, I’m marking time until I am—as if my own life has ceased to exist and is only the time in between him and him. It angers me, this endless jangling. I picture my stomach cavity filled to the brim with little pieces of bitten fingernails. A lifetime's worth of pain that never got digested. When they cut me open, that's what they will find. Strange deposits, sharp and brittle.

Jack is curled up beside me on the sofa, his head in my lap, reading something on his phone. From this angle, he looks like a sweet little boy, and my heart breaks. I lean down to kiss him, but he swats me away with the back of his hand.

"I'm still mad at you," he says.

"Rude of them to make us wait. Make some room." Peter squeezes in next to us on the sofa, trying not to spill his drink. "Sip?"

"After my swim."

"I'll have one," Jack says.

Peter starts to hand Jack his glass.

"Don't even think about it." I stand up, shaking them both off me. "I'm going for my swim. Tell Jonas and Gina I'll see them another day."

"Should you be worried?" my mother asks from the kitchen.

"Thanks, Mum. Yes, they've probably all drowned. Or died in a fiery car crash." I slam the screen door behind me.

"Your wife has been a complete nightmare since she woke up this morning," Mum says to Peter. "Is she having the curse?"

"I heard you," I shout, and storm down to the water's edge.

Twelve swift strokes bring me out to the deep. I turn onto my back, arms akimbo, using only my frog legs to push me out deeper. Listen to the muffled sound of water bubbling past me.

In the middle of the pond, I turn over and do a dead man's float, facedown, open my eyes and try to see. But my eyes can't adjust to the pond-green gloam. My senses fail me here, in over my head. I imagine what it would be like to drown—to sink down into the underneath, trying to fight back to the surface, drink in water as if it were air.

1979. October, New Hampshire.

Outside the car window, New England autumn rushes past in a blur of yellow and red, the occasional dark punctuation of pine. It is Parents' Weekend at Anna's boarding school. Dixon, Mum, Becky, and I are driving up for the night to see her. I've never been to New Hampshire. "Neither have I," Anna tells me when I call to say we're coming. "We never leave campus. I'm stuck in a redbrick time warp with girls who play field hockey and live on Ex-Lax." But the truth is, Anna is much happier now. She almost never comes home to visit. On long weekends, she stays with a roommate who lives closer to school.

Going up for Parents' Weekend was Dixon's idea. Mum wasn't planning to go, but Dixon insisted. Anna is his goddaughter. He likes Leo a lot, he tells Mum, but marriages end, children don't.

"Well, that's not technically true," Mum says.

"Don't be grim. You're starting to sound like your mother," Dixon says, poking her in the ribs.

Frizzy Andrea and Dixon have split up. When their baby was born (at home in the bathtub), it was immediately clear it wasn't Dixon's. "I am many things," Dixon tells us. "Brilliant, a sex god, an expert on Walt Whitman. But Asian is not one of them."

"You'll find someone," Mum says. "You always do. In about two seconds."

"True," Dixon says. "But nothing that sticks."

"That's because you have terrible instincts and only date morons," Mum says.

"It's my Achilles' heel," Dixon says. "If I'd had any sense, I would have married you."

"Obviously."

"To be fair to Andrea, she was just following her own truth."

"I rest my case."

Dixon laughs. "Whatever. It was a cute baby, right, Becks?"

"Kind of," Becky says. "His head was a weird shape."

"That was temporary. Andrea's birth canal was very narrow."

Becky makes a gagging noise. "Can we please not talk about Andrea's vagina, Dad?"

Becky and I are squeezed into the back seat between Dixon's waxed-canvas duffel and a big Mexican straw bag of Mum's that she's filled with last-minute things Anna forgot to pack when she left in September.

"Why can't it go in the trunk?" I ask.

"The trunk is full of crates. We're going apple picking on the way home," Mum says. "We'll make apple butter," she says when I groan. "Don't let me forget to pick up some pectin, Dix."

"Cool," Dixon says. "Apple butter." He turns on the radio, spins the knob past several staticky stations.

"Please keep your eyes on the road," Mum says to him.

"No backseat driving."

The only local station he can get to come in clearly is playing "Time in a Bottle."

"Not this," Mum says. "I can't bear Jim Croce. Too maudlin."

"Give the poor guy a break, Wallace. He was killed by a pecan tree."

"Well, that certainly didn't improve his music."

Dixon grins and turns the volume up all the way. My mother puts her fingers in her ears, but she is smiling. She is always more relaxed around Dixon.

We turn off onto a country road bordered by running stone walls and stands of maples. It twines its way through open pasture, red-painted barns, endless apple orchards, trees still heavy with fruit. Anna's boarding school is on a narrow lane, its entrance marked by two massive granite pillars and a discreet bronze plaque, tarnished and almost unreadable. Lamont Academy. The long gravel driveway opens suddenly onto wide lawns punctuated by trees so thick-waisted it would take three people to put their arms around the trunks.

Lamont is bigger than I'd imagined, more formidable. Redbrick dormitories and classroom buildings climbing with ivy, a white clapboard chapel next to a marble-columned library. In the parking lot, students swarm their parents in relief and happiness. Anna is nowhere in sight. We find her sitting in the sun on the steps of her dorm. There's a paperback in her lap. She is crying.

"How can Phineas have died?" she says, closing the book and getting to her feet. "I hate this book."

"*A Separate Peace* is the ultimate preppy downer. Everyone knows that," Dixon says.

"He was so handsome," Anna says. "He was perfect."

"Only the good die young," Dixon says.

"That's complete rubbish," Mum says.

Anna and Mum stand slightly apart, like kids at a school dance, each waiting for the other to make the first move. It has never been the same between them since Anna was sent away. Mum has tried to make it up to her, but there's a distance in Anna, a coolness that will never thaw—as if her past life is in the rearview mirror, still visible, but her eyes are only on the road ahead.

Mum breaks first, crossing the ground to where Anna is standing. "I'm so happy to see you," she says, hugging Anna. "You look wonderful."

"I wasn't expecting you to make it," Anna says.

"Of course we made it," Mum says, bristling.

"You didn't turn up last year."

"Well, we're here now." Dixon puts his arm around Anna. "And what a gorgeous day. I need to find the john before I piss myself, and then I want the grand tour."

"Jesus, Dad," Becky says.

"Lily's parents invited us to have lunch with them at the Inn," Anna says.

"I thought we were having a family lunch, but that sounds lovely, too." She smiles, but I can tell she's disappointed.

"I want to show Elle my dorm room first." Anna takes my hand in hers as if we've always been best friends.

Becky starts to follow, but Dixon stops her. "Have you seen the size of that tree, Beck? It must be two hundred years old."

Anna has a triple—a big room with tall windows, a battered wood floor, and three single beds pushed up against the walls. On the windowsill, an avocado pit sprouts hoary white roots into a glass jar filled with cloudy water. Anna's bed is unmade—I recognize her purple Indian bedspread. Two photographs are tacked on the wall above it. One is of Anna and her roommates standing in front of a swimming pool. The other photo is of the two of us climbing a tree in Central Park. We are laughing.

Anna sits down on her bed cross-legged. Pats the space beside her. The mattress sags at the edge when I sit down.

"So, guess what?" she says. "And you have to promise not to tell anyone."

"Okay."

"I'm serious," she says. "On pain of death." She leans in. "I lost my virginity last weekend." She sounds so proud of herself, as if this is some great achievement, and I want to say the right thing—something that sounds casual, grown-up. Anna is confiding in me. But all I can think of is mustiness, damp sweat, my mother begging. I pull at a loose thread on Anna's bedspread. An accordion of cloth gathers in its wake.

“I didn’t know you had a boyfriend,” I say.

“I don’t. He’s a friend of Lily’s brother. He’s nineteen. We were all there for Columbus Day.”

“What was it like?”

“Not great. But still—I’m not a virgin anymore.”

“What if you got pregnant?”

“I didn’t. I borrowed Lily’s diaphragm.”

“Gross.”

“I washed it first, duh. For, like, two hours,” she laughs.

“That’s still gross,” I say.

“Whatever. Better than getting PG.” She hops off the bed and walks to the window, picks up the avocado plant, holds it to the light. “I need to change this water.”

“I’m going to wait,” I say.

“Wait for what?”

“Until I fall in love.”

Anna puts the jar back down, says nothing, stands with her back to me, whatever window she opened between us, shut.

“Maybe I won’t wait. I don’t know,” I scramble. “I guess it sounds dumb.”

“No, I think it’s a good idea,” she says, turning to me.

“You do?”

“For *you*. Just not for me. I doubt I’ll ever fall in love. I’m not the type.”

We drive home in the dark. The car smells of fresh apples. Becky and I sit in back playing coochie catchers.

“Pick a number,” she says, going first.

“Three.”

She opens and closes the beaky paper mouth three times.

"Pick a color."

"Blue."

She unfolds the blue triangle to reveal my fortune.

Inside she has written: *You will go to third base with a fat oily pig.* She has the handwriting of an eight-year-old.

"You're so gross," I laugh. "Your turn." I pick up my own catcher and put my fingers into the paper triangle slots. Open. Shut. Open. Shut. Open. She points to red.

I open the flap.

"*A mysterious stranger will soon come into your life.*" She reads what I have written in a whisper. "And he will put his penis in you."

"I did NOT write that. Psycho," I say.

"Wait." Becky leans across me and unzips her father's duffel, careful not to let him hear. She pulls out a white book with no cover. "You think *I'm* gross?"

The book is filled with black-and-white drawings. Picture after picture of a couple doing it. The woman looks like the wife on *The Bob Newhart Show*, except naked. The man has long dark hair and a beard. He is wearing an open shirt and nothing else. His penis dangles out from the bottom of his shirttails. He's revolting. I think about Anna having sex with that college guy. The thought of her with someone she barely knows makes me feel sad for her, and I wonder if, deep inside, she regrets it. Because once you do it, you can never undo it.

Becky turns the page to a different illustration: the woman is leaning against a wall. The man is on his knees with his face in her crotch.

"Blech," Becky whispers. "Can you imagine anything more disgusting? She probably tastes like pee."

"*Ewww.*" We start laughing so hard it hurts.

"What's the joke?" Dixon asks from the front seat. "I want in."

Becky shoves the book back in her dad's duffel.

"We were reading," I say.

"Elle, you know reading in the car makes you sick," Mum says. She opens the glove compartment and takes out a plastic baggie. "Just in case." She hands it to me. "But for god's sake, if you do feel sick, try to hold it until we can pull over. The smell of vomit makes me want to vomit."

4:10 P.M.

I let my lungs ache until, unable to bear it another second, I wrench my head out of the water, breaking for air. Something bites my ankle, sharp, quick. I panic, feeling its pull. Jonas pops up out of the water in front of me. He laughs at the look of panic on my face.

"Are you insane? I thought you were a snapper." I swim away from him, furious, but he grabs my bikini bottom.

"Let go."

"I'm not letting go."

"You're a jerk."

"I'm not." He yanks me closer to him. "You know I'm not."

"You were late."

"Your children are fish. They wouldn't come out of the water."

"I know." I sigh. "Sometimes I want to put their boogie boards through a wood chipper. I don't know how Peter has the patience."

We tread water, apart but together.

"Gina senses something," I say. "There was a weird moment when I first got there." In the distance, Maddy and Finn chase each other around on the shore. Behind them, my mother hangs a white linen tablecloth on the line. I hear a door slam, the linger of Gina's laugh. Jonas hears it, too. I look away from him.

"It's all right," he says.

"It's not all right. There's something wrong with me. I should be filled with agonizing guilt. Instead, on the beach with Gina, I felt smug. Like I'd won. That heart in the sand."

"You have."

"That's a terrible thing to say."

"It is," he says. One of the things I've always loved most about Jonas is his ability to admit his fault lines, a shrug-shouldered peace with who he is. "I love Gina. But I carry you in my bloodstream. This isn't a choice."

"Of course it's a choice."

"No, it's what I have to do. And I accept that. That's the difference between us. Acceptance of the choices we made."

"I don't want to talk about that." Whatever secrets my stepsister Rosemary revealed when Peter and I were in Memphis last week, however much it may have changed how I think about the past, Jonas and I will always have to be the sacrifice, the penance. "I'm not going to leave Peter."

"So that's it? This just ends?" Jonas says. He looks away from me to the wild, uninhabited side of the pond. Gazes at the reeds, the rushes, the place where we first became true friends: a small boy, hidden in the tree line, straddling the low-hanging branch of a tree, patient, pin-drop quiet; and a gangly, angry girl who wanted to die that day. The tree is still there, but its branches now reach high into the open sky.

Jonas sighs. "So many years."

"Yes."

"It grew so tall."

"That happens."

He nods. "I love the way trees grow up and down at the same time. I wish we could do that."

All I want to do is kiss him. "You should swim back."

"I told Gina I'd walk home from the far side of the pond and meet her back at the house."

"No. Swim back to her."

Jonas looks at me, his expression unreadable. "All right," he says. "Maybe I'll see you at the camp."

"Maybe," I say, hating everything about this: the distance left by the shift of his body away from mine, the familiar hole I carried for so many years inside of me opening back up. But I have to let him go, even if this, us, is what I've wanted my entire life. Because Jonas is wrong, *this* is wrong, and it *is* too late. I love Peter. I love my children. There isn't any more than that.

I watch him swim away, watch the space between us widening. And then I'm swimming after him, pulling him under the water with me, kissing him hard and long, there in the blur, hidden from the knowing world, telling myself it will be the last time.

"Are you trying to drown me?" he says when we come up gasping for breath.

"It would make things easier."

"For fuck's sake, Elle. I spent my whole life waiting for last night. Don't take it back."

"I have to. I'm going to. I just can't face it quite yet."

"Don't," he says.

We butterfly our way across the pond, tandem-legs splashing, winging for lift, throw ourselves onto the little sandy beach, sit side by side in the warm air.

12

1980. April, Briarcliff, New York.

Sunday. We've had a wet spring, but today is perfection, the sun strong, everything green and blossoming. Joanne has asked my father to clear out his boxes from her parents' attic. We drive up the Hudson with all the windows rolled down. Since Joanne and my father split up, we've been spending much more time together. He's been making a big effort with me and Anna—he even drove up to visit her at boarding school. But I can't help knowing that if Joanne were still around, he probably wouldn't be.

Dad has packed us a picnic: ham-and-tomato sandwiches, pears, sweet pickles, a bottle of beer for him, a Yoo-hoo for me. He's in a great mood.

"I couldn't see the back of Joanne fast enough, but I *am* sorry to lose Dwight and Nancy. They've been good to me. We'll stop somewhere first to have our lunch. I don't want to turn up early."

"I loved that house. It had the nicest smell."

"Nancy will be glad to see you. She's been in a bit of a blue patch since Frank went away to college."

I'm relieved Frank won't be there. The thought of his moist upper lip, his revolting thick-bodied snake, still makes me nauseous. "I haven't seen them in so long. Anna and I used to stay there all the time."

"Not *all* the time," Dad says. He pulls off into the parking lot of the Tarrytown train station. "There's a decent little picnic area on the other side of the tracks."

As I get out of the car, something sad shudders through me, indistinct but clear. It's been years since I've been here, but this is the stop where Anna and I would get off the Harlem-Hudson Line when we came to visit Dad and Joanne before they moved to London—the stop where we learned not to expect to see more of our father than the short car ride to and from the Burkes' house.

We cross the tracks and find a bench overlooking the Hudson. The river is shrugging off the last of winter, stretching itself awake for spring. I watch a large branch moving downstream, pulled by the slow, heavy current. My father fishes his old Swiss Army Knife out of his pocket, pries out the bottle opener, and opens his beer. I've always loved his knife—its hidden treasures: the teensy pair of scissors, the nail file, the doll-sized saw. He pulls out the large blade and begins peeling a ripe pear in a tight, precise spiral.

"Why did we stop staying with the Burkes, Dad?"

"Because I wanted my girls with me."

"Then why did you always leave us there?"

"Well," he says, "that was Joanne." He slices off a piece of pear and offers it to me on the blade of the knife. "Careful. That blade is sharper than it looks. There's a hunk of Muenster in the bag."

With my father, everything is always someone else's fault.

"Have I ever told you the story of how I got this scar?" He holds up his thumb. Leans in. A dramatic pause. My father doesn't *tell* stories, he performs them. Narrates. Puffs up like a frigate bird, red and barrel-chested. Waits for his audience to settle in. Usually, when he's repeating a story, I pretend I've never heard it before. I don't want to hurt his feelings. But right now all I want to do is pinprick him. Deflate him. *Yes, you've told it to me about twenty times.*

"Pop gave me this knife when I turned ten. Told me knives were for men, not boys—to use it with respect. I cut my thumb wide open the very first time I used it. Trying to pry the cap off a bottle of cola with that same blade. Had to get twelve stitches. Blood all over the damn shop. Like a jugular vein. Pop took the knife away for a year. Told me he'd made a grave error. Said a boy who can't tell the difference between a bottle opener and a blade was just masquerading as a man. That was a powerful lesson." Behind him, a train slows to approach the station, heading south. "Your grandfather taught me to whittle, you know. And to shoot straight. Do you remember that little wooden turtle I made for you?"

I shake my head no, though it is on the shelf above my bed, where it always is. I hand my father the cheese, take a sandwich from the picnic bag. I pull off the top slice of bread. It is stained wet with pink tomato juice. One by one, I pick off the seeds, flick them into the grass. On the river, a sailboat fights the current.

We pull into the Burkes' circular gravel driveway at two on the dot.

"Perfect timing," Dad says, pleased with himself.

A chocolate Lab is lying on the front porch, napping in a patch of sun. It ambles over, rubs against my father's leg, then stands there motionless, as if that simple gesture has left it stunned.

"Hello, old girl," Dad says, patting her. "You remember Cora?" he asks me.

"The puppy?"

"She's an ancient lady now. Dog years." He knocks on the door.

"Hello-o?" he calls out. "Nancy? Dwight? Anybody home?" But there is only the silent house. "Nancy's car is here. She must be gardening out back." He opens the front door and we let ourselves in.

Everything is exactly as I remember it: the shiny brass tongs and cinder scoop for ashes leaning against the white brick fireplace. The WASPy threadbare wingbacks, worn Persian rug. A vase of garden peonies sits on the coffee table, loose petals strewn over art books.

"Hello, hello?" Dad calls out, again. I follow him into the kitchen. The Mr. Coffee has been left on, giving off the faint sour odor of burnt coffee. My father turns off the machine, holds the glass pot under the tap. It hisses and steams as water hits the caramelized ring, tinting the water brown.

"She's not in the garden. They must be out for a walk. I'll start bringing my boxes down from the attic. Go have a look at your old room."

"Maybe we should wait. It feels like we're trespassing."

"The Burkes are family, Joanne or no Joanne."

The hidden door that leads to our room is open. I pause halfway up the wooden staircase on the landing where Anna and I used to sit and play with our dolls, before heading upstairs. Nothing has changed—the same flowered pillowcases we used when I was six, the same lace doilies on the bureaus. Dotted swiss bedspreads. I picture Frank's agonized face, the day we found his hamster Goldie squashed behind Anna's bed. The way he cried. His high-pitched gurgle. Sun streams in through the mullioned windows. Above the dour rock face, the sky is brilliant. Nancy's rhododendrons are in bloom. Nothing has changed, and yet now our old room feels sad and hollow, one-dimensional—like a stage set for a happy childhood, which, when you look behind it, reveals itself to be false walls and empty spaces. Suddenly all I want is to be with my father.

Downstairs in the pantry, I stop in front of the door to Frank's old hamster room. A yellowing sign in faded Magic Marker is still tacked to the door: DO NOT ENTER ON PAIN OF DEATH. I turn the knob, step into the forbidden, windowless room. My eyes take a little while to adjust. It's a storage room now, the walls stacked high with crates. Frank's hamster cages are gone. But in the far corner, illuminated by the pale glow of neon, is a glass aquarium. It is five times larger than the one I remember. As I walk toward it, I see a subtle shift, a movement, sinuous, reptilian. I back out of the room.

Nancy is sitting at the kitchen table, slicing apples. "Well hello, dear," she says brightly. "There you are."

I feel caught in the spotlight of her benign smile.

She puts down an apple core and wipes her hands on her apron. "Hasn't Waldo gotten big?"

"We knocked." I say. "Dad said it would be okay to start moving his things."

"Of course, dear. I lay down for a quick catnap. You've certainly blossomed into a lovely young woman. You must be fifteen by now."

"Thirteen—I'll be fourteen in September."

"I imagine you're thirsty after that drive. I made iced tea. Dwight should be back any minute now. He drove down the hill to return a book to his friend Carter Ashe." She goes to the refrigerator and stands there without opening it, gives her head a little shake as if she's trying to get rid of a passing thought. "He missed luncheon," she says. "You must be thirsty. I made iced tea."

I find my father in the attic surrounded by boxes and piles of old photographs. The air is hot, stuffy. It smells of the past.

"Have a look at these." He passes me a thick manila envelope. "All my old contact sheets and negatives. There are some wonderful ones of your mother."

I pull out the black-and-white contact sheets and look through them. Endless photos of my mother in a cocktail dress and pearls, lying on a sofa, smiling into the camera. Anna in the bathtub, covered in soapsuds, with a colander on her head. Me and Mum in the playground. Mum is pushing me on the baby swings; one of my red buckle-up shoes has fallen off. At the bottom of the stack, I find a series of photos of the four of us. We are on the steps of the Natural History Museum, Anna and I in matching smocked dresses and Mary Janes. Dad is carrying me on his shoulders. I have no memory of any of it.

In the shadows of an eave, pushed up against the crawl space, are three open boxes with my father's name scrawled across them in black marker. They are filled with record albums. His collection of 78s in brown paper envelopes, LPs in worn cardboard covers. I run my finger across their spines. I like the sound it makes. I remember these.

My father picks up a faded color photograph from the pile in front of him. "Come look at this one." Hands it to me.

It is a photo of Dad with Mum. They look so young. They are in a field. My mother is lying in the grass, her head resting on my father's lap. She's wearing sailor shorts and a frilly white blouse, its top three buttons unbuttoned. Her eyes are closed. He is staring down at her. He looks happy in a way I do not recognize. Behind them, in the distance, a volcano rises up into a faded sky.

"Acatenango." He points to the volcano. "Your mother and I flew to Guatemala so I could meet your grandmother Nanette and your uncle Austin. What a disaster *that* was. You never met her, did you?"

"I'm not sure. Maybe. When I was a few months old."

My father nods. "Of course. It was while you were still in the hospital. After your operation. She came for Christmas. Brought me an embroidered folkloric tapestry of Mary and Joseph riding a donkey. She tried to claim it was a valuable Mayan relic," he laughs. "Matter of fact, it's probably at the bottom of one of these boxes. She was a force of nature, that woman. Couldn't stand me. Said your mother was marrying down. She was right, of course. Your mother was way out of my league." He pauses. "Wallace and Leo seem very happy."

"I guess."

He takes the photo from me. Stares at it for a long time. "I was so in love with your mother."

"So, what happened? I mean, you're the one who left."

"Believe me, that was the last thing in the world I wanted."

"Then why did you get divorced?"

"I suppose your mother finally realized Nanette was right about me." He laughs, but I can tell there's a part of him that believes it's true.

"That's completely idiotic," I say. "And Nanette sounds like a bitch."

Dad smiles. "Well, about that, Miss Elle, you are right." He stands up, dusts off his trousers. "Let's load this stuff up and get the hell out of Memory Lane."

Nancy hugs us goodbye at the door. "I wish you didn't have to leave," she says. "I'm certain Dwight will be home any minute now. He was just returning a book." She stands on the porch, waving.

I watch her dwindle out of sight. "Nancy seemed so sad. Lonely."

"Dwight's a good man—great poet—but he has his demons. Marriage isn't always bliss," my father says.

Two days later, my father receives a panicked call from Joanne. Dwight Burke's body has been pulled out of the Hudson River. He had been missing since Monday morning.

"He went to see his friend Carter Ashe," Joanne tells my father. "They ended up having one too many bourbons. You know how he is. Mother didn't want him driving, convinced him to stay the night. According to

Carter, Daddy drove down to the river at sunrise. 'To shake off the night before.'"

"No better cure for a hangover than a cold swim," my father says when he tells me about the drowning. "But that river can be a mighty beast."

4:30 P.M.

There is nothing more beautiful than Jonas wet from a swim. Black hair slapping at his neck, dripping and rough-cut. Barefoot, wearing nothing but old shorts, his glowing skin, watchful pale green eyes. He picks a leaf off a bush and carefully removes its spine, its tracery, lays the delicate silhouette on the palm of my hand. He crushes the torn-away green of the leaf and waves it under my nose.

"*Mmm.*" I breathe in its raw, minty smell. "Sassafras."

"Did you know Native American tribes used it to cure acne?"

"Very romantic." I laugh.

"Quick walk to the sea?"

The sun has poured a molten river onto the ocean. A cormorant plunges into liquid gold. Waves swell without cresting. Plovers peck their way around the sandbars in search of sea lice and razor clams. There are still a few late-afternoon stragglers. We sit in a hollow at the top of the dunes, hidden behind a screen of poverty grass. I am in love.

"There was a seal hauled up on the beach earlier," Jonas says. "Finn and I walked down to see it. Huge gash in its blubber. Looked like a shark had tried to take a bite out of it."

"Why do all those idiots at the beach still get excited when they spot a seal in the water? They're everywhere now—they're like the pigeons of the sea."

"Seals are quite extraordinary. They can drink salt water and distill it into fresh. They separate out the salt in their urine. I wrote a paper about it in fifth grade. As I recall, I posited the idea that someone should figure out a way to make a saltwater distillery out of seal bladders."

"What a peculiar child you were."

Jonas trickles grains of sand through his fingers. "So, what did you and Peter do after you left the beach?"

"I don't know. Nothing really."

"When we arrived, he thanked us for hanging with the kids. Said it was nice for you two to have some 'alone time.'"

"Jonas."

"Sorry." He looks ten years old. "I can't help it."

"You can."

He threads a sharp blade of grass between his thumbs, strings it tight, blows through the hole, a low foghorn tone.

"Fine," I say. "But you asked. We threw our wet towels in the back of the car, pulled off onto a dead end in the woods, and had sex. It was nice. It's been a while."

"You're lying."

"He's my husband, Jonas."

"Don't." He stares at the ground, hair falling across his face. I can't see his eyes.

I sigh. "We went to Black Pond for a quick swim, and then I sat on the porch and read my back-issue guilt pile of *New Yorker*s while I waited for you. What took you so long? I was going crazy."

Jonas looks up now and smiles. "God, I am so fucking in love with you."

Far away, on the flat glassy sea, a fat seal head breaks the water's surface. I watch it appear and disappear up the shoreline.

"I'm in love with you, too," I say. "But I'm not sure it matters."

1980. October, New York.

Orchestra has gone late. We are rehearsing for the middle school winter concert. I am second flute.

"Stands away, everyone," Miss Moody, our music teacher, calls out as students begin filing toward the door. "Chorus is in this room first period." She comes over to where I'm sitting, putting away the pieces of my flute. "I'd like you to work on that first movement over the weekend, Eleanor. And do those exercises I gave you last week in our lesson. You need to strengthen your embouchure if you are going to hit the high C. We wouldn't want you to go sharp, would we?"

I like Miss Moody, but she can be so annoying. I pull on my down jacket, shove my flute in my book bag.

It's only four thirty, but already it feels as if night is falling. I hate Daylight Savings. The late October wind bites through my clothes as I trudge home alone down Madison Avenue. At Eighty-eighth Street, I stop at the stationery store to get a 3 Musketeers bar. When I exit the store, a young guy is leaning against the wall of the building. He is tall, his face covered in acne scars, wearing a Varsity basketball jacket—St. Christopher's, the Catholic high school in our neighborhood.

"Hey." He smiles at me, so I smile back. "Nice tits," he says as I walk past him.

"I'm wearing a parka, moron." But I hunch my shoulders and walk away as fast as I can, down the darkening street. I'd run, but I know better than to look afraid. I'm waiting to cross at the light when I hear footsteps behind me. It's him, and he has a twisted, creepy smile on his face. I look around for a grown-up to walk with, but there's no one else on the street. He reaches into his pocket. He has a switchblade.

"Here, kitty, kitty," he hisses.

Cars are coming in both directions, but going into the traffic seems the safest option. A Checker cab barely misses me, and the driver rolls down his window to shout. But I keep going, running so hard that the cold air burns my lungs. At the bottom of the hill I make a sharp turn and run into the lobby of a doorman building.

"Can I help you, miss?"

I can't catch my breath. "There's a guy following me," I gasp.

The doorman goes out onto the street, looks both ways. "No one out here," he says.

I sit down on a radiator bench.

"Is there someone you'd like me to call?"

"No, thank you," I say. Mum is sitting in on Leo's sound check at the Village Gate. It's Thursday, so Conrad will still be at wrestling practice. "I live around the corner."

The doorman checks the street again and gives me the thumbs-up. "All clear, miss."

I follow him out and look down the block toward Park Avenue. There's a church on the corner. Its lights are on.

"I'll be okay," I say.

But the moment I hear the heavy doors closing behind me, I wish I had stayed put. I walk down the street checking every stairwell, walking close to the cars. The Christmas trees are already up on the center islands of Park Avenue, their fairy lights making a path down the middle of the avenue, all the way to Grand Central. In the spring, beds of tulips bloom there. They come back every year with the cherry blossoms. On our block, the tulips are bright red. When their petals begin to fall, they leave behind rows and rows of naked stalks crowned with small black clusters that look like eyelashes.

When I turn onto Park, he is there, waiting for me in the shadows, his back up against the wall of the church. His hand darts out and grabs my arm. "Here, kitty, kitty." He flicks open his switchblade.

We've been watching public service messages in school. Short black-and-white movies that warn us about rubella, eating lead paint chips, the dangers of heroin, the importance of self-defense. And I remember, now, that I am meant to face my attacker.

"I don't like Catholic boys," I say. "They have pink skin. It's disgusting." I look directly into his mean, close-set eyes, his acne-scarred face. I stab the instep of his foot with the heel of my shoe as hard as I can. And then I run—panting, terrified, harder than I have ever run in my life—until I reach the safety of home.

5:00 P.M.

"I need to get back." I stand up and brush the sand off.

"I want to show you something first."

"I told Finn I'd take him canoeing."

"Ten minutes."

I follow him along the top of the dune to where it reaches the edge of the woods. He takes my hand and plunges us into the tree line. Jonas stops in front of an overgrown thicket. "Here."

There's nothing but a rage of green.

"Look underneath."

I get down on the ground and peer under the thicket. There, hidden by the overgrowth, is the old abandoned house. The house Jonas and I found when we were kids. All that's left now is a foundation and two stone walls; the rest has been devoured by blackberry brambles and catbrier. Indigo weed climbs up the crumbling walls, strangling them in beauty.

"How did you find this again?"

He lies down on the ground beside me. Points to a hole where a door once was. "Remember the kitchen? And that room in the middle was going to be our bedroom when we got married."

"Of course I remember. You promised to get me a double boiler. I feel kind of cheated."

He rolls on top of me, pulls the string of my bikini top with his teeth so that it falls away, licks my breasts like a big sloppy dog.

"Stop that." I push him away, laughing. But I can feel my sex swelling.

"Sorry. I have to." He stares into my eyes, intense, never once looking away, as he spreads me wide, open. Enters me. When he comes, I can feel it pulsing out of him, filling me.

"Don't move," I whisper. "Stay inside me." Without moving, he reaches down and, like the slightest breath, barely touches the tip of me until I sob, cry out, aching in eternity.

We lie like that, enmeshed, two bodies, one soul.

I wrap my legs tighter around him, trapping him, forcing him even deeper up inside of me. Food and water. Lust and grief. "You should never have left me," I say. "This is a disaster."

"You said you wanted Peter."

"Not *then*. After that summer. You never came back."

"I left for your sake. So you could start your life fresh."

"But I didn't. I had no one but you to talk to, no way to get any of it out of my head. Even moving to another country did nothing."

He looks away. A steadying sadness between us. The wind has come up, ruffling the trees. A speckled alder sways, raining miniature grass-green pinecones down on us. Jonas plucks one out of my hair. "Have you ever told Peter about Conrad?"

"Of course not. We swore a blood oath. You practically cut off the tip of my finger."

"I only meant to say." He hesitates. "You've been married a long time. I would understand."

"I wish Peter knew. I hate that there has always been a lie between us. It isn't fair to him. But he doesn't. And he never will." I listen to the silence of the woods, the subtle seeping away of the day. Syrupy light spills across the forest floor, turning pine needles into splinters of copper. My words fill me with remorse. I roll free of Jonas, sit up and re-tie my bathing suit top. A dog tick makes its way up a piece of grass. It looks like a tiny watermelon seed. I put it on my thumbnail, crush it in the middle, and watch its legs splay out until I am sure it's dead. I dig a hole in the soil and drop it in, bury it, pat the soil firm. "Anyway," I say.

Jonas sits up, wraps his steady arms around me. "I'm sorry."

"I have to get going. Peter will start to worry."

"No." I can hear my own pain in his voice. He takes my hair in his fists, kisses me. Rough, hard, unhinged. I don't want to give in, but I kiss him back with a love that feels like drowning. The breathless desire to breathe. Moonlight and sweet junk and sharks and death and pity and vomit and hope all combined. It is too much. I need to get home to my children. To Peter. I break away, scramble to my feet, desperate.

"Elle, wait," he says.

"Conrad ruined everything," is all I say.

Book Two

◆

JONAS

13

1981. June, the Back Woods.

There are snapping turtles in our pond—massive prehistoric creatures lurking on the bottom, beneath the cool mud. Late in the afternoon, they dig themselves out and make their way to the pond's glassy obsidian surface, where swarms of water boatmen zip around like quick, febrile catamarans. From the screen porch, you can see the snappers rise: first the ugly black fist of a head, then the cusp of a carapace floats into view. It's the distance between the two silhouettes that tells you whether you are seeing the Big One—the grandfather of snappers–or just one of his smaller, Galápagos-sized progeny. Few people have ever seen him. Back Woods people say he's a myth, or long dead—and anyway, snappers are harmless. In a hundred years, no one has ever been bitten. But I've seen him. I know he's out there, living off bullfrogs and baby birds, praying for the quick flash of an orange webbed foot, the soft crunch of duckling.

The first time I saw Jonas, that day by the spring, he was a lost, tangle-headed boy following a bird. I was almost eleven, only three years older, though in my mind old enough to be his mother, when I took him by the hand and led him back to the path. I could never have imagined then that the second time I saw him, four years later, this strange child would irrevocably change my life.

That day I woke up anxious—a hollow, homesick feeling in my chest. My dreams had scared me: a man wanted me to eat jacket potatoes. He said he was going to kill me. I begged to see my mother one last time. There were banjo players. I pounded on the glass, but no one could hear me.

Anna was still asleep. Her spiral-bound journal had fallen open on the floor beside her bed. I was tempted to read it, but I already knew everything it would say. I reached under the mattress and pulled out my own journal. Jade silk, with a teensy lock and key. Mum had bought it for me in Chinatown after our annual New Year's Day dim sum. Anna had chosen a red T-shirt covered in what looked like Chinese characters, but when you tilted your head sideways it said, *Go Fuck Yourself!* Mum bought herself a lavender bathrobe. By the time we got home, I'd already managed to lose the key to my journal. I pried open the lock with a safety pin and broke it. Which didn't matter, since pretty much all I did was make lists of things I needed to do to make myself a better person. Things like "practice the flute for an hour every day!!" or "read *Middlemarch*!"

It had rained heavily the night before, and the air was waterlogged. Early morning heat raised steam off the damp pine needle paths around the camp. Already our cabin smelled of mildew. I needed to pee.

I closed the cabin door quietly behind me and headed to the bathroom, kicking away sharp, squirrel-nibbled pinecones with my bare feet. The towels we'd hung on the line to dry were soaked and heavy, flecked with bits of debris from the overhanging trees.

When I sat down on the toilet, I noticed blood on my shin. I wiped it off with a wodge of toilet paper and got a Band-Aid from the medicine cabinet. I had one leg up on the toilet seat, struggling to open the frustrating wax-papery wrapper, when I saw drops of blood on the floor. I lifted up the hem of my nightgown. The back was stained with blood. Finally. I'd waited so long for this, checking my underpants every day, hoping to catch up with my friends.

I dug around in the linen closet, found Anna's box of Playtex, and sat down on the toilet seat, little plinks of blood dripping into the water. I knew what to do. I'd stolen her tampons a few times before, practiced inserting them. Becky said I was being an idiot, but I was worried that if I did it wrong, the tampon would break my hymen. I'd studied the little pamphlet in the box with its pictograms of a lunglike vaginal canal, squat legs bent at the knees for just the correct positioning.

I was peeling off the plastic wrapper when there was a knock on the bathroom door.

"Don't come in!" I shouted. "I'm in here!"

"Well, hurry up, I need a piss." It was Conrad.

"Pee in the bushes. Are you a girl?"

"Are you a total bitch?"

I listened to him stumbling away into the woods. There were moments when Conrad was bearable. At times I even felt sorry for him. But he had this creepy, insinuating way about him—the kind of guy who's constantly washing his hands. Recently he'd started following me and Anna when we walked to the beach, always just out of sight. Sometimes, lying on the hot sand, we would catch him spying on us from the top of the dunes, hoping to see our boobs.

I made sure the bathroom door was locked. Sat back down on the toilet, pulled my nightgown high up around my waist and took my underpants off so I could spread my legs wide enough apart. I positioned the pink plastic applicator and was pushing the plunger when I heard a noise. On the opposite side of the bathroom, Conrad's face was smashed tight against the clerestory window, eyes wide, staring between my open legs. I dropped the tampon applicator and it skittled away across the bathroom floor.

"Get away, you freak!" I shrieked, my entire body vibrating with rage and shame. I listened to Conrad's sickening laugh as he ran off. By tomorrow, every one of his weirdo friends would know. I sat on the toilet weeping, wanting to die. The second I heard his cabin door slam shut, I ran for my cabin, shoved my bloody nightgown out of sight under my bed, yanked on my bathing suit, and raced to the pond. My only thought was to put as much distance between me and Conrad as possible. I would never be able to face him again, that much was clear. A stack of paddles was leaning against a tree. I grabbed one, pushed our fiberglass canoe off the spongy green undergrowth into the water as hard as I could, lay down on the bottom of the boat as the canoe drifted away from the beach. I hugged my arms to my chest, stared up at the early morning sky. *This must be what it's like to be a Viking dead person,* I thought as the boat glided out unmanned.

When I was far enough from shore, I sat up and paddled away as fast as I could. By the time I reached the middle of the pond, I'd decided the simplest option was to drown myself. I would need something heavy to weigh me down. I was a strong swimmer and I knew that, in the end, I would fight for the surface. If I had a big rock, I could tie it to the boat's painter, wrap the rope round my ankle, and jump. Conrad might never admit what he had done, but he would know, for the rest of his miserable psycho life, that he was responsible for my death.

I paddled toward the swampy, uninhabited side of the pond, where the horsetail reeds stalked out into the pond like an army, and hair-thin tangles of lily pad stems waited to trap your oar. The shoreline here was scattered with glacial debris, ancient rocks and pebbles deposited in the wake of the slow-moving glacial ice.

As I neared the shallows, I dug my paddle hard into the water, gathering momentum, then lifted it high and clear over the lily pads, gliding silently over their spidery web. The crunch of the sandy floor scraped the bottom of the canoe. I was about to leap out and drag it the rest of the way in when I heard a quiet voice.

"Don't move. Stay in the boat."

I looked up, startled. Jonas was sitting perfectly still on the lowest branch of a pitch pine that jutted out above my head, over the water. Almost completely camouflaged. Shirtless, wearing a pair of faded army-green shorts, long legs dangling. He was leaner than the last time I'd seen him. Taller, of course—he must be at least twelve by now—his thick black hair tangled below his shoulders. But his eyes had the same older-than-his-years intensity that had struck me the day he found me in the woods.

"Hand me your paddle," he whispered.

"Why are you whispering?" I whispered back.

He pointed to the reeds beneath my boat.

I leaned over the edge of the canoe, trying to see what he was pointing at, but from my angle I couldn't make out anything.

"The paddle?" he whispered again.

I stood up, careful not to rock the canoe, and passed the paddle up into the tree. Jonas took a plastic bag of something that looked like raw hamburger meat out of his pocket and slathered it over the end of the oar.

"Watch." He lowered it down directly in front of me.

The sound will always stick in my brain—the sudden, violent crack of wood as the paddle split. Jonas leaned backward on the branch with his full weight, hanging onto the oar. And then I saw it, rising from the murk, jaws clamped shut around my paddle. It was the Big One, the granddaddy—an ugly snapper as wide as a rowboat. Prehistoric. Chicken-headed. And he was angry. Jonas jumped down onto the shore, pulled on the paddle with all his might. Teeth gritted.

"I need help."

Giving the snapper a wide berth, I made my way to Jonas and together we dragged the snapper toward dry land.

"I need to unhitch your painter," he said. "Don't let go." He ran to the canoe and undid the thick rope clipped to its bow.

"Hurry, please," I said. The snapper was slowly eating his way up the paddle toward me.

Jonas made a slipknot in the painter, crept behind the turtle, and lassoed its thick-scaled tail.

"Got him," he said.

"Now what?"

"We need to get him into the boat."

The snapper hissed and thrashed, pulling against his bonds. His long neck twisted and turned, groping impotently for the rope, his razor-sharp jaws never letting go of the paddle. He turned his attention back to me with a dead-eyed anger—humiliation at being caught; fury at having been exposed to the world, stripped of his dignity—and began to make his way farther up the oar. He was coming for me now, coming for his pound of flesh, and I understood what he was feeling completely.

"Let him go," I said.

"No way." Jonas pulled harder at the rope.

"It's wrong," I said. "And he's going to eat me."

"I've been trying to catch him for two years. My brothers say he doesn't exist."

"Well, you caught him."

"Yeah, but they won't believe me."

"Then they're idiots."

"According to them, I'm the idiot."

"This isn't a great time to argue the point," I said as the snapper inched toward me. "But if your plan was for us to lift a one-hundred-pound enraged killer turtle into a tippy canoe, then maybe your brothers are right."

Jonas stood assessing the situation: the massive beast pulling at its yoke, my frightened face, the fiberglass canoe. With a deep sigh, he untied his trophy. I let go of the paddle and we backed away.

For a few long moments, the snapper kept coming. Then, slowly realizing he had been given his freedom, he dropped the paddle from his jaws, gave us a last wary look, and turned his enormous body toward the safety of the deep. We watched as he made his arthritic crawl into the shallows, and when the water was deep enough, we watched him swim for his life.

Nothing was left of the paddle but a shredded stick. We reattached the rope and dragged the canoe around the edge of the pond toward my camp. At some point Jonas took my hand, just as he had done years before, when I led him out of the woods.

Conrad was sitting by the water, watching us approach, a nasty sneer slashed across his flabby face. His sickening cackle from this morning still echoed in my head, but my distress and shame had been replaced by a cold front of anger.

"Who's that?" Jonas asked.

"My hideous stepbrother. I hate him."

"Hate is a strong emotion," Jonas said.

"Well then, I hate him strongly." I paused. "He's a pervert. I caught him spying on me this morning when I was in the bathroom. I'm planning to kill him later."

"My mother says it's always better to take the high road."

"There isn't any other road to take with Conrad. He's always the low road."

"What happened to the paddle?" Conrad asked as we neared him.

I walked past him without answering.

"It got attacked by a snapper," Jonas said.

"Sounds exciting," Conrad's snide tone made me want to throw the paddle in his face, but I kept walking.

"It was," Jonas said. Together we pulled the canoe onto dry ground, turned it on its side in case of more rain.

"I had an exciting morning myself," Conrad said.

My jaw tightened. Whatever happened next, I was not going to let him bait me.

"I keep picturing it in my head, over and over," Conrad said. "Who's your little friend?"

"Jonas, meet my stepbrother Conrad. He is living with us temporarily while his mother decides whether or not she wants him back. I have a horrible feeling we're going to be stuck with him forever."

"You wish," Conrad said. And though I had ended up on the low road, the genuine look of pain on his face was almost worth my tampon humiliation.

"Come," I said to Jonas. "Let's go tell your brothers what happened."

That summer Jonas became my shadow. When I swam or canoed across the pond to go to the ocean, he'd be waiting for me on the shore, knowing I'd appear. When, instead, I walked to the beach along the path through the woods, I would find him sitting on a fallen tree trunk, drawing in the little sketch pad he always carried with him—a broken branch on a pitch pine, a darkling beetle. It was as if he had an internal compass—a magnetic field that picked up true north. Or maybe, like a carrier pigeon, he could smell my odor on the wind.

Sometimes he would point out coyote scat or a trail leading into the bearberry hollows, where the low brush still held the imprint of a deer. We spent most days lying in the hot sand on the wide empty ocean beach, daring each other to swim out too far at high tide, riding the waves, trying not to get taken by the undertow. Often we didn't even talk. But when we did, we talked about everything.

I knew our friendship made no sense. I wasn't a loner, or even lonely. Becky was down the road, and I had Anna. I was fourteen and a half, he was twelve. But for some reason that summer, when so many things were falling away, when I began to feel like prey, Jonas made me feel safe.

We were an odd pair. Me—tall, pale, plodding around in Dr. Scholl's and a bikini, hiding my uncomfortable breasts and new curves under fray-collared shirts I'd inherited from my father. Jonas, easily a foot shorter, always barefoot, in the same filthy green shorts and Allman Brothers T-shirt he wore every single day. Once when I suggested this habit was repulsive and that a washing machine might help, he shrugged and told me swimming in the sea and the ponds was antiseptic.

"Also," he said, "you're being extremely rude."

"I'm being maternal," I said. "I feel responsible for you."

"I'm not a baby."

"I know," I said. "You're a child."

"So are you," he said.

"Not anymore."

"Meaning?"

The second I opened my mouth I wanted to punch myself. "Nothing," I said. "I'm just older than you."

Jonas wouldn't let me off the hook. "No. You said *you* are no longer a child, but *I* am. You don't have to hang around with me if you don't want to. I'm not your responsibility."

"Stop acting like a baby."

"Apparently, I am a baby," Jonas said.

"Fine. Whatever," I said. "I'm a *woman* now, as my mother keeps telling me. It honestly makes me want to puke when she says it. 'Eleanor, be proud. You're a woman now.'"

He looked at me with a serious, unwavering expression. Then he reached up, put his hand on my shoulder, and gave me a reassuring squeeze.

"I'm so sorry," he said. "That really does sound vile. Come on, I found something cool yesterday. By the way," he said over his shoulder as we walked, "they teach sex ed in fifth grade, so I do understand that women bleed."

"Gross."

"The power to create life is a beautiful thing."

"Oh my god!" I swatted him.

"Be proud, Eleanor, you're a woman now," he said in his best imitation of my mother, and ran ahead before I could tackle him to the ground.

Deep in the woods, in a grove of locusts, Jonas had discovered an abandoned house, the walls and roof long ago rotted away, leaving only the stone outline of two small rooms. Wild roses and woodbine had tangled themselves over everything. We jumped the low walls and stood in the center of what had once been someone's home. Jonas found a stick and scratched at a bump in the sandy soil until he unearthed a sapphire-blue bottle, worn like beach glass. He cleared a space on the floor and we lay down beside each other, looking up at the white mackerel clouds. I closed my eyes and listened to the whisper of the pines, smelled the samphire and juniper. It was comfortable lying there with him in the quiet. Silent but connected, conversing without words—as if we could hear each other's thoughts and so had no need to speak them aloud.

"Do you suppose this is where the marital bed was?" Jonas asked after a while.

"You're such a peculiar child."

"I was just thinking how lovely this spot is, and that we could rebuild the house and live here when we get married."

"Okay, first of all, you're twelve. And second of all, stop being weird," I said.

"When we're older, our age difference won't matter. It barely matters now."

"I guess that's true."

"I'll take that as a yes," Jonas said.

"Fine," I said. "But I want a double boiler."

"My brothers tease me about you," Jonas said one afternoon as I walked him home from the pond. I knew his brothers a bit: Elias was sixteen. He and Anna had taken sailing lessons together two summers ago, and one time they had kissed during a round of spin the bottle. Hopper was my age, fourteen. Tall, with thick red hair and freckles. We'd said hello once or twice at the Friday-night yacht club dances, but that was it.

"They tease you because I'm old enough to be your babysitter. And they're kind of right. It is a bit weird."

"Hopper has a crush on you," Jonas said now. "I think that may be why he's giving me such a difficult time. Though I don't suppose that explains Elias's behavior."

I laughed. "Hopper? I've barely ever spoken to him."

"You should ask Hopper to dance sometime," Jonas said. "Look." He crouched down and picked up a tiny blue eggshell that had fallen into the tall grasses on the roadside. "The robins are back." He handed it to me carefully. It was weightless, paper-thin. "I was worried the jays had chased them all away."

"Why would I be nice to him when he's being a jerk to you?"

"He's only being a jerk because he sees me as a threat."

"What I *should* do is tell him to stop teasing you."

"Please don't," Jonas said. "That would be humiliating."

We slowed as we came to a bend in the road. Beyond it was the Gunthers' house—the only property in the Back Woods with a keep-out fence around its perimeter. The Gunthers were odd. Austrian. They kept to themselves. They were both sculptors. Sometimes I would meet them on the road when they were walking their two German shepherds. The dogs terrified me. When anyone walked past the house they would come to the edge of the fence, barking and salivating. Once, one of the dogs had gotten loose and bitten Becky on the leg.

As we neared the Gunthers' driveway, I could already hear the dogs barking, racing down the hill toward us.

"Fine," I said. "I'll ask him. But I seriously doubt he thinks of you as a threat." I laughed.

Normally, when we passed the Gunthers' house, we ran. But now Jonas stopped dead in the middle of the road. "Thank you, Elle, for clarifying that."

The dogs had reached the fence and were frantic, angry. They threw themselves against it, not used to being ignored.

"We need to move," I said. "They're going to break through the fence." But Jonas just stood there while the dogs upped their pitch. "Jonas!"

"I can make it home from here on my own," he said coldly. And headed down the road away from me.

At the top of the hill, Mr. Gunther emerged from his studio. "Astrid! Frida!" he called to his dogs. "*Herkommen! Jetzt!*"

When I walked to the beach the next day, Jonas never appeared.

"Dad," Conrad says, "did you know Eleanor is a cradle snatcher? She's in love with a ten-year-old."

It's late in the summer. Mum has gone to the dump before it shuts. Leo is at the sink, deboning a bluefish he caught this morning—they've been running up the coast, churning the waters close to shore.

"He's just some kid who follows me around. And he's twelve, not ten," I say, but I can feel my cheeks turning red.

"Who follows you?" Leo asks. He's been on tour with some jazz band most of the month. I'm glad he's here. Mum is much happier when Leo is home.

"That kid Jonas who's always hanging around," Conrad says. "He's Elle's boyfriend."

"That's nice," Leo says, disappearing into the pantry.

I hear things falling. Leo curses.

"Stop being a jerk. He's just a little kid," I shove my chair away from the table and clear my plate.

"Exactly," Conrad says. "Cradle snatcher."

"Does anyone know where your mother hides the Saran wrap?" Leo calls out. "Why does she keep buying wax paper? Who uses wax paper?"

Anna has been sitting on the sofa trying to put her puzzle ring back together. Now she looks up, smelling blood in the water. "Wow, Conrad," she says. "Jealous, much?" She smiles. "I think Conrad has a crush on *you*, Elle."

Conrad's face twists into an odd shape. He forces a laugh.

"What do you think, Elle?" Anna says. "Do you like Conrad? He wants you to be his girlfriend."

"Stop it, Anna," I say. "That's repulsive." And yet I feel a disconcerting ding of recognition, as if what she has said reminds me of something I already know but can't remember.

"Screw you," Conrad spits at Anna.

She can sense his weakness and circles in for the kill. "Incest is quite a few levels worse than cradle snatching, Con."

Conrad leaps up and grabs Anna's arm hard. "Shut up. Shut up or I'll break it."

"Calm. Down," Anna says, baiting him. "I'm only trying to help. I want to make sure you know it's a sin before you do anything you'll regret."

Leo walks out onto the porch just as Conrad punches Anna in the face.

"Conrad!" In two strides he is there, grabbing his son by the shirt, pulling him off Anna with his huge, fish-smelly hands. "What the hell is wrong with you?!" He drags his son across the porch, shoves him out the door so hard that Conrad falls to the ground. "Get up!"

We watch as Conrad tries to fight back his tears.

"Baby," Anna says with a snide smile. She goes back to the couch and picks up her book, keeps reading as if she has no idea she has just set the house on fire.

Dixon's end-of-the-season beach picnic has always been my favorite night of the summer. The whole Back Woods gathers for a massive bonfire at Higgins Hollow. We collect crisp sun-blackened seaweed from the tidemark for tinder, drag gnarled driftwood into a pile, watch the fire spit embers into the night sky. Everyone dances and sings. At dusk, we light sparklers and run around like fireflies. The grown-ups drink too much. We spy on them from the dunes and play capture the flag. People cook lobster and steamers in enormous speckled-enamel pots, wrap seawater-soaked raw corn in tinfoil and throw it onto the fire.

We are hamburger people. My mother always insists on bringing sweet relish, mustard, and raw onions that make her breath unbearable. She passes around radishes with salt as if they are some kind of delicacy.

This year, Conrad isn't allowed to come. He's been grounded for a week. He begs his father not to leave him behind. Even Mum tries to convince Leo to change his mind, but he won't budge.

"God knows he *has* been extremely difficult lately," Mum says. They are getting out of the pond after a swim.

Anna and I are sitting on the porch eating strawberry ice cream.

"And must his room smell of feet at all times? Isn't there something he can do for that? That athlete's foot remedy they sell might help, don't you think? I gave him a bottle of talcum powder, but he says it makes him itchy. You need to talk to him."

I watch Leo dry himself off with a towel as if he's buffing a large white car. His bathing suit is saggy, and his belly jiggles as the towel moves back and forth. He looks like a big toddler. Leo isn't much of a swimmer, but my mother has him on a new exercise regime.

"It can't be easy for him in this house, Leo. All these women. You've been away nearly half the summer. It's hard belonging to a family that isn't your own. He needs you to take his side."

"What he *needs* is to understand the consequences of his actions."

"What you're doing is alienating him even more. It just makes it harder on all of us."

"This isn't about you and the girls, Wallace. It's about my son."

"Let him come. It makes him so happy to do the Bear Hunt with you. It's a tradition."

"No son of mine gets away with hitting a girl," Leo says.

"She probably deserved it," Mum says.

I lie in bed the next morning looking up at the skylight. A misting of yellow pollen has collected at the edges. We need a good rain to clear it. It's been blue skies for days. I watch a spider fiddling around in its web. A desiccated moth hangs from a single loose filament, swaying with each bit of breeze. My hair smells of bonfire smoke and ketchup. Someone is taking a shower. A rush of water splatters on dry leaves. The water groans to a stop. Conrad curses as he steps on a catbrier. I pick up my book and open to the dog-ear. It will take a few minutes for the hot water tank to refill.

Our camp only has the one shower, attached to a smallish tree outside the bathroom house and enclosed by a weathered stockade fence that's always crawling with daddy longlegs. No one uses the rotting shaker pegs to hang their towels. We hang them over the lower branches of the tree. A stream of soapy water runs directly from your body onto the leaves and out to the path, pine needles swirling in its wake, so we have a strict no-peeing-in-the-shower rule. Otherwise, the path to the bathroom starts to smell like the back of a Greyhound bus.

After ten minutes, I grab my towel and my Wella Balsam conditioner. There's a soapy puddle in my way, slowly seeping into the ground. I jump across it and land with a splatter on its far edge, covering myself in what I instantly realize is pee water. I storm back down the path and bang on my mother's cabin door.

She appears a few seconds later, pulling on her bathrobe, looking exhausted. "Leo is sleeping," she whispers.

"Do you smell that?" I hold out my leg.

"Eleanor, I'm not in the mood to smell you," she says. "It was a late night. One too many gin and tonics."

"Conrad peed in the shower."

"Well, at least he's bathing. That's a plus."

"Mom. It's disgusting. I stepped in it."

"I'll talk to him. But he's already being punished, so God knows what good it will do."

"Why does he even have to be here?"

My mother comes outside, closing the cabin door behind her. "You know, maybe if you and Anna were nicer to Conrad, he wouldn't behave this way." She rubs her temples. "Can you go to the kitchen and bring me water and an aspirin?"

"Why is he *our* problem? Why can't he go back to Memphis to live with his own family?"

"We *are* his family."

"I'm not."

"Just try, Elle. For Leo." She looks back into the room to make sure Leo is asleep. "Invite him for a swim occasionally. Ask him to play Parcheesi. It won't kill you."

"He cheats. And he can't even make it to the middle of the pond."

"Try. For me."

"Fine," I say. "I'll ask him to come to the beach today. But if he acts like a jerk, you owe me a hundred dollars."

"I might as well pay you now." My mother sighs. "But thank you."

The remains of last night's bonfire are still smoldering in the sand. Someone has made a barricade of driftwood around it to keep people from burning their feet. There's a paper plate lying facedown, a few half-buried corncobs.

"So?" Conrad asks. "Was it fun?"

"Yes."

"Who was there?"

"The usual suspects."

Conrad flicks sand at the paper plate with his big toe. It makes a whisking noise as it lands, slides. "Did my dad do the Bear Hunt?"

"Of course."

Conrad looks upset. "Who was the dog?"

"I don't know. One of the kids. Sorry you couldn't come," I force myself to say.

We spread out our towels well above the waterline. The tide is coming in. I sit down and take a sweating can of Fresca out of my bag. When I pull the pop-top, the ring breaks off in my hand, leaving the metal teardrop sealed shut.

"Give me that," Conrad says, and stabs the can open with a sharp piece of shell, hands it back to me.

"Thanks."

"Do you want to go in?" Conrad asks.

"I need to get hot first. I might not go in at all. The surf looks rough."

"I thought you liked it rough," Conrad says, and laughs at his own bad joke.

I ignore him and open my book. He sits there, scratching a mosquito bite on his leg. After a while he gets up and walks toward the water. I lie down on my stomach, relieved that he's gone. Close my eyes and rest my head on my arms. I'm drifting off when I feel something wet drop on my back.

"Look what I found," Conrad says. "I think you and Jonas left it here last night."

I reach back and take the thing off me. It's a used condom. I shriek and jump to my feet. "What the hell is wrong with you?" I shout, and rush into the sea to clean myself off.

The first wave blindsides me and I go under. When I try to come up, I'm tumbled again and again. I need air, but I force myself to sink. I find the bottom and push myself off the sea floor as hard as I can. I break the surface sputtering for breath, grab for the shore, and stumble my way out before another wave can hit me. A few adults have seen me struggling and run over to pull me in.

"I'm okay," I say. "I'm okay."

My bathing suit is like a sandbag. I shake out grit, krill, seaweed. A pinkish rock falls to the ground around my ankles. Conrad is doubled over, laughing. I walk past without acknowledging him.

"It was a joke," he says. "Lighten up."

I grab my towel and my book, shove them into my bag. "You should go for a swim," I say. "It's a perfect day to drown."

"You owe me a hundred dollars," I tell my mother when I get home.

"Where's Conrad?" she asks.

"Dead, if I'm lucky."

"I'm making clam chowder for dinner," she says.

In the morning, when I walk to the main house for breakfast, I find Jonas sitting outside on the deck. Conrad is inside at the table eating a bowl of cornflakes in his revolting brown terry-cloth bathrobe, reading *Spy vs. Spy*.

"Hey." I sit down next to Jonas. "What are you doing here?"

"I came to say goodbye."

"Oh."

"We were supposed to leave on Saturday, but my mother caught Elias up in the dunes with some girl at the bonfire and, as she put it, 'didn't like what she was seeing.' Otherwise known as my brother's naked butt." He sighs. "Anyway, we're going back to Cambridge this afternoon."

On the porch, Conrad puts down his comic and stops eating, spoon suspended above his bowl. I know he's eavesdropping, but I don't care.

"When does school start?" I ask.

"Like, two weeks, I guess."

"Middle school, right?"

"Yeah."

"Wow."

"Yes," Jonas laughs a bit ruefully. "Big Boy School."

In all the days I have spent with Jonas, this is the first time it has felt at all awkward. The thought of school, of real life outside Back Woods—his in Cambridge, mine in New York—suddenly makes the difference in our ages seem huge, an unbridgeable gap.

"I know," Jonas says, reading my thoughts. "It's weird." He rubs his toe into the damp sand. "I was thinking we could take one last swim across the pond."

"I have to go into town with Anna and my mom."

"Well then, I guess this is it." Jonas stands up and puts his hand out to shake mine. "See you next summer."

"Why don't you kiss him goodbye?" Conrad calls from inside the screen porch.

"Shut up, Conrad," I say, taking Jonas's outstretched hand.

"Give him a big wet tongue kiss."

"Ignore him," Jonas says.

"You know what," I say to Jonas, "I do have time for a quick swim. One sec." I run and change into my bathing suit. Jonas is already swimming out when I get back. I dive in and catch up to him. "I'm sorry. He's a complete idiot."

"Boys his age have a one-track mind," Jonas says.

I laugh. "You really are so weird."

"It's been a great summer, Elle. Thank you," Jonas says, treading water in front of me.

"It was a pleasure," I say. "One last breath-holding contest?"

"It's not a contest if I always win," Jonas says. "Though I'll admit you've gotten marginally better."

"Please." I laugh. "I'm the state champion."

"One, two, three, under?"

I nod.

We duck underwater and hold our breath. Then, without thinking, I pull him to me and kiss him.

I wait until Jonas has left before confronting Conrad. "Why do you do that?"

"Do what?" Conrad flips the pages of his comic, eats a last spoonful of soggy cereal. Milk dribbles from the corner of his mouth. I watch it run down his chin onto his neck like a bead of white sweat.

"Act like a pig."

"You shouldn't be hanging around with a twelve-year-old."

"It's none of your business."

"It makes me sick."

"Why do you care?"

"I don't," Conrad says. "But you're embarrassing the family." He stands up and gets in my face. "Did you let him get to first base?"

My mother and Anna walk past the house, heading to the car. "Put pears on the list," I hear Mum say. "And minute steaks. Oh—we're almost out of bourbon."

"Did you let him finger you?" Conrad says.

I turn on him now. "I'm embarrassed to be seen with *you*," I say. "You're the embarrassment in this family. Not me."

"Yeah, right."

"It's true. No one wants you here, creeping around in the bushes like some pervert with your disgusting blackheads. Why don't you move back with your mom? Oh, right," I say. "She doesn't want you either."

Conrad's face turns a dark shade of red. "That's a lie."

"Really? What's her number? Let's call her and ask." I walk over to the black rotary phone and lift the receiver. There's a list of important numbers on a scrap of paper, thumbtacked to the bookshelf. I scroll down it and find the number. Dial. "It's ringing."

"Screw you," Conrad says, and runs outside. He is crying.

"Baby!" I shout after him.

In my hand I hear a tinny, faraway voice: "Hello? Hello?" someone is saying. I put the receiver back in its cradle.

Retribution for my cruelty to Conrad comes quickly. It begins with an itchy feeling under my eyelids. My throat swells. By late afternoon my face is oozing with blisters. I can't open my eyes at all. The doctor tells us there is only one way to contract this kind of poison ivy: someone at the picnic must have thrown a vine-covered log into the fire when I was sitting in the path of the smoke, which carried the poisoned oil directly into my ears, my mouth, my nostrils. My mother has set up a camp bed for me in the darkened pantry. She covers my face and neck in wet cheesecloths soaked in calamine lotion. I look like the leper from *Ben-Hur*. She brings me cold chamomile tea and a straw. Puts a bowl of ice next to the bed. Swallowing is torture.

Everyone is in the living room playing poker. I hear wooden chips being tossed into the pot. Anna and Leo arguing about who had the better bluff. My mother laughs. Conrad laughs. My bandages are drying out, sticking to the painful sores. I try to call out, but my voice won't work. More laughter. I bang on the floor with my foot, and at last hear footsteps approaching.

"Mum?"

"She sent me to see what you need." It is Conrad.

"I need Mom!" I whisper. "My bandages are stuck."

"Okay," he says, but instead of leaving, he sits down on the edge of the bed. A bubble of panic rises in my throat. I lie there, helpless, and brace myself for whatever is coming.

"Get Mom!" I croak. I can feel him staring at me.

"Here," he says. He peels the cheesecloth off my face gently and replaces it with a damp washcloth. "I'll go get her."

Anna calls out from the other room. "Conrad, it's your turn!"

"Coming!" But he doesn't leave. "I could read to you or something," he says.

"I just need Mom."

He stands up. His foot shifts back and forth across the gritty wood floor. I wait for him to go.

"I'm sorry about the rubber," he says finally. "I don't know why I did that."

"Because you want everyone to hate you."

"That's not true."

"Then why do you act like such a jerk all the time?"

"I don't want you to hate me," he says quietly.

"Kind of late for that, isn't it?" Anna says from the door. "Stop bothering my sister, Conrad."

"It's okay," I say.

"That's because you can't open your eyes, so you don't realize he's standing there ogling you like some creepy freak."

I can feel Conrad go rigid.

"C'mon, lovebird, everyone's waiting."

"Stop it, Anna," I say. "He wasn't bothering me."

"Fine," she says. "Your funeral. And if you don't come right now, Conrad, we're dealing you out."

"I'll be there in a sec," he says.

"Sorry about that." I pause. "And I'm really sorry I said that about your mom."

Conrad sits down on the side of my bed.

14

1982. January, New York.

I climb into bed and wait. Soon I hear my mother's stockinged footsteps pause outside my door in the long book-lined hallway of our apartment. She should be wearing shoes. The old floorboards splinter and attack anyone reckless enough to wear socks in the house. A quick run down the hall, a skid, and a thin shiv of dark wood pierces your foot, too deep for tweezers. The soles of my feet are covered in tiny scars. By now I can perform the ritual myself: light the match, sterilize the needle until its point glows red, tear open a line of flesh above the splinter's shadow. Dig.

Mum switches off the hall light as she passes my room. She hates wasting electricity. I wait for the shush of her bedroom door. In the living room Leo closes his book, pulls the chain on the old Ming vase lamp, shoves back his heavy wooden armchair. Their bedroom door opens, shuts again, more firmly now. Hushed good-night voices, water running in the bathroom, the soft *crunk* of the plastic rinsing glass being replaced onto the edge of the porcelain sink. I count the minutes. Listen for the creak of the bed as it takes Leo's weight. My breath rises and falls. I listen to the shift of my cotton sheets. Wait. Wait. Silence has fallen. Careful not to make the smallest sound, I get out of bed, turn the door handle slowly. Still silence. I reach into the pitch-dark hallway and feel around for the light switch, turn the light back on. Wait. Nothing. They are asleep or too tired to bother. I close my door tight, climb back into bed, pull the covers up around my neck. I have done what I can. It's always safer when the hallway is lit.

One night in October, a month after we got back from the Cape, I surfaced from a deep sleep. What woke me was a breeze on my thighs. I remember thinking I had kicked off my covers, but when I reached down to pull them up, I realized my nightgown had gotten scrunched all the way up, legs and stomach and breasts exposed. And there was wetness all over my panties. My period had come early. I wiped my hand off on my nightgown and was getting up to go to the bathroom when a thought occurred to me: there was no dark streak, no blood where I had wiped off my hand. I put my hand to my nose, confused. A strong bitter smell I didn't recognize. A thick, gruel texture. And then I saw something move in my closet. Someone was in there, hidden in the shadows, the hollow darkness. I could not see his face, but I could see his penis, a fleshy white against the blackness, still erect. He was squeezing it, the last drops of semen glistening on the tip. I froze, paralyzed. Afraid to breathe. In the past three months, four women had been found raped and strangled to death in the city, and they hadn't caught the killer yet. The most recent victim was only about eighteen years old. She had been found naked, floating in the river, hands tied behind her back. Carefully, slowly, I lay back down. Maybe if he thought I hadn't seen him, he would leave without hurting me. I closed my eyes tight and prayed. Please get out. Please get out. I won't yell. I won't tell anyone. In the quiet inside me, I was screaming so loud that sound filled the void, a terror I could barely control. Minutes passed. Finally, a movement. The swing of my bedroom door. I allowed myself to open my eyes a crack, to make sure he was gone. Just as the door was shutting, Conrad turned around.

February

Outside my door I hear the smallest creak of a floorboard.

"Elle?" Conrad whispers my name, testing to make sure I am asleep. "Elle, are you awake?"

He opens the door and stands beside my bed in the dark. After a few seconds, he reaches down, pulls my nightgown up past my thighs, unzips his pants, touches himself. A soft, gummy sound. Lie in silence. Swallow. Don't dare stir. I must pretend to be fast asleep. Conrad thinks I have no idea he comes into my room at night. Looks at me. Masturbates. As far as he knows, I'm dead to the world, completely unaware of what he is doing. I might as well have taken a heavy sleeping pill. And he must *never* know. As long as he thinks his visits are his secret alone, I can act normal, sit at the family dinner table with him, walk past his room to go to the bathroom. Because as far as I'm concerned, nothing has happened. Maybe if I had not been paralyzed in terror that first night, if I had screamed and yelled. But then it would be out there—the humiliation, the filth. When I woke up that night he had already jerked off on me, all over my panties. I had seen the tip of his penis. That part could never be undone, even with a scream. Everyone in my family would be stuck with that disgusting image in their heads. I would be tainted forever—an object of pity. So, I will carry the weight of this shame rather than tell on him.

I know my silence protects him. But it also protects me: Conrad is terrified of getting caught—exposed to his father, rejected forever. That is the one power I have. Whenever he comes too close to me now, I pretend to wake up, and he slithers out before he gets caught. Back to his rat hole. I am safe. I just can't ever fall asleep.

March

Leo and Conrad are fighting. "Goddammit," Leo is yelling. "I can't take it, I can't take it . . ." I hear the thud of a wall being punched. "It's a disgrace," Leo shouts. "Do you understand? Do you understand?"

"Dad, please."

"Pick up this room!" More crashes, kicking.

I've just gotten home from my babysitting job and I desperately need to pee. I peer down the long hallway. Conrad's bedroom door is wide open. It will embarrass him if he knows I've overheard, but I have to go past his room to get to the bathroom. I put my things down, hang my down vest on a coat hook, and tiptoe down the hall hoping to get by unnoticed.

"Dad, please, I've tried. I just don't get it."

"Don't get what?" Leo yells. "That Des Moines is the capital of Iowa? It's geography, not rocket science. If you fail again, they will kick you out. *Do you understand?*"

"Yes, sir."

"There are no second chances here."

"I didn't flunk it on purpose, Dad," Conrad says, so upset. "I'm just bad at it."

"There's no such thing as *bad at geography*. There's only *lazy*."

"That's not true," Conrad says, his voice cracking.

"Are you calling me a liar?"

"No, I—"

Leo spies me as I'm sneaking past. "Ask Eleanor to tutor you. She got straight As this semester. Eleanor, come in here."

I stop, but don't come in.

"I don't need her help," Conrad says. "I can do better, I promise."

"Your sister does well because she has gumption. She works hard and respects our expectations."

"I'm just good at memorizing things."

"She's not my sister," Conrad says. When he looks at me, there is venom in his eyes.

"I have to go to the bathroom," I say.

"Leo?" My mother calls out to him from somewhere in the bowels of the apartment. "Can I make you a drink?"

My eyes are closed, but I can feel Conrad's damp breath. He leans his face close to mine, looking for signs of life. I keep my breathing even, slow. He leans in closer now and strokes my hair. I stir; pretend to be on the verge of waking. He pulls his hand away and steps back into the shadows, waits to see if I will move again. I turn over onto my side and re-settle. It's enough to unnerve him. As he is about to go, he says something, so softly I can barely hear him. But I do. "One of these days I'm gonna put it in you for real," he whispers. "I'm gonna get you pregnant. And *then* who will they think is the perfect child?"

Vomit rises in my throat, but I keep it down. Don't move a muscle.

April

The clinic is packed with women. Older women, young pregnant women. Three Puerto Rican girls sit opposite me. "Yo, mamacita," one of them taunts. "You got a man friend?" and the others laugh. I stare at the orange plastic seat of my chair.

Outside, snow is falling, killing off the first of the cherry blossoms. My hiking boots are soaked through. On the walk from the subway to the free clinic, through the blooming snowdrifts, I almost lost my nerve. But I'm here now, waiting for my pink ticket number to be called, as if I'm at a Baskin-Robbins.

The nurse calls us in five at a time. I hand her the signed letter I've forged on my mother's stationery, giving me permission to get birth control, since I am only fifteen. She barely glances at it before tossing it on top of a pile of what are probably similar letters. I am taken to a curtained-off area with the Puerto Rican girls and a pregnant woman. A counselor talks to us about the risks of birth control, the option of adoption, and then gives each of us a pregnancy test to take. The pregnant woman protests that this is a waste of a test, but the nurse explains that it's part of the protocol. The three girls eye-fuck me the entire time. "What's the matter, blondie? Daddy won't pay for a real doctor?" I take my test into the bathroom and pee on the strip.

My mother thinks I am spending the day with Becky, going to see *Victor/Victoria*. She even gave me money for popcorn and a soda. I want to tell her the truth, beg her to save me, but I can't do that to her. It would break her heart, destroy her marriage. She's so happy with Leo, and I am stronger than she is—strong enough to carry this. It is my responsibility. I was nice to Conrad, I let him in the door. "It's your funeral," Anna had said that poison ivy night. And she was right. Now everywhere I go, I'm trapped by the weight of his body, his moist breath, his smelly hands, his hideous fleshy parts.

We are ushered from the information session to a changing room and given paper dresses. "Take everything off, leave on your shoes," the nurse tells us. There is a line of women in thin paper dresses and heavy snow boots sitting on a long bench waiting their turn. It is two hours before my name is called, and the nurse brings me into an exam room.

The doctor has a mask over his mouth. I never see his face, just his distracted eyes.

"Please ask the patient to get on the table and put her feet in the stirrups," he says to the nurse.

"I just need a prescription for birth control pills," I say.

He turns to the nurse. "Did you explain that she cannot get medicine prescribed until we examine her?"

The nurse nods and gives me an impatient glare. "Of course, Doctor. She signed the forms."

When I climb up onto the table, I feel my dress tear. How will I get back to the changing room without exposing myself? I lie back and let the nurse place my wet boots into the metal stirrups. It is hot in the room, but I can't stop shivering.

There's a knock on the door.

"Come," the doctor calls out.

A young Asian man in a white coat enters the room.

"We have a medical student here from Kyoto studying our birth control methods. You don't mind if he observes?" the doctor says. He beckons the man over to the end of the table, ignoring the look of horror in my eyes. Hands him a mask.

The man gives me a formal bow, arms tight by his side, before putting his head between my legs and looking at my vagina.

"Interesting," he says. "The hymen is still intact."

"Yes," the doctor says. "This will feel cold."

15

1982. November, New York.

Water sluices the windows. My room is tomb-like, sealed. I yawn, sit up in bed, stare down into the interior courtyard. The heavy rain has puddled to the middle, forming a square-shaped lake. A waxy Dixie cup skitters across the surface, dragging a piece of Saran wrap behind it like a jellyfish tail. I reach for my clock. I have a history test first period and I've set the alarm for six a.m. so I can finish memorizing. 7:45. A flash of panic sweeps me as I realize I've slept through my alarm. I rush around my room, throwing things into my backpack, drilling myself out loud: Stamp Act Congress, Taxation Without Representation, "the shot heard round the world." I pull on whatever clothes I've left lying on the floor and am almost out the front door when I remember my birth control pills. I race back to my room, reach into the way-back of my closet, grab the nude oval container from inside the old ice skate where I keep it hidden, and swallow *Tuesday.*

The week I started taking the pill, Conrad stopped coming to my room at night. At first I thought it was the timing. Six days after my visit to the clinic, Conrad had left to spend spring break in Memphis with his mother and weird Rosemary, whom I hadn't seen in three years and, for all I knew, was probably a bride of Christ by now. The first few weeks after Conrad got back, I lay in bed at night, forcing myself to stay awake, waiting for a floorboard to creak, the whisper of his clothes, the unzipping. But nothing happened. It was as if I had taken a magic pill.

Conrad was different when he got home from Memphis. He was happy. The trip had been a big success. His mother had asked him to come again in June and stay for the whole summer.

"We're gonna drive to New Mexico to visit my uncle," he told us at dinner. "Rosemary figured out it's exactly nine hundred and ninety-nine miles from Memphis to Santa Fe. We're choosing a one-mile detour so it'll be an even thousand."

"Cool," Leo said. "Uncle Jeff?"

"Yeah."

"Is he still married to the stewardess?"

"Linda."

"Right. With the big hair."

"They're separated," Conrad said.

"Your mother could never stand her. Said she was a fortune hunter. Though marrying an orthopedist isn't exactly hitting the jackpot." Leo served himself a big glob of mashed potatoes. "Can someone pass me the butter?"

Conrad *looked* different, too. He stopped buttoning the top button of his shirt tight around his Adam's apple, which always made him look like a serial killer, and finally started using the dandruff shampoo my mother kept putting in the bathroom. He had made the varsity wrestling team. There was even a girl he liked at school. Leslie. A sophomore who had transferred in midyear.

In June, right before he left for Tennessee for the summer, Conrad, Leslie, and I went to see *E.T.* together. As we sat in the dark movie theater eating popcorn and watching a small boy communing with a long finger, I realized that, for the first time in a long time, things felt almost normal.

It's been over six months, and still no quiet tapping at the door, dark shadow next to my bed, whispered threats. I don't know if it's because spending the summer with his mom and Rosemary made him realize what a disgusting perv he was, or because he and Leslie are dry-humping all the time, or because the hormones I'm taking change the way I smell. But whatever it is, the pills are working.

I run the eight blocks to school, rain pelting down on my umbrella, dirty puddle water splashing my ankles. I'll probably flunk the test. I can't remember why Paul Revere is so important.

December

"*There* you are," Mum says, pushing her way through the heavy velvet stage curtains and plonking herself down on a metal folding chair in the now-empty viola section.

"You're not supposed to come back here," I say.

"The concert was a great success," she says, ignoring me completely. "Though that conductor has no sense of rhythm. At these prices, the school really should hire someone more musical."

"Mom!" I give her a fierce look and mouth *Shut up*. Half of the school orchestra is still backstage, putting their instruments away. Mr. Semple, our conductor, stands nearby, chatting to the oboes.

"I should have a word with him. He may not know he's off tempo."

"If you speak to him, I'll kill you." I pull apart the pieces of my flute, thread a white handkerchief through the tip of my cleaning rod, and shove it into the hollow lengths of silver pipe. A thin stream of saliva drips from the head of my flute when I hold it upright.

"And why on earth do a movement from Brandenburg four when you could do five?" She takes a ChapStick out of her purse and applies wax all over her lips. "In any event, Eleanor, you stole the show. Your piccolo solo has always been my favorite part of *The Nutcracker*: that quicksilverish slide up the scale: *Bada bada bada bah . . . blrump, ba ba badladladladl bloom-pah*," she sings, at the top of her lungs.

"Oh my god. *Mom*. Stop." I pick up my flute and piccolo and shove them in my backpack.

"The bassoons sounded like curdled milk."

Leo and Conrad are waiting for us in the lobby outside the auditorium.

"Bravo!" Leo says. "You've turned into an excellent flautist, young lady." He turns to Conrad. "What'd you think?"

"It was fine."

"Only fine? I thought Elle was terrific."

"I'm not into classical stuff."

A few of my friends have run over to congratulate me, twittering with excitement: *You were amazing . . . Who knew you could do that? . . . Is it hard?* I like my friends, but I know they are not here to see me play a wind instrument. They're here because Jeb Potter, the hottest guy in school, plays timpani in the orchestra.

Conrad edges his way into our circle. "Hey," he says to my friends.

"How's it going?" He puts his hand on my shoulder. "I'm Elle's brother, Conrad."

"*Step*brother," I say.

1983. January 1, New York City.

If I eat another dumpling I will burst. We are in a crowded dim sum restaurant in Chinatown, sitting at a big round table. Mum and Leo are hung over and are being mildly unpleasant to everyone. A waiter with a big metal steam cart is bashing around the restaurant flinging small white plates of unrecognizable food onto tables. The air is thick with cigarette smoke, sweat, and din. The waiter puts a beer down in front of Mum and she gulps it straight from the bottle.

"Hair of the dog," she says. "Not even twenty-four hours and I've already broken my first resolution."

I look over at Anna and groan. "I'm so fat."

"Please," Anna says. "I feel like a tick."

Anna is home from college. She's a freshman at UCLA. She's sharing my room over the break, since Conrad has her room now. Mum set up the folding bed for Anna, but the mattress is lumpy, thin in the middle – you can feel the metal bar coming through. So, I've given her my bed instead. At night, we lie there talking until we pass out. Ever since I visited her at boarding school, when she confided in me for the first time, we've become friends.

"Who wants a pork bun?" Leo grabs two plates off the cart. Conrad reaches out to take one, but Leo bypasses him—Conrad has been gaining weight. "Rosemary?"

Rosemary is spending the holidays with us. She's still mousy, with dull dirty-blond hair. Small for her age. Sad. She's fourteen, but she wears sensible brown lace-up shoes and pleated wool skirts. She looks like her mother dresses her. Rosemary didn't want to come for Christmas, but Leo insisted. He's happy having both his children under one roof again, but Mum is going out of her mind. She keeps finding reasons to go to Gristedes. For Christmas, Rosemary gave each of us a different ceramic souvenir bell from Graceland. Leo played carols on his saxophone and we all sang. Then Rosemary asked if she could sing her pageant solo, "Lully, Lullay," which always sounds to me like someone playing the recorder. Rosemary insisted on singing every verse, eyes closed, rocking back and forth to the music. At one point, tears began to roll down her cheeks. Anna pinched my thigh so hard I almost screamed.

"It's like she never grew up," Anna says later that night when we are lying in bed. "Her skin is translucent. It's probably all that religion."

"We should talk about the summer, Rosemary," Leo says now. "It would be wonderful if you could come for a proper long visit this year. We've missed you."

I can see Mum mentally kicking him under the table, but she smiles at Rosemary, nods in agreement, polishes off her beer, and waves to a waiter.

"I can't. I have band camp in June," Rosemary says. "And then Mom and I are going to Lake Placid."

"Mom didn't say anything to me about Lake Placid," Conrad says.

"It's a girls' trip. You're not invited."

Conrad takes the pork bun off her plate and bites into it. Small bits of liquid brown meat ooze from the white, doughy corners.

"Are you sure you need that, Conrad?" Leo asks.

February

The playground is still full. It's freezing out, and dusky evening is setting in, but Mrs. Strauss, the woman whose daughter I babysit after school, insisted I take five-year-old Petra to the park for fresh air, even though I'm sure Mrs. Strauss could see I had frostbite and my nose was about to fall off. She's one of those women who only *seems* nice—the kind who shops at snotty stores like Bendel's and Bergdorf's, but not Bloomies. The Strausses live in a modern white-brick building on East Seventy-fifth, with a beige awning that stretches all the way across the sidewalk to the curb, so the tenants can step into a cab without getting wet in the rain. Their apartment has sliding doors onto a balcony that overlooks the park. When Mrs. Strauss and her husband are too lazy to walk their Weimaraner, they let it shit out there, and then the shit freezes in horrible gray-brown clumps.

I follow Petra around the playground, from jungle gym to slide to swings. Children run around in thick wool coats and mittens, scarves tied around their necks, noses running with snot. The nannies sit together on a park bench, ignoring them, trying to fill the gap between after school and dinnertime with the least effort possible.

"Push me!" Petra says.

I've forgotten my gloves. My hands are turning blue as I push the metal chain of the swing, flinging her higher and higher into the wind. The trees are bare. Inside my coat pocket, I can feel the weight of the roll of quarters I have stolen from the kitchen drawer where Mrs. Strauss leaves change for the housekeeper to use in the basement laundry machines.

I step off the elevator, waving good night to Pepe, our elevator man. A few flights up, someone else is ringing for him. Pepe slides the heavy brass gate closed. The outer elevator door shuts behind me. I stand in the foyer, feeling around in my book bag for my house key. Even from here, outside on the landing, I can hear Conrad and Leo fighting again. It's so loud, everyone in our building must hear them. Conrad is screeching that his father understands nothing—he was just "holding" for some kid at school. It wasn't his pot.

I slide down to the worn black-and-white mosaic-tiled floor of the foyer and lean my back against the front door. There is no way I'm going in.

"You're grounded for a month," Leo is yelling.

"You can't do that! I have tickets to WWF at the Garden. It's André the Giant," Conrad screams. "I'm taking Leslie."

"Give them to Elle."

"I bought them with my own Christmas money from Mom." Conrad is sobbing now. "You're such a dick. I hate you."

I'm at my desk doing my algebra homework when Conrad appears at the door. "Here, bitch," he says, and throws his tickets at me.

"What did *I* do?" I say. "I hate sports."

March

The sound of paper wakes me. An orange-and-white paperback book cover is sticking through the crack of my closed door, which now has a hook-and-eye lock. I watch in dread as *Of Mice and Men* slides slowly upward. It catches under the metal latch, lifts it up and out. The book cover disappears. My door handle turns.

"Mum?" I call out before he has time to open the door. "Is that you?"

I listen for the creep of his footsteps receding down the hallway before relocking the door.

April

The doleful drizzle hasn't let up since we arrived at our grandparents' house in Connecticut. My grandmother insists April showers bring May flowers, but this feels more like a heavy heart than the twiggy greenness of spring. Anna and I are spending two weeks with Granny and Granddaddy. Granny Myrtle has been having fibrillations and she's feeling a bit wobbly. She could use some extra hands around the house. Anna is on spring break and wants to spend most of her time with them.

"Who knows if I'll ever come back from California. And by then they might both be dead," she says when she calls me from school to tell me the plan.

"Lovely. We'll all miss you so much."

"You know you will," Anna says.

"I know. I already do."

Now Anna and I lie on our old twin beds, where we have spent most of the past three days reading the books Granny Myrtle took out of the library for us. "These should keep you occupied until the nasty weather lets up," she said, handing each of us a thick book. *War and Peace* for Anna, *Wuthering Heights* for me.

I hold my book up to my face, sniff the pages. I love the way library books smell: more important than regular books, a grand olden-days smell, like the steps of a marble palace, or a senator.

Anna yawns, stretches. "This book is too long. And too Russian. All that male, thrusty prose. I'll never finish it. I'm going to go find something else on the bookshelves."

Alone in our room, I watch raindrops slide down the window. Stare out into the brume. The crabapple tree has become a specter in the mist, its black-wet branches tapping at the pane. I don't care if it rains for a month. I'm just happy to be here where I'm safe, where I can spend time with my funny, brusque, sardonic sister; where I can fall asleep without dread, where I know that my grandmother, no matter how frail, will love me fiercely, make fresh waffles, insist on washing my hair in the kitchen sink with Johnson's Baby Shampoo, as she has done since I was little, rinsing out its sweet-kerosene smell under the warm tap, my head leaning back at an unnatural angle, neck pressed against the sink's cold porcelain edge. And yet even here, I'm prodded awake all night by my unconscious vigilance. I lie in the darkness comforted by Anna's snores, before at last falling back into a restless sleep.

"You look like shit," Anna said when she got back from California.

"I've been having trouble sleeping," I said.

"I thought someone had punched you in both eyes."

When Conrad first started coming into my room at night, I wanted to call Anna and tell her. But I knew Anna would tell Mum, even if I made her promise not to. Anna's not like me. She thrives on confrontation. She doesn't give a shit what other people think. She doesn't need to be liked. Anna is a warrior. She would never, ever have allowed Conrad to get away with it. Nor would she have understood why I had allowed it to go on—that the only way I could protect myself from the shame and humiliation I felt was by denying any knowledge of it. But if I told Anna, she would attack him, tear everything open, expose me to him in a different way. Conrad would know I had known his dirty secret all along. And then it stopped, and I thought: Nothing terrible really happened. He touched himself, but he never touched me. No one ever needs to know. But recently, his visits have started again, and I wish I had told her when I could.

Anna wanders back holding my grandfather's copy of *The Great Gatsby*.

I glance up as she comes in. "Haven't you read that book a hundred times?"

"This is a first edition," she says reverently.

"Did he say you could take it?"

"I didn't want to bother him. He's upstairs in his study." She settles down on her bed. "Anyway, I'm not going to read it, I just want to lie in bed and stroke it. Who knows, maybe we'll even get to second base."

"You're such an idiot." I laugh.

"I am," Anna says. "'That's the best thing a girl can be in this world, a beautiful little fool.'"

"Can one of you girls come help me get supper on the table?" Granny Myrtle calls from the kitchen. "The potatoes need peeling."

"I'll go," I say to Anna. "You stay and get felt up by your book. Can I do the carrots instead?" I ask, coming out of our room. "I'm bad at peeling potatoes." I always end up with pale pentagonal lumps, most of the potato still attached to the peels. I will disappoint Granny Myrtle, which I hate.

"Why don't you run down to the road and get the mail," Granny says. "I've left it all day." She goes to the sink and starts peeling potatoes. Their razor-thin skins fall elegantly into the basin. I come up behind her and nuzzle her cheek, making soft, burring pony noises.

"Oh, for heaven's sake, you silly girl," she says. But she's smiling. "My rubbers are in the front hall if you need them."

Outside, the drizzle has turned to pelting rain. Lightning cracks the sky, silhouetting gravestones across the road. Seconds later, a thunderclap.

May

I wake in a flop sweat, my back to the door. I have fallen asleep on my watch. A streetlamp casts tree shadows on the wall above me—witch fingers. I can't see him, but he's there behind me, beside the bed. Watching me. Deciding. I shift my position, murmur in REM, wait for him to leave. But he doesn't move. The tip of a finger touches my ankle, draws a line up my leg, stops at the border of my hem. It presses into my thigh. A damp, squishy press. And I realize then, it's not his finger. I jerk away before I can stop myself. Too quick. Too aware.

"Elle?" softly.

I curl away into an inverse proportion, shoulders concave, knees to chest, whimpering at a nightmare. "It's not a peacock," I mumble. My arm thrashes at nothing. "Your house is here."

Conrad steps away into shadow. He waits for me to settle. When my breathing slows, he lets himself out. The door sighs behind him.

16

1983. June, New York.

Eight a.m. and already the city is stifling and muggy, giving off the dusty gray smell of warm sidewalks, dog piss, oil stains on asphalt, the sweet, pale scent of linden trees. We are leaving for the Back Woods today. The car is double-parked. I'm helping Leo load. He's anxious to get on the road. We have a six-hour drive ahead of us and he wants to beat the traffic. But Mum still hasn't managed to catch the cat, and the car is only half packed because Conrad, who's in charge of bringing our bags downstairs, is moving so slowly he looks like he's swimming through honey.

"Can you move those short legs of yours a bit faster?" Leo says.

"Asshole," Conrad says.

Leo says nothing.

My mother leans out the window of our third-story apartment. "Elle, did you want me to pack your Waterpik? Oh, and I need you to run across to Gristedes and get me one more cardboard box. Something I can use for kitty litter in the car."

When the car is finally packed, Mum comes out of our building holding a picnic basket and the cat-carrying case.

"He was hiding under the bed." She puts the cat case on the back seat, hands me the picnic basket. "Can you fit this at your feet, Elle? Leo doesn't want to stop for lunch. There's an apple and three nectarines. I made peanut butter and mayonnaise, or roast beef." She settles into the front seat, fans herself with a piece of junk mail from the dash.

I move the cat case to the middle of the seat to make a wall between Conrad and me.

"Why can't we get a car with air conditioning?" Conrad says.

"You'll be swimming in the pond in a few hours." Leo slams the rear door shut.

I roll down my window letting in the swampy breeze. I can't wait to get to the woods. Anna is spending the summer at a kibbutz in Northern California, so I'll get our cabin to myself. I'm signed up for sailing lessons. And Jonas will be back this summer. Last year his parents were on sabbatical in Florence. His mother is working on a biography of Dante. I'm excited to see him again. I wonder whether he will have changed a lot, or if I will have outgrown him.

Traffic is bumper to bumper. Somewhere in Rhode Island, our radiator overheats. Leo pulls over onto the scrubby verge, cursing.

"I needed to stretch my legs anyway," Mum says.

Twenty yards ahead of us another car has broken down. Beyond it, on a massive billboard, a man in a zebra suit advertises a car dealership. I watch the cars creep past, feeling vaguely resentful, as if we have lost our rightful place in line.

"I filled up an empty half-gallon milk jug with water, just in case," Mum says. "It's somewhere behind you, Conrad."

"Hand me that water, would you, Con." Leo unbuckles his seat belt.

"I'll need to let the heat out from under the hood. Cool down the radiator."

Conrad glances over his shoulder. "It's too far back. I can't reach it."

"Then get out and go around."

"You're getting out of the car anyway."

"I'll get it," I say before Leo has a chance to respond. I wiggle my way over the back of the seat, stretch over paper bags filled with groceries, suitcases, a basket of pears, strain to grab the water. "Got it," I grunt.

"Elle, you're an angel," Leo says. "I'll deal with you later, Conrad." His voice is stony with contempt.

"*I'll deal with you later,*" Conrad mocks his father under his breath. He looks at me with loathing. "Kiss ass."

Between us, on the seat, my mother's cat howls and scratches at its box.

By the time we reach the Woods it's almost midnight. The camp has been locked up all winter. Our canoes are stacked on the porch. Everything is covered in pollen and spiderwebs. Some large animal has managed to get in over the winter, knocking plates off the open shelves. Shards of ironstone are skittled across the living room floor. The mice have made their annual nest in the silverware drawer. Mouse shit in the fork tines, afterbirth on the teaspoons. The hot water needs to be turned on. The flashlights are all dead. No one feels like making beds.

I pee in the bushes, walk down the path to my cabin, and throw myself onto the bare mattress. I'm so happy to be here. I lie there listening to the boom and croak of bullfrogs, the stillness of the trees, as the full moon shines through the skylight. A twig snaps. Something is moving outside my cabin. I hold my breath. Wait. Footfalls shuffle past toward the edge of the pond. Soon I hear splashing and a sound like a soft baby's cry. I climb out of bed and creep to the screen door, peer out into the darkness letting my eyes adjust. A large mother raccoon and her four kits are fishing in the shallows. She stops, sniffs the air, sensing me, before turning back to her task. She swipes her paw across the surface of the water and brings up a fish. Careful not to make a sound, I step out onto the path. She freezes, wary now. I take a step forward. She turns her bandit face toward me and snarls. Within seconds, the raccoons have disappeared into the trees. No sign of them. Only the slight warble of the pond. The moon is so bright I can see pebbles under the water. I pull off my nightgown and wade out until I am waist-high among the reeds, and then I melt into the pond. I've never swum alone like this—at night, naked, in the silence. It feels luxurious, secretive.

I step out and shake myself dry, grab my nightgown from the branch, dash up the steps into my cabin, and pull the door shut behind me.

A hand comes out of the darkness then, covers my mouth.

"I was watching you," Conrad whispers in my ear.

My stomach drops into my feet. My entire body cold with panic. I scream, but all that comes out is a muffled moan.

"You should skinny-dip every night." He rubs his hand over my naked body, sighs. "Your skin is soft, rubbery."

He pushes me onto the bed.

I struggle to get free of him, but his grip is too tight.

"You knew I was watching," he says.

"Stop it, Conrad," I beg.

"Cocktease. You like it. You let me come into your room at night. You never tell me to leave. I know you just pretend to be asleep."

I shake my head, no, thrashing, desperate. "That's a lie," I manage to whisper.

"I told all my friends you let me touch you."

He stabs himself into me then. I feel a searing pain as he tears through my hymen. Rips me open. I think about the mother raccoon listening to my soft baby-like cries from the tree branches above. When he comes, I weep.

A bluebird flies across the sky, wings from tree to tree. I lie on the mossy ground deep in the woods by my secret stream in a fetal curl. After Conrad left, I ran to the bathroom and washed myself from the hot tap. Scorched him from me. But it did nothing. I am no longer myself. I can't go home. I can't stay here. I won't let him ruin this place for me. The pond is mine. The woods are mine. I need to sleep. The night hates me. I am walking death.

Hours later, I come to, my body frozen, teeth chattering, clothes drenched in sweat, numbed. I can't get my bearings, still caught in the fog of a dream that lingers and evades. I want to stay there, but the here won't allow it. I wash my face in the cool stream, smooth my hair. My flesh revolts me. I have to go home. I can never go home.

I approach the camp in stealth, hover in the bushes outside the pantry. My only objective is invisibility—to creep past, find a hole, crawl into it, shut my eyes too tight, see nothing but floaters. Leo's station wagon is gone. My mother is alone in the kitchen making dinner. I watch her from my leafy blind. She is humming, filling a large pot with water. I take a step toward her. She looks up, alert, like a deer, as if she senses my presence. She shuts the tap, comes to the window, peers out. I wait for her to turn away before emerging from the woods, letting myself in through the pantry door.

"There you are!" she says. "I haven't seen you all day. I was starting to worry."

"I walked into town."

"Your friend Jonas dropped by earlier."

"Where is everyone?"

"Leo and Conrad went to the package store. I forgot beer. We're having bluefish tacos."

"I think I might skip dinner. I have a terrible stomachache."

My mother shreds a cabbage on the counter; a pile of pale green bones.

"Mum?"

"Mm-hmm," she says without turning around.

"I need to tell you something."

"Can you grab me the sour cream?" She cleans off the blade of her knife with a dish towel and picks up a pile of washed parsley. Gives it a quick shake.

"*Mom.*"

"Please don't call me that, you know I hate it."

I hear a car coming down the driveway.

"Oh good," she says. "They're back. I can put the bluefish on the grill." She pours a bit of olive oil into a cast-iron pan, throws in a few crushed cloves of garlic. "So. Tell," she says.

The car doors slam.

"I think I have a fever."

She feels my forehead with the back of her hand. "You *are* a bit hot." She goes to the sink and pours a glass of water. "Take this. I'll bring you some aspirin as soon as I get the fish on."

I walk down the path toward my cabin, stand outside it, afraid to go in, afraid of what I will find.

The strange thing is, nothing has changed. There are no traces of violence, no smell of fear. My yellow floor is bright and cheerful. Mum has left a pile of fresh cotton sheets and floral pillowcases on the end of the mattress. Nothing has changed but me.

I stay in my room for four days, shaky, weeping, managing to avoid Conrad the entire time. At night I lock my door, put a chair in front of it. Mum thinks I have a stomach virus. I put my finger down my throat, force myself to throw up into the garbage can any food she brings me. I flush the toilet over and over again, faking diarrhea. Mum keeps everyone out of my cabin. "The last thing we need is you infecting everyone else." She brings me bowls of chicken broth with rice, and cool compresses. My mother isn't a warm person, but she has always been an excellent nurse. Each day, Jonas comes to visit, but she turns him away.

Monday morning, the first day of sailing camp, I make a miraculous recovery. My mother is dubious, but I promise to call home if I feel sick. The sea air will do me good, I tell her. She drives me to the bayside yacht club and drops me at the dock.

"Leo will be here at five to collect you."

"I thought you were coming to get me."

"Leo will already be out of the Woods. He's taking Conrad to Orleans to get new swimming trunks. Apparently, the ones Conrad packed no longer close at the waist."

"Why does Conrad need a bathing suit? He barely ever gets in the water. I don't want to be sick in the car with Leo."

My mother sighs. "Fine. Five o'clock."

I watch the station wagon pull away before heading down to the boat slip. My body feels foreign to me, weak, see-through. But I'm glad to be away from the camp, from *him*.

A group of kids are standing around on the dock, waiting for our instructor. Beyond them, legs dangling in the water, Jonas is sketching something in the harbor that has caught his eye.

"Hey," he says, as if we just saw each other yesterday.

"Hey, stranger. What are you doing here?"

"Learning to sail."

I stop a few feet away from him, afraid he will smell the shame on me, but he jumps up, a huge smile on his face, and comes over to give me a bear hug. I'm shocked by how much he has changed—he's still tan and ramshackle, shirtless, but he looks so much older than fourteen. He must be six feet tall, and he has gotten very handsome. For a moment, as we hug, I feel oddly shy. I wish I had washed my hair.

"You look different," I say, pushing it away. "Same shitty shorts."

He laughs. "About ten sizes bigger, but yeah, you know me, a creature of habit. How have you been?"

I am saved from dishonesty by the arrival of the sailing instructor, who yells at us to grab a life jacket and climb aboard, three to a boat. Five Sunfish are moored in the bay. They look like hard candies, their sails striped in green, turquoise, lemon, orange, red, and lavender.

"I hope you don't mind me being here," Jonas says as we climb aboard. "Your mother told me you signed up. I got all your postcards. Thanks."

"Are you kidding? Of course I'm happy to see you," I say. And I am.

"You look different, too," Jonas says.

"I've had stomach flu." I am an Untouchable.

He considers me. "No," he says, "I don't think it's the diarrhea."

"Yuck."

"Indeed."

"I'm probably fatter."

"That's not it. You're lovelier than ever."

"You are more ridiculous than ever." I laugh. But I'm glad he thinks so.

An older girl climbs onto the boat and squeezes in between us. "I'm

Karina," she says. "I did this last year." She takes hold of the mainsheet. Shoves us aside.

We sail out onto the choppy bay. Beyond us, a boat capsizes. Someone stands on the centerboard and rights it. The wet sail thwacks against the mast. The kids pull themselves out, drenched and happy, squeezing water out of their T-shirts. They pull the boom in, grab for the line. Our instructor dodges in and out around our flock of boats in a small white skiff with an outboard motor.

"Ready about! Hard alee! Watch the boom! Pull the sheet!"

"Is he speaking Mandarin or ancient Greek?" Jonas asks. "I can't quite make it out."

We laugh, but within an hour Jonas is captaining our boat like a pro, marginalizing the bossy Karina, shouting at me to trim lines, make knots, lean out. Our sails luff, we turn and zip, slow to nothing. None of it matters. I'm happy to be breathing. Happy to be here with Jonas. Safe from Conrad. *I can do this,* I think as we sail out farther and farther. I can survive this. No one needs to know. I'll put a kitchen knife under my mattress. If he touches me again, I'll kill him. The thought of that uplifts me. I close my eyes and let the salt wind coarse my face.

17

July

Sunday. Our day off from camp. Jonas and I have made a plan to take a picnic to the beach. We'll canoe across and walk to the ocean from there so Jonas can fish on the way home. When he arrives, I'm in the kitchen making ham and Muenster sandwiches. I have a jar of dill pickles already packed in the basket, a thermos of iced tea. I throw in a bag of cherries, some paper napkins, and a baggie of Milanos. Jonas leans against the counter and watches as I fold wax paper around the sandwiches, making hospital corners.

The screen door slams open and shut. Conrad sits down at the porch table. I head into the pantry, bury my head in the icebox, pretending to look for something.

My cabin door has stayed locked every night since that night, but I've started to feel safe in daylight, as long as we aren't alone. As long as I never, ever look at him. I have become a blindered horse. Conrad pretends to act as if nothing happened, but he has been unusually solicitous—pulling out my chair at the dinner table, refilling my water glass.

"Quite the young gentleman," my mother says, smiling at him.

"Hello, Conrad," Jonas says now.

"What's up?" Conrad grunts.

"Not much. Elle's making us a picnic to take to the beach."

"What's she making?"

"Ham and cheese."

"Maybe I'll come with you."

"Okay," Jonas says.

The mustard jar I'm holding slips from my hand, shatters on the floor, splattering everything around me in Dijon yellow.

I crouch down and pick up shards of glass.

"Are you all right? Did you cut yourself?" Jonas asks, coming into the pantry to help me.

"I'm fine," I mutter. "Just glass and mustard everywhere."

"Conrad wants to join us."

"We can't fit three people in the canoe."

"I can fish later. It's not as if the bass are going anywhere."

"You should have asked me first."

"What was I meant to do? Say 'Hold on a sec while I go ask Elle if she wants you to come? . . . Sorry, she says no?' That would have been marginally awkward, to say the least."

"I need wet newspaper and a broom," I snap.

"Are you sure you're okay?"

"I'm fine," I say, turning away from him. "Stop asking."

We take the path that leads from the camp to the beach, walking single file through the woods—Conrad, then Jonas, then me.

Jonas keeps up a patter of conversation with Conrad. I slow down and let them drift ahead. When they are out of sight, I double over, dry-heaving. I was wrong. I can't do this. I can't be with him. Smiling, naked except for my bikini, swimming, knowing. Knowing that he knows. The panic in me feels like a snake slithering out of my mouth.

Somewhere up ahead, Jonas is calling me.

"I stubbed my toe," I yell. "I'll catch up."

I want to turn around and run home, lock myself in my room. Instead, I close my eyes and will myself to calm down, move forward. I've been down this path so many times I recognize every root, every tree. I know when I round the next corner I will see wild grapevines climbing into the trees and scrub, clusters of sweet Concord grapes hanging down from the bay laurel, crops left over from a hundred years ago when this wooded hill was still farmland. I know that beyond the vines, the path will widen and steepen. I will crest the hill and come down into a hollow between the dunes, where an old fire road runs parallel to the sea. Beyond, at the top of the next dune, I will come to a wooden hut, dilapidated but still standing, built during the war as a lookout for approaching German submarines. Anna and I played there with our dolls when we were little. I will stand there, looking out at the wide ocean, my ocean. I know this place. This is my place, not his.

The beach is beautiful and broad. Low tide. Conrad is already knee-deep in the water, wading out. The skin on his back is bright white against his ugly red bathing suit. There's a smattering of acne across his shoulders. I scan the ocean, looking wistfully for a shark fin. I run down the steep dune, letting my towel out behind me like a sail.

I sit down a few feet away from Jonas.

"Hey." He pats a space on the towel next to him, but I ignore it.

Conrad dives under a wave and gets tumbled. His fat legs poke out of the water like a giant's fingers giving us the peace sign before the sea finally rights him.

"Did you two have some big fight?"

"No. Just the usual: he's a jerk and I hate him."

"So why are you acting so mad at me?"

"I'm not acting like anything. You ruined a nice day. It's no big deal."

"I didn't ruin the day, Elle. It's beautiful, perfect. Look at that water. Even Conrad's glad to be here."

"Well, thank God for that." I stand up. "I'm going to take a walk down the beach. You two have a nice time. There aren't enough sandwiches for three of us."

"You can have mine if you promise to stop acting like an insane person."

"Don't talk so loud," I snap, and storm down to the water's edge, hating myself. Conrad has ruined the pond, ruined the Paper Palace, ruined me. But I will not let him come between me and Jonas, stain the one thing that is still mine with his black squid ink.

Conrad is jumping waves, his back to me. I reach down to the tide line, pick up a chipped-flint stone—*my heart,* I think as I hurl it at him with all my strength, aiming for his head. The stone misses, disappears into the sea a yard short of him. I have always thrown like a girl, and I hate it. It's a weakness that others can see. I look down, searching for a better rock. Each time the tide recedes, a hundred little holes appear in the smooth wet sand where clams have hurriedly dug themselves down, hiding from the sharp-eyed gulls above. I find the perfect stone: gray, tangerine-sized, with a raised white streak running across its middle. When I stand up, Conrad is looking at me. I put the stone in my pocket for later, and walk away, follow the edge of the sea until I am so far from him that when I look back, he is nothing but a meaningless speck.

When I get home from the beach, Jonas is waiting on the steps of my cabin, something cupped in his hands. "Look." He's holding a tree frog the size of a button.

"Sweet," I say. "I'm fairly certain you are touching frog piss. They pee in your hand whenever you pick them up." I push past him and shove open my cabin door.

"Yes," Jonas says. "It's an instinctive reaction to fear."

"So, see you Monday, I guess."

"Elle, wait. I'm sorry." He puts the frog on the ground, watches it hop away.

"For what?"

"I don't know. You're so mad at me. Please don't be mad. Haven't I already been punished enough? All that guy talks about is wrestling and Van Halen, my two least favorite subjects."

He looks like a little boy. I feel terrible. None of this is Jonas's fault, but there's nothing I can say that will make him understand, because there is nothing that can be said. "It could have been *Best of Bread*." I sit down beside him. "I'm sorry I was mean."

Three weeks into sailing camp, Jonas and I are upgraded from a Sunfish to a Rhodes. We each receive a small iron-on badge. Jonas is the natural sailor, but I'm a decent second mate, and I feel peaceful when I'm out on the water with him. The boat typically holds six of us, but our instructor wants us to be "self-sufficient," able to navigate with a two-man crew. So, today, Jonas and I get to team up on our own. It's been drizzling all morning, and we are far out on the bay in our bright yellow slickers. The wind is fickle, changing direction every ten seconds. I've been hit by the boom so many times that even Jonas stops laughing at me.

"This is ridiculous," I shout.

"I agree. Let's head back." He trims the sheet and tries to come about, but the wind refuses to cooperate. Our boat bobs around in the surf, its sail flapping slack.

"We should call out for a tow," I say. Our instructor will come get us if we need him.

"No way. It's our first two-man. It'll pick up."

Instead, the rain begins to bucket down on us so hard that my ears fill with the water dripping off my hair. I can no longer see the dock. Nearby, in the mist, our teacher is towing in another boat.

"I'm calling him over."

"Give it five more minutes."

"I'm freezing to death."

He stands up, fiddles with the jib.

"Fine. Five." I pull my collar up and scrunch down in the cockpit.

Jonas leans against the mast, gazing out at the rain as if he is looking for answers.

"Penny for your thoughts?" I say.

A sea gull flies out of the fog and lands on the bow. It cocks its head and looks at Jonas, unblinking. Jonas looks away first.

"I don't want you to get mad," he says.

"I won't."

He sits beside me, with a resigned breath. "Have you and Conrad ever, you know, done anything together?"

"Done anything?" I spit-take the words. "Done anything how? What does that even mean? Why would you ask me that?"

"It's just, he said something that day after you left the beach."

I brace myself. "What? *What* did he say?"

"He said you let him feel you up. He said you fool around. He said I shouldn't get my hopes up."

A hysterical laugh escapes from my mouth. My windpipes start to close in on themselves. "That's so disgusting."

He laughs, relieved. "Well, technically you aren't related, but the thought did make me want to puke."

"What's wrong with him? I hate him so much. I would die before I ever let him touch me," I say, voice shaking.

"I never really thought you had."

I will myself not to cry in front of Jonas, but the tears start slipping out against my will.

"Elle, forget it. He was joking around, being a jerk." He takes the bottom of his T-shirt and wipes the rain and tears off my cheeks. "So, I can get my hopes up again?"

"I'm too old for you," I say, though I'm not sure I believe myself.

"I know you think that, but you're wrong."

"And you're way too good for me." And this I know is true.

He reaches into his slicker, pulls out a smushed Peppermint Pattie and tears it in half. "Lunch?"

There is something so sweet about everything he does, something in his gesture that breaks my heart and makes me start crying again.

"What? You hate mint?"

A sob bursts out of me, half laughter, half pain. Conrad has stolen everything from me. I will never be sweet again. I will never be clean again. I always imagined my first time would be with someone I loved. Someone like Jonas. I'm sobbing uncontrollably now, all the terror and shame I have held vomiting out of me in massive heaves and gulps.

"Elle. Stop, okay? I'm sorry I brought it up. I'm an idiot."

I try to stop, to catch my breath, but the more I try, the harder I cry. The sea fog rolls in now, so thick it muffles my sobs, turns us both into specters.

"He enjoys belittling me. We know that. I shouldn't have said anything. Please stop crying."

I want to tell him everything, to unshoulder this burden, but I can't. He's barely fourteen, and this murder of crows in my belly is mine alone to carry. The wounds inside me will scab over and heal, however lopsidedly. And next time I will be prepared, armed with more than pills. In the distance, I hear the toll of a warning bell.

"We should head in," I manage to gulp out, through my snot and tears and sobs.

"Elle, I don't understand. Please stop crying. It's not like it's true." He is anguished, confused. "Did something happen that you aren't telling me?"

I stare down at my waterlogged sneakers. An inch of seawater has collected in the bottom of the boat. I tap at it with my shoe, making little splashes, wipe my face with the sleeve of my plastic slicker.

I feel him scrutinizing me, trying to weigh things up. "Did Conrad hurt you?"

"No," I say in a whisper.

"You swear on your life?"

I nod, but my face must betray me, because all of a sudden his body slumps, as if the sharp blade of discovery has de-boned him.

"Oh god."

"You can't say anything. Ever. No one knows."

"Elle, I promise, he will never touch you again."

I laugh, but the sound is bitter, hollow. "That's what I promised myself after the first time he came into my room."

A large shadow passes under our boat. It hovers for a moment before slipping off into the mists. Our boat rocks gently as I tell Jonas everything.

18

August

The most beautiful days in summer come after a heavy rain. White cumulus clouds hover in a deepened blue; the air is crisp enough to drink. Today is one of those days. Yesterday's storm has washed the skies clean. I wake up having forgotten—I may even be smiling before memory strikes and I wish it away. A stick cracks outside my cabin door, the steps sag with a hollow groan. My mother's face appears in the screen door.

"Why is this locked?" she says, rattling the handle.

"It catches sometimes." I jump up and unlatch the door.

"Put this stuff away, please." She dumps a pile of fresh folded laundry on my bed. "Leo thought it would be fun to take my father's old boat out today." My grandfather's sailing dinghy has been parked on a trailer at the bottom of our driveway collecting pine needles all summer. "We're thinking eleven-ish to hit the outgoing tide, so up you get. No dawdling."

"I think I'll skip it, if that's okay. I'm not really in the mood."

"Leo wants a family day. We'll have a picnic and then sail out to the Point."

The Point is the literal end of the Cape, a dwindling spit of sand that curves around the wide harbor in a protective embrace, the final barrier between civilization and the wide-open ocean. From the launch at the town beach you can sail out to the Point, drop anchor in the warm, glassy shallows of the sheltered bay, watch scuttling crabs in the sea grasses, dig for clams when the tide recedes. But three minutes' walk around the point and you are facing out to sea, nothing between you and Portugal but an occasional yacht coming in for safe harbor, fishing boats in the far distance heading out to the rich waters of the Stellwagen Bank in search of bluefin tuna and halibut, the breaching whales.

"Why do I have to come? Why can't you and Leo go by yourselves? Anyway, we won't all fit." The dinghy is barely big enough for two, three tops. And Leo is so huge, he's basically two people already.

"We'll go out two at a time. Conrad's coming."

"No way. I'm not going sailing with Conrad."

She sighs. "Elle, I'm asking you to do this."

"It's a terrible idea. He's like a big fat cat in the water."

"Don't be nasty, it doesn't suit you."

"It's true."

"Why are you being so unpleasant? What has Conrad ever done to you?" My mother shakes her head in dismay.

"Fine. But only if Jonas comes, too."

"I told you. It's a family day."

"Mum. Seriously. Think about it. If we capsize in the bay, Conrad will be useless. I won't be able to right the boat by myself if the water gets remotely choppy. So, either you, me, Leo, and Conrad squeeze into the boat, in which case it will definitely sink, or I need Jonas to help me sail."

"Fine," she says. "It's too beautiful a day to argue."

In the driveway, Conrad and Leo are trying to hitch the boat trailer to the car, but it keeps slipping out of their hands. I watch them belly-laughing at their own ineptitude, transfixed by the strangeness of normality, the flat line of the everyday.

"Never ask a sax player to do a man's job," Leo says when he sees me standing there. "Come give us a hand with this. Conrad, you hold it in place while Elle puts the pin in."

I hesitate, trying to think up some excuse, but nothing comes.

"Any time now, Elle," Leo says. "This trailer isn't going to hitch itself." He hands me the metal pin. "Hold this while Conrad and I lift."

"Okay, kiddly-winks." My mother appears, smiling. She throws a cooler into the back seat.

Conrad and Leo slot the trailer into place. As he stands up, Conrad accidentally knocks the trailer pin out of my hand. He reaches down to get it for me. "I'm sorry, Elle," he says, his voice so quiet I barely catch it.

Jonas is waiting for us at the end of his driveway, sitting on the verge of the road. He looks relaxed, shirtless as always, but there is a wariness in his eyes, a knitting.

"Hop in, Jonas," Mum says. "Conrad, you squeeze over."

Jonas gets in beside him, leans his body away against the car window, pretending to watch the trees go past. I have never seen Jonas look away from anything, never seen his body blanch. And I know it is because I have tethered him—taken away the whitetail dart, wild green-leaf spring of his marrow: forced him to collude, to carry my lie. It's as if I have stolen his virginity.

"We may need to use the spinnaker," I say to him, "so we can run in front of the wind."

It was lovely and calm in the woods—only the perfect luff of a breeze—but when we get to the bay, the wind has picked up. Waves crisscross the harbor, chopping at boats on their moorings. There's almost no one out on the water.

The first few times we try to put the boat in, it is whipped back to shore before we can get the dagger board down. Conrad yelps in pain as the boat crashes into his shin. My mother watches from the beach, calling out useless directions.

"You all hop in," Leo says. "One last push."

"This isn't going to work, Leo," I say from the boat. "It's too rough."

"You're probably right. But we've come this far."

"I think I'm going to bail." Conrad is clearly nervous.

"Come with us. It'll be fun," Jonas says. But there is a meanness I've never heard before.

At that moment, Leo catches a break between the waves, shoves us hard, and suddenly we are heeling, ripping out to sea. The wind cracks the white sail taut. Conrad sits on the bow, his legs dangling over the edge, skimming the water like thick pink lures.

"I can't look at him," Jonas says to me under his breath.

"You have to pretend everything's fine. You promised me."

"Why?" Jonas whispers. "How can you even talk to him?"

"I can't. But I don't have much choice, do I? I live with him."

"As a matter of fact, you do. If your mother knew—"

"My mother will never, ever know."

"You can't let him get away with it, Elle."

"Shut up!" I hiss. "Pull in your legs!" I call out to Conrad. "You could get bitten by a shark." Jonas turns away from me, his lips an angry pinch. The waves froth and nip at our little boat as it picks up speed.

Conrad pulls himself into a crossed-leg position. The bottoms of his feet are thickly calloused, and I can see small hairline splits running up his heels where he has picked the dead skin away. He looks over at me, smiles. "You were right. This is pretty cool."

He spits his chewing gum into the ocean. I watch it sink in the foam of our wake. I pull a Fresca out of the cooler. "Want one?" I toss Conrad the can.

"Thanks." He pulls off the aluminum pop-top and throws it overboard.

"You shouldn't do that," Jonas calls out. "A bird could choke on it."

"Right. Like anyone can see me," Conrad scoffs.

"That's not the point," Jonas says. "*I* see you."

"I think I'll live."

"Asshole," Jonas mutters under his breath.

The shoreline dwindles away behind us. I can barely make out my mother waving from the beach.

A large swell lifts us up and then drops us with a thud.

"Jesus," Conrad yells at Jonas as the water soaks his clothes. "I thought the whole point of dragging you along was you know how to sail."

"Be my guest," Jonas says, and lets go of the tiller.

"Dick." Conrad stands up and starts inching toward us.

I feel a shift in the sea as our little boat loses its grip on the waves. "Jonas, please don't be an idiot. We'll breach."

Jonas says nothing, but he grabs the tiller.

Another wave brings us crashing down.

"We're getting too far out," I say. "Loosen the sheet, or we're going to pass the Point."

"Fine," Jonas says. "I'll come about." He pulls in the ropes and prepares to turn. "Conrad, sit down. Watch out for the boom," he yells.

Conrad gives him the finger. He smiles at me. His teeth look like Chiclets.

When the boom hits him, I watch him topple, then lurch into the sea. He comes up a moment later, flailing behind the boat.

“Stop,” I scream at Jonas. “Stop the boat.”

Jonas slacks the mainsheet, and our boat slows. There’s an orange life preserver in the well, and I try to untie it, but my fingers fumble on the wet knot.

“Help!” Conrad screams as our boat drifts farther and farther away from him. “Get me out of here!” He is panicking, gagging for breath.

“Take your sweatshirt off, it’s weighing you down,” I yell, struggling to get the life preserver free.

“Jesus Christ, you stupid bitch. Just throw me the thingy.”

“I’m trying,” I say. But I sit down, numb. Jonas puts his hand over mine, holds it still.

When the next wave comes, Conrad is lifted up out of the water, his face white with terror. He reaches for me.

Book Three

PETER

19

1989. February, London.

I am racing down Elgin Crescent toward the Ladbroke Grove tube station, trying to make the last train back to Mile End. It's late, and the damp night air is bone-chilling. I've had too much to drink and my bladder is about to burst. I'm considering squatting between two cars, when a heavyset man steps out in front of me and asks for my wallet. He has a shaved head and a swastika tattoo on his neck. The pubs have just closed, and there are people falling into the streets, but there is no way I am saying no to a man with a knife. I hand him the cash in my pocket.

"Your ring," he says.

"It's nothing," I say. "It's worthless."

"Fucking ring, slag," he says, and punches me in the stomach.

I double over. There's a scroll going across the inside of my head, reading *Stop being an idiot*, but somehow I can't seem to connect thought to action.

The man grabs my hand and tries to twist the ring off my finger.

"Fuck you," I say, and spit in his face.

He wipes his face with his sleeve before backhanding me so hard my teeth rattle.

I deserve this.

1983. August, the Back Woods.

It is three days before Conrad's body washes up on shore, a few miles down the coast. A local mother and her two small children find his body. At first, they think the bloated corpse is a dead seal. His ears have been nibbled at by crabs. I am in my cabin under a blanket, hiding from Leo's wails, when the door opens and Jonas comes in. He is shaking, pale-faced. I crawl out from under the covers and wrap my arms tight around him. Rest my head on his shoulder. I cannot see his face, but it doesn't matter. I know he is crying, because I am, too.

"I'm sorry," I whisper. "I'm so sorry."

We sit like that for a long time, holding each other in the quiet, Jonas's heart beating against mine.

"No one can ever know," Jonas says. "Blood oath."

"No one," I say. There's a safety pin on my bureau. We prick our thumbs, each squeeze out a drop of blood, press them together.

Jonas wipes his hand off on his shorts. He reaches into his pocket and pulls out a silver ring with a green glass stone, puts it in the palm of my hand. I squeeze my fingers tight around it. It feels cold; one of the metal prongs that holds in the glass bites at my life line.

"I love you, Elle," he says.

I slide the ring onto my ring finger, put my hand in his.

I love him, too.

The following summer Jonas doesn't come back to the Woods. He's at a camp in northern Maine, his mother tells me in a curt voice when I call the house. Jonas writes me only one letter that summer. The blackflies are terrible, he says, but he is learning to make a birchbark canoe. He has seen a giant moose. Did I know that a group of bears is called a sloth? There are snappers in the lake. He misses me more than anything, he says, but it is better this way. And though I know he's right and that I am the one who did this to us, I feel devastated, abandoned. As if he has chosen camp *over* me, not *because* of me.

1989. February, London.

I stumble to the ground, drooling a mouthful of blood onto the sidewalk.

"I've had enough out of you, stupid twat," the man says.

I take Jonas's ring off my finger and am handing it over when someone steps out of the shadows behind him.

"Hey. Stop that."

"Fuck off, ya cunt," Pig Face says, and then collapses to the ground in front of me.

A man stands over him looking slightly shocked. He is holding a tire iron in his hand. "I had it in the boot," he says, nodding toward a banged-up Rover parked behind him. He's tall and rangy, late twenties maybe, wearing a moth-eaten corduroy jacket and a thin woolen scarf on a freezing February night. Brits always insist on acting as if weather doesn't exist. It starts pouring rain and they just turn their collars up. I notice, as I get to my feet, that his brown leather brogues look custom made.

"We might want to fuck off out of here," he says. "He'll be a bit cross when he comes to. Can I walk you somewhere?"

"Shouldn't we call the cops?"

"Ah." He smiles. "American. That would explain the stupidity of wandering London streets alone at night."

I still haven't quite gotten my breath back, but I manage to spit, "Maybe I'm safer here with him."

"Right, then. As you like." He fishes a pack of Rothmans out of his jacket pocket, lights up, drops the tire iron back in his trunk, and slams it shut. "Sure you don't want a lift somewhere? Oh, for fuck's sake." He pulls a parking ticket off his windscreen.

Pig Face is still unconscious at my feet, but now he moans. I watch, fascinated, as a thin stream of white breath, like cigarette smoke, exhales from his slack mouth. I am tempted to kick him.

"Are you an axe murderer?"

He laughs. "Yes, but not tonight. Too cold."

"Actually, a lift would be great."

"Peter." He holds out his hand.

1983. August, Memphis, Tennessee.

The funeral is in Memphis. My mother meets Leo's ex-wife for the first time in the shade of an old magnolia, beside an open grave. I watch droplets of sweat run down the priest's neck into his stiff white collar. Leo plays out taps on his saxophone as Conrad's coffin is lowered into the moist soil. Halfway through, his breath falters. The saxaphone echoes a ragged sob. My eyes are dry. I know I should cry. I want to, but I can't. I have no right. The ex-wife looks at me with hatred, and I'm certain she knows. She is wearing nude hose and little pinched-toe pumps. She holds pop-eyed, pasty Rosemary tight against her thin black cotton dress. Rosemary smiles at me and gives a little wave, as if she's just spotted me across the bleachers at a basketball game. Her mother's knees buckle. Rosemary steadies her, looks away.

Afterward, Leo takes me, Mum, and Anna for a quick lunch at a Chinese restaurant, where every dish is full of hearts of palm and none of us speaks. At three o'clock we drop him at his old house for the reception. It is slightly dilapidated—white clapboard with a covered porch held up by big columns. Corinthian, Leo tells us, distracted. They seem too fancy for the house, too hopeful, and it makes me sad. In the front yard are two crepe myrtles, the ground below them carpeted with flowers that have dropped off and turned into bits of colored paper. Next to the front door is an umbrella stand shaped like an alligator with its mouth wide open. I can't imagine Leo ever living here.

Mum gives Leo's hand a squeeze. "Sure you don't want me to come in with you?"

"Best not. I need time with them."

Mum nods. "When should I collect you?"

"I'll take a cab back to the motel," he says.

We sit in the rental car and watch him disappear into the sagging wooden house. Inside, I can hear a floor fan whirring. Someone is sobbing.

We are almost back at the motel when Mum pulls off the highway into a strip mall.

"I need to make a pit stop." She hands me and Anna five dollars each. "Treat yourselves." She disappears into the pharmacy.

"What the hell are we supposed to do with ten dollars in a Memphis strip mall?" Anna says.

"Ice cream?"

"The last thing I need is more calories. I'd rather die."

"Nice," I say.

"What?" she says. "You want to be fat?"

"'I'd rather die'?"

She looks at me blankly.

"Very sensitive," I say.

"Oh. Right. Crap." For a second her face freezes. Then she starts to laugh. Suddenly I'm laughing, too, a high-pitched hysteria, so hard that, at last, tears stream down my face.

"Girls?" Mum walks up to us. She's carrying a small white paper bag from Fred's Pharmacy. Her beautiful face looks tired, worn thin. "Care to share the joke? I could use a good laugh."

"It must have been the week before Conrad died," I hear my mother talking on the phone in her bedroom. "We haven't made love since."

We've been back in New York for a few days. The city is sticky. The banana-vomit smell of rotting garbage rises from the streets. No matter what we do, we end up with big sweat marks in the armpits of our shirts. Air conditioners drip rancid water onto the sidewalks below. Our apartment is sweltering and close with dust and mothballs and the sweet odor of cockroaches in the walls. Everyone hates being here, but Leo can't go back to the woods. He blames himself for the accident: he's the one who insisted we go sailing that day. He pushed the boat out even though the waves were too rough. At night his thoughts, his blame, spiral outward. He stomps back and forth in the living room, scotch in hand, ranting at my mother, a broken record of what-ifs, looking for answers he can't find. Why didn't I make him wear a life jacket? Why was the life preserver tied with a double knot? How could no one have noticed? Did Conrad see the wave that took him? Did he know?

"No," I say, my throat constricting on itself. "He never saw it coming."

Now that Conrad is gone, Anna has her old bedroom back. Every time Leo walks past the room he looks at her as if her presence there is a betrayal.

"I need to get the fuck out of here and go back to L.A.," Anna says to me. "It's like we're living in a morgue with an angry goat."

It makes no sense, but I know what she means.

"Don't ask me that," Leo screams. "I can't stand it. I can't stand it."

"It's not my fault," my mother pleads.

The door to their room is closed, but I can hear the shouting through my bedroom wall. There's a loud crash and then the sound of glass breaking.

"Get rid of it," Leo shouts.

"Stop it," Mum yells. "Stop it! That was my grandmother's lamp."

"Fuck your grandmother."

"Please. I love you."

The bedroom door opens and Leo slams past me, runs out of our apartment, out of the building, into the hot night. My mother sobs in her room. I force myself to listen until, unable to stand another second, I put my pillow over my head.

Five weeks later, Leo tells us he's moving out. He packs his bags, his saxophone, and kisses my mother goodbye.

"Don't go. Please don't go," she begs.

She stands there, gripping his arm, lonely already, even before he has gone. When the door shuts behind him, she goes to the window and waits until he appears, watches as he trudges down the street, away from her. She is already beginning to show.

1984. May, New York.

The baby dies during my mother's labor. The umbilical cord tears, the baby cannot breathe, suffocating in amniotic fluid. They try everything to save it. They rip and pull, tear her vaginal wall, her perineum; doctors screaming, nurses running. It is a boy. Tiny and blue, like a Picasso child. Leo has disappeared and left no forwarding number, so he never learns that both of his sons have drowned.

My father comes with me to the hospital to collect Mum. He pushes her wheelchair out to the curb, careful not to hit any bumps. There's a Checker cab waiting for us. My mother's layette bag of washed and folded baby clothes is slung over the back of the wheelchair. She doesn't notice, as we drive away, that my father has left it hanging there. Out the rear window, I watch it swinging back and forth before it finally stills.

The cherry blossoms are in bloom along Fifth Avenue, bathed in sunlight.

"I love this time of year," my mother says. "We should have a picnic. We can make cucumber sandwiches." Her eyes are hollow.

"Let's just get you home," my father says. "Elle made soup, and I put a ripe avocado and a head of Boston lettuce in the icebox. I'll run out after we get you settled and pick up some bourbon. We can all use it."

"I need to find Leo. I need to tell him."

"Yes," my father says, "I'm working on it."

There is something different in his voice, an authority and a tenderness I don't recognize. As the taxi speeds us toward home it occurs to me that for the first time in my life, I have parents.

The cab meter ticks up slowly. "Do you think this would have happened if he had stayed?" my mother says. Her hair is flat, her strong beautiful face puffy and red.

My father takes her hand. "Don't be ridiculous," he says. "They did everything they could. It's no one's fault."

"It has to be," she says.

And I know she's right.

20

1989. February, London.

Halfway back to Mile End I ask Peter to pull over so I can pee. It is London, which translates as: every fucking place in the city is closed after eleven.

"Can you wait five minutes?" he asks.

"If I could wait, I wouldn't be suggesting that I pull my pants down in front of a total stranger to piss in the street."

"Right. Duly noted. Lovely." Peter pulls the car over on a narrow, cobbled street. "Off you go, then."

I squat down behind a tree, praying that no one looks out of the row house windows behind me. My thighs glow white in the pale light of a streetlamp. I groan, stomach sore from Pig Face's beating. A puddle forms beneath me on the freezing ground. I move my feet out of the way as it makes a break for my shoes. I have never felt such pure relief. When I stand to pull up my jeans and underpants, Peter is watching me from the car. He laughs when I catch him, covers his eyes in mock dismay.

5:45 P.M.

My mind is filled with bees—the raw, sweet stinging of the day. I cannot seem to shake it. The swim home from the far side of the pond has washed Jonas off me, but he is here, stuck inside my head, as I stand at the kitchen stove in my wet bathing suit and towel waiting for the kettle to boil. I picture myself butterflying away from him, leaving him behind me on the shore. His stricken face. In the deep center of the pond where the green water blackens, I stopped to catch my breath, treading water, afraid to turn back and see Jonas standing there, afraid to swim home to Peter, to my life.

"You must be an absolute prune," my mother says, taking an old black tin of Hu-Kwa tea down from the shelf. "You and Jonas were gone for hours. We were about to send out the Donner Party."

"I'm not sure how useful that would have been." I laugh. "And it was hardly hours. We walked over to have a quick look at the ocean. The afternoon light was so beautiful."

"It's a full moon tonight," she says.

Behind us, Peter and all three kids are playing Parcheesi. I glance over to see if Peter is listening, but he has just rolled doubles and is busy trying to create a blockade.

"Anyone there?" my mother asks.

"I saw the Biddles camped out to the right, toward Higgins. And I could just make out her purple skirt, but I'm pretty sure it was Pamela, way down the beach taking her daily walk. Other than that, it was pretty empty. The piping plover signs are finally down."

"Thank God." She pries the lid off the tin of tea with the back end of a spoon. "Here." She hands it to me, takes the kettle off the stove. "The water must be hot enough by now."

"For god's sake, Wallace," Peter says, "wait until the water boils. You might as well just hand me a cup of warm piss. And do not even think about plying me with that Lapsang Souchong rubbish. Filthy stuff."

"It's smoked over pine needles," Mum says.

"Even worse."

"He's a bit bossy, that husband of yours," my mother says, but I can tell she likes it. She puts the kettle back on the burner and goes in search of some plain English tea.

Finn gets up from the table and comes to give me a hug. "I found a shark egg on the beach."

"A shark egg?" I ask, dubious.

He sticks his hand in his pocket and brings out what looks like a small, crispy black pouch with devil horns on each end. "Here. Gina says it's an egg sack. For a baby shark."

"Everyone thinks that, for some reason. But it's actually for a skate. It's called a mermaid's purse."

"Which makes no sense unless the mermaid is Goth." Peter laughs.

I hand it back to Finn. "Put it up on the shelf so it doesn't break."

"Maybe I should be a mermaid this year for Halloween," Maddy says.

"Excellent idea. Though it might be hard to walk around the neighborhood with no feet," Peter points out. "Come play the next round with us, wife."

"I'm not really in a Parcheesi mood. I need to get out of this wet bathing suit."

"You certainly do. You'll get a urinary tract infection." My mother comes out of the pantry holding a ten-pack of toilet paper. "Put this in the bathroom, would you? We're out. I don't know how you all manage to go through things so quickly. You're like a bunch of locusts."

"Your daughter has a bladder the size of a pea," Peter says. "It's all her fault."

"Untrue," I say. "I don't think you've ever changed a roll of toilet paper in your life."

Peter turns to the kids. "On our first date, your mother pulled down her pants and peed in front of me."

"Gross," Jack says.

"It wasn't a date," I say. "You were just some guy giving me a lift back to my dorm. And it was that or pee in your car—which probably would have gone unnoticed, because that car was disgusting. It smelled like rotten meat."

"No, no." Peter laughs. "You wanted me. The moment I saw you squatting under a tree in your white underpants, I knew."

"So deeply not."

"You *guys*." Jack makes a gagging noise.

"Also, I had just saved your life."

"Your father was very heroic," I say. Which, of course, makes the little kids laugh.

"Dixon and Andrea invited us for hamburgers," my mother says. "They're having an impromptu barbecue. I told them we'd walk over around six thirty or seven."

"Ugh," I say.

"Don't let me forget—I said we'd bring a red onion."

"Can't we have a quiet dinner at home? I'm still recovering from last night."

"Our cupboards are bare," Mum says. "No one went to the supermarket." There is blame-lust in every syllable.

"I know we have a packet of pasta. And frozen peas."

"At any rate, I'm not in the mood to cook."

"I'll cook. It's supposed to rain tonight."

Peter looks up from the Parcheesi board. "I'm happy to take the kids if you want to stay home."

"It's just—we've barely been home from Memphis for twenty-four hours and it's been nonstop socializing. I need an early night." I need time to think.

"Then you shall have it," Peter says.

I walk over to him, put my hands on his shoulders, lean down, and give him a kiss. "You're a saint."

"Don't distract me," he says. "This is a very serious game we're playing," and sends one of Finn's little yellow pieces home.

Outside the Big House, I pause, watch my family. Finn rolls dice out of a small cardboard canister. My mother pours boiling water into an old brown teapot. A trail of steam rises from its spout. She watches the tea steep before pouring it into a chipped ironstone mug through a bamboo strainer. She peers into the sugar bowl, frowns, and wanders off.

Peter pushes up his shirt sleeve and makes a muscle. "See that?" he says to the kids. "See that? No one messes with this man." He ruffles Maddy's hair.

"Stop it, Daddy."

"Grump." He grabs her in a bear hug and kisses the top of her head, growling.

"I'm *serious*." She laughs.

Jack gets up from the table and walks over to the kitchen counter, takes a plum from the fruit bowl.

"Hand me that cup of tea, would you, honey?" Peter says to Jack. "Your senile grandmother forgot to bring it to me."

"I heard that," my mother calls out from the pantry.

I make my way down the path, feeling the familiar crunch of pine needles under my bare feet. I can smell the promise of rain in the air. There's a wet towel dumped on the steps of the kids' cabin. I pick it up and hang it on a tree branch. They've left the light on inside their room. I go in and turn it off before the screen door becomes covered in a sea of moths and rattling june bugs. The cabin is a mess. When Anna and I lived in here, it was the same: a chaos of bikini bottoms and lip gloss and clogs and arguments. I collect their dirty clothes off the floor and throw them in the laundry basket, stuff a sweater back in Maddy's drawer, hang a damp bathing suit on a hook. I know it's *Bad Mothering 101*—they should clean their room themselves—but right now it's soothing to concentrate on something simple and straightforward. My mother's cure for all woes: "If you're feeling depressed, organize your underwear drawer."

Jack's scratchy oatmeal-gray blanket has fallen halfway to the floor; his pillows are crumpled between the mattress and the wall. I pull his bed out. Something drops with a thud. With one blind hand, I grope around the spiderwebby floor, pull out a black notebook. His journal. My cryptic son, who barely acknowledges me these days, who side-steps, shuts down. And I'm holding all the answers in my hand.

The Braun travel clock on the bookshelf ticks out seconds. I close my eyes and put the book to my nose, breathe in the smell of Jack's fingerprints, his innermost thoughts, his longings. He would never know. But I would. Knowledge can be power, but it can also be poison. I put the book back where I found it, push the bed against the wall, and unmake the covers. I do not want the weight of any more secrets.

1984. October, New York.

In our dark, heavy apartment, something is cooking. If I'm lucky it will be hamburger, frozen corn, and creamed spinach. But I'm not holding my breath. Last night my mother cooked a whole chicken, still wrapped in cellophane. She's been distracted lately.

"I'm home," I call out.

I find her in the kitchen stirring chicken livers and onions in a cast-iron pan, an apron over her jean skirt. There's a bowl of rice and some ketchup already waiting on the table, glazed terra cotta pots hanging on the walls, spices, dried hot peppers in a glass jar that never get used. A stained potholder has fallen to the floor.

"Orchestra went late," I say, reaching down to pick it up.

"Hand me the oregano, would you?" she says, without looking up.

I open the food cupboard. The panes of glass in the doors have been painted white so we don't have to see what's inside: a box of Shredded Wheat, three cans of jellied consommé, cat food, an expired can of Metrecal. I shove aside a tin of Colman's Mustard and grab the oregano.

"I spoke to Anna earlier," she says. "She called me from Los Angeles. She sounded well. Though I still cannot understand how communications can be considered a major. It's like majoring in eating. Or walking. Go wash your hands for supper."

The apartment is dim. I head down the hallway, flicking on lights. Since Leo left last year, Mum has become obsessed with saving energy. I tell her it uses more energy to turn the lights on and off than to leave them on, but she says that's an urban legend.

It takes a while for the hot water to come out of the bathroom taps, and when it does, it scalds me. I wipe my hands dry on my jean jacket, dump my backpack in my room. The cat has curled up on my bed. Across the interior courtyard, I can see my mother through the kitchen window, setting the table for the two of us. I watch her place a fork and knife beside each plate, then a wineglass. I'm halfway to the kitchen when I stop and run back to turn off my bedroom light. It's a small thing, but she cares about it.

It's odd that I didn't notice it before, I think. My old journal is lying out open on my desk. I approach it cautiously, as if it might jump up and bite me. I pick it up, afraid of what she has found, heart beating hard in my chest, and riffle through time.

Today is the last day of school!! Becky and I are going to Gimbels tomorrow to get new bathing suits. I'm using my allowance. Mum says she'll contribute an extra $15.00. Becky told me they're teaching Transcendental Meditation every Wednesday night at the Town Hall this summer and she wants us to try it.

I flip forward a few pages.

Back Woods tomorrow!!! I can't wait to see Jonas.

<u>Summer to-do list:</u>

Read 12 books
Practice flute every day
Vegetarian?
Learn to sail
Lose 15 pounds

Then, below the list:

I'm so scared. What if he does it to me again. What if he comes to my room again? I hate him. I want to die . . .

Mum can never, ever know. It would ruin her whole life if she knew.

I hate him
I hate him
I hate him

I turn to the next page.

my period is late. what if I'm pregnant? Please God don't let me be pregnant.

After that there is one more entry, the page tearstained, blue ink blurred.

They found Conrad's body on the beach today. The lady said his eyes were open. I can't breathe. Why didn't I throw him the life preserver? I'm sick.

And then nothing but blank pages.

I turn off my bedroom light and stare out the window. Somewhere, on a higher floor, a neighbor starts vocalizing, running soprano scales up and down the courtyard walls. My mother slams the kitchen window shut, pours herself a glass of wine, puts it to her lips and drinks it down in one shot. Pours herself another glass. She knows. The courtyard hasn't been swept in a while. The ground is littered with takeout menus, plastic bags. At the edge are two empty tins of cat food—one of the doormen feeds the strays, strictly against building policy. From somewhere above comes a sudden rain of green peas. They hit the concrete like hailstones. Anna and I used to do the same thing: scrape peas, broccoli, cooked carrots, fish sticks—whatever we didn't want to eat—out the window into the courtyard as soon as Mum turned her back. If she knew, she never said a word.

When I walk into the kitchen she doesn't look up. The room is airless, oppressive. I shove the window back open a few inches. There's a pile of rice and chicken liver and onions already dished out on my plate. Beyond the kitchen door I hear the rumble and wheezy breath of the service elevator as it stops on an upstairs floor.

Mum puts her wineglass on the wooden table, pulls out a chair for me, hands me the bottle of ketchup. We sit in the silence. "I was in your closet today," she says finally. "I thought it would be nice to donate your old ice skates to the school charity drive. You've outgrown them." She shakes her head, as if she's trying to scramble whatever image is inside. "How could this have happened?" There's an unbearable edge of desperation in her voice.

"I'm so sorry. I'm so sorry." A teardrop of salt water lands in my rice and disappears, swallowed up in a sea of white.

"Why didn't you tell me?" She searches my face.

"I didn't want you to hate me." I stare at the kitchen floor.

"I could never hate you. It's *him* I hate."

"I'm sorry, Mum."

"It wasn't your fault. I'm the one who brought him into your life. If I had known he was hurting you . . . I'm glad he's gone." She takes my hand and grips it too tight. "Jesus. I should have seen it. How did I not see it?" The tips of my fingers turn pinkish, then white. There is something in her face that I haven't seen in a long time. Steel. A spark of light.

"If I ever see him again, I swear to God I'll kill him."

"What?"

"I should take out a warrant for Leo's arrest. I should call the police."

6:15 P.M.

I shut off the kids' light and close the door behind me as fast as I can so the mosquitoes won't get in. The surface of the pond is quieting, inky, the evening air pushing out the last warm motes of late afternoon. I head to our cabin to get out of my bathing suit. From the Big House, I hear Peter's bellowing laugh. Once, after that night, Leo called my mother, drunk, from some bar. He begged her to take him back, swore he still loved her—she was the love of his life, he said. She hung up on him.

21

1989. March, London.

Peter and I have sex on our third date. He takes me to a hole-in-the-wall Indian restaurant on Brick Lane, full of steam and cloves. "Westbourne Grove is for tourists. This is proper Indian," he assures me. Afterward, he invites me back to his flat for a quick drink, and I surprise myself by saying yes. I rarely date, let alone go home with a man. But Peter is a financial journalist, and for some perverse, old-fashioned reason, the fact that he writes about money makes me trust him—as if anyone with a job that boring couldn't be dangerous.

We drive back to his house in the endless rain, windows steamed up, the smell of diesel, a warmth. Peter lives in Hampstead, which is practically the opposite end of London. At a zebra crossing, Peter stops for an old man. He rolls the window down an inch, lights a cigarette. The old man shuffles his way across the high street, inch by inch, collar pulled up tight against the downpour, his pale wrinkled hands clutching a broken umbrella. Peter doesn't look at me when he takes my hand for the first time, his eyes trained on the blinking yellow lamppost, the sheeting rain.

"Is this all right?" He seems almost shy, and it surprises me.

We turn down a narrow street and make a hairpin turn onto a lovely cobbled square, stop in front of a row of Georgian houses.

I'm drenched before I'm halfway out of the car. Water funnels down on us from all sides, puddles, rises against his front door. "This rain is nuts," I say.

"What rain?" Peter laughs as we run for cover.

Peter's flat is beautiful—much larger than I'd expected: high ceilings with ornate plaster moldings; huge windows looking out onto the dark heath, the glass so old it has dripped; six-paneled doors with brass knobs the shape of eggs; rough pine floorboards. A working fireplace. Along the front hallway, wooden pegs hang thick with tweed and corduroy jackets, a mud-covered Barbour. Beneath them, toes to the wall, a line of beautiful worn-leather shoes and boots.

"Apologies in advance," Peter says, throwing his keys on a chest in the front hall. "It's in a bit of a tip." Old newspapers are strewn everywhere, ashtrays full of cigarette butts, an open jar of seeded mustard on the coffee table, a pinstripe suit flopped over the back of an overstuffed chair.

"My mother," he explains as I take in the heavy velvet curtains, ancestral portraits, scattered Turkish rugs. "She's very tasteful."

"You're right. It is a pigsty," I say.

"To be perfectly fair, I wasn't expecting company."

"I'm glad."

"What strange creatures you Americans are."

"No etchings," I explain.

"Ah." Peter laughs. "Don't underestimate me. Come, I'll show you the bedroom."

I hesitate, part of me wanting to follow, part of me wanting to run for my life. But I follow.

Unlike the living room, Peter's bedroom is surprisingly neat, the bed properly made, hospital corners.

"God, you're lovely," he says. His voice is frank, direct, secure in its own knowledge. "Let's get you out of these wet clothes."

I wince as he starts to unbutton my shirt. It has been six years since Conrad. And though I've had a few drunken kisses, I have never let a man touch me underneath my clothes.

Peter goes to unzip my jeans, but I stop his hand.

"Sorry. I thought—" he says.

"No. It's okay. Just . . . I'd rather do it myself." My fingers shake as I finish unbuttoning my shirt, pull down my jeans, step out of them. I stand in front of Peter in nothing but my underwear and bra. The rain is coming down harder now, a latticework of rills streaming across the enormous windows. Behind Peter, on a tall Tudor dresser, there's an unopened carton of Rothmans, a half-eaten pear. I unclasp my bra, drop it to the floor. He comes to me, cups my breasts in his hands. My entire body is shaking.

"You're cold." He lifts me up, carries me to the bed.

He makes love to me slowly, fingers tracing my curves, letting me respond to him, our tall, lanky bodies wrapping into each other, the rain on the windows, the tang of tobacco, his powerful, muscular arms. I close my eyes tight, brace myself as he enters me. My sharp inhale of breath betrays me.

"Do you want me to stop?" he whispers.

"No."

"We can stop," he says.

"It hurt a bit, that's all."

Peter goes completely still. "Are you a virgin, Elle?"

I wish I could tell him the truth, but instead I say, "Yes."

And so we begin on a lie.

1989. December, New York.

The 86th Street subway station is a bleak and dirty place, filled with gum-rubs and lifeless bits of paper on the tracks. The station empties out onto the four corners of a wide, ugly street. Anna and I exit the northwest corner into a blast of icy wind that whips up under the bottom of my down jacket. I've forgotten how cold New York gets. Outside on the street, the chestnut man is huddled by the warmth of his open stove, roasting fat, gaping nuts on a brazier. The night air smells sweet and delicious.

We turn the corner onto Lexington Avenue, picking our way around black-speckled snowdrifts in our high-heeled boots. At six p.m. the light is gone, replaced by the sheer acid halos of streetlamps and a swampy darkness.

"So, she was a total douche," Anna says.

We've just had our annual Christmas Eve tea with Dad at his Greenwich Village apartment, where we were introduced to his new girlfriend. Mary Kettering is a redhead from Mount Holyoke with thin lips and a pencil-sharpened nose. When she smiled at us, her mouth became an angry line, revealing everything she was in an instant.

I'm carrying a shopping bag full of our presents. They are wrapped, but I know from the dead weight that it is books again. Our father pretends they are specially chosen for us, but we know he gets them for free from the giveaway table at his publishing house. Every year he gives us meaningless books with meaningful inscriptions written in blue fountain-pen ink. He has graceful, memorable handwriting and a way with words, if nothing else.

"She couldn't stand us, either," I say.

"Understatement of the year," Anna says. "Could she have hated us any *more*? And when she started talking about the Hamptons?" Anna sticks her finger down her throat and gags. "And Southampton, not even Water Mill. How can he kiss her? Ugh. She's like this horrible little bird skeleton."

"You really are a cow." I laugh. I have missed my sister more than words since I've been in London. "She might have been nicer to us if you hadn't rolled your eyes every time she opened her mouth."

To his credit, my father stuttered past the awkwardness, seeming genuinely happy and proud to have brought us all together. After tea, he poured two inches of bourbon into his teacup and played "Rock the Casbah" on his new turntable, dancing in embarrassing, awkward little jerks. He was barefoot, in a pair of old Levi cords, and the tops of his feet were hairy. Thick tufts grew up from each toe. It was mesmerizing. Mary beat the rhythm out with her Belgian loafer.

"She's just another Dad horror story in a long line of Dad horror stories," Anna says.

"Maybe she's nicer than we think." My foot slips on a patch of black ice and I go sprawling.

"I think that's God's way of telling you no." Anna laughs.

The shopping bag has ripped open, spilling our gifts onto the slushy sidewalk.

I get on my hands and knees and crawl around collecting the presents. "Help me with these."

Anna is already fifteen yards ahead. "Leave them. We're going to freeze to death. We don't want his stupid books anyway," she says, and keeps walking.

"Seriously?" I call after her. "Fine. I'll tell Dad you didn't want his presents."

"Be my guest," she says over her shoulder. "He can give them to Mary instead. Ooh la la, what joy she'll feel. What laughter. A hardcover copy of *Bartlett's* fucking *Quotations*."

A woman walking a greyhound clothed in a houndstooth sweater-cape and booties stops, watches as I crawl around picking up the parcels. Next to me, her dog balances on his shivering hind legs and takes a shit in the snow.

I catch up to Anna as she's entering the lobby of our building. "Nice," I say. "Thanks for the help."

The bitter wind follows us in through the swinging double doors, and the new doorman, Mario, rushes to close them shut. A fake fir tree in the lobby twinkles with colored lights. On the marble mantle-piece beside it, a menorah with fat, flickering orange bulbs is plugged in.

"Ladies," Mario says, ushering us toward the elevator. "Merry Christmas."

"Happy *Hanukkah*," Anna corrects him.

Mario looks confused.

"We're Jewish," Anna says.

We get onto the elevator.

"Jewish? What was *that*?"

"We could be. He doesn't know."

"Why are you being such a total asshole?" I say.

"Because he makes me sick."

"Mario?"

Anna gives me her best "how can you be such a fucking idiot" look. "*Dad*."

We stamp the snow off our boots, leave them outside on the mat to drip. The front door to the apartment is, as always, unlocked. The lights are out. Mum is sitting in a chair in the middle of the hallway, backlit by a living room lamp, the tabby cat curled in her lap.

"You look like Anthony Perkins," Anna says, taking off her coat. "We brought you some ginger cookies."

"Please don't take another step into the apartment," Mum says.

"Do you think she's being held hostage?" Anna asks me in a stage whisper. "Mum," she says in her normal voice, "you're acting weird." She hangs her coat up in the closet and tries to push past, but my mother blocks her.

"Your father called me after you left. It seems his new girlfriend Mary left a large bag of marijuana in a coffee canister and it disappeared after your visit."

"Mary smokes pot?" Anna says. "You've got to be kidding me."

"I wish I were kidding. I really do," Mum says. "I don't want to do this, but your father made me promise. Please get undressed, both of you, and empty your bags."

"You're out of your mind." Anna laughs. "What am I, five?"

Mum sighs. "I know. It's ridiculous. But he gave his word to Mary, and he asked that I respect her request."

"I don't even smoke pot," I say.

"Tell her to take her nickel bag and shove it up her vagina," Anna says.

"Anna."

"You haven't met her, Mum. She's repugnant. She has sharp little pterodactyl teeth."

"I have no doubt." My mother dumps the cat out of her lap and stands up. "In any event, I promised your father I would insist you let me search you, and now I have insisted. I didn't promise him I would do it. I'm going to make myself an eggnog and climb into bed."

"Wait," I say. "He really asked you to strip-search us? On Christmas Eve? You know what? Fuck it. Fine." I take my clothes off, step out of my underwear, and throw them at her.

She hands them back to me with a beleaguered sigh. "I'm too old for this."

"*You're* too old? I'm twenty-three, for fuck's sake. Tell Dad I'm never speaking to him again."

"You need to wax," Anna says, and heads down the hallway.

I call Peter from my bedroom. It's almost midnight in London, but I know he'll be awake, trying to finish his piece before deadline.

"My mother just tried to strip-search me. Merry fucking Christmas."

"Sorry?" Peter says.

"Dad's new girlfriend accused us of stealing her stash."

Peter laughs. "Did she find anything?"

"Fuck you, Pete. It's not funny."

"It's spectacularly funny. Though if that's how you do things in your family, I may have to rethink coming over for New Year's."

"Don't bother coming," I say. "I'm getting on the next flight back to London. I'm done with these people."

"That's an awful idea. You'll have to eat my mother's cold salmon with dill mayonnaise that tastes like vomit. And attend midnight mass. And sleep in an icy room with stone walls and medieval windows. Alone. Because my mother does *not* approve."

"I thought your mother liked me now."

Peter's parents are very posh. His father is an MP. When they aren't at their country home in Somerset, they live in a large house in Chelsea overlooking the Thames. They hunt and have a Pimm's Cup with lunch. They take brisk, tweedy walks across the moors. His mother is a classic battle-axe in pearls. After my fifth date with Peter, she insisted he bring me over to be inspected. We drank sherry in a large sitting room with polished hardwood floors—mahogany inlaid with fruitwood, she explained. A tasteful abstract painting hung over the marble fireplace. She'd recently taken an interest in "the Moderns." I perched on a sage-green velvet sofa and thought about Becky Sharp as I crossed and uncrossed my legs. Peter's mother could barely conceal her disdain when I confessed that I had never been on a horse. I redeemed myself somewhat when she learned I was getting a postgraduate degree in French literature at Queen Mary and planned to teach. "Though, of course, you would do much better to read German. Far more depth, less of that vulgar excess," she said before refilling only her own glass.

"She does like you," Peter says now. "Very much, for an American. That said, she has made it abundantly clear to me, abundantly," he says with emphasis, "that she believes it inappropriate for me to be with a young woman I picked up on a street corner. You could be *anyone*."

"Ha-ha."

"Look, stay calm. I'll be there in four days. We'll work all this out. Incidentally . . ."—Peter laughs—"I'm very much looking forward to getting high with your father."

"You aren't going to meet my father," I say. "Because I am never speaking to him or seeing him again."

"I thought that was the entire point of this visit," Peter says, "so I could ask him for your hand in marriage."

"Oh, for fuck's sake. Stop turning everything into a joke. I'll meet you outside baggage claim." I hang up the phone, lie back on my bed, and stare at the ceiling. There are cracks in the plaster. Bits of peeling paint. Garlic and onions are cooking in an upstairs apartment. The interior courtyard smells thick with it. My single bed—the same bed I have slept in since I was five—is too short for me. On the bookshelf above my desk, next to the wooden turtle my father carved for me when I was little, is an entire set of useless *Encyclopaedia Britannicas* that my mother rescued from a Dumpster when I was ten, thrown away because it was out-of-date. "Knowledge is knowledge," my mother said. I get up and pull volume 4, *Botha to Carthage*, off the shelf. Hidden deep inside it is a single sheet of paper, folded into a tiny square, entirely covered in words. One sentence, written over and over. Part punishment, part incantation: *I should have saved him*. I refold it, put the encyclopedia back on the shelf. Outside, the wind blows up gusts of dry snow from the cement ground. I head down the hall to find Anna. The door to her bedroom is partly closed. She's at her desk, her back to me, rolling a joint.

22

1989. December, New York.

Peter's flight arrives on time, but I'm hideously late. The Train to the Plane goes out of service at Rockaway, and we all have to wait outside on the platform for the next one to arrive. Sleet is turning to heavy snow and I can feel my eyelashes beginning to ice over. This is why I hate picking people up at the airport. It's a gesture that almost always backfires. Peter will be pissed off and sulky that I'm not there, jumping up and down, when he comes out of the international tunnel after an eight-hour flight. And even though I'm trekking all the way out to fucking JFK and getting pierced in the face by thousands of freezing sleet needles, I now feel guilty *and* resentful. I should have told him to take a cab.

By the time I reach the International Arrivals gate I'm sweaty, breathless, and ready for a fight. I see him before he sees me, sitting on top of his duffel bag, back against the grimy airport wall, reading a book. He smiles when he spots me.

"Right on time," he says, and gets up to give me a massive kiss. "God, I've missed you, beautiful."

I've prepared Peter for our dark apartment, my depressed mother's obsession with conserving electricity, the slow, heavy way she moves—as if she's sagging under the weight of her own boards.

"Must have been a cheery Christmas all-round," he says.

But when we get there, every light in the apartment is on. A Duraflame log makes its noiseless crackle in the fireplace. A scratchy LP plays bossa nova.

"Mum? We're back," I call out.

"In here," she singsongs from the kitchen. "Leave your boots outside if they're wet."

I shake my head, puzzled. "Maybe *she* stole Mary's pot."

Peter gives me a wry look as we head into the kitchen.

My mother is standing at the icebox. Her hair is up in a bun. She's wearing lipstick and a red silk blouse.

"Peter." She gives him a kiss on both cheeks. "You made it. How was your flight?"

"Fine. Bit bumpy, but nothing."

"It's been blizzarding on and off all day. We were worried they might divert you."

"Where's Anna?" I ask. "She said she was going to be here."

"Some friend of hers from law school called. She went rushing out."

"Sorry," I say to Peter. "I really wanted her to be here when you arrived."

Mum pulls a silver shaker and three martini glasses out of the freezer. "Olive or twist?"

"Twist, thanks," Peter says.

"A man after my own heart." She pours him a drink.

There's cheese, pâté, and a small bowl of cornichons on the kitchen table. She has brought out the special rosewood cheese board with the irritating little curvy knife that she and my father were given, a million years ago, as a wedding present.

She raises her glass. "Here's to a new year. It's so good to finally put a face with a name. You never told me he was so handsome, Elle." She is practically batting her eyes. "Chin-chin."

I feel like I've stepped into one of those black-and-white society movies where everyone lives in an apartment with fifteen-foot ceilings and wears fur stoles to lunch. Any second now, Cyd Charisse will stick a black-stockinged leg out from behind a door, while a maid in uniform serves canapés and a little white dog scampers about.

They clink glasses. I raise my glass to toast, but they are already drinking. My mother takes Peter's arm. "Let's go sit in the living room. I've made a fire. Elle, grab the hors d'oeuvres. I got a piece of Stilton at Zabar's. I figured that was a safe bet."

Peter follows her out, leaving me standing there with my glass in my hand.

"Oh, and your father called. Twice," she says over her shoulder. "You're going to have to call him back sometime. It's so nice to have a man in the house, Peter," I hear her saying as they disappear into the other room.

I know all her efforts—Peter's warm welcome—are meant for me. And the last thing I want is Peter's first instinct to be "Escape from Horror Castle." But listening to my mother howling with laughter at something Peter has just said, all I want to do is slap her.

"I like her," Peter says later as he drags his duffel down the hallway to my room. "She's not at all how you described her."

"A narcissistic bitch?"

"What you *said* was that she's been very sad. And she likes to conserve energy. You never mentioned what an attractive woman she is."

"Stilton? Because you're English? We've been living on saltines and peanut butter and soup out of a can since Christmas. Believe me, this is not normal life."

"So, just my British charm?"

"No. She's a male chauvinist pig. Also, she asked me to take my underpants off in front of her on Christmas Eve. And gave me ugly gloves and a bottle opener for Christmas. So, it might be Yuletide guilt."

Peter stops to scan the bookshelves that line the hall. Pulls out an old grade-school textbook of mine. "*Caribou and the Alaskan Tundra*. Perfect bedtime reading." He opens it and riffles through. "Oh good. You've underlined the important bits. That'll save me time."

"My mother doesn't believe in throwing away books."

He shoves the book back onto the crammed shelf. "I think she's very glamorous. Elegant. I'm surprised she hasn't remarried."

"You're welcome to sleep in her room tonight. Her bed is bigger than mine."

"Now, now."

"I finally bring a man home to meet my mother and her first instinct is to flirt? What does that even mean? My mother has barely had the energy to wash her hair the past few years. Between losing Leo, and losing the baby. She's been wandering around the house in a defeated trance for so long, I forgot she was ever attractive. She spends most of the day in her nightgown. The only reason my mother bothers to get dressed is to go across the street to Gristedes for whatever meat is on sale because it's reached its sell-by date."

"Sounds like she lives life on the edge." Peter laughs.

"Don't," I say, and walk away down the hall.

He follows me into my room and tries to put his arms around me, but I shrug him off.

"Elle, I've just flown across the Atlantic, in a raging storm, to see my beautiful girlfriend. Who, for the record, I am sickeningly, utterly in love with. I'm exhausted. All I've eaten in the past twelve hours is a piece of moldy cheese. And my socks are wet." He sits down on my bed and pulls me onto his lap. "Be nice."

"Ugh. You're right." I burrow my head into his chest. "I should be glad you've cheered her up. I *am* glad. It's just been a shitty few days. And I missed you."

"I know. That's why I'm here." He lies down on my ancient twin bed. His feet stick out two feet off the bottom. "Hmm," he says, "I may need to sleep in your mother's bed after all."

"I fucking hate you, Pete."

"I know. All the women do. That's my particular charm."

And I laugh, despite myself.

1990. January 1, New York.

New Year's Day, and if today is anything to go by, this will be a truly shitty year. It's below freezing, I'm sick to my stomach after our annual family dim sum at a loud, overheated restaurant in Chinatown, where I ate ten too many steamed meat-ish things I didn't even want, and my mother got into an argument with the waiter over the check. Now Peter is pressuring me to return my father's calls.

"It's New Year's. Perfect time for an olive branch," he says as we head down Mott Street in the biting wind.

"Shit. I left one of my gloves in the restaurant."

"They're probably feeding it to some poor sucker," Peter says.

"Don't be an ass."

Twenty minutes later, we're squeezed inside a telephone booth a few blocks from my father's apartment. I feel like kicking Peter. I cover the receiver with my hand. "This was a terrible idea," I hiss.

"This is between you and Mary," my father is saying.

"How can it be between me and Mary?" I snap.

"You two need to work this out."

"There's nothing *between* me and Mary. I've met her once."

"I know," my father says. "I want that to change. She's important to me."

"And I'm what?"

"Elle—"

"She convinced you your daughters were drug-addict thieves."

He's quiet on the other end of the phone. "Look, Mary made a mistake. I know. I made a mistake. And I am very sorry. Can we please move past this?"

"Fine. But if you think there is a world in which I will ever set foot in a room with that chicken-lipped woman, you're insane."

"Please don't make this any worse."

"Do *not* try to make this my fault."

He sighs. "Mary and I are engaged. We're getting married in March."

"You just met her."

"I know it's soon, but Mary says there's no reason to wait. We love each other."

"Wow." A piece of greasy dumpling rises in my throat.

"I need you to tell me it's okay."

"You're pathetic." I slam down the phone.

"That went well," Peter says.

I stare at the receiver in my hand. Someone has scratched the word *cunt* on the back of it. And a smiley face.

"They're getting married."

"Ah."

"Why did I listen to you? I should've hung up the second he mentioned her name."

"Do *not* try to make this my fault," Peter says.

"Mocking me? That's your choice? My father just told me he's marrying a woman Anna and I have met once. Who's awful. And obvious. And fake."

My steam-breath covers the glass in front of me. I rub a small window in it with the back of my glove, stare out at the street. "And, yet again, he doesn't choose us." I know I'm about to cry, which infuriates me even more. Weakness is the only thing I've inherited from my father. The afternoon sky is turning to flint. An angry gust of wind pushes a *Happy New Year* bugle down the sidewalk. I watch until it rolls off the curb and disappears.

"Elle, you're the one turning this into an either/or."

"What does that even mean?"

"She made the accusation, not him. He's in a tough spot. He loves you. And apparently he loves her, too."

"You don't even know him," I snap. "I need an ally, Pete, not some impartial witness."

"I know it feels like treachery now, but once you calm down, you'll realize this isn't about you."

"Calm down? Very useful."

Peter opens his mouth to say something, but reconsiders. "You're right. I'm sorry. Now can we please get out of this phone booth? As much as I enjoy being sweaty and pressed up against you, it's starting to smell like a whorehouse in here."

"How would you know?" I push open the accordion door and walk away.

Peter follows me out into the bitter cold. It's starting to snow. "Elle. Stop." He catches my sleeve. "Please. I love you. This isn't our fight." He pulls me into a doorway, out of the wind. "I'm defending your father because I want you two to make up. So I can meet him before I go back to London. That's all. It's entirely selfish. But there it is. I don't want to have to come back to this hellishly freezing city."

Up the block, a Checker cab appears. Peter steps out into the street and hails it. "Let's go home. We can tuck up in that miserable little bed of yours and make our New Year's resolutions." The cab pulls over. "Mine is to stop trying to win an argument with you."

"You go. I'll meet you back there."

"Elle—"

"It's okay. We're okay. But you're right: I need to calm down. I need to walk this off."

"And just like that, I win my first fight." Peter takes both ends of my scarf, wraps them around my neck, pulls my hat down farther on my head. "Don't be long."

I watch the taxi's taillights round the corner away from me into a halo of snow. The street is deserted. No sane person wants to be out in weather like this. Tears have dried in piss-thin icicles on my cheeks. I put my head down and start walking up Bank Street to my father's building.

All the lights in his second-floor apartment are on. I ring the buzzer and wait. Through the etched-glass windows of the brownstone's heavy mahogany front doors I can see a stroller parked in the stairwell, my father's bicycle locked up behind it, leaning against a peeling radiator. It looks warm and clanky inside. I buzz again. My toes are beginning to feel like ice cubes inside my boots. I stomp my feet to get the blood moving, buzz one more time, lean on the bell. Nothing. I know he's there, but he can't hear the buzzer if his bedroom door is closed. There's a pay phone in the Greek coffee shop around the corner I've had to use before.

I make my way down the salted stoop, sludge up the block. Most of the brownstones are lit up and cheerful. I get glimpses of parlor ceilings, messy kitchens, exposed brick walls. The air smells of firewood and contentment. My breath condenses like white smoke into the dun-gray whirl. Trash cans, overflowing with empty champagne bottles and pizza takeout boxes, are already blanketed in snow. It is fucking freezing.

It's only one block, but by the time I get to the coffee shop, my face has been petrified by the cold.

"Close the door," a man behind the register says before I'm even inside.

The place is half empty. A few saddies sit in the red vinyl booths eating eggs and bacon for their hangovers. Two old men are drinking coffee at the counter.

The pay phone is all the way in the back, next to the bathroom. I make my way past the booths, past a stack of sticky high chairs, the cigarette vending machine. Some guy is on the phone having a heated argument. His hair is thinning, greasy. A rat tail. There's a tall stack of dimes on a ledge next to him. I take off my glove, pull off my hat, and fumble around my purse, shaking change. He feeds a few more coins into the slot and turns his back to me. I lean against the wall, wait for him to finish his call.

A waitress sets a piece of banana cream pie down on the counter, refills a coffee cup. The manager sticks a pencil behind his ear and rings up a pistachio-colored check.

"Excuse me?" I say when I see the man at the pay phone reaching for more coins. "Are you going to be much longer?"

"I'm on the phone, lady."

"I just need to make a quick call. Two seconds."

He covers the receiver with his hand. "I'll be done when I'm done." He leans into the phone and keeps talking. "Sorry," he says. "Just some crazy lady."

There's a cheap antiqued Coca-Cola mirror on the wall next to me. I catch a glimpse of myself. My hair is flailing out in all directions, staticky, my cheeks red with windburn and dry heat. I look like a bag lady. Behind me I hear coffee hissing into the brewer. The door jingles and a gust of air hits the back of my neck.

I've just about decided my father isn't worth this when pay-phone guy shouts, "Screw you, you twat," into the phone and slams down the receiver. It's that kind of day. He hits the coin-return lever a few times and checks the box until he's satisfied that he hasn't left a nickel behind by mistake. I fish out a dime and move toward the phone.

"You really are in a hurry, aren't you, lady?" He takes his time buttoning his coat, blocking my way.

"Asshole," I call after him as he heads for the door. A few people look up, but most of them just keep eating.

The phone rings six times before someone picks up. It's Mary.

"Hello, Elle. Happy New Year." Her voice is like treacle. Even through the telephone, I can hear her smiling a lie.

"Happy New Year, Mary. Can you put my father on the phone, please?"

"Your father's resting."

"I need to talk to him." I picture her in her kelly-green twin set, her small, calculating eyes.

"I'd rather not disturb him."

"I'm just down the street. I rang the buzzer, but no one answered."

"Yes."

"Can you please get him?" I try to stay calm.

"I don't think that's a good idea. You made him very upset. He tried to run out of the house with no shoes on. I was worried sick."

"Just put him on, please." I can't keep the anger out of my voice.

"I think you both need some time to cool down."

"Excuse me?"

"You were extremely rude to him earlier."

"This is between me and Dad."

"No," she says. And this time she doesn't bother to disguise her venom. "This is between you and me."

I take a deep breath, try to control my hatred of her, the heartbreak of all my father's broken promises—of the promise he made the summer after he and Joanne had finally split up.

It was August. Anna had a summer job as a mother's helper in Amagansett and Conrad was in Memphis, so I was going to stay with my father while Mum and Leo were on tour in France. Dad had sublet Dixon's apartment for the summer.

Mum and Leo put me on a Greyhound bus on their way to Logan, with enough money for a sandwich and a drink if the bus stopped at a rest area and a taxi from Port Authority to Dad's apartment.

"Why can't he pick me up at the bus?" I asked.

"Oh, for god's sake," Mum said. "You're thirteen years old. He said he'd have supper ready."

"Fine. Don't blame me if I get kidnapped by some pimp looking for runaways and end up as a fourteen-year-old hooker."

"You watch far too much television," Mum said.

When I woke the next day, it took me a moment to recognize where I was. A dark room. Dim, air-shaft light. The smell of someone else's laundry detergent. The bunk bed, crayon marks on the walls, brown floral sheets. Becky's room. The last thing I could remember was my father giving me one of his sleeping pills. I rubbed a dreamless sleep from my eyes and wandered down the long hallway looking for him. He was sitting at a big oak table in the cavernous, sun-washed living room of Dixon's apartment reading a manuscript, wearing his usual weekend uniform—Levi's, bare feet, a faded navy-blue Lacoste, the faint smell of peppermint castile soap.

He looked up and smiled. "Hey, kiddo."

"What time is it?"

"Almost three. You slept for seventeen hours. Hungry? There's half a turkey sandwich in the icebox."

"No, thanks. Why didn't you get me up?"

"Or I can make a pot of coffee." He put the manuscript down. "Do you drink coffee?"

"I'm not allowed."

"New rules."

I followed him into the kitchen and sat down on one of the stools at the counter. He took a bag of coffee beans out of the freezer.

"You have to keep them in the freezer or the beans lose their flavor."

I watched him grind the coffee, stopping the electric grinder twice to give it a shake. "Makes sure it's evenly ground," he said, getting two glass coffee cups from the cupboard, heated up milk in a saucepan. My father is fastidious about the details of cooking.

"I love this song," he turned up the radio, started humming "Rhiannon." "English muffin?"

"Sure."

He took a fork out of a drawer, made little holes in the muffin all the way around, split it in half and put it in the toaster. "It's so good to have you here," he said, reaching into his pocket. "I made you a key." He beamed at me as if this was an extraordinary achievement, pulled up a stool beside me. "So. My divorce is finally final."

I wasn't sure what I was meant to say—whether I should be happy for him or sad. I opted for silence.

"Joanne made it a pretty easy decision. She gave me an ultimatum: my marriage or my girls. And obviously that was a no-brainer." He took a dramatic pause. "You and Anna didn't know this, but Joanne never liked my having kids."

I feigned a look of surprise, tried not to laugh.

The toaster popped up. "I'm so sorry I disappeared on you girls. Joanne made it all so difficult. Anyway," he said, taking a stick of butter and a jar of English marmalade from the icebox, "good riddance to bad rubbish. Never again. From now on it's you, me, and Anna. No one will ever come between us again. And that's a promise."

"Mary," I hiss into the pay phone now. "Go tell my father I need to speak to him. And tell him if he doesn't come to the phone, I'm never speaking to him again." I hear her taking a mental pause. "Do not make this decision for him, Mary, if that's what you're thinking. Believe me, it'll backfire."

She puts the phone down on the counter. I listen to her steps moving into the bedroom. I can hear her talking to my father. After a few minutes, she picks up the receiver. "He says, 'Fine, if that's what you want.'"

"You told him that would be *it*?"

"Yes," she replies sweetly, "I repeated your exact words."

I feel sick, sucker-punched. "Well then, I guess there's nothing else to say. Have a lovely wedding. Last time Dad got married, the bride wasn't wearing any underwear. I think he likes that bare-crotch thing."

I hang up the phone and run into the coffee-shop bathroom, dry-heaving over the bowl a few times until the nausea subsides. I've never been able to make myself throw up, no matter how hard I try. I hate him. I hate his weakness. Everything he has never done for us. Everything he has promised. The endless betrayals. I splash my face with cold water. I'm splotchy and bloodshot, but at least I can breathe. I need to get out of here. I need Peter.

I'm almost out the front door when someone in the booth behind me says, "Elle?"

His voice has changed. Deepened, of course. But I would recognize it if it were in a chorus of a thousand voices. I've imagined this moment for so many years. What it would be like. Who we would be now. In my version, I'm carrying a rough draft of my thesis on Baudelaire, running to meet a corduroy-clad professor; or coming out of the pond after a vigorous swim—tan, fit, mature; no regrets. I run my fingers through my wild staticky hair. I could walk out the door, let him think he's made a mistake.

"Elle," Jonas says again, in his soft, easy voice—monosyllabic but perfect, like a pressed shirt.

And I turn around.

He looks different. Less woodland, less feral. His thick black hair is cut short. But his eyes are the same sea green: unwavering, pure.

"Wow," I say. "Wow. This is so weird."

"Indeed," he says. "Wow."

"What are you doing here?"

"I was hungry."

"Shouldn't you be in Cambridge with your family? It's New Year's."

"Elias had a baby. They're all in Cleveland. Hopper is the godfather. I had too much work. What's your excuse?"

"I was breaking up with my father. He lives around the corner."

He nods. "That was always kind of in the cards. Who was that greasy-haired guy you were shouting at?"

"Just some asshole."

He smiles. "So, not your boyfriend?"

"Funny," I say, and slide into the booth across from him. "I can't believe it's you. You got old."

"I always told you I would, but you refused to believe me." Under his ratty wool overcoat, he's wearing a faded work shirt and jeans, stained everywhere with thick blobs of colored paint.

"You look like an insane person," I say. But if I'm being honest, he looks amazing.

"You look good," he says.

"I look like shit and we both know it." I pull a few paper napkins out of the metal dispenser on the table and blow my nose. I look at him, trying to take in what I am seeing. He stares back at me, expression wide-open—that same vaguely unnerving look he had the very first time we ever met—an old man's eyes in a young man's face.

"I heard you were living in England," he says.

"I am. London."

Jonas points to a bland tenement building on the corner. "I live there."

"You hate the city."

"I'm at Cooper Union. Studying painting. I have one more year."

The waitress comes over and hovers until we acknowledge her.

"Coffee?" Jonas asks me. "Or are you a tea person now?"

"Coffee."

"We'll have two coffees," he tells her. "And two sugar donuts."

"No donut."

"K. One donut," he tells the waitress. "We'll split it. So. What's in London?"

"Grad school. French lit."

"Why there? Why not here?"

"Farther away."

Jonas nods.

"So," I say. "Seven years."

"Seven years."

"You never came back to the Woods. You disappeared."

"I liked camp."

"Don't do that. You've never been good at glib."

He takes my hand, touches my ring. "You still have it."

I tug the ring from my finger, put it down on the table. The silver plate has worn off in places, and the prongs are barely holding the green glass in place. "This is the first time I've taken it off since you gave it to me."

"I'm surprised you haven't died of gangrene."

"I got mugged last year. In London. By a skinhead. He tried to take it, but I refused. I told him it was worthless. He punched me in the stomach."

"Christ."

"There was a man there. He saved me. He's the reason I still have it."

The waitress drops two cups of coffee on the table between us. "He's out of sugar donuts. We have a cinnamon cruller or a Boston cream."

"I think we're good," I say. "Can I have some milk?"

She reaches across to an empty booth. Grabs a bowl of fake creamers.

"Cinnamon cruller," Jonas says.

I watch her walk away. "I'm with him now. The ring guy. Peter. He's here. Well, at Mum's."

"Cool." Jonas seems unconcerned. He takes a little creamer from the bowl, peels off the foil top, dumps it in his coffee. "So, what does he do?"

"He's a journalist."

"Is it serious?"

"I guess so."

Jonas takes a bite of his cruller. It leaves a dusting of cinnamon on his lips. "Well, I hope you made it clear to him you're already engaged to *me*."

I laugh, but when I look at him, his face is completely serious.

"I should probably go. He's waiting for me."

"Stay. If he loves you he'll wait. I did. I have."

"Jonas, don't."

"It's true."

"You didn't wait. You left."

"What was I supposed to do, Elle? Come back the next summer and pretend nothing had happened? Take sailing lessons? Put a lie between us? You know I couldn't do that."

All these years I've thought about him, missed him, wanted to walk next to him on the quiet paths, souls twinned together. But now that he is here with me, all I see is how far apart our lives have grown.

"Maybe you're right. I don't know. Except that now there is no *us*." And the truth of it is almost unbearable. "We don't even know each other. I don't even know where you live."

"Yes, you do. I live across the street in that shitty building."

"You know what I mean."

"I am exactly the same person I was back then. Possibly a bit less peculiar."

"I hope not," I laugh. "Your weirdo-ness was always your best quality."

Jonas picks up the green glass ring, holds it up to the light. "You should be careful with this. It's valuable. I used all my allowance money to buy it."

"I know. It's worth a lot."

"I don't regret what happened."

"Well, you should. We both should."

"He was hurting you."

"I would have survived."

Jonas puts the ring back down on the table in front of me. It lies there between us. This tiny thing—so ugly, so beautiful.

"I don't wear it because you gave it to me. I wear it to remind me of what we did."

The waitress comes back to our table, holding the Pyrex pot of coffee in her hand.

"Freshen your cup?" she asks.

"We're good," I say.

"Anything else you want?"

"Just the check." I put on my coat and stand up. "I really do have to go."

He hands me the ring. "Take it. It's yours. Even if it reminds you of him."

"No."

"Why not?"

I could lie. I would, to anyone else. "Because it also reminds me of you," I say sadly.

Jonas takes out a pen and tears off a piece of napkin. "I'm giving you my number. For when you come to your senses. Don't lose it."

I fold the fragile paper, put it in my wallet. "It's insanely freezing out there." I pull on my hat, wrap my scarf around my neck.

"I miss you," he says.

"Same," I say. "Always." I lean down and kiss him on the cheek. "Gotta go."

"Wait," Jonas says. "I'll walk you to the subway."

Outside the diner, snow is falling in great heaps, dumping fistfuls at a time. Jonas puts his arm through mine, sticks my cold, un-mittened hand into his coat pocket. We walk the seven blocks without speaking, listening to the silent snowfall. The quiet between us is easy, familiar—like walking single file down the path to the beach, roaming around the woods—everything between us resonant but unspoken.

The gray, gaping mouth of the subway comes sooner that I want it to, exhaling bundled, bedraggled people in its stale concrete breath. Jonas takes both of my hands in his.

"You don't have to miss me, you know."

I take my hand out of his and put it on the flat of his cheek. "Yes. I do."

He pulls me to him so quickly I have no time to react. Kisses me with the intensity of every day, every month, every year we have loved each other. It is not our first kiss. That was long ago, underwater, when we were children—when we said goodbye for the first time, knowing it would not be the last. But this time when I pull away from him, it is agonizing. Not found, but lost. I pause, stand on the precipice of memory, wanting so desperately to fall into it, knowing I can't. Jonas is animal, Peter is mineral. And I need a rock.

"I'll see you," I say. And we both understand what that means.

"Elle . . ." Jonas calls out as I head down the steps into the subway.

I stop, but this time I don't turn around.

"Peter isn't the ring guy," he says. "I'm the ring guy."

23

1991. February, London.

The Heath is empty. Just a few grim-looking dog lovers, who stand apart from one another watching their shivering pets run off leash, chicken-bone legs covered in mud, having fun at their owners' expense. It's raining. Not a lush, fertile deluge, but that endless drizzle from a leaden lowering sky specifically designed to make you pull your socks up. A black dog charges across the field chasing a red ball through the mizzle.

I've moved into Peter's Hampstead flat, with its grand, soaring ceilings and plaster cornices. Bookshelves line the walls, filled with leather-bound volumes on shipbuilding or Agrippa that Peter has actually read. At night, when he gets home from the City, we build a proper fire in the fireplace, curl up together on the sofa under feather duvets while he reads aloud to me from the most boring book he can find, until I beg him to stop and make love to me instead.

The flat would be heavenly if it hadn't been decorated by his mother in austere velvet sofas with lion's paws for feet, and prints of hunting dogs carrying limp dead fowl in their mouths. Peter has taped a Clash poster over one particularly heinous Br'er Rabbit death scene, and thrown kilims over the backs of chaises. But I can still feel her here, spying through the eye of the formidable-looking ancestor whose portrait hangs above our bed. I know she wasn't happy when I moved in. A young American girlfriend is acceptable as long as it ends when she returns to her ghastly country.

On days like today, when Peter is at the office and I'm alone at home trying to finish my thesis, pacing the rooms, eating Nutella from the jar, getting nothing accomplished, I can feel her staring back at me from the walls, the ceilings, as if she has skim-coated them with her disapproval. If only she knew how right she is.

At the bottom of our street there's an old pub with a hopeful outdoor terrace for sunny days. Beyond it is the vast Heath, its wild, reckless fields and forests smack in the middle of the city. The woods here are gnarled, druidic, their roots extending out around them like fingers seeking blindly for a past they still remember. Little paths lead between them, worn trails that disappear into deep hollows, fecund, rotting, overgrown, hiding fox dens and the men who come here to cruise for blow jobs after dark.

Most afternoons, I walk on the Heath, letting my mind air out after too many hours staring at a typewriter. I've planned to take a proper long walk this afternoon, from Parliament Hill to Kenwood House, but the rain starts coming down, heavier now, waterlogging the world, so I change course and make a diagonal cut across the field toward home, past the men's swimming ponds.

Two old men in matching blue rubber bathing caps and baggy trunks stand at the edge of the public pond, their white, crepe-paper skin translucent, dull rain pattering their backs. I see them here almost every day. It's a British thing—taking pleasure in duty, maintaining a citizen's right to swim in a cold, unappetizing pond in the middle of a public park because one *can*. The same reason Peter's mother insists on walking directly through her neighbor's garden or the farmer's pigsties, ducks and geese scattering as she climbs a wooden turnstile: because it is a public right of way, and the pleasure in walking through, legally trespassing, is so much purer than the ease of walking around.

Now, as I hurry past the swimming pond, I can see the old men laboring across the water, strokes in perfect synch; two bright blue snapping-turtle heads in a dreary sea. It must be freezing.

I'm almost out of the park when I hear shouts behind me. A woman with a small dog is waving her arms, screaming. A man on the far side of the field hears her, breaks into a run, but I am closer and reach her first.

"He's drowning," she screams, pointing to the pond, frantic. "I can't swim."

Down below in the pond I see only one blue head.

"He was over there." She points. "He was right there, calling for help. I can't swim."

"Call 999," I shout.

I'm in the pond before I have time to think, kicking off my sneakers, leaving my raincoat and heavy sweater somewhere on the ground behind me. The water is warmer than I expected, fresher. I surface six quick strokes from the old man. He is treading water, shivering with shock. His terrified eyes search the surface for a sign of his friend.

"It was our third lap," he says. "We always do six laps."

"Get back to shore," I say.

I go under, eyes searching the gloom for a spot of inconsistency, of color. I break surface for air and dive again, deeper this time, down to the reedy bottom. Ahead of me, I see a hint of blue.

The paramedics arrive just as I reach the shore, breathless, dragging the old man's limp weight. Two of them wade in to pull me out, but I shake them off. "Save him," I gasp. "Please save him."

His friend stands shivering on the little wooden dock. The woman has wrapped her coat around him. We watch the paramedics pummeling his sad white chest, breathing into him. I hold my breath, wait for that sputtering of water to cough from his lungs, his eyes opening in surprise, as if he has just spat out a live frog. In the muddy shallows, his blue rubber cap laps the shore.

Peter is already home when I come in, lying on the uncomfortable sofa, reading. He must have just gotten home, because there's only one cigarette butt in the ashtray and his mug of tea is still steaming. I stand in the doorway, barefoot, dripping a puddle onto the coir mat.

"You got caught in the rain," Peter says, putting his book down. "I'll light the fire."

I'm frozen in place, my heart a sodden heavy thing.

"C'mon then," Peter says, coming over to give me a sloppy kiss, "let's get you out of those wet things."

"An old man drowned in the swimming pond."

"Just now?"

"He swims there every day. With his friend."

"And you saw this? Poor possum," he says.

I am numb, too numb to feel. "He hadn't even reached the bottom of the pond. He was still floating down when I got to him."

"Hang on a minute," Peter says. "Wait. You mean to tell me you went in after him yourself? Into the men's swimming pond?"

"The water was dark, but I saw his bathing cap."

"Christ, Elle." Peter fumbles for a cigarette, lights it.

"The paramedics were already there when I got him to shore. He looked like a fetus—one of those things they keep in formaldehyde."

"You could have drowned. What the hell were you playing at?" he says, his voice gruff with love and worry.

I look away from him. I wish I could tell him, explain it. I needed to save him. A drop in the bucket. But I can't.

He wraps me in his arms, holds me tight. "Let's get you into a hot bath."

"No. No water."

Peter peels my wet clothes off where I stand, carries me to our bed. He climbs under the covers with me, fully dressed, spoons me. I like the feel of his shirt, his belt buckle, his pants, so cloth-like, so concrete, pressing against my naked flesh.

"You should take off your shoes," I say.

"I'll go make you a cup of tea. Don't move. In fact, I'm never letting you out of this flat again."

My skin refuses to warm. I pull the covers closer around me but my body keeps shaking. I can't stop thinking about his body drifting down, the amniotic embrace of death, how graceful he looked as he fell. I listen to Peter filling up the electric kettle, the jangling of silverware as he opens a drawer. I imagine every little movement he is making: carefully choosing a teacup he knows I will like, dropping in two PG Tips bags instead of one, steeping the tea forty seconds longer than I would, pouring in enough milk to make it the correct shade of pinky-beige, not too pale, stirring in a heaping teaspoon of sugar.

"Whiskey in or on the side?" he says, bringing me my tea.

"I need to go home," I say. "I'm sick of the rain."

"What rain?" he says.

24

1993. September, New York.

The cat has stretched herself out on a sun-washed windowsill next to a pot of red geraniums. Her long tail brushes back and forth like a trailing vine, strewing loose flower petals from the sill onto the hardwood floor below. One of them has landed on her back and perches lightly atop her soft tortoise fur, a splash of red paint. The telephone rings, but I ignore it. There's no one I'm in the mood to talk to. I hate everyone today.

Peter is drinking his coffee, reading the paper in the kitchen of our East Village walk-up. "Can you get that?" he calls out. "It could be the office."

I'm hating Peter most of all. The apartment stinks of cigarettes; there are newspaper fingerprints on the walls, on the light switches, on the backs of the chairs. We had plans to go upstate this weekend for my birthday, but Peter had to cancel. Too much work. And yet somehow he has time for the Sunday paper and coffee. His dirty underpants lie in a heap next to the bed, waiting for me to pick them up and throw them in the laundry. He bought skim milk. I hate skim milk—its thinness, its blue-vein color.

I let the phone ring twice more, just to irritate him, before reaching over to answer it, but the machine gets there first.

"Eleanor?" a small shaky voice asks, confused. "Eleanor? Is that you?" I grab for the phone.

"Granny, I'm here," I shout, afraid she is already hanging up the receiver—as if my voice can catch her hand midair.

Now that my grandfather has died, my father and the Bitch have decided to move Granny Myrtle from her Connecticut farmhouse into a nursing home. Not a nice one, with a big circular driveway lined in sweet-smelling privet and reassuring nurses who tuck you in with a bowl of hot soup and read to you. Just some shithole in Danbury that smells of urinals, with a bunch of underpaid nurse's aides—cinder-block institutional, dirty floors, windowless puce hallways.

I've given her my word that I won't let it happen. She will stay in her own house. She's already told my father and Mary that they won't have to pay for round-the-clock nurses, if it comes to that. She's fit as a fiddle. She can look after herself. There's a local girl who can bring groceries in, do light cleaning, carry the mail in from the box at the bottom of the hill. She'll manage. Because that's what the Bitch is worried about: spending any of their potential inheritance on private nurses. My father has promised me they won't move her if I can figure out a solution that makes everyone comfortable. They are worried that she will fall, he says, and unless I'm willing to spend every weekend with her to spell the girl. "I'll do whatever it takes," I say.

"Eleanor," she says now, her voice quivering. "Is that you?"

"It's me, Granny."

"I'm frightened." She is crying. I have never heard her cry before.

"Granny, what is it? What's happened?"

"I don't know where I am." She starts to sob.

"Don't cry, Granny, please don't cry."

"They've put me in this place. It's cold here. I can't find my reading light. Where is everyone? I'm scared, Elle. Please come get me."

A rage rushes through me, crimson-red fury. "Wait. Where are you, Granny? Who moved you?"

"I don't know. I don't know. They came and brought me here." Her voice is frail, childlike.

"Who came?"

"Mary and her friend. She said my blood pressure had spiked. She said I had a doctor's appointment at the hospital. I called Henry. He told me to go with her. I don't know what to do. Where are my blankets?"

"Granny, I need to call Dad. I'll sort this out. You'll be out of there by tonight. Don't worry."

"It's dark here. There's no window. I can't breathe. You must come now!" She sounds confused, panicked, like a tethered horse in a burning barn.

All I want to do is hug her frail, bony Granny self. "I'm going to fix this. I'm coming to get you."

"Who's there?" she says.

"I'll be there in a few hours. Just try to stay calm."

"I don't know you," she says.

"It's me. It's Eleanor. I'm calling the nurses' station right now. I'll make sure they move you to a room with a window."

"I don't know you," she says again.

Now I hear a man's voice in the background, telling her to stay still. The phone drops, but I can hear her thrashing in her bed. "Get away from me," she screams. Whoever it is hangs up the phone.

When I get to Avis, there's a line. The woman behind the counter seems to think she works at the post office. A manager wanders in from a back office and we all breathe a collective sigh of relief. But instead of opening up a second line, he taps some override code into her computer, says something that makes her give a nice, round fake laugh, and then disappears into the back.

"Excuse me?" I call out. "Can you get someone else to help?"

"Ma'am, I'm working as fast as I can." As if to underline this point, she gets off her stool and, slow as mud, walks over to the printer. Waits for a contract to spool out.

"Sorry," I say, hoping to get back on her good side. "I need to get to my grandmother in the hospital. I don't mean to make a fuss."

"We all have places we need to be." She turns to the man in front of her and gives him a long-suffering smile, rolls her eyes. She's on his side, she wants him to know, just not on mine.

I arrive at the nursing home with fifteen minutes to spare, grab my purse, and run. I'm breathless when I get to reception.

"I'm here to see my grandmother."

The woman behind the counter stares at me blankly, as if she has never seen a visitor before. She looks at her watch. "Visiting hours are over."

"No. I still have fifteen minutes. Myrtle Bishop?"

She sighs. They don't pay her enough to deal with this crap. "Sorry," she says. "You're too late."

I practically stamp my foot. "I just drove up from New York. It was bumper-to-bumper traffic. She's old and frail, and she's waiting for me. Can you just be nice?"

"Ma'am," she says, "Mrs. Bishop passed away an hour ago."

Granny is buried next to my grandfather in the old cemetery across the road. It occurs to me that she spent most of her life looking out at the place where her body will rot. We stand under a threatening sky next to a raw hole in the ground. The graveyard has expanded up the hill. The old suicide grave where Anna and I used to play is now surrounded by the tombstones of nice, normal people. Anna stands beside me, looking elegant and thin in a black wool dress. Granny would approve. She squeezes my hand tight as the first shovel of dirt thuds heavily on ebonized wood. Rain begins to fall, tat-tatting the coffin like an accompaniment. My father stands across the grave from me, shoulders heaving with tears. His umbrella lists away from him. Raindrops land on his black felt hat. I have been sick at heart since Granny died, my mind stuck in a loop of regret and self-recrimination. Why didn't I act sooner, rush to protect her the minute my father and Mary threatened to move her? She was the one person in my life who made me feel safe when I was a child, who protected me from ghosts, read me to sleep, fed me protein and a vegetable, whose love never wavered. And I failed her. She was, literally, scared to death.

The minister closes his dog-eared *Book of Common Prayer*. My father's sobs have turned desperate, guttural. He stumbles toward Mary. She opens her arms wide to embrace him, but he passes her by and throws his arms around me instead. I feel a momentary triumph when I see her red-slash lips tighten in humiliation.

I hold my father close, feel the sodden chill of his trench coat against my cheek. "You have no right to cry," I whisper in his ear.

After the funeral, we all walk across the road, up the steep driveway to the house. The rain has let up, but the trees in the orchard—the crabapples and plums still heavy with unpicked fruit—weep into the tall grasses under their boughs.

I leave Anna and Peter mixing drinks in the living room, discussing the case Anna is working on. Anna is a litigator at a fancy law firm in downtown L.A. "Well, I would have preferred you did something in the arts, but I suppose it's good you found a way to put that frightful argumentative streak of yours to work," was Mum's congratulations when Anna first called to tell her she'd gotten the job. I wander down the hallway to our old bedroom off the kitchen. It is exactly as it has always been: our twin beds made, our favorite children's books still on the shelf, a red tobacco tin filled with crayon stubs. I know if I go into the guest bathroom and reach up blindly onto the top shelf above the toilet I will find a pack of menthol cigarettes, hidden where she thinks no one will find them. The most wonderful thing about my grandmother, among many wonderful things, is that everything is always the same. The lovely lemon-wood smell of the house, the little bottles of ginger ale pushed to the back of the icebox for hot days. The silver thimble her mother gave her when she was a girl, nestled in a lavender box on her bureau.

I open the cupboard in our room. As far as I'm concerned, my father and the Bitch can have everything. They'll take it anyway. Anna can fight them for the four-poster bed and the first edition of *Gatsby*. There's only one thing I want to keep. I reach back behind the dusty pile of board games—the old Scrabble box and Chinese checkers. The Game of Life. My hand searches for our treasure box filled with the paper dolls Anna and I made. But the box isn't there. I take everything out of the cupboard and pile it on the floor in a heap. Check the closets, under the bed. Nothing.

Anna is in the dining room on her cell phone. "No. You stay on the 22. Past Pawling," I hear her say as I walk past. Her new boyfriend Jeremy has just flown in from L.A. "And don't rush. The roads are wet and you've already missed the funeral."

In the living room, mourners are eating Triscuits and Brie, stiff drinks in their hands. My father sits alone on the sofa, staring into space. There's a streak of mud on one of his polished black leather shoes. He looks perplexed, as if he's waiting for his mother to appear from the kitchen, apron still tied around her waist, holding a plate of sugar cookies.

"Dad." I sit down next to him. "I've been looking for a brass box that lives in our bedroom cupboard. It was there last time I looked. Can you think where Granny might have put it?"

"The paper dolls?" he says.

"Yes," I say. "I looked everywhere."

"Mary's niece was here with us a few weeks ago. She liked them. Mary said she could take them home with her when she left."

I stand up. "Well, I should go. The sooner everyone's out of the house, the sooner you can sell it."

I reach over to the bookcase behind his head, pull my grandfather's treasured first edition of *The Great Gatsby* off the shelf. "I'm taking this for Anna."

Peter drives us home, taking the slick curves of the blacktop roadway too fast. Our high beams cut a path through the rainy night. Ahead of us, trees lean in on either side like massive shadow puppets. The radio is off. I close my eyes. Listen to the windshield wipers back-and-forthing. I cannot speak. I cannot even cry. We hydroplane around a steep S curve, but Peter pulls us back to center, accelerates. I don't tell him to slow down. I am grateful for the distance he is putting between my past and the present.

"I hate him," I say finally.

"Then I hate him, too." Peter takes a hand off the wheel, puts his arm around me. "Scooch over," he says, and pulls me tight to his side.

The car swerves slightly, but I don't mind.

25

1994. April, New York.

I push my chair back from my desk, stretch my back. I've been correcting papers for what feels like ten hours. I pick up the phone and call Peter at the office.

He answers after one ring. "Hello, gorgeous. I'm missing you."

"Well then, it's a good thing you're seeing me very soon. I'm done here. If I have to read another obvious undergraduate essay on 'Feminism and Colette' or 'Homosexual Apologism in Gide,' I may have to shoot myself. Do you want me to come up to your office and we can go together?"

"I have to finish this piece. Best meet there in case I get stuck."

"Don't get stuck. I hate these things." Crowds of art-parasites pretending the emperor is wearing clothes. Peter's parents are flying into town for the opening of the Whitney Biennial, and we're meeting them there.

I hear him light a cigarette, inhale. "Just because *you* don't like conceptual art doesn't mean the rest of the world is wrong."

"Three words: Michael. Jackson. Bubbles."

"My mother says the show is meant to be very 'political' this year."

"Where are they taking us for dinner?"

"Somewhere nice. They're looking forward to seeing you."

"They're looking forward to seeing *you*. I'm the woman who kidnapped their son and brought him to live amongst the savages."

Peter laughs. "I'll be there as soon as I can. Promise."

I get off the local train at Seventy-seventh and Lex. It's a perfect spring evening—the golden smell of honey locust, brownstones taking in the last of the sun. Around the corner from the Whitney, I sit on a stoop and change my running shoes for a pair of flats, put on some red lipstick, adjust my boobs up and out a bit. I'm wearing my favorite pale blue linen cocktail dress, but the neckline is a hair too low, and if I don't lift and separate, my boobs end up looking like a baby's bottom.

The Whitney is a madhouse, the concrete bridge to the entryway thick with bodies, an express train at rush hour. I'm not even inside, and already I'm pissed off. At the door, a woman hands me a button that reads *I can't imagine ever wanting to be white*. I grab a glass of wine from a passing tray and head into the crowd. If there's a fire, I will be trampled to death.

We've arranged to meet Peter's parents at the elevator bank, but they aren't here yet. I find a bit of open space on the wall and lean against it, slug down my wine, watch the beautiful people shoving their way across the room. A dark-haired waiter carrying a tray of champagne moves away from me into the throng.

"Can I grab one of those?" I say, but he doesn't hear me above the noise. I tug his sleeve to get his attention before he is swallowed up. The tray slaloms in his hand, and for a second it looks like he will lose control of it, but he manages to follow its sway, keeping all of the full flutes upright. Not even a slosh.

"Idiot," I hear him mutter as he presses forward without letting me take a glass of champagne from his tray.

I know this voice. "Jonas?"

The waiter turns, scowls at me. It's not Jonas.

As I watch him walk away, a sadness comes over me, a disappointment I didn't know was there, a gut-punched feeling—as if I've been given a pardon on my death sentence and then, seconds later, been told it was a mistake. It's been four years since the coffee shop. Since Jonas kissed me that way. Since I ignored the message he left on my mother's answering machine the next day, knowing—as I erased it, as I toasted a bagel, as I brought Peter coffee in bed—that Jonas was what might have been. Maybe even what *should* have been. Knowing it was too late.

Peter is what *is*. Our life together is good. Great. In love with the realness of each other—with toilet plungers and morning breath and running to the bodega to get me Tampax, falling asleep to Letterman, yelping at wasabi. But none of that matters right now. I reach into my bag and pull out my wallet, thick with receipts I need to throw away—taxi drivers' cards I take rather than hurt their feelings and admit I'll never call, a few old photos, a maxed-out credit card. My fingers feel around the recesses behind the window pocket where my hideous license photo stares out at me. I pull out the folded paper napkin. His number is faded but still legible.

There's a pay phone in the lobby corner near the gift shop. Jonas answers on the fourth ring, and this time I know the voice is his.

"It's me," I say.

Silence. The din of the lobby behind me is deafening. I press the telephone receiver hard against my ear, plug my other ear with my index finger, trying to create a bubble of silence. "It's me," I say again, louder this time. A man enters the Whitney wearing a pink vinyl suit; the woman on his arm is a head taller, dressed in a Chanel jacket and sheer stockings that do nothing to hide her nakedness underneath. I watch them air-kiss their way across the lobby.

"Jonas? Are you there? It's Elle."

I hear him sigh. "I know who it is. Are you drunk-dialing me?"

"Of course not. I'm at the Whitney."

"Ahh," he says. "I thought you were in London."

"We moved back. I thought I saw you just now. There was a waiter. I was so sure it was you."

"No."

"I know. You're there."

He waits for me to say more.

"Anyway, I was standing by myself in this crowd of assholes in vintage Fiorucci, waiting for Peter, and I thought—"

"—you thought: *assholes . . . Jonas. I never returned his call, but I'm sure he'll be happy to hear from me in the five minutes before my boyfriend arrives.*"

"Don't be an asshole," I say. "I'm calling you now."

"Why?"

"I don't know."

He is quiet on the other end of the phone.

Behind me, there is a cloud of sound.

"Fine," he says.

"Thank god. I was worried you were going to keep sulking."

"I was. But apparently I have the backbone of a snake. How are you?"

"I'm good. We came back last year. I was homesick. It rains in London."

"I've heard that."

"Peter got a job at *The Wall Street Journal*. We live on Tompkins

Square Park, so I look out at green. And junkies." I pause. "I wanted to call you back."

"Then why didn't you?"

"You asked me to choose," I say.

Jonas sighs. "I asked you to choose *me*."

The operator interrupts, asking me to please deposit ten cents for the next three minutes. I feed a dime into the slot, wait for the reassuring chunking.

"Anyway," Jonas says in an "I want to get off the phone now" voice, "I'm working, so I'd better get back to it."

"Can I see you?"

"Sure. You have my number." There's a retreat, a coolness in his voice, and I feel a sudden acute panic. I haven't lost him yet, but I know in every atom of my body that he's about to shut the door.

"How about tomorrow?"

"Week after next is better," he says.

Across the room, I see Peter and his parents pushing through the crowd, heading for the elevator bank. I turn my back, so he can't see me. "For what it's worth, I called because I was so excited when I thought that waiter was you. I was so happy. Then he wasn't you, and I couldn't think of anything else except I needed to see you right that second. It couldn't wait. I couldn't breathe if I didn't hear your voice immediately. I still had your number in my wallet. I walked over to the pay phone. I dialed."

"That's sounds a bit dramatic, even for you," Jonas says.

I laugh. "Yeah, a bit. But it's true."

"Then come *now*," he says quietly.

Peter looks at his watch, scans the lobby. I duck down behind a large man in a purple tuxedo. If I can slip out the side door before Peter sees me, I can call him from the street—tell him I'm feeling too sick to come. I can go downtown to see Jonas and be back at the apartment before Peter gets home. The big man turns, stares down at me as if he is looking at a small, blinking mouse. His face is painted in clown makeup.

"Good evening," he says. His voice is high-pitched, like a little girl's.

I smile up at him, trying to act as if squatting in a crowd is perfectly normal. He cocks his head, considers me, lipstick-red clown mouth pursed, before moving on. I hear my name being called. Through the window Clown Man has left in his purple wake, Peter has spotted me.

"Oh good," Peter's mother air-kisses me on both cheeks. "We were beginning to worry."

"I dropped my keys," I say to Peter.

Peter's elegant father stands next to him, thick silver hair brushed back, Savile Row suit. He looks older than the last time I saw them. Tired around the eyes.

"You must be jet-lagged." I give him an awkward hug. Even after all these years, Peter's parents still intimidate me in their properness, their adherence to a mysterious Upper-Class Brit code of manners. As much as I have tried to learn its rules, whenever I'm with them I have the feeling I am making a faux pas. And worse, I don't know what the faux pas *is*.

"I had a bit of a nap at the hotel," Peter's father says.

"We don't believe in jet lag," his mother says.

"I thought *I* was late. I ran all the way from the subway. Almost killed me." Peter gives me a big wet smooch. I can feel his mother's eyebrows raising. Public displays of affection are definitely frowned upon. Almost worse than visible panty line.

"It's the cigarettes," she says. "Eleanor, you really must make him stop."

"I've *been* here," I say. "I went to the ladies' room." I pause, trying to think of some excuse, anything that will get me out of here. Jonas is waiting. If I stand him up, he will not forgive me again. Peter takes my hand.

"Shall we go up?" His father pushes the elevator button. "We booked at Le Cirque."

The elevator begins to rumble down. I listen to its approach, knowing it's now or never. "I'll meet you up there," I blurt as the doors open. "I need to use the bathroom."

Peter looks at me, confused. "I thought you just came from the bathroom."

"I'm feeling a bit ill," I say. "Tummy."

"You do look flushed." He reaches out to feel my forehead, holding the elevator doors open with his free hand.

"If you aren't feeling well, Eleanor, you should go home. No use getting the rest of us sick," Peter's mother says.

"*Mother.*"

"She's probably right," I say. His mother looks so thrilled by her petty triumph that I almost feel absolved.

"Then I'll come with you," Peter says.

"No. Stay with your parents. I'm fine. I'll be fine."

The elevator dings impatiently.

"*Peter,*" his mother says. "Other people are waiting."

"Go," I say. "I'll see you at home."

I wait for the elevator doors to clang shut before running out to the street and hailing a cab.

Jonas is outside his building, hands in his pockets, staring up at a scraggly tree boxed into the sidewalk. I almost don't recognize him. He's still

Jonas, but he's broad-shouldered now, muscular: a *man* man. I follow his gaze to a large hawk perched on an upper branch.

"It's a redtail," Jonas says. "Must be hunting rats."

"How disgusting."

"Still," he says, "a bird of prey in Greenwich Village."

"That could be the title of my stepmother's memoir."

Jonas laughs. "How do you do that?"

"Do what?"

"Manage to make me laugh even when I hate you." He looks at me, gaze direct, no lies behind his water-green eyes. "To be honest, I was hoping you'd gotten really old and fat. All doughy and English. But you look beautiful." He frowns, runs his fingers through his dark hair. It is long again, wilder. He's in his work clothes, jeans and T-shirt covered in paint. He smells of turpentine. There's a smear of ocher on his cheek. I reach out to wipe it off, but he stops my hand midair.

"You have paint," I say.

"No touching."

"Don't be stupid." I put my arms around him, don't let go. It feels good to be close to him. When I step away, there is wet oil paint on my linen dress.

"That's all I meant," he says.

"Shit. I liked this dress."

Far down the street I see a couple crossing at the light, arm in arm. For a second, I think it's my father and Mary, and a rotten, crumpling feeling clenches my insides.

"What?" Jonas asks.

"I thought I saw my father," I say. "I don't speak to him anymore."

"What happened?"

"He put Granny Myrtle in a home. Against her will. She died the next day. She called me. She was so scared and alone. I tried to get there, but I was too late. I'll never forgive him."

Above us, the hawk takes wing, chasing after a smaller bird. I watch it circling in. "I lied to Peter and his parents. Told them I was feeling sick to my stomach."

"Sorry," he says. But I can see in his eyes it makes him happy that I lied to Peter so I could see him.

"Don't lie to me," I say. "It's pointless."

He smiles. The truth of everything between us. "I was thinking we could grab some beers on the corner and walk down to the river."

The windows of my father's apartment are open. Someone—Mary, obviously—has attached tasteful window boxes filled with trailing ivy and white geraniums. Jonas and I walk, arms entwined, through the narrow cobbled streets. Down Perry and across West Street to an old pier littered with desiccated dog shit and crack vials. We find a cleanish spot and sit down. Legs dangling over the edge.

"I thought it would be romantic, but it's actually kind of disgusting," Jonas says.

"I forgot how much I like you."

"Same," he says. "I kind of hate everyone else." He hands me a beer. Opens one for himself.

"I've never seen you drink before. Funny," I say. But it doesn't feel funny, it feels sad, all the things we have missed.

"Yes." He slugs his beer. "So many things."

We sit in silence, watching the current. A small pink plastic spoon drifts by. Baskin-Robbins, probably. There's no awkwardness. No tension. Just familiarity—the bond between us that nothing will ever replace.

Jonas looks down at his knee, rubs at a paint stain. "I wasn't expecting your call. I think I thought . . . I waited a long time. And then I stopped."

"It was too hard," I say.

"And now?"

"I don't know."

He drains his beer, reaches for another. "So, are you planning to marry this guy?"

I look away from him. Behind us, on the West Side Highway, traffic has come to a standstill. In the near distance, I hear the rise and fall of a siren. A taxi driver leans on his horn, a pointless gesture, like pushing the elevator button again when it's already lit. Another driver honks at him for honking, shouts, "Fuck *you,* moron," out of his window. A quarter mile behind them, I watch the circular flashing light of an ambulance trying to wedge its way forward between the grudging cars.

"Maybe." I sigh. "Probably."

He stares out across the heavy river. "Promise you'll warn me beforehand."

"Okay."

"Don't surprise me. I hate surprises."

"I know. I promise."

"Mean it."

The sun has set, leaving behind a fiery orange sky. Pylons that once held up the long-gone piers stalk out into the river in rows of two, black against the burning sky.

"It's painfully beautiful," I say.

"Just so we are clear," he says, "I will never love anyone the way I love you."

26

1996. August, the Back Woods.

It's Anna, not me, who insists we go to the end-of-summer bonfire. I can't remember the last time I went, and I don't particularly want to go. But Anna has come to the woods for a solo visit. She rarely comes back east anymore—it is practically impossible for her to get time off from work now that she's on the partner track—and Jeremy, her Orange County boyfriend whom I cannot bear, thinks the Paper Palace is a decaying slum: the sagging cabin steps, Homasote ceilings stained brown with small circles of mouse piss or the slow drip drip of their afterbirth. No one has ever had the guts to investigate what lies above. And mosquitoes, which, Jeremy insisted, the one and only time they came to the camp together four years ago, do not exist in Manhattan Beach. He has not been back since.

"We *live* on the beach, babe," he said to Anna at breakfast after their second night. "This place is great, but why be here when we can be at home in the condo? Frosty AC, chilling on the deck, a good chardonnay."

"That's the reason we love it here," I said. "No Chardonnay." I have tried to understand why my sister is with Jeremy. As far as I can tell, he represents everything we detest. But maybe that's the point.

"It's odd," my mother said, coming onto the porch with her coffee and a novel, "*Manhattan* and *beach* are two of the greatest things on earth. But put them together and all you have is mediocrity."

"*Mom*," Anna said.

"It's such a treat having you both here." Mum sat down on the horsehair sofa and settled herself in, opened her book to the middle. "Anna," she said without looking up, "I hope you explained to your young man that we don't flush for pee." She took a sip of coffee. "Don't let me forget to call the plumber about replacing the septic tank. Clearly, tainted groundwater is leaching into the pond." She pointed out toward the lily pads. "How else do you explain the algae bloom?"

This summer, by some miracle, Jeremy's bosses have invited him to attend a marketing conference in Flagstaff the same week he and Anna had already booked to come to the Cape.

"I can't believe you managed to resist the dramatic-but-healing landscape and the all-you-can-eat buffets to come to the 'shithole,'" I say now as we canoe across to the far side of the pond. On bonfire night, it's impossible to park at the beach—much quicker to canoe and walk. We've packed a bag of marshmallows, Cape Cod potato chips, red wine, and a moth-eaten army blanket to sit on when the sand goes cold.

Anna laughs. "Harsh."

"He insulted my favorite place on earth."

"You can't condemn him because he doesn't 'get' the pond. It was my fault. I forgot to tell him the name Paper Palace was ironic."

"It's not just the camp," I say. "It's his whole outlook on the world. Like everything should be made of Saltillo-fucking-tile and polished granite countertops."

"That's why I like him. He's predictable. I know exactly what I'm getting."

I roll my eyes.

"Elle, we all have different shit. Jeremy makes me feel safe. Anyway, not everyone can fall madly in love with a rich, dashing English journalist. Some of us have to settle for a kind-if-boring Californian guy with good pecs. So, don't be such a judgmental cow."

"That's fair." I will never like Jeremy. Not because, as Anna says, he's predictable or, as Mum says, "bourgeois." But because he makes her be less-than, and it pisses me off.

We are both quiet for a bit, our paddles cutting the glass-still surface of the pond, the canoe gliding silently into a reflection of pink sky. A heron stands statue-still in the reeds, letting us pass.

"What time is Peter driving up tomorrow?" Anna breaks the silence.

"Right after lunch. He wants to beat the rush hour."

"If he's taking the Merritt, ask him to pick up some bagels from H&H."

Our canoe hits sand on the far side of the pond. I hop out into the shallows, trying not to soak the cuffs of my jeans.

Anna winces as she climbs out. "I shouldn't have ridden my bike into town this morning. That dirt road is one big pothole. I think I bruised my vagina bones."

"Gross." I laugh.

We drag the canoe up onto the shore, into the thick grasses beyond the rough scrape of wet sand against metal, stash it in a gap between the trees.

"I haven't seen any of these people in so long," Anna says as we walk down the red clay road toward the beach. "It's going to be weird."

"It's like riding a bike, only more boring," I say. "And less painful."

Anna laughs. "I wish I didn't feel so fat." She pulls her hair up into a ponytail. "I'm not in the mood to be judged by these fuckers."

Anna has been model-thin for years, but she still thinks she's a fat kid. "Fat thighs are like a phantom limb," Anna tells me. "Years after you lose them, you can still feel them rubbing together."

"You look amazing, Anna. I, on the other hand, spent the winter holed up in the apartment with Peter eating Milanos. I need to starve myself between now and the wedding."

We walk on the road single file, Anna in front, skirting thickets of poison ivy. The back ends of her flip-flops raise little puffs of red dust.

"You know which ones are underrated?" Anna says. "Brussels."

"And Chessmen."

"Dad's favorite."

"Have you talked to him recently?" I ask. I haven't spoken to him since our grandmother's funeral.

"He calls me every once in a while," Anna says. "We have these awkward conversations where all I want to do is get off the phone. The whole thing is ridiculous. You two are the ones who've always been close, not me."

"Not anymore."

"The only reason he calls is because Mary forces him to. She likes to tell her friends what a doting husband and father he is. She's trying to get them into some country club in Southampton. One of those no-Jews places."

"I hate her."

"Anyway, I've told him *he* needs to call *you*. He's the father, for fuck's sake."

"That's the last thing I want. Honestly? It's a relief. I don't have to wait for him to disappoint me all the time."

We stop at the top of the high dune. Down below us, a hundred yards to the right, there's a crowd of linen. Someone has planted Chinese fish flags on poles in the sand—a brightly colored circle of wind socks. The bonfire has been lit, its flames mostly invisible in the still-light summer evening, heat oiling the sky above it.

"P.S., I know you're mad at me because you think I acted like a total pussy for forgiving him. I just don't care enough about him to care. I'll freeze him out if you want me to," Anna says.

"I *did* want you to, but thinking about it, I'd rather you be the one getting Belgian loafers for Christmas, stuck in a needlepoint chair in the sitting room drinking eggnog with the evil cunt."

"That's fair."

"Merry Christmas!" I laugh. "Here are some book galleys."

"'And a nickel bag from me!'" Anna squeaks in a high voice, imitating Mary.

We run down the steep dune toward the sea, shouting into the wind, ecstatic, faster than our legs can carry us. At the bottom, our momentum is slowed by the deep crunch of flat beach.

Anna falls forward onto her knees, raises her arms into the sky, victorious. "*This*, I miss."

"This, *I* miss." I fall onto my back next to her, making a snow angel in the sand. Anna's cheeks are flushed pink, hair wind-tangled. "You're looking absurdly gorgeous."

"Don't let me get drunk and fuck some hot guy in the dunes," Anna says.

"I think you're safe. Everyone here's a thousand years old."

"Still."

I push up onto my elbows, look out at the sea—the pooling sun, the whitecap flecks, the crest and swell. Every single time I see the ocean, even if I've been there in the morning, it feels like a new miracle—its power, its blueness always just as overwhelming. Like falling in love.

The wind shifts, carrying the smell of burning driftwood and brine. Anna gets to her feet, brushes sand off her knees. "Right. Let's go get our linen on."

"I refuse to be seen in public with anyone who says, 'get our linen on,'" I say.

"It's repulsive, I agree," Anna says, cracking herself up.

I worship my sister.

The first person to come into focus as we walk up the beach is Jonas's mother. She's standing slightly apart, her back to me, but I recognize her grizzled, aggressively undyed hair, the worn-suede Birkenstocks she's holding in one hand, the line she's drawing in the sand with one big toe. She must feel the vibration of our steps in the sand, because she turns, like a snake, and smiles. She's talking to a girl I've never seen before: young—maybe twenty—pretty, petite, dark hair frosted blond at the ends, skin tanned a perfectly even brown, wearing shorts and a cropped T-shirt. Her belly button is pierced with a large diamond stud.

"Cubic zirconia," Anna says as we approach them. "Do we know her?"

"No."

"Hello, Anna, Eleanor," Jonas's mum says, lips tightening. She's always disliked me. "I had no idea you two were here."

"I've been avoiding the beach," I say. "It's like Coney Island this summer."

"I got here yesterday," Anna says.

Jonas's mother puts a proprietary arm around the girl she's been talking to. "This is Gina."

Anna puts her hand out to shake, but instead Gina steps forward and gives her a big hug. "I'm so happy to meet you finally," she says, hugging me next. Behind her back, Anna gives me a look of mock horror that Jonas's mother catches.

"I ran into your mother at the A&P," Jonas's mother says. "I gather you're planning a *winter wedding*." She says the words as if they are in quotes, making sure I don't miss her tinge of disdain.

"Yes," I say. "We're thinking ice statues and a chocolate fountain."

"And not a moment too soon."

"I'm sorry?" I say.

"Well, let's face it, none of us are getting any younger."

"Elle still has a few weeks left before she becomes a withered crone of thirty," Anna says, sweet as a punch. "But we take your point. Are any of your boys here?"

"They're *men* now," Jonas's mother says, as if she's explaining something to a dunce. "No climbing on the dunes," she shouts at some children playing at the bottom of the steep dune.

"It could collapse on them," she says to Gina. "I do worry."

"How's Jonas?" I ask her.

"He's very well."

"He's awesome," Gina jumps in. "He got a gallery in Chelsea. We are both totally psyched. And we found this amazing loft. It was a ribbon factory."

"What kind of work is he doing these days?" Anna asks.

I vaguely hear Gina saying something about acrylics and found objects, but my mind refuses to focus. The thought of Jonas living with this Gina person fills me with a jealousy I have no right to feel. Physical, palpable. Jonas belongs to me. It's all I can do not to kick her in the shins.

Jonas's mother looks as if she's just swallowed a large tasty bird. "We are all absolutely delighted."

Every bit of dislike I've ever had for her—her lack of generosity, her sanctimony, the way she implied to everyone in the woods, back then, that Jonas would never, ever have been out sailing with me and Conrad that day if I hadn't pressured him into it—comes roiling to the surface. "She had him wrapped around her little finger," my mother once overheard her saying. I force myself to think about Peter, my lovely, gallant Englishman. His easy intelligence, his beat-perfect irony, the way he cooks a pork roast with salt-crunchy crackling, his worn leather brogues, the way he tugs on my hair when we make love. I manage a clear smile. "That's great news. You must be so happy for Jonas."

"Yes," she says. "And for Gina, of course."

I see him then, walking in our direction through the throng. He's carrying a brown-paper grocery bag under one arm. A jumbo pack of hot dog buns teeters out of the top. I watch as he scans the crowd. He finds Gina, her back to him, smiles. Then he sees me. He stops where he stands. We stare at each other across the sand. He shakes his head, more in anger than in sorrow—some combination of pain and disgust, as if he cannot believe what I have done, cannot fathom that I broke the promise I made two years ago as we sat on that broken-down pier, drinking beers, looking out over the Hudson, accepting our fate.

Jonas's mother sees him now, his eyes locked on me. She taps Gina on the shoulder. "Jonas is back."

Gina's face lights up as if she has never seen anything so wondrous.

He comes over to her, bypassing me, gives her a long, deep kiss. "I was looking for you," he says.

"Anna." He hugs her hello, hands his mother the buns. "They only had a jumbo pack."

"They'll all get eaten. No one ever brings enough buns to these things." She heads over to the food table, hands them to a man cooking linguica and burgers. "Buns!" I hear her announce, as if she has just delivered the Holy Grail.

"Hi." Jonas turns to acknowledge me last. His tone is friendly, no trace of what I saw on his face. He smiles at me, composed, benign.

"Hi," I say, giving him a what-the-fuck look.

He puts his arm around Gina's waist. "Gina, this is Eleanor. Elle and I knew each other when we were kids."

"We've met," I say.

"My mother said none of your gang were up this week."

"I know your mother hates it when people disagree with her," I say, my voice bitchier than I'd intended. "But we're here. I've been here."

"Gina and I drove up last weekend. I gather from my mother that you're planning a winter wedding. She ran into Wallace at the A&P." His voice is cold.

"I tried to reach you."

Gina looks back and forth between us, as if sensing that she is suddenly on the outside looking in. "Jonas is taking me squid fishing later," she says.

"Cool," Anna says.

Gina looks dubious. "Fishing for squirming things off a pier at midnight?"

Anna laughs. "It's very satisfying. You shine a flashlight into the water, and they swarm. You barely have to move the jig. Like shooting fish in a barrel."

"Jonas and I used to go all the time." I smile at him, trying to break through. "You were obsessed."

He doesn't give an inch, just stands there looking through me.

"If you love it, I'll love it." Gina pulls him into her and kisses him like she owns him.

"Just don't get inked," I say.

"And marinate them in milk overnight before you grill them," Anna says.

"I don't eat seafood," Gina says.

Anna looks at me and Jonas. She hooks her arm through Gina's. "I'm going to go grab a beer. Come. I'll introduce you to the only two interesting people here." She pulls her along before Gina can think of a reason to say no.

The summer after I graduated from high school, Anna and I decided to go for a midtide swim at Higgins. The sea was perfect that day. No mung. No churn. We floated in the ocean, cradled by the rise and fall of the swells, as Anna droned on and on about how totally in love she was with her Dyadic Communication professor.

"I have literally no idea what that means," I said.

"It means I want to fuck my professor."

"Dyadic." I laughed, diving under the water. I came up where I could stand.

"So, what about you, Miss 'I'm going to wait until marriage'?" Anna called over to me. "Still a virgin?"

"Of course," I lied. "And I never said anything about marriage. I just said I wanted to wait until I fell in love."

"Then why do you have birth control pills in your bureau drawer."

"Why are you looking in my bureau drawer?"

"I needed to borrow a pair of underwear. All of mine are dirty."

"Gross."

"Don't change the subject."

"Whatever. I have them just in case."

"Just in case you suddenly fall in love for the first time?"

"No," I said. And this, at least, was the truth. I hesitated a breath before saying, "Anyway, I already have."

"Have what?"

"Been in love."

"Huh. That's news. But then, why no sex?"

"It's Jonas."

Anna looked confused. "Wait. That kid who used to follow you around?"

I nodded.

"Okay, that's a bit pervy. Excellent choice on the no-sex thing."

"He grew up. But yeah."

"So, what happened?"

Standing there in the familiar sea, looking at my beautiful sister, dark hair against the infinite blue, I thought about telling her everything. It would be such a relief. But instead I said, "His mother sent him to camp in Maine."

"That woman is so unpleasant. Every time I see her I feel like shitting on her shoes," Anna said.

I watch Anna and Gina walk away in search of beer, feeling sick to my stomach. I have never felt anything with Jonas but our unique symbiosis, but I don't know this man. *This* Jonas has dead eyes.

"I had no idea you would be here," I say.

He stands there, letting me dangle.

"Jonas. Don't do this."

He stares at me. Says nothing.

"I called to tell you, but your number was disconnected. I was planning to call your mom to get it. I'm sorry."

"For what?"

"My mother is a stupid bigmouthed cow. I told her not to say anything to anyone."

"It's not a big deal." He pulls open a bag of potato chips and shoves a handful into his mouth. Offers me the bag.

"You have every right to be mad at me."

"Please. Don't worry about it. That's ancient history."

"I saw the look on your face when you saw me."

"I didn't expect to see you here. That's all."

"Don't lie. I hate it when you lie."

"I'm not lying, Elle. I was angry at you for disappearing on me again. It was rude. *You* called *me*. You're the one who said we should be friends. It made me feel like an idiot. But I'm over it. It was a million years ago. I was a stupid kid with a stupid crush."

"Wow," I say, my voice teeth against teeth. "That's a truly shitty thing to say."

"I don't mean it to be. I'm trying to tell you it's fine. The past is the past. I'm with Gina now. I'm in love with Gina."

"She's *twelve*."

"Don't do that," Jonas says. "It's beneath you."

"She doesn't even eat fish."

When the night sky is black, and everyone has gathered close around the warmth of the bonfire, I move away into the darkness. I need to pee. I sit on the uphill slant at the base of the staggering dunes, pull my jeans down to my knees, dig a little hole underneath me. The stream of pee vanishes into the sand. As Anna has always said, peeing on the beach sitting down is even better than peeing in the shower standing up. I pull my pants back on and move two feet to my right, sit down again on safer ground. I can barely see my hands, it's so dark out here. Moonless dark. Jonas and Gina are huddled together at the far edge of the fire. Their faces glow in the golden-orange flicker. He looks around the gathered circle, scanning, and I know he's looking for me. He starts to stand, then changes his mind. I watch him stare at the deepening embers, watch his eyebrows knit together because he's had a thought that bothers him, and I know he is thinking about me. This man who saved me. Who I have hurt. Whose trust I've now lost. I promise myself that, somehow, I will find a way to make things right.

High above the tallest dune, a star appears in the sky, faint at first, then gaining strength until it becomes a brilliant jewel. And yet I know it is death I am seeing. The flickering out. The silent gasp. The sputtering beauty. A desperate flame—massive, transcendent—fighting for its last breath.

27

1996. December, New York.

Dawn comes sooner than it should. I lie naked on top of my duvet, stare out the window of our East Village apartment, listening to the spits and hisses of the radiator. They're predicting heavy snow and the sky has that breathless, dry-ice blankness, as if the air is taking a pause. It's my wedding day.

Peter has spent his last night as a single man at the Carlyle Hotel on Madison Avenue with his best man, a posh friend from Oxford who has always seemed suspicious of me—as if the fact that I am American means I must be a fortune hunter.

Anna is asleep in the living room. I can hear her soft snuffling. She must have passed out lying on her back. Last night we put on our ancient Lanz nightgowns, the ones Granny Myrtle gave us every year for Christmas until we were too old to appreciate their old-fashioned coziness, drank shots of tequila, and talked so late into the night that I'm going to have hideous purple bags under my eyes. Anna is my maid of honor. She and Jeremy have been staying with Mum, who has been characteristically horrible to him, much to my delight. Jeremy has made it almost impossible for me and Anna to have any time together. He makes her do a full hour of yoga with him every morning after breakfast, and even insisted on coming to my dress fitting. On Wednesday, when Anna and I had plans to go to the Russian Tea Room for a girls' lunch, he surprised her with matinee tickets to *Cats* at the Winter Garden—even though Anna hates musicals and the show has been running since 1982. "It's tiresome," Mum said when I called her to complain. "But that's what people from California *do* when they come here. For some unfathomable reason, watching actors singing on stage dressed as animals makes them think they're getting culture."

My cream silk velvet dress hangs on the closet door, still in its dry-cleaning bag. It is long, with a train, cut skintight against my body, the neckline low enough to reveal just too much. Next to it, on the floor, are the $300 satin pumps Anna insisted I buy. They're the kind of shoes that will never be worn again—the kind you swear you'll have dyed black after the wedding, but you never get around to it. Instead, dust will settle into the white—dull them, dim them, and they will live like that for years in the back of your closet, slowly going gray.

Dixon walks me down the aisle, handsome and dapper in a morning coat. My father is still excommunicated, though he's here at my mother's insistence, sitting in the family pew next to Jeremy. I refused to bend for Mary the Bitch. As I walk up the aisle to my future life, I smile, thinking about how cruelly she will take her revenge on my father for agreeing to come without her. Peter is waiting for me at the altar, and he smiles back at me across the length of the church, happy and proud. I wonder if he would love me if he could see inside my head—the pettiness, the dirty linen of my thoughts, the terrible things I have done. The church is festooned in lilies and thick white cabbage roses that smell like the perfume counter at Bloomingdale's. I have a sudden image of Anna holding my hand on the steep up-escalator when I was little. She had taken me to try on new Keds while our mother shopped for Christmas presents. We found Mum in Accessories, trying on a pair of red leather gloves lined in cashmere.

"Elegant, aren't they?" she said, and put them back on the table. Later, as we stood on the subway platform waiting for the express train, I saw a flash of red peeking out of her coat pocket. On Christmas morning, she opened a narrow box, tied with a green satin ribbon. It was the red gloves. "From your father," she said. "How on earth did he know?"

The organist plays Pachelbel's Canon, possibly my least favorite piece of music. Peter's request. When I argued that it was pedestrian, he laughed and told me it was a family tradition and that I sounded like my mother, so I had no choice but to relent. Now, pacing myself down the aisle to its treacle strains, I'm annoyed.

Peter's mother sits on the Brit side—a sea of women in ugly hats, tulle-ed and feathered, clutching their men closely to them, lips pinched in disapproval at my skintight dress. As I walk, my train collects strewn rose petals from the marble floor. I search the rows for Jonas, hoping he is not here—I've invited his entire family. But the snow is coming down hard now, and the church has dimmed to shadows, a stark Netherlandish gray. I face forward, walk toward Peter, so handsome in his lanky old-world self-confidence. I love him—everything about him. The way, when he is excited, the tips of his ears flush red. The length of his gait. The way he steadies me, makes me safe. His long, elegant hands. The way he always gives money to beggars, looks them in the eye with respect. The person he sees when he looks at me. Peter's best man stands too close beside him. *He is right to protect his friend from me,* I think as I take Peter's hand.

It must be very late. Out the window, the sky is coal-black. The snow has stopped. Peter is in the shower. I know this because I can hear the water running from the Plaza Hotel bed where, apparently, I have just regained consciousness. I'm still in my wedding gown. My two feet poke straight up from the mattress in silk pumps, as if a house has fallen on me. I have no idea how I got here. I close my eyes, trying to remember our wedding reception. A blur of colorful hats. Platters of oysters on crushed ice. Peter's mother in a plum-tweed Chanel suit talking to Jonas's mother. A tuxedoed waiter handing me a crystal flute of champagne, me throwing it back in one gulp and grabbing another from the tray. Earth, Wind & Fire. Anna and I slow-dancing together, slugging champagne directly from the bottle. Watching my father sneak out the back before the toasts began. "Once a douche, always a douche," Anna had said.

"Peter?" I call out now.

"Sec," he calls back. He emerges from a billow of steam, a plush hotel towel wrapped around his waist. "The prodigal alcoholic returns." He leaps on top of me and kisses me. "Hi, wife." He sniffs me. "You smell of baby-sick. Might want to take off those shoes. The splatter."

"Oh god."

He reaches down and takes them off me, one at a time, throws them in the wastebasket. "You'll never wear them again, anyway. White satin heels? You'd look like a hooker at Charing Cross."

"Did I puke at the party? In front of everyone?"

"No, no. Just the hotel staff and the limo driver. It took three liveried bellhops to carry you into the elevator."

"They carried me?"

"I insisted you were luggage."

"I need a cheeseburger," I groan.

"For my beautiful blackout-drunk bride, anything." Peter wipes my hair back from my brow.

"It was the champagne. I can't drink champagne. It's the sugar. I'm sorry."

"Don't apologize. Watching you throw your garter to my father was the highlight of the day."

"I'm going to shoot myself."

"That, and marrying the woman of my dreams."

I reach up and put my arms around his neck, look deep into his eyes. "I need to brush my teeth."

When I wake much later, a dream lingers on the tip of my mind. I'm on a cloud, scudding across the sky. Below me the sea is bright blue, infinite. A pod of whales migrates north, grandly oblivious to the smaller creatures in their wake. A white sail appears, riding fast on the chop. There are two children on the boat. Behind them, an enormous sperm whale dives, sounds the depths. I am underwater. I watch as the whale torpedoes toward the surface, aiming for the triangular shadow of the boat. A house floats by. Red ribbons flow through a broken screen door.

The room service tray is on the bedside table. Peter is passed out next to me, a smudge of ketchup on the corner of his mouth. Most of the fries are gone. I am married.

1997. February, the Back Woods.

Two months after the honeymoon I get a call from Anna. At first I'm not certain it's her—she's crying so hard I can't make out what she's saying, and Anna doesn't cry.

"Slow down," I say. "I can't hear you."

I listen to her sobs for a moment or two before she hangs up the phone. When I try to call back, it rings and rings until the machine picks up. I call Jeremy at his office.

"She's good," he says brightly. "She's been doing a lot of work on herself."

My throat constricts in knee-jerk disgust. "That's great." I force myself to keep the judgment out of my voice. "She sounded pretty upset when she called me just now."

"She had group therapy today. That might have loosened up some silt."

"When you get home tell her to call me, okay?" I loathe him.

"So, how's it going?" he says, not taking his cue to hang up.

"Fine. Great."

"*You* certainly had a good time at your wedding."

"Tell her to call me," I say.

The highway is desolate, barren—a cindery streak, salted for black ice, its sandy verges frozen hard and flat. A few dark pines punctuate the woods, but most of the trees here are bare, their last remaining leaves, rattle-dead brown, waiting sorrowfully to be taken by the next icy gust. It's not even three p.m., but already the winter light is fading. Anna hasn't spoken since I picked her up at Logan airport in a rental car. She looks haggard, empty, her eyes rubbed red. Anna is tough. A rock. Caustic and funny. The Creature from the Black Lagoon. This is not my sister. I listen to the swish of tires on wet road, the salt spray. Fiddle with the radio. Nothing but AM. I hate the Cape in winter.

Every house we pass on our way into the woods is closed up for the season. Not a single sign of life. Just beyond the turnoff for Dixon's house, a fox runs across the road in front of the car carrying a small animal in its mouth. It freezes in our headlights, looks at us for a moment, before moving on.

The pond is thick ice. Hoarfrost covers the dead brush, bright red berries on a thin silvery branch. The camp looks naked, all its faults exposed. I pull in next to the back door, turn off the engine. We sit there in the quiet, the warmth, the deepening hues. Anna rests her head against the window glass.

"Stay in the car. I'll get the heat on."

The back door is padlocked. I go around the side of the house, wade through a pileup of dead leaves, reach up under the eaves. Even after all the years, I'm always amazed and relieved when my fingers find it—a single key hanging on a rusty nail. The same key to the same ancient Master Lock that has been here since we were children.

"Got it," I shout to Anna. I open the door, stumble over the doorsill into the dark pantry, make my way to the fuse box on the far wall. My fingers feel their way down the braille of circuit breakers until they find one switch thicker than the others—the main. It takes a bit of force to turn it over from left to right. The refrigerator has been propped open with a broom to keep it from moldering, and the interior light goes on as it rumbles to life. The living room is clean-swept, empty of color, the sofa pillows and throws stored inside big black contractor bags. It feels colder inside than out, like a walk-in freezer, filled with the boxed-in chill of dead air. The water has been turned off, so the pipes don't freeze. I'll have to wait until the house has warmed up before flushing out the antifreeze and getting the water going. For tonight, we will get water from the pond.

I walk around the room turning on lamps. It is far too cold to stay in a cabin with no heat but we can make a fire, sleep in the Big House on the sofas. Tucked under a table are two electric heaters. I plug them into living room outlets. They come on like old-fashioned toasters, thin coils heating to orange-red, filling the room with the smell of burning dust, and always the spark of worry in me that they will burn the house down while we sleep. There's a pile of wood and kindling beside the fireplace and a stack of fading newspapers—mostly last summer's *New York Times*es, a few *Boston Globe*s mixed in. Someone, probably Peter, has laid a fire in the hearth, in anticipation of next summer. I take the tin of strike-anywhere matches from the mantelpiece, get down on my knees, light the crumpled newspaper, the tinder. The fire hisses, crackles, blazes alive. Behind me, I hear Anna come in.

"We should ice-skate," she says.

"I'll open a can of soup. There might be sardines." I pull a big pile of feather pillows, blankets, and cold sheets out of an old captain's chest.

We go to sleep listening to the flicker of the fire, the occasional thud of wood chunks falling into the embers. Outside, in the winter moonlight, the world is cold, stark—a bare echo of the place I love, the place where, for me, life begins and ends. Yet, lying here next to my anguished, perplexing sister, her hand within reach, breathing in the smell of woodsmoke and mildew and the winter sea, I can begin to feel its heartbeat. I have no idea what has happened to break Anna like this. I only know that whatever it is, it led her back here. Like a homing pigeon, who, deaf to everything but pure instinct, hears the wind blowing across a mountain range two hundred miles away and sets its course.

At dawn, sodium light seeps in through the porch windows, waking me. The fire has gone out during the night, and already I can see my breath. I put my socks on under the covers, grab my down jacket from the floor, and pull it on over my nightgown. The coals are still red. I add dry wood, stoke the embers, careful not to wake Anna, grab a jug and go down to the pond. I need coffee. There will be an unopened can of Medaglia d'Oro in the pantry. My mother always makes sure to leave coffee, olive oil, and salt. The pond is frozen solid. The ice must be six inches thick. Small twigs and leaves are paper-pressed into it, caught in motion like fossils. But where the ice meets the shoreline, it thins to a sheer brittle. I shatter the surface with a stick, cup my hands and drink from the pond before filling my jug.

The smell of coffee wakes Anna. "Oh good," she says, yawning.

"She speaks."

Anna cocks her head, a small gesture, like a winter sparrow. Then her face flushes gray with remembered sorrow.

"Talk to me." I bring her a mug of black coffee. "There's sugar but no milk." I sit down on the edge of the sofa beside her. "Shove over."

She shifts to make room for me, a hollow space beside her hip. "I'd like to walk to the beach while the sun is out."

"There must be extra sweaters in the chest," I say.

She sits up, adjusts a pillow behind her back. "I went to the gynecologist last week. I missed my period."

"And?"

"I was sure I was pregnant."

"I spoke to you last week. You didn't say anything."

"I was afraid if I said anything, I'd lose it again. I kept thinking 'third time's a charm.'" She takes a sip of coffee, makes a face. "We should have stopped at Cumby's for milk. Anyway, I'm not."

"Anna. Fuck. That sucks. I'm so sorry."

She puts her coffee on the windowsill, looks down at her hands, turns them over, staring at them. She traces her finger across the upper line of her right palm. "Remember life lines?"

I nod. "Remember love lines??"

Anna laughs. "Mine had all those little feathers off it. Lindsay called them my slut lines."

"Whatever happened to Lindsay?" I say.

"I'm never going to have a baby," Anna says.

"Of course, you will. You're only thirty-three. You just have to keep trying. You'll probably end up with four brats that look and act like Jeremy."

She shakes her head. "I missed my period because I have the Big O."

"Why would that make your period late?"

"Ovarian cancer," she says.

"The Big O means an orgasm, you idiot." The words are out of my mouth before I realize what she has said. The room stops breathing, dust motes freeze in place, sunlight balks at the windowpane, waits. Inside me there's a silence like cement.

I shake my head. "You don't."

"Elle."

"How do they know it's not just a fibroid?"

"It's stage four. It's already spread."

"Have you even gotten a second opinion, because if you haven't, you have to do it right away."

"Elle, be quiet and let me talk. I mean it. Just. Shut up, okay? They saw spots on my liver. They are going to go in next week, but the doctor says to prepare for bad news."

"That's just one possibility. It could also be completely operable. They don't know yet. You'll do chemo and radiation. We'll get the best doctor in New York. You are going to be fine."

"Okay," Anna says. "If you say so."

"I say so."

"Well then, we have nothing to worry about. Let's walk to the beach." She throws off her bedding, pokes me in the hip. "Move, please, so I can get out."

"I know you hate physical affection, but I'm going to give you a really big hug, and you're going to have to deal with it."

"Fine. Give me a second to prepare myself."

I put my arms around her and hug her so close. "I love you, Anna. It's going to be fine. I promise."

"Love you back," she says. "I don't know why I hated you so much when you were little."

"I was annoying."

"I was angry."

"You were terrifying. You still sort of are." I laugh.

"Do you remember that time Conrad sucker-punched me on the porch?" Anna asks.

"Yeah."

"Leo grounded him and he fell down and cried. I still feel bad about it."

"Why? He hit *you*."

"Because I goaded him. I wanted to get him in trouble." She stares out the big plate-glass window at the pond. The sun is hitting the ice at a perfect angle, so that it shimmers like crystal, throwing off sparks. "I was so mean to him," Anna says.

"You were mean to everyone."

"After Leo sent him to his cabin, I locked myself in the bathroom and cried. I have no idea why." She gets up and goes over to the stove, picks up the metal jug, pours water into the kettle. "I saw some mint tea in the pantry," she says.

"I'll get it," I say.

"It's weird, the things we remember. There were probably a million worse things I did back then, but when the doctor told me about the cancer, that day with Conrad was what came into my mind. How horrible I'd been. And then he died the next summer."

"It was two summers later," I say. "You were working at that kibbutz in Santa Cruz."

"Why was I doing that? A kibbutz? I must have been on acid." She laughs, and for a moment she's entirely herself again. "I keep thinking if I'd been a nicer person, this wouldn't be happening to me. What if that whole karma thing is true? I could come back as a centipede. Or a blood clot."

"This is not your fault," I say. "And there's no such thing as karma."

"You don't know that."

But I do. Because if karma existed, I would be the one with cancer, not Anna. I take a deep breath, knowing what I have to do. All the years, I've kept my promise to Jonas. But Anna has to know this isn't her fault. "Do you remember how Leo kept ranting around the apartment screaming *why?* Breaking things and yelling at Mum?"

Anna nods.

"He blamed himself for Conrad. But it had nothing to do with him. It was my fault." I take a deep breath. "That day on the boat, when Conrad died—"

"I don't want to be dead, Elle," Anna says, interrupting. "I don't want to be *nothing* anymore . . . no more trees, no more you—just a pile of flesh rotting away. Remember Mum? And the worms?" She's half laughing, half crying.

"You won't," I say. "I won't let you."

"Poor Conrad," she says, her voice barely a whisper. "I wasn't even sad."

28

1998. May, New York.

The top of my mother's kitchen table was once an old barn door, its sharp edges softened by decades of family dinners. There is still a keyhole where a lock once fit, and woodworm boreholes like pinpricks, filled with years of food grime turned the consistency of earwax. When I was little I loved to root around in each hole with a fork, making tiny piles that seeded the tabletop like termite droppings. I sit here now, poking at the table with the tip of a ballpoint pen. Peter should have been here by now. It's Mum's birthday and we're taking her out for dinner. Our reservation is at eight. I pick up the kitchen phone and call the time. "At the tone, the time will be . . . seven . . . twenty-five . . . and fifty seconds. . . . At the tone, the time will be . . . seven . . . twenty-six . . . exactly." The new kitten walks into the kitchen. Marmalade back, white paws, yellow eyes. He looks up at me, wanting attention. I put him on the table and he starts eating the termite crumbs. Somewhere in the apartment I hear a crash. I push back my chair and go down the hall.

Mum is on a stepladder, alphabetizing the bookshelves.

"Oh good," she says. "You can help me with the poetry section." She pulls a stack of books off the shelf and hands them to me.

"Peter's running late." I sit down on the floor and start sorting books. "Does Primo Levi go in poetry?"

"I can never decide. Put him in philosophy for now."

I pick up *The Collected Poems of Dwight Burke* from the top of a pile and open it. On the front page is a handwritten dedication, scrawled in faded blue fountain pen: *For Henry's girls, who are sweeter than pachysandra, with hope that your lives will be filled with poetry and spice. Love, Dwight.*

"This is mine."

Mum glances down from the ladder. "I believe it's yours and Anna's."

"You're right. I'll send it to her."

"I'd keep it here. It's probably worth a fortune by now—a signed first edition of Burke. Jeremy will just want her to sell it."

On the back cover of the book is a faded black-and-white photo of Dwight Burke in a seersucker jacket and polka-dot bow tie. His face has the same kindly expression I remember from my childhood, a pleasant WASPiness.

"He was a nice man," I say.

"Such a tragedy," Mum says.

"He wore penny loafers with nickels in them. I should write to Nancy."

"Your father always thought he was a homosexual."

For years after Dwight Burke drowned, there were rumors he had killed himself—that Carter Ashe, the man he had gone to return the book to that spring day when my father and I went to collect his boxes, was Burke's lover. That Burke, a devout Catholic, was overcome with shame and guilt. My father insisted the rumors weren't true. Burke's clothes had been found in a careful pile on the banks of the Hudson, perfectly folded—everything but the boxer shorts he was wearing when they pulled him out of the water. "If he were planning to drown himself," my father had said, "why keep on his boxers? Dwight would have wanted to go out of the world the same way he came in. He was a poet. He loved symmetry."

"Author or subject?" Mum says. She's holding a book about Gandhi. She has moved on to biography.

"Subject. No one really cares who wrote it." I open the book of poetry in my hand. The poems are alive, odd, buzzing with insects and tender grasses. As I skim through, a verse catches my eye.

At the crest of the hill two stallions
backs black against a nectar wash
graze on the green-tang clover,
acorns to sniff out.
We lie together beneath the flowering hawthorn,
your white collar unbuttoned.

Once, I heard the sound
of wind under water, breathed in the sea
and survived.

I hope my father was right, that Dwight's drowning was an accident. I hope he left his lover's house that morning wanting nothing more than a bracing swim; that he lay on the banks of the Hudson River, listened to the water flowing past, breathed in the crocus blossoms, the sour-tart smell of crabgrass. He stripped down to his underwear and waded out into the muscular water, floated, watched clouds run across the sky, the flocking birds. He turned to swim back, but the landscape had changed.

Now he was drifting past an unfamiliar shore, pulled by a current too strong for him to fight.

The doorbell rings twice.

"Anybody home?" Peter calls out.

"We're back here," Mum calls. "Don't let the kitten out. He keeps trying to escape through the front door."

Peter is carrying an enormous bunch of flowers, daylilies and pale pink garden roses.

"Happy birthday, Wallace," he says, handing them to my mother. He looks around at the piles of books everywhere, my mother on the stepladder, alphabetizing. "Very festive."

"I'm too old for birthdays. I'll change my blouse and then we can go." She hands me the flowers. "Can you put these in water?"

Most of the streetlights on our block are out, deliberately broken by crackheads, who prefer the shadows. Peter and I walk home from dinner down the center of East Tenth Street, arm in arm, making ourselves a larger, less appealing target. Half the ground-floor apartments have BEWARE OF DOG signs in their windows, though we rarely see anyone walking a dog.

"Your mother was on excellent form tonight," Peter says. "She was practically beaming when we put her in the cab."

"She loves to be pampered. She pretends to scorn it, but take her to an overpriced restaurant and pick up the check? She acts like a delighted little girl who just got a new doll from Daddy. Also, she adores you. You make her feel young."

"And you?" Peter asks.

"I *am* young."

"Do you adore me?"

"Most of the time. Sometimes you're just irritating."

He pulls me to him, breathes me in. "You smell good. Lemony."

"Probably the cheese-clothed lemon wedge they gave me to squeeze on my fish."

"*Eau de Sole. Because every woman has one.* I think we could market that." Peter laughs.

"Not *every* woman," I say.

When we open the door to our apartment the air in the room feels charged, staticky. A faint metallic tang in its molecules. The phone is ringing and ringing, unanswered. Next to it, on the bookshelf, a vase of tulips has overturned, water pooling.

"Fucking cat stepped on the answering machine again. I'm going to strangle that damned cat." I throw my coat on the table and storm into our bedroom. There are two large windows in our bedroom. One on the right, over the bed; the other, which opens onto the fire escape, mostly obscured by heavy metal security bars that can only be opened from the inside, in case we need to make an escape. The window above our bed is now lying across it. Above the bed, a gaping hole, a splintered wooden frame. There's a man squatting on the windowsill. He grins at me, eyes glazed, seemingly unaware that he is teetering on the edge of a four-story drop. His greasy hair is matted, weeks of unwashed filth webbing the surface, as if spiders have nested in it, their microscopic eggs warmed by his damp, cradle-capped scalp. Somehow the man has managed to climb across the side of the building from the fire escape, span the free fall, and bash in our entire window frame. On the fire escape, outside the unlocked window bars, I can see our TV and VCR, the tangled cords of the answering machine.

The man follows my gaze, then looks back at me, cocks his head, as if deciding whether to go or stay. He wets his lips with the tip of his pink tongue and smiles. I scream for Peter, but it comes out as a whisper. Leering, the man starts to climb back into the room. My entire body coils. If I run at him right now, take him by surprise, body-slam him, he will fall backward into the night sky, splatter onto the cement, lie there, eyes wide open, while some other crackhead picks his pockets. I hurtle toward him like a battering ram before I can change my mind. And then I'm flat on my face, legs kicked out from under me. Peter strides past, tall, menacing. He is holding a kitchen knife. When he speaks, his voice is measured, blade-cold.

"Go out the way you came in," he says. "You can have the television—it's a rabbit-eared piece of crap. But you will leave the answering machine. There's a number on there I need." He takes a few steps forward. He is terrifying, powerful in a way I have never seen. A wolf, transformed by the full moon. "Now," he growls. "Before I have your blood on my hands."

The man backs out, leaps like a cat from the window onto the fire escape, picks up the TV under one arm, VCR under the other. I listen to the clang of his shoes descending the metal stairs, the rasp and rattle of cords dragging behind. On the floorboards beside my face, there's a spray of red. I've cut my chin. In the far corner of the room, the closet door slowly pushes open.

"Peter," I warn. "Behind you." Then I close my eyes to whatever is coming, wait for the creak of heavy footsteps on wooden floors. Instead, something silky brushes my face. I open my eyes. Next to me, the cat is licking my blood off the floor.

Later, after the police have come, after the answering machine has been dusted for prints, after we have swept up shards of glass and splintered wood, after I have forgiven Peter for shoving me to the ground, for the scar on my chin that I will carry the rest of my life, Peter asks, "If I hadn't stopped you, would you really have pushed him out the window?"

"I guess so. I don't know. I just reacted."

Peter frowns, looks at me as if he's seen something just under the surface of my skin, tiny broken capillaries, or a bluish hue—something that shouldn't be exposed to the light, and I feel the creep of shame, of exposure.

"You would have *killed* a man over a TV and VCR?"

"Not the TV. He was coming back inside for *me*," I say. "His eyes were black."

"We need to get out of this neighborhood before you end up in prison for murder."

"Screw you, Pete. I was terrified."

"I'm *joking*," Peter says. "Well, mainly." He laughs.

I grab the answering machine from the bureau and head into the living room. "You said there was a number you needed?"

Peter follows behind me. "Elle. Please. Come on." He picks a pack of cigarettes up from the coffee table, pats himself down for a lighter. "You risked your life to save a drowning man, for fuck's sake. You're hardly a killer. I'm the one who threatened him with a knife." He looks around for somewhere to put his ash. Settles for the geranium pot.

I turn away, pretend to look for something on the bookshelf.

"Bastard must've nicked my ashtray."

"It's in the dishwasher," I say.

Peter comes over to me, turns me around to face him, serious now. "I wouldn't give a toss if you had drawn and quartered that pig, hung his innards on a flagpole. The only thing I care about is that you are safe. You're my wife. The love of my life. There's nothing you could ever say or do to change that. I was just surprised, is all. I've never seen that side of you."

I wish so badly that I could believe him. But I don't. Some things can be forgiven—an affair, a cruel comment. But not the dirty, vile instinct lurking like a tapeworm in the dark folds of my gut, ready to emerge the moment it smells bloody meat. Until tonight, I thought it was gone. Pulled from my mouth inch by inch, foot by foot, year by year, leaving only the hollow space, the memory, of where it had once nested.

Peter pokes the tip of my nose with his finger. "Now, no more grumping, missy." He goes into the kitchen, comes back with an ashtray and a saucer of milk. "Here, kitty, kitty," he says, placing it on the radiator.

Tell him, I think. *Let him see you. Kill the worm. Be clean*. But instead I say, "Cats are lactose intolerant."

That night when we get into bed I feel a distance from him far greater than the crumple of sheets between us. The fault line I have cemented. I love him too much to risk losing him.

1999. July 31, Los Angeles.

My plane clears the last spiky, desolate ridge of mountains. Below me, an endless suburban sprawl, a drab blanket on the earth, the low-hung shimmer of the Pacific barely visible in the distance. The plane shudders through a gyre, lowers its landing gear with a rough throat clearing. Moments later, we hit tarmac and the passengers cheer. We are always expecting the worst.

I go straight from LAX to the hospital, dragging my heavy carry-on behind me, pushing through air and space with aggressive, panicked need. *I cannot be too late. I cannot be too late*. There's a taxi waiting for me—Jeremy has arranged everything—but the driver is lazy, unobservant. He manages to miss every light, slows to let other cars merge, carefully picks out the Murphy's Law route. By the time we pull up in front of the hospital, my teeth are ground to a chalk, and I've gone from 15 percent to 10 percent to shoving a few dollar bills in his hand and saying, "Asshole," under my breath.

Inside, a guard points me to the elevators and I run, air-lifting my suitcase off the polished palazzo floor. A crowd of people are ahead of me at the elevator bank, all looking up, hoping to divine which elevator will arrive first. By some miracle, the doors directly in front of me open. I press 11, then hit the doors close button repeatedly, hoping they will shut before anyone else gets on, but nothing happens. A woman in a head scarf and wig steps in just as the doors are closing. Cancer. The elevator sits there. Shut, tomblike.

"I think this one is out of service." I press the open button. Press it again. I can feel a claustrophobia rising inside my chest, as if my body itself is trapping me. But then the elevator starts to move. It rumbles slowly up one floor and stops, opens its doors. When it is clear that no one is getting on, the elevator pulls away and heads up one more flight. Again, we stop, wait an interminably long time.

"Some kid must have pushed every button," I say.

"It's Shabbat," the woman says.

"You must be fucking kidding me." I'm on the Sabbath elevator, which stops on every floor. "I don't have time for this shit."

The woman looks at me as though I have contagion. Moves away.

"I'm sorry," I say. "I didn't mean—" I'm finding it impossible to breathe. "You don't understand. I can't be late. My sister is dying."

The woman stares at the ceiling, mouth pinched in sour contempt.

I have always considered myself a tolerant person. Each to her own. Yet right now, when what's on the line is not punishment for turning on a light switch but whether I will get to my beautiful sister in time to say goodbye—to climb into the hospital bed beside her, hold her in my arms, admit it was me who tore her Bobby Sherman poster, make her laugh with me one last time—right this second, I feel only pure rage at the stupidity of all religions. I close my eyes and pray to a God I don't believe in that Anna will wait for me. I need to tell her what I did.

Book Four

THIS SUMMER

29

Six Weeks Ago. June 19, the Back Woods.

Every morning on the pond, before Peter and the kids come in, I sweep the floorboards, making tight neat piles of dust and sand and earwigs that I then transfer into the dustpan, pile by pile, before shaking the whole thing outside underneath the nearest bush. And every morning on the pond, in that moment, I think of Anna. The briefest flash. Not so much a memory of her, as the recognition of a tiny but indelible mark, a living piece of her that still lives in me. Anna taught me how to sweep when I was seven. "Not like that, moron," she corrected from the porch as I swung the broom around the room like a pendulum, lifting billows of dirt and dust ahead of me. "You have to do small strokes close to the ground. Make lots of little piles. Sweep inward. Otherwise *that's* what happens."

This morning when I put the broom away in its place between the refrigerator and the pantry wall, it slips sideways, falls into the cob-webby gap behind the fridge. I sigh, knowing I have no choice but to retrieve it from the spidery darkness. My mother always cleans the camp before we come, but only the places she can see. When we arrived for the summer yesterday, the first thing Maddy noticed was a massive mouse nest in the rafter above the pantry shelves.

"I'm pretending I haven't seen it," I overheard my mother saying to her as I passed the back door, lugging bags of our clothes in from the car. "I leave the truly horrible things for when your mother arrives."

"I heard that," I said.

"A family of muskrats is living in the water lilies," she said to Maddy, ignoring me. "They're very sweet—three little ones swim out behind their mother every morning. There were four, but I found one floating in the weeds when I was out in the canoe. His body was like a fur log. Full rigor mortis."

"That's nice, Mum. Thanks for sharing that with my daughter," I called out over my shoulder.

"Are you planning to move in permanently? I've never seen so much stuff."

I stopped at the end of the path and stood looking out at the pond, the bright June sky. A perfect day for a swim. "I'm so happy to be here, I can't stand it," I said to no one.

But this morning is gray and overcast, too cold for a swim. I leave the broom where it has fallen, walk down the path to our cabin, and fish around my canvas duffel for running shoes and a jog bra. Peter's clothes are in a little heap on the floor where he took them off last night. I hang his white cotton shirt on a hook, fold his threadbare moleskin trousers and put them over the back of the chair.

Peter stirs behind me.

"It's early," I whisper. "Go back to sleep."

He turns over, smiles at me, hair matted to his forehead, his pillow sleep-wrinkled onto his cheek. "Cozy," he says. He looks so sweet, like a little boy.

"Back soon." I kiss his eyelids, breathe in his familiar smell of salt and cigarettes.

"I'll make breakfast," he mumbles.

I jog up our steep driveway, dodging roots and winter potholes in the soil, before heading down the dirt road that skirts the pond and ends at the sea. The woods are quiet, barely stirring. Most of the houses haven't yet been opened for the season. June can be rainy and damp. The fresh morning air feels like a splash of cold water. With each thud of my feet on the sandy ground I can feel my body waking up, as if I'm coming back to life after a long hibernation, sniffing for bees in the clover, looking for just the right tree to scratch. It's this way every year.

As I near the ocean, I pick up speed, eager for the dense woods to give way to low scrub and cranberry, eager for the sea. Around the last bend in the road, I'm surprised to see Jonas sitting on the shoulder, binoculars dangling around his neck.

"What are you doing here?" I'm panting when I reach him. "You said you weren't coming up 'til next week." I sit down beside him.

"Last-minute decision. One hundred percent humidity, the whole city stank of armpit, and then the air conditioning in the loft decided to stop working."

"Oh, c'mon. Admit it. It's because you missed me so much." I laugh.

Jonas smiles. "Well, that too. It seems impossible for us to get any proper time together in the city. We're all so crazed. And then suddenly it's summer. Thank Christ. Kids happy to be here?"

"Hardly. We haven't even been here a day and already they're complaining about no Wi-Fi. Peter's threatening to send them all to military school."

"He up for a bit?"

"Two weeks. Then the usual back-and-forth on weekends. Are you on your way to the beach, or already been?"

"Been. I went to check on the nesting shorebirds."

"And?"

"They're nesting."

"Are the fences up?"

He nods. "They've cordoned off half the beach."

"I fucking hate piping plovers."

"You hate anyone who doesn't understand that *you* own the Back Woods," Jonas says.

"The whole thing is ridiculous. The paper says the plover population has *decreased* since they started roping off those sections of beach to protect them."

Jonas nods. "It's possible the smell of humans was keeping the coyotes away from the eggs."

"So, what's been happening at your end? Gina good?"

Jonas hesitates a hitch before answering, almost imperceptible, but I notice it. "Ecstatic to be here. And already looking for ways to avoid my mother. She left to go sailing before I woke up. Took the Rhodes out to check the rigging."

"Sailing." Even after all these years, the word sticks on my tongue, as if I'm speaking a Namibian click language.

"Sailing," Jonas says.

It hangs in the air like a slow-falling rock. I feel the unpeeling of something tender and awful and sad and shameful between us, as I always do. But Jonas breaks its fall, and the moment passes.

"She wants to buy a Cat 19. I'm on the fence."

"Jack will be psyched if she does." My bright voice rings false, and I know he hears it, too. But it's what we do, what we've done for years now. We drag our past behind us like a weight, still shackled, but far enough back that we never have to see, never have to openly acknowledge who we once were.

Above us, a peregrine wings the sky. We watch it peak into the clouds, turn, and plunge headlong toward the earth, sighting its prey.

Jonas stands up. "I need to head back. My mother wants help planting marigolds. The mosquitoes are terrible this year. Stop by for a drink later. We're home tonight."

"We'd love that."

He gives me a quick kiss on the cheek and heads off. I watch him walk away until he rounds the bend, out of sight. It is easier this way.

Mum is in her usual spot on the porch sofa when I get back. Peter is in the kitchen making coffee.

"Morning, gorgeous," he calls out. "How was the first run of the summer?"

"Heaven. I feel like I can finally breathe."

"Coffee's on its way. Did you make it to the ocean?"

"I did. The tide was just going out. I found this." I walk over to him, hold out my open palm. "I've never seen a horseshoe crab this teensy. It's perfect."

"How was the water?" my mother asks.

"I didn't swim—I was in my running clothes."

"You could have swum naked," Mum says. A criticism.

"I could have," I say. It has begun. "I ran into Jonas on the road. He invited us all for a drink later."

"Excellent," Peter says.

"Did you notice? The gypsy caterpillars are back," Mum says.

"The road to the beach looked fine."

"They'll get there. They're like locusts. Half the trees between here and Pamela's are bare. It's too depressing. That horrible pattering sound of droppings raining down onto the path. I had to put my rebozo over my head and run, yesterday morning."

"Caterpillars shit?" Peter asks.

"It looks like beige coffee grounds," I say.

"That happened to me once," my mother says. "It turned out I had an ulcer."

"Your mother is speaking in tongues again, Elle," Peter says.

"Your husband is impertinent," Mum says. "In any event, if you ever find what appear to be coffee grounds in the toilet bowl, you'll know."

"That's disgusting," I say.

"Nevertheless."

"Coffee, Wallace?" Peter asks, coming out of the kitchen with a fresh pot.

I adore my husband.

Four weeks ago. July 4, Wellfleet, Massachusetts.

We hear about the dead child at the Fourth of July parade. A five-year-old girl, buried alive this morning when a dune collapsed on her at Higgins Hollow. Her mother was out on a sandbar doing yoga. When she turned to check on her daughter, all she could see was her daughter's pink bucket, which at first appeared to be floating four inches above the ground.

"I will never get that image out of my head. That little hand sticking up out of the sand." I'm standing with Jonas and his mother under the shade of a towering maple, watching the parade. Gina, Maddy, and Finn have waded into the crowd hoping to get a front-row view.

"What did I always say to you kids about climbing on the dunes?" Jonas's mother says now, with a tone of smug "I told you so" satisfaction. "See?"

Jonas looks at me in amazement and bursts out laughing.

"That's *extremely* insensitive of you," his mother says, and turns her back to us. "You're disgraceful."

I've been trying my best to keep a straight face. But I can't help it. I feel like I'm fourteen again, standing in Jonas's living room being chided by her for ever having liked an overtly racist television program like *Little House on the Prairie*. Or the time she preached at Anna on the beach about the evils of wearing a bikini. "You're allowing yourself to be objectified by men." Anna had pulled off her bikini top and shimmied at her like a stripper, before walking down to the water topless. Once, Jonas's mother made the grave mistake of chastising my mother for bringing a bag of charcoal briquettes to a bonfire. "Charcoal, Wallace? There's barely a tree left in the Congo. You might as well go to Virunga and shoot the mountain gorillas yourself."

"I would, but the airfare is extravagant," Mum had said.

Then she'd dumped the entire bag of charcoal onto the bonfire, which rose in a glorious blaze. "You're *disgraceful*," Jonas's mother had spat. Jonas and I had stood there, jaws dropped, thrilled by the sight of our mothers doing battle, before running away down the beach, laughing and shouting, "*You're disgraceful!*" at each other.

Jonas grins at me. "You're *disgraceful*," he mouths.

"*You're* disgraceful," I mouth back.

A float of teenage girls in lobster suits drives by. They wave and smile, throw candy corn into the crowds. Behind them, the local middle school marching band plays an off-key version of "Eye of the Tiger." Gina approaches us with Maddy and Finn in tow. All three of them are waving plastic American flags stapled to balsa sticks. Maddy is wearing a candy necklace.

"What's so funny?" Gina puts her arm through Jonas's.

"Look!" Finn waves his flag at me. "Gina bought us flags."

"You shouldn't have," I say to Gina. "Those things are a waste of money."

"It's for the war veterans," Gina says in a tone that makes it clear I've offended her.

"Of course," I say quickly. "It was very generous of you."

"It was *three* dollars."

"I just meant: look how happy you made them." Maddy and Finn have run back down the hill and are waving their flags excitedly at four weather-worn old men in a brown Oldsmobile holding up a Rotary Club banner.

Jonas puts his hand on my arm. Points to the Oldsmobile. "I could swear those are the same old geezers *we* used to wave at."

"I'm pretty sure they swap them out every ten or twenty years. Remember the guy in the Uncle Sam hat who screamed at me for wearing a Walter Mondale T-shirt and chased us down the street?"

Jonas laughs.

"So," Gina says, pushing back into the conversation. "What was so funny?"

Jonas's mother turns, purse-lipped. "A small child died on the beach earlier today. Your husband and Elle seemed to think it a cause for merriment. Anyway, I'm leaving. It's like an oven here. I'd appreciate it if you could stop at the store on your way home and pick up rice cakes and Clamato juice. And we need paprika." She stalks off without saying goodbye.

"Whoa," Gina says. "What's up with *that*?"

"She's in a huff because we were laughing at her," Jonas says.

"About a child dying?"

"Of course not. She was being tone-deaf."

"So . . . what?" Gina presses.

"Something she used to say when we were kids," Jonas says. "It wouldn't translate."

"I'm sure I can keep up." Gina bristles. "Whatever. You two can keep your secret code."

Jonas takes an irritated breath. "She called us disgraceful."

"She's right," Gina snaps.

I feel like I've been slapped in the face. I look over at Jonas for an explanation, but he is intent on Gina, his eyes a slow burn.

"Sorry," Gina says quickly, backpedaling. "I have no idea why I said that. It's hot and I barely slept."

"It's fine," I say. But it isn't. Her hostility, her insecurity makes no sense. Gina has always had an unquestioning self-confidence, a complete lack of superego. She *likes* herself. When Gina and Jonas were first together, I knew she felt threatened by me. Not because she had any idea how much Jonas had once loved me, he has never told her. What made her jealous back then were the ancient roots of our friendship—a shared history that would always exclude her. But that was a hundred years ago. We've all made our own history together. We've grown older together. As couples. As friends. Yet it feels as if just now, for a quick second, she lost control and revealed her true feelings, a jealousy and deep resentment of me that she has kept hidden all these years. Then, realizing what had escaped, tried to put it back in the bottle. Something must have triggered this. It's about more than lack of sleep, the heat. Something is going on between them, some strain that Jonas hasn't acknowledged to me.

"I'm going to get the kids and head off," I say, backing out. "You're right, Gina. This place is a furnace. Maybe see you at the fireworks later?"

"We're skipping it," Gina says. "I have the regatta tomorrow morning. Six a.m."

"*I* might come," Jonas says.

Driving out of town with the kids, I pass Jonas and Gina outside the grocery store. They are arguing. Gina gesticulating at him, livid. She's crying. Jonas has a plastic bottle of Clamato under his arm. The appeal of tomato juice laced with clam has always puzzled me. Jonas shakes his head angrily at whatever she is saying. Cars inch forward in front of me. I know I should look away, but I don't. The yellow light turns to red. Above the low thrum of the air conditioner, through the closed car window, I hear Gina shout, "Fuck you!" I glance behind me to see if the kids have heard, but they are deep in their phones. Jonas says something to Gina, then turns and walks away down the street. Gina calls after him—begs him to stop—but he keeps going. I watch her shoulders slump. I feel like a Peeping Tom. She wipes the dripping snot from her nose with the back of her black shirt-sleeve, leaving a streak of mucus that glistens and shimmers in the sun like a snail trail. There is something so defeated in her posture—a vulnerability I have never seen before—and it makes me sad for her. I look away, begging the light to change before she notices our car. Behind me, Maddy rolls down her window, waves to Gina, calling out. Gina looks up just as the light changes.

"Mom," Maddy says as we pull onto the highway into an endless line of post-parade traffic, "Gina told us there are alligators in the sewers in New York. Is it true?"

"Did she?" I laugh. "Did she also tell you that when you play the *White Album* backward it says, "Paul is dead?"

"Who's Paul?" Finn says.

"I don't think there are alligators down there, Maddy. Although you never know. When I was four years old I watched my mother's boyfriend flush a baby alligator down the toilet."

"How big was it?" Maddy says. "Wouldn't it have gotten stuck?"

"Like a gecko."

"What if they climb out onto the sidewalk and kill people?" Finn asks.

"I'm pretty sure you're safe, bunny."

"I don't want to walk to school anymore."

Traffic creeps along. Bicyclists pass us on the verge.

"You know," I say, "when Anna and I were little, our father gave us Sea-Monkeys for Christmas. They came with a plastic aquarium and a packet of Sea-Monkey eggs. It said on the box that when you put the eggs in water, they would grow into instant pets. There was a little packet of food with a tiny spoon."

"They still have those," Maddy says. "We should get some. They sound cool."

"Well, *-ish*," I say. "They were supposed to turn into creatures that looked like naked sea horses with long human legs and crowns and lived in underwater castles."

"Can we get some?" Finn asks.

"No."

"Why not? I want a pet."

"Because they are bullshit."

"Mom!" Maddy says. "Language."

"Fair enough." I laugh. "Anna and I waited and waited for the Sea-Monkey family to appear. We ran home every day after school to see if they had hatched into little kings and queens. And lo and behold, after about a week these microscopic shrimp-like things began to dart around the water."

"So, then what happened?" Maddy asks.

"Nothing. They didn't grow. They stayed that way. It turned out they were just microscopic krill."

"That's what whales eat," Maddy says to Finn.

"I *know* that," Finn says.

"End of story: One day we got home from school and they were gone. My mother had poured them down the sink. She said most of the Sea-Monkeys were dead on the bottom of the container, and the aquarium was turning into a breeding ground for mosquitoes."

"That's so sad," Maddy says.

"Maybe, maybe not. We never got to see them grow, but who knows—maybe they finally grew after she flushed them. Maybe there are kingdoms of Sea-Monkeys in the sewers, full of teensy kings and queens and princesses in their minuscule crowns."

"I hope you're right," Maddy says. "That would be the best thing ever."

"I do, too, sweet pea. Anyway, my point is, maybe Gina is right about the alligators. Maybe they are down there living on tiny Sea-Monkeys."

"No!" Maddy says. "I hate that. That would be horrible."

It's been years since I've thought about the Sea-Monkeys. How Anna and I watched that plastic aquarium every day. How we hoped and waited and clapped when tiny things began to move, and felt bitterly disappointed when that was all. The waiting begins early, I think. The lies begin early. But so do dreams and hopes and stories.

I pull off the highway onto our one-lane dirt road, head into the

Back Woods, praying I don't meet another car coming out. I hate backing up, and this stretch of road has no turnoffs.

Every year the town sets off fireworks from an old wooden barge in the harbor, testing fate, sparks aiming for shore as the barge creaks and groans. My favorite place to watch the fireworks has always been from the end of the pier that juts farthest out into the bay from the town wharf. Walking out past the line of briny trawlers, their nets piled damp, tethered to the dock like horses outside a saloon. Past the dinghies, bobbing on their moorings. Out to where the deeper water licks the tops of the pylons, far from the crowds. The smell of fishiness and wet timber. Most people gather at the town beach to watch the display: cascades of color rocketing into the night, illuminating the roof of the sky, comet tails and giant sparklers reflecting onto the bay like a million stars, so that for an instant, the sea becomes the sky. Sitting at the end of the pier, legs dangling down above the dark water, the stars appear right beneath our feet, slipping past us under the pier, into that mysterious world. It was Jonas who first brought me to this spot.

The blank, unbearable heat of the day has alchemized into a perfect summer night. Soft breezes in the dark. The kids have run off somewhere to watch the fireworks with their friends. Peter, Mum, and I drink white wine from paper cups, waiting, anticipating that first spiraling whistle. Any minute now, my mother will start to complain.

"Mind if I pull up a chair?" Jonas materializes out of the night, a phantom, silent approach, just as he used to do when we were young and I walked to the beach on my own. I have rarely if ever heard his footfall.

"They said nine p.m. on the dot, but as usual they're making us wait," Mum says.

"Gina not coming?" Pete asks, as Jonas sits down beside him.

"She sends her love. She badly wanted to come, but she's been feeling a bit under the weather."

I look over at Jonas, surprised by the white lie. It is unlike him. I know he can feel my steady gaze, but he doesn't turn.

An hour later, when all that remains in the air is the tang of gunpowder and the skies have regained their gravity, we head back to round up the kids. Peter and Mum are in the lead, laughing and bickering. I slow to let them pull farther ahead of Jonas and me before bringing up his lie.

"I wasn't lying," he says, annoyed. "I was making Gina's excuses. It's called being polite."

"Actually, it's called lying, when you lie," I say, not letting him off the hook.

"She was having a shitty day. Am I really required to explain that to Peter and your mother?" he snaps.

"Don't be a jerk. I was just asking. I saw you shouting at each other outside the grocery store."

"Sorry."

"So? What's going on?"

"Gina lost her gallery in May. She hasn't told a soul—she feels too humiliated. Meanwhile I'm having my big show in the fall. She thinks I told you, and she's upset."

"But you didn't."

"Well, I have now."

We slow to a stop, stand together looking out at the sleeping boats. I wait for him.

"The fight was my fault," he says. "I was extremely angry with her for speaking to you that way. I lost my temper."

Jonas championing me over Gina gives me a jolt of cat-cream pleasure I shouldn't feel, but I say, "That was dumb."

"Gina loves you, you know that. But she knows we talk about everything. I think that if my oldest friend was a man, it would be easier for her."

"That's ridiculous," I scoff. "Gina is the Rock of Gibraltar." But I know what he says is true. I've seen it: a fissure; the vulnerability she revealed today when she thought no one was watching; the way her body luffed, wind knocked from her, as Jonas walked away and didn't look back. And yet some lizard-brain instinct in me recognizes that openly acknowledging even the slightest rift between Gina and me will leave all of us more exposed—though to what, exactly, I don't know. A nervous energy.

"You should have stayed home with her tonight," I say. "Patched things up."

"We did. We're good. And you and I always watch the fireworks together."

"We could have skipped a year."

"It's our tradition."

"So is eating turkey at Thanksgiving. But frankly turkey is dry and bland. Who really likes it?"

"I do," Jonas says. He links his arm tightly through mine and we head down the pier to join the others.

Five Days Ago. July 27, the Back Woods.

Sunday. Peter, Mum, and the kids have gone off to the flea market, their weekly ritual of looking through tables of other people's junk to find pearls, usually in the form of some hideous laminated reproduction of a Gibson girl drinking Coca-Cola, or a book about fly-fishing that Peter thinks might one day come in handy. Afterward they have lunch at the Clam Shack, where every time Peter tries to convince the kids to eat raw oysters and lobster rolls, and every time they order foot-long hot dogs in buttered buns.

I walk down to the edge of the pond, take off my bathing suit, lay my towel on the warm sand. Above me, the trees wave their branches to me as if they are greeting an old friend. I'm thinking about Bain de Soleil, its thick, orange oiliness, burnt caramel smell, zero sun block—how Anna and I used to try to attract the sun rather than block it—when the phone starts ringing in the Big House. I try to ignore it, but it doesn't stop. Mum doesn't believe in answering machines. "If they want to reach me they can call back."

It is Peter's office. They need him to fly to Memphis in the morning for a story. Flight details. Hotel information. Local telephone numbers.

I look around for a pen and something to write on. All I can find is a takeout menu and a flyer for a local production of *The Silver Cord*. Nearby, thumbtacked to a wooden shelf above the phone, is my mother's list of important phone numbers. It has been there since I was a child, by now covered in scribbles and corrections, names of local plumbers and electricians, the Park Ranger station; numbers crossed out in ballpoint pen, rewritten in pencil; a peace sign Anna once drew in green Magic Marker. In the middle of the list, written in faded blue ink, Conrad's mother's phone number in Memphis is still visible. The handwriting is Leo's.

"Wasn't your stepfather from Memphis?" Peter says, throwing a few things into a carry-on bag. "Socks."

"He was." I pull open a lower drawer and take out four pairs of socks.

"Have you ever been?"

"Once. For Conrad's funeral."

"Of course. I wasn't thinking."

"It was a long time ago."

"How old was Conrad when he died?"

"Jack's age," I say. "Do you need undershirts?"

"Christ. How do you ever get over something like that?" Peter throws a few last things into the bag—a pack of gum, a comb, the book from his bedside table—and zips it.

I sit down on the edge of the bed. "You don't."

Down the path, I hear Finn and Maddy arguing. "No shouting on the pond," my mother yells from the porch.

"I can't believe you're abandoning me with that crazy woman." I chip at the red nail polish on my big toe. My heels look like they are made of rhino horn. "I need a pedicure."

"Come with me. We can have a romantic getaway."

"In Memphis?"

"Anywhere we can have sex without your mother hearing us."

"Much as I love you, Memphis is the last place on earth I ever want to see again."

Peter sits down beside me on the bed. "I'm serious. It'll be cathartic. I'll take you out for barbecue spaghetti."

I stare out the cabin door, mind searching for a simple excuse. The pond is golden, glassy, tipping toward evening. Here and there a few small turtle heads have popped up like thumbs, basking in the last of the sun. I wonder whether Peter is right—whether there could ever be such a thing as catharsis.

"*Come*," he says again. "You'll be rescuing me from four depressing days on my own in the murder capital of America. We can have loud sex. You can get a pedicure."

"I doubt Mum's willing to watch the kids," I say. But even as I sidestep, I hear my mother's voice in my head, the pep talk she would always give me and Anna when we were afraid of anything—the dark, a bad grade in social studies, the idea that, one day, she would die and rot: "We are not a family of cowards, girls. We face our fears head on."

"Let *me* ask her," Peter says. "You know if I ask, she'll say yes."

"True."

"And you can visit Conrad's grave."

30

Three Days Ago. July 29, Memphis.

The cemetery is prettier than I remember—an arboretum of mature flowering trees and shaded slopes giving way to wide lawns dotted with the gray teeth of the dead. Carved angels cling to the edges of tombstones. It takes me half an hour to find Conrad's grave. I make my way through row after row of Chinese headstones and crumbling Confederate graves. Groups of tourists wander the cemetery listening to an audio tour of *Dead People Greatest Hits*. I watch them move like lemmings between the tombstones.

His marker is small, strewn with spongy fallen petals—pale pinks browning to rot. A flowering dogwood towers above, shading and littering his plot. Nearby is a large granite obelisk with a nice low ledge to sit on, the ground around it carpeted with thick green grass. Someone has recently left a bouquet of fresh flowers. I move the flowers to one side and sit down on the cool stone seat. Anna hated grassy graves. "They're grassier because there are more worms in the soil. Think about it." Instead, I think about the picnic lunches Anna and I had as children, when we would visit our grandparents. Sitting on the cool marble tombstone of the suicide grave, playing with our paper dolls. Mine were awkward, bulbous stick figures with rounded feet and simple faces. Anna's were always magazine-perfect—girls with Susan Dey hair, boys with brown shags. An endless wardrobe of miniature clothes—hip-huggers and purple clogs, French sailor sweaters, bandana bikinis, Fair Isles, kilts with teensy safety pins. Our secret one-dimensional world—the world we pretended was ours as we sat on a sad man's grave eating ham sandwiches on buttered white bread, looking out across the old cemetery to our grandparents' house on the hill, the fields of cows and cud beyond.

I stand up, brush off the back of my skirt, walk over to Conrad's grave. The grass here is weedy, sparse. This at least would have made Anna happy. The headstone is plain. No inscription. Only Conrad's name and dates: *1964–1983*. He was barely eighteen when he died. A stupid kid who dreamed of being Hulk Hogan, who loved his mother more than she loved him, who wanted his father's approval. It would have made him so happy to see Leo desperate, falling to pieces, after he drowned—to know how much his father truly loved him. I try to picture Conrad doing pull-ups in his doorway, arguing with Anna, his ugly terry cloth bathrobe, reading a comic on his cabin steps. Anything. But all I can see is his face, white with fear, terrified, pleading, while Jonas sat beside me on the boat and stayed my hand. The sudden understanding in his eyes before the waves sucked him under. I think about the choices I've made—the ones I've spent my life hiding from. The choice Jonas and I made that blustery day. The choice I made to keep Conrad's secret from Mum; if I had had the courage to tell my mother—to allow *her* life to fall apart instead of mine—Conrad would still be alive. It wasn't only Conrad's dreams that died. Stupid, stupid children.

Conrad ruined everything. Jonas ruined everything. I ruined everything.

I lie down on Conrad's grave, put my mouth to the ground, and though I know he will never hear me, talk to him. I tell him I'm sorry. *You didn't deserve this. You did something terrible*, I say, *but I did something worse*. I tell him about the prices I've paid, hoping it will count for something, though I know the burden of carrying a secret is nothing compared to the burden of earth he carries. I tell him about Peter, about the kids. And, for the first time in almost thirty-five years, I cry for him.

Peter is at the hotel bar, shoulders slumped, drinking something amber on the rocks. I can tell from the doorway that he's had a long day. I know he's waiting for me, looking forward to unburdening himself. But all I want is to go up to the room and crawl under the covers, hide from him, from myself. I am backing out when he turns, sees me.

"Memphis is a truly crap city," he says as I pull up a barstool next to him. "And I can't smoke in the bar."

"What are you drinking?" I pick up his glass and take a sip. "Rum? That's a weird choice. You okay? You look tired."

"I spent the day talking to the dead. It's no wonder this city has fallen into economic ruin. These people are so numbed by poverty and violence. It's tragic. I interviewed a schoolteacher who's already had three of his students murdered this year. Kids. It's like a war zone, but even more pointless. And you?"

"I spent the day talking to the dead, too."

Peter drains his drink and signals the bartender. "You went to the cemetery?"

"I did."

"How was *that*?"

"It was strange to see it after all these years." I picture the grave—Conrad's headstone already worn by time, my tears watering bare patches of dirt. "It took me a while to find it. In my memory, he was buried on top of a hill. But the grave was down in a low hollow. All I really remember about the funeral is how muggy it was, and Anna complaining that her hair was getting frizzy and refusing to say the Lord's Prayer."

"Classic Anna."

"Conrad's mother never said a single word to any of us. Not even to Mum. And my stepsister Rosemary, clinging to her mother—this little white ghosty thing."

"Do they still live here?"

"I have no idea. We never saw them after that. Leo left Mum a few months after Conrad died."

"How old was Rosemary?"

"When Conrad died?"

Peter nods.

"Maybe fourteen?"

"Were you friends?"

"With Rosemary? God, no."

"Why not?"

"She was . . . I don't know. Odd. Spectrum-y—like she missed all the normal social cues, if that makes sense. I remember she liked to sing hymns."

"You should look her up, see if she still exists."

"She probably moved away ages ago."

"Maybe, maybe not."

"Anyway, it would be too awkward. Calling out of the blue after all these years of making zero effort."

"Better late than never." Peter gets up off his barstool. "I'm going outside for a smoke."

"You really should quit."

"One of these days," he says. I watch him cross the lobby away from me, push through the revolving doors out onto the sooty sidewalk.

Two Days Ago, July 30. Memphis.

Rosemary lives in a quiet, nondescript neighborhood on the east side of the city. Block after block of almost identical ranch houses with tidy front yards. But I know her house the minute the taxi pulls up: on the front landing is the alligator umbrella stand from her mother's porch, its mouth still agape after all these years. Rosemary comes to the door holding a small dog—a rescue, she tells me. Her hair is beige, cut short. She's a professor of musicology. Her husband Edmund teaches quantum physics. They have no children.

"My area is Baroque," she says as I follow her into the living room. "I have herbal tea or decaf. Caffeine makes me jittery."

"Decaf's great."

"Make yourself comfortable. I made a carrot cake." She heads into the kitchen, leaving me alone in the living room. The mantelpiece is covered with framed photographs: Rosemary looking drab in a cap and gown; Rosemary and her husband on their wedding day; Rosemary as a young girl riding on a trolley car with Leo. There isn't a single photo of Conrad. I pick up a silver-framed photo of Rosemary with an elderly couple on a cruise ship. It takes me a moment to realize the man is Leo. He has his arm around a woman I recognize as Rosemary's mother.

"They remarried," Rosemary says, coming up behind me.

"I didn't know."

"A few years after my brother died." She takes the photo from me and puts it back on the mantel. "They've both passed."

"I'm sorry."

"Well, it's what happens." She hands me a slice of carrot cake. "I use applesauce instead of sugar. And how is Anna?"

"Anna died, too. Almost twenty years ago. As a matter of fact, tomorrow is the anniversary of her death."

"You two never really got along, as I recall," Rosemary says.

I bristle. "She was my best friend. I feel her absence every single day."

"Life can be lonely."

We sit there together silent, each pretending to concentrate on eating.

"This is delicious," I say after a while.

"The applesauce makes it moist. So, what brings you to Memphis?"

"My husband Peter. He had to come here for work. Mum's at the pond, taking care of the kids. We have three."

"And is this the first time you've been back?"

I nod. "I should have come sooner. I visited Conrad's grave yesterday."

"I've never been. Cemeteries depress me. Mother visited him once a week. She never quite recovered from it all. I think she blamed you."

I feel as if she's thrown a glass of ice water in my face.

"I'm sorry," I say, feeling the inadequacy of those words. "I couldn't save him."

"Oh, well. If you'd jumped in he probably would have pulled you down with him in his panic. He was that type." She takes a big bite of cake, chews slowly. "You saw him drown."

"Yes."

"That must be a hard thing to get out of your head."

"I never have."

Rosemary fingers a small cross that hangs around her neck. She seems to be considering something. "I've tried to picture it: Conrad falling off the boat into the cold open ocean. He was a terrible swimmer. What was it like, watching him go under? I wish I'd been there to see it myself."

It is such a bizarre thing to say. "I don't understand."

"Don't you?" She gives me a long hard look. "You remember that summer he came home to stay with me and Mother?"

I nod, feeling a dull dread.

"Well, that was my idea. I was quite lonely after Con left. Mother was in a mood half the time. I'd sit on the porch swing, try to stay quiet as a mouse. She said noise made her nervy. Anyway, Conrad, Mother, and I made a plan to drive across country to my uncle's home in Santa Fe. I was so excited. The first night Conrad was home, he came to my room after Mother was asleep. I woke up with him on top of me. I could barely breathe. I tried to call out for help, but he kept his hand over my mouth. I sobbed into his palm." She pauses, picks a bit of lint off her trousers. "The whole time he was raping me, he kept saying your name."

The room bleeds into a white blur. I feel as though I am being sucked slow motion through the center of a star. I can vaguely hear the low hum of the air conditioner. Somewhere down the street children are shouting. I imagine them playing with a hose, dousing each other in cool water. A car drives past. Then another.

"He came to my room almost every night that summer. I was thirteen years old." Her face is impassive, bland. She could be talking about cats. "My brother was a monster. Every night I prayed to God he would die. And finally God answered my prayers." She pauses. "Part of me has always wondered if it wasn't God who answered my prayers, but you."

Rosemary reaches over to the coffeepot and pours herself another inch of decaf, carefully adds two sugar cubes with a little pronged tong. "Edmund wanted children, but I could never see the point. More coffee?"

I am too numb to respond.

The front doorbell rings. "Oh good," Rosemary says, standing up. "That'll be the dry cleaning."

Outside Rosemary's house, the sun is still shining, the air dripping with heat and the exhaustion of being. A boy bicycles past, ringing his tinny bell. Weeds grow up from a crack in the sidewalk. I come to a crosswalk. The smell of banana peel, a vacant brown lot strewn with plastic bags that float and settle like a broken laundry line of wife-beaters. I need to call Jonas.

31

Yesterday. July 31, the Back Woods.

"What time are people coming?"

"I said sevenish." My mother has her head deep in the refrigerator, hunting for a lost tube of tomato paste.

I grab a white linen tablecloth from a drawer and throw it over the porch table. "Are we eight or ten?"

"Nine, including Jonas's insufferable mother. I don't know why we had to include her. I hate odd numbers."

I take a stack of pasta bowls from the shelf, carry them carefully to the table, and set them around. "What about Dixon and Andrea?"

Mum hands me a pile of cloth napkins. "Dixon, yes. Andrea, no. Use these. And the brass candlesticks."

"Why not?"

"That dreadful son of hers is visiting from Boulder for the weekend. She asked if she could bring him, and I said no."

"You truly are the absolute worst."

She hands me a breadboard. "Why on earth would I include him? He didn't know Anna."

I bring wineglasses to the table, two by two. Forks and knives. Salt. Pepper. I concentrate on each small task as if it is a lifeline, anchoring me to the present, to my life *right now.* I cannot get Rosemary's words out of my head, her mundane, unvarnished voice as she handed me absolution, a pardon for my crime.

"What else needs doing?" I say.

"You can open a few bottles of claret to let them breathe. And grate the cheese. There's a hunk of Parmesan on the door of the refrigerator." She places a white ironstone compote filled with limes and bright green pears in the center of the table.

"That looks nice," I say.

"You must be exhausted."

"I am."

"I still don't understand why on earth you wanted to go to Memphis with Peter."

"He asked me. He never asks." I wander into the pantry. "I'm glad I went. Do you have any idea where the corkscrew has gone? It's not here."

"Last time I looked it was right there on its hook. It may have fallen down. Grab me a head of garlic while you're in there."

"Got it. I saw Rosemary," I say, bringing it to her. "I went to her house."

"Rosemary," she says. "I'd practically forgotten she existed."

"It was Peter's idea."

"She was such a strange little girl. The way she clung to her father. Those hollow eyes. I remember there was something about her that drove Anna running out of the house every time Rosemary came to visit."

"She hated the way Rosemary smelled."

"That's right," Mum says. "Anna said she smelled of formaldehyde. Sickly sweet." She crushes five fat cloves of garlic with the wide flat of her knife and throws them into a cast-iron pan. Finely minced carrots, celery, and onions are already caramelizing in olive oil and browned butter. She opens a package of ground meat wrapped in butcher paper—veal and pork—and adds it into the pan bit by bit, then milk, to make the meat tender. An open bottle of warm white wine sits on the counter for deglazing.

"Hand me that, would you?" She points to a slotted spoon. "What's she like now?"

"Still an oddity. Direct. She's a musicologist. Lives in a ranch house. Short feathered hair. Slacks. That sort of thing."

"Married?"

I nod.

"And her mother?"

"Died a few years ago."

"Poor woman. What a sad life."

I watch my mother stir the sauce slowly, round and round. I hesitate. "Leo went back to her. Did you know that? They got remarried."

"I did not know that. I assumed he was dead or in prison."

"There was a wedding picture on the mantel. A photo of them on a cruise. Just an ordinary-looking older couple."

She picks up a cucumber and starts peeling it. "Let's not talk about Leo. As far as I'm concerned, he died a long time ago. He was a bad man. I don't like to think about him, and you shouldn't, either."

She takes the bottle of white wine from the counter, pours some into a glass.

"Isn't that cooking wine?"

"It's wine," she says, drinking it down.

"I need to talk to you about Leo, Mum."

"Eleanor, people will be arriving soon and I'm trying to cook. So, whatever it is will have to wait."

Jonas and I haven't spoken since I called him from Memphis yesterday, from the dizzying sidewalk outside Rosemary's house. When I see his mother and Gina appear at the door, my stomach does an odd drop—something familiar and yet forgotten. It takes me a moment to realize what it is: I am nervous, excited, anticipating his arrival. It is the strangest sensation, like a sense memory from my past—something I haven't allowed myself to feel in so many years; and yet there it is.

But Jonas isn't with them.

"He insisted on taking a shower even though he'd just had a swim. Complete waste of water," his mother says, coming in through the screen door.

"He's right behind us." Gina hands my mother a bottle of wine. "I brought white."

"We're drinking red," my mother says, taking it to the kitchen.

"Ignore her." Peter comes over and gives Gina a hug. "She's been an utter cow all afternoon."

"Be fair," I say, though I completely agree with him. "This is always a difficult day for her."

"You're right," Peter says. "I take it back."

"I'm sorry I never got to know Anna," Gina says. "She seemed like a cool person."

"She was," I say. "The coolest."

My mother comes out holding a platter of cheese and crackers.

Jonas's mother waves it away. "I've cut out gluten and dairy. My arthritis."

"You should have told me," Mum says, annoyed. "I'm serving pasta. But we have olives."

"How was Memphis?" Gina asks.

Peter sighs. "Muggy. Tired."

"I've never been," Gina says.

"Elle liked it."

"I did. It's a city full of ghosts," I say.

"Do you want wine or a 'drink' drink?" Peter asks Gina.

Over Gina's shoulder, through the screen, I see Jonas walking down the sandy path. His hair is wet and messy. He's barefoot, in torn Levi's and a blue chambray shirt. His cheeks are flushed. He looks like he did when we were young. Lighter on his feet, clear. When he sees me, he smiles: not his usual "happy to see his old friend" smile that I have grown so accustomed to, but something more, intimate and open, as if to say: finally, after all these years, we can look at each other without the scrim of shame between us.

Peter gets up from the dinner table, stretches. "That was delicious, Wallace. What's for pudding?" He lights a cigarette and wanders inside to the shelf where Mum keeps a stack of old LPs next to what may be the world's only living Victrola.

"We have fresh pears and sorbet. Who wants coffee?"

A scratchy Fleetwood Mac song comes on. "Did you actually purchase this album, Wallace?" Peter calls from the living room.

"It was Anna's," she says. "Aren't you going to read the Shelley?"

Every year, on the anniversary of her death, Peter reads us Anna's favorite poem, "To a Skylark," the prayer she asked for at her funeral. It is a sacred ritual.

But tonight Peter says, "I'm too tired and too drunk. Can someone else do it?" and flops down on the sofa.

Gina pulls her chair over to him, and they start some pointless conversation about restaurants in Bushwick.

I feel like punching them both in the face.

Dixon picks up the battered book, peers at it, then hands it to Jonas. "My eyes aren't what they once were," he says.

Jonas finds the page.

"For beautiful Anna," he says. "We hail to Thee, blithe spirit." And he begins.

"I just don't believe in psychiatry." My mother holds forth to the last of her guests.

"That's because you're afraid you'll be sent to the nuthouse," Peter says from the sofa.

"As far as I can tell, the only thing it's good for is making children blame their parents for everything that's ever gone wrong in their lives."

"The only thing I blame you for is making me take sailing lessons," I say, and everyone laughs, forgetting. Everyone but Jonas.

"Watch. Now she's going to say she wasn't given enough love from me as a child," Mum says, getting up from the table and heading into the kitchen to start on the dishes. "Of course she's absolutely right."

"Not everything is about you, Mum," I say.

Jonas stares at me, his eyes burning.

I get up from the table and go out the back door into the dark night. Then I lean against the cold cement-block wall and wait, for what feels like a lifetime.

Book Five

◆

TODAY

6:30 P.M.–6:30 A.M.

32

Today. August 1, the Back Woods.

6:30 P.M.

I strip out of my damp bathing suit, leave it on the cabin floor, and lie down on the bed. From the Big House, I hear Peter's deep laugh, my mother calling to the kids to stop playing Parcheesi and get ready for the barbecue. The ceiling of our cabin is crawling with carpenter ants, brought out by the heat, the impending storm. A dusting of cardboard covers Peter's bedside lampshade. I stare up through the skylight at the evening sunlight breaking through the trees, the dappled twigginess of the branches. Nimbus clouds float past, pregnant with rain.

When Anna and I were very young, our father planted a delicate birch sapling outside our cabin, its trunk as thin as a pussy willow. A tree planted in a forest. He said it would grow up with us, grow tall with us. Back then, before it reached beyond the roof line, the skylight above my bed was an uninterrupted rectangle of blue. I loved to lie there, staring up at the open sky, watch gulls flying the wind shear. After Conrad died, I prayed to that open sky—not for forgiveness, but for guidance, a way to move beyond the past, a clear path forward. By then, the split ends of birch branches had begun to appear in the corner of the skylight—tiny sharp strands that poked at the air. Inch by inch, year by year, the birch's unruly mane grew into frame until it covered the windowpane, blocked out the sky. I had begged for answers, for the clarity of glass. But the passage of time brought only a messy tangle of branches marking my failure to heal.

"It's a window," Jonas had said, that long-ago day by the stream. And I had said, "I know."

Last night I stared at him across the crowded table, his green eyes darkening beyond the candlelight. He stared straight back. No one flinched. Finally his lips curved into that ironic smile—relief, regret, the absurd, sad inevitabilities. We were always meant to be together. Marriage, children—nothing has changed this essential truth. If I could take back what I have done, I would do it. Every bad decision when the road forked. Every terrible choice that led me away from him. Every terrible choice that led me away from Peter. Not just fucking Jonas last night, or what we did today, what I can't stop thinking about, what I want to do tomorrow, but Conrad—that day, that bright choppy day, when the winds turned. The truth I have kept from Peter. The lie I carried into our marriage. I picture Rosemary, her prim, bland living room, her moist cake, the rage behind her eyes. The way she thanked me for saving her life. I have never thanked Jonas for saving mine. Only blamed him. Blamed myself. Kept Peter at arm's length, punishing him for my own sin. Built my entire life on a fault line. If I had told Peter about Conrad, about that day on the boat, I know he would have forgiven me. And that is why I couldn't tell him. Because I did not want to be forgiven.

And the choice Jonas is asking me to make now. To leave my wonderful husband. To cause my children pain. Peter is not vindictive—whatever happens, he would never take them away from me, never create a rift between me and them. He loves us all too much for that. He is a man with backbone. It is his gravity that holds my orbit steady when I falter. I am in love with Jonas. I always have been. I cannot live without him, cannot give him up now, after waiting for so long. But I'm in love with Peter, too. I have two choices. One I can't have. One I don't deserve to have.

I get up off the bed. I need a hot shower and too many Advil. My body is sore. My head hurts from trying to think, going around and around in circles. Does letting go mean losing everything you have, or does it mean gaining everything you never had? I wrap myself in a towel. I should go to Dixon's. Be with Peter, with my children.

Outside the bathroom, I turn on the shower to let the water run hot, then go in search of Advil. I root around my mother's deep, disorganized cabinet. My hand grazes something in back, and I pull it out, already knowing what it is. One of Anna's ancient Playtex tampons. No one else ever used that brand. The plastic wrapper has yellowed, but the little pink plastic applicator inside has held its pink. I think of Conrad peering in through the bathroom window, my legs spread wide, tampon skittling across the floor. The day I met Jonas. And I think of Anna, always shouting at me for touching her things—that I was the one she told when she lost her virginity. How sad and scared she was those last months. How Peter held me fast, every day, when the tears came. I step into the shower, stand under the hot, gushing water, hoping it will drown out my guttural animal sobs, my salted-wound despair, begging the water to make me clean, to scald away the past. Knowing that there is only one choice to make.

6:45 P.M.

We walk up our steep driveway, stop at the dirt road, wait for Mum at the triangle.

"Don't wait for me," she yells from halfway up the driveway.

But we wait. I'm barefoot, in a linen dress, flip-flops shoved in a straw bag, flashlights for the walk home, trying to keep my insides at bay. Maddy has run on ahead—she likes to be first—with Finn racing down the dirt road behind her. I watch my mother's slow progress. Her knees aren't what they once were. She's wearing her same old jeans—slightly too short, slightly too wide, and a cotton Indian shirt that covers her behind, as she likes to say. The pond frames her ascent: a glass-blue horizon line, waist-height, behind a fretwork of trees. I pretend to listen to Jack arguing with Peter about why we need a beach sticker for White Crest Beach. The surfing is better, and it only costs thirty dollars for residents.

"We'll see," Peter says.

I swat at my ankles. I'm being bitten alive by blackflies.

A horsefly lands on my arm. Its quail-speckled wings settle. Horseflies are slower than blackflies—bigger and easier to kill, but their sting is ten times worse. I swat it. Kill it. Watch it tumble to the dirt road and twitch once before dying.

"Who has the bug spray?"

Peter reaches into a canvas bag.

"Here I am," my mother announces. "The flies are back. I'm glad you decided to come with us, Eleanor," she says. "Though I wish you'd put your hair back. It looks so much nicer when it's out of your face."

We are coming up to the Gunthers' house when my mother stops. The Gunthers' vicious German shepherds are long dead. So are the Gunthers. I don't know the family who bought the house. Yet I still feel a tinge of nerves, expecting the high-pitched barking, the saliva, the growling, gums exposed for the kill, every time I approach their white wooden fence, now partially rotted away, fallen into the dark underbrush along with everything else.

"Oh, for heaven's sake," Mum says. "The red onion."

"Jack can run back," Peter says. "It'll take five minutes."

"Why am I always the one who has to do everything?" Jack grouses. "Why can't Maddy or Finn go?"

I can see the muscle in Peter's jaw clenching. "Because you are currently making up for your utterly shit behavior to your sainted mother this morning."

"I *said* I was sorry."

"It's fine. I'll go." I start back without waiting for Peter to contradict me. I know every fucking family is unhappy in its own fucking way. But right now, for a few hours, I need Happy Family. Until I am safely on shore, I need to hold on to this truth like a life preserver. Not let go.

"Can you grab me a sweater?" Peter calls after me. "It's going to get chilly."

A white cat I've never seen before is sitting on the deck outside the screen porch. There's something about a white cat that revolts me—a ratlike porn-y quality. The cat disappears into the bushes when it sees me coming. The bottom half of a chipmunk lies on the deck, its furry tail dangling between the wooden slats. I know I should clean it up, but it's disgusting and I may as well let the cat finish his dinner. I leave it there and go to our cabin to grab Peter a sweater.

The top bureau drawer is open. *Peter,* I think, annoyed. I'm always careful to shut it tight to keep the moths and spiders out. I shove the drawer closed. My jewelry box is out on the bureau top. Odd, because I know I didn't leave it there. I open it to check if anything is missing. Nothing has been taken, but something has been added. A piece of folded paper lies atop my tangle of earrings and necklaces. It has been cut in the shape of a snapping turtle. Inside is my green glass ring. Jonas has had it all these years. Since we stumbled back into each other in the Greek coffee shop. Since that spring evening on the pier. Since the beach picnic where I first met Gina—Anna's last summer on the pond. I wonder where he has kept it. Hidden away. A tiny secret. It's such a small thing, a worthless tin thing, its gilt long gone. Yet, when I put it on my finger I feel a powerful sense of completion—as if I've finally been made whole, restored—like a Venus de Milo whose missing arm has been found, trapped under the earth for centuries, and, at last, reattached. I close my eyes, allowing myself this, at least. I remember the moment he gave it to me. His clammy, shaking hand. Saying goodbye. Two children who would always love each other. I stick the ring in my pocket, crumple the paper turtle, toss it into the wastebasket, and grab Peter a sweater.

7:15 P.M.

I catch up with the others as they approach the turnoff to Dixon's. His driveway is actually a section of the Old King's Highway. Past Dixon's house, the road dead-ends at a wide field, overgrown with goldenrod and Queen Anne's lace. But beyond the far edge of the field, hidden under the shade of the woods, the ancient road reappears. When we were young, this was our secret route into town. We could walk the whole four miles—all the way from Becky's house to the Penny Candy store—without ever going on the tar road. Sometimes, after a heavy rain, we would find bits of pottery or arrowheads unearthed from the steep banks. One year I found a small medicine bottle, plum purple, sea-glassed by time. I imagined some Pilgrim tossing it from a wagon or saddlebag into the thick woods with a quick glance over his shoulder to make sure no one had seen him littering. The bottle had lain there untouched for two centuries—gone directly from his hand to mine.

The trail comes out of the woods at the Pilgrim cemetery, a long-deserted graveyard. It fascinated us: the rows of small sunken tombstones carved with winged death's heads, wind-worn and pitted, their epitaphs barely visible, filled with lives, with resignation. Most of the dead were children. *Temperance, Thankful, Obediah, Mehetable. Aged 3 wks, aged 14 mo. and 24 d's, 2 yr 9 months, 5 d's.* All facing east. On Judgment Day, the children would arise to face the dawn, hoping to be placed on God's right hand, to be judged among the righteous.

The smell of mesquite and hamburger wafts up the driveway. "Yum," I say, catching up to the kids. "I'm starving."

"You must be, after that long swim," Mum says.

"I want three hamburgers," Finn says. "Can I have three hamburgers, Mom?"

"It's not up to Mom," Jack says. "You have to ask Dixon."

"What about hot dogs?" Finn says.

"What I need is a stiff gin and tonic," Peter says. "And I'll shoot Dixon if all he has is that Almaden swill."

"He uses them for lamps," my mother says.

Peter looks at her, confused.

"You fill them with sand," she says.

"Sand."

"Clearly you missed the seventies."

"Elle, I think your mother may have incipient dementia."

She swats him with her hat. "Given the amount we used to drink, we had to use them for something."

"If you're not feeling well, Wallace, I'm happy to walk you home."

"Your husband is intolerable." She laughs. "It might be time to think about divorce."

Finn and Maddy look distressed.

"*Mum.*"

"Oh, for heaven's sake, I'm *joking*. It was a joke," she says to them. "I adore your father, as he knows perfectly well."

"Your grandmother has always been a great wit," Peter says.

I take Finn's hand, crouch down beside him. "Your grandmother was being silly—you know how silly she can be. Daddy and I love each other. We always will."

About fifteen people are milling around on the front lawn, the usual Back Woods crowd, chatting, eating Kraft cheddar on Wheat Thins, drinking out of plastic cups. A makeshift bar has been set up on a round picnic table, citronella candles burning.

"Right, then," Peter says. "Into the fray?"

The first person I see is Dixon's wife Andrea. Even now, all these years later, every time I see her I think of that Monopoly game and Dixon walking across his living room naked. Dixon and Andrea got back together three years ago after running into each other at a rare-book auction. They were bidding against each other for a signed first edition of *Jonathan Livingston Seagull*. Dixon says he didn't recognize her at first, she was so changed. Andrea's mass of curly red hair is now a tidy gray bob. She's traded in her African tribal earrings for tasteful pearl studs, replaced her Peter Max dove button with a pink ribbon. Her son is an investment banker. He lives in Colorado and trades in clean energy, she says, as if that makes it ecologically acceptable. She still believes in world peace. Andrea is deep in conversation with Martha Currier, a fraying ex-jazz singer from New Orleans who has a modernist house overlooking the beach and is never without her turbaned head scarf. Martha is smoking a Virginia Slim through a long ivory cigarette holder. Andrea waves the smoke away from her face every time Martha exhales, but Martha ignores her and, if anything, seems to exhale more directly into Andrea's face each time. I have always enjoyed Martha.

My mother ducks behind me as we approach the gathering. "Shield me," she says. "Just until I'm safely past Andrea. Before she corners me and asks me how I am, in that 'interested' way, and then waits for me to give her a sincere answer. As if anyone ever wants to get stuck in an actual conversation at a cocktail party."

I laugh. "I couldn't agree with you more. Which is rare. Small talk and move on."

"How he can stand spending more than ten minutes with her is beyond me. The woman is as boring as a box of salt."

"It's mysterious," I say, steering her clear.

"Well, he claims she's still a dynamo in the sack. Which I assume means she gives good blow jobs."

"Mum, that's disgusting."

"I agree. It is very disturbing. She has such a small mouth."

"I meant, *you* are being disgusting." I laugh.

"Don't be such a prude."

"I don't want to talk about Dixon's sex life. He must be almost eighty."

From across the lawn, Dixon waves to us. Mum waves back. "He's still a very attractive man. He could have any woman he wants."

"Any woman over sixty-five."

"Don't be so sure. He's always been very sexual."

"And now I'm stuck with an image of Andrea with a penis in her mouth."

"At least it means she's not talking. Can you be an angel and get me a vodka? Rocks, no soda." She sits down in an Adirondack chair. "And if you happen to see any peanuts. Oh, thank God," she says as she sees Pamela approaching. Pamela is wearing a long lavender caftan and chunky amber beads. "Pamela, sit." She pats an empty chair next to her. "Save me from these people."

Pamela laughs at Mum in her lovely, good-natured way. She thinks my mother is wonderful, for reasons I cannot fathom. But then, Pamela is the kind of person who always sees the best in everyone. Even Conrad.

The summer after Conrad moved in with us, Pamela took me and Anna into town for fried clams. "Now then, you two," she said when we'd settled into a booth, "I want all the news. Is Leo behaving himself? He can be a bit of a scoundrel, that one. But what a lovely man. Your mother seems exactly herself, as always."

"I think they're okay," I said.

"And Conrad? It must be a bit of an adjustment having a brother."

"Stepbrother," I said.

"Do you want the truth or the lie?" Anna said.

"I'll leave that up to you. Clam strips or whole bellies?"

In the end, we decided on the truth.

We told her how awful he was. How he was always creeping around. Stood at the icebox drinking milk straight from the carton so neither of us could ever have cereal for breakfast. The gross pubescent beard that he refused to shave.

"He uses up all the hot water every morning," Anna said. "Jerking off in the shower. It's disgusting. I mean . . ."—she put her finger down her throat, pretending to gag—"imagine what he's thinking about."

I was sure Pamela would be horrified. Instead, she told Anna she sympathized—the situation sounded positively beastly. Was it possible, though, that Anna might be blaming Conrad for her having been sent away to boarding school, Conrad's taking over her bedroom? "Because," Pamela said, "however repugnant his behavior, *that* is not his fault. In fact, it's the last thing on earth he wanted. All he wanted was for his mother to love him. So, if you can, try to remember that he is suffering. Be kinder. Both of you." She bit into a clam belly, squirting juice all over the table. "You have the most beautiful eyes, Anna. I'm always meaning to tell you. That pale gray. If you see our waitress, I need hot sauce."

Dixon is manning two kettle-shaped Webers, dressed, as always, in white duck pants and a blue linen shirt, barefoot and tan, tongs in one hand, a martini in the other, not a splatter of grease on him. His gray hair, still damp from the beach, is pushed back slick over his head. Three roughed-up surfboards are leaning against the side of the house, his wet suit flopped over a wooden sawhorse, drying. He's the only man I know who still swims straight out into the sea at high tide without hesitation. Mum is right—he is a handsome man, even now. A Downhill Racer, a Hubbell. He waves Jack over, gives him a firm handshake and hands him a spatula.

Peter is at the bar. I watch him pour two inches of gin and a small splash of tonic water into a glass. Only then does he add three sad little cubes of ice. They float around like turds on the sea. Brits love to drink, but they make tepid, vacuous cocktails. I come up behind him, put my arms around his waist.

"Who that?" he says.

"Ha-ha."

He turns around and kisses the tip of my nose.

"My mother is requesting vodka. One ice chip."

"Roger that. You?"

"I'm going inside to find where Andrea has hidden the decent wine."

"I'll whistle three times if I see her coming."

I let myself in the kitchen door. I have always loved the Dixons' kitchen—the poppy-red floorboards, the worn breadboard counter, the musky smell of Band-Aids and cumin and glasses of ginger ale. Every time I'm in this kitchen I have an urge to pull a stool up to the counter and eat a bowl of cornflakes with milk and heaps of white sugar. I open a cupboard above the sink, grab a wineglass. High up on a shelf is a yellowing Cuisinart base that probably hasn't been used since 1995. Beside it, an old Salton yogurt maker gathers dust. Seeing it makes me think of curdled milk, sanctimony, and other people's parents having sex.

There's a just-opened bottle of decent Sancerre in the fridge. I fill my glass and wander into Dixon's study. Beyond the windowpane Peter brings my mother a can of Spanish peanuts. He has stolen the vodka bottle from the bar and hands it to her. She takes it without a flinch, glugs. Hands it back. He laughs, sits down on the arm of her Adirondack chair. Lights a cigarette. Whispers something in her ear that makes her swat him. But she is laughing, too. No one else can make my mother relax into her old self the way Peter does. He has some perfect combination of kindness, mean-spirited wit, and I-don't-give-a-fuck that makes her happy. In a way, Peter saved her all those years ago, after Leo disappeared, after her baby died, after she found my journal. Peter woke her up from a daze, turned the lights back on in our old apartment. Made all of us feel it was safe to be happy again.

Maddy and Finn come running over and clamber around him, flocking to him like baby ducks. He swats a mosquito that has landed on his left arm, opens his palm to show the kids that he got it. And in that tiny gesture, I feel an overwhelming sense of relief. And of gratitude.

I head past the living room to the upstairs bathroom. A few of the older crowd have come inside. They are sitting around a fire, engrossed in a conversation about birdcalls.

"For me, it's the chickadee. *Chick a dee dee dee* . . . So sweet. Like little hopping bits of corn," someone is saying.

"The chickadees are disappearing from our property in droves," I hear Andrea say. "I'm convinced it's the neighbor's cat. They refuse to bell it. I've called the National Park Service, but they insist there's nothing to be done."

"I'm partial to the blue jay's screech." I hear Martha Currier, her deep, raspy southern accent. "Though I know that puts me in a minority."

Dixon's house has two staircases. The wide stairs I climb now lead to the formal part of the house—the grown-ups' side. Here the rooms are beautiful, elegant. Each of the guest rooms has antique wallpaper—sprays of pale rosebuds or lily of the valley against a robin's-egg blue. The master bedroom has always been my favorite room in the world. As a child, I used to dream that one day I would have a room exactly like it. Hand-painted wallpaper with lush white peonies drooping in jade-green leaves; a romantic canopy bed, eyelet curtains, a worn wide-board floor; a fireplace with a neat stack of wood and kindling beside it; a claw-foot tub in the bathroom.

The kids' stairs are steep and dark with no banister—just the close press of walls on either side to steady you. They lead directly from the kitchen to the "dorm"—a loftlike room with high windows and bunk beds lining every wall. This was the sleepover house when we were kids, the place where we could sneak in boys for spin the bottle, smoke clove cigarettes. The only way to access the dorm from the grown-ups' part of the house was through a Jack and Jill bathroom that we could lock from our side.

The guest bathroom is occupied, so I go to use the one in Dixon's bedroom. When I open the door, my heart sinks. Andrea has redecorated. The old-fashioned peony wallpaper has been stripped, the room painted in an eggplant tone. The beautiful canopy bed is gone, replaced by a beige-linen upholstered bed, plank floors tastefully covered in herringbone sisal. There are matching mid-century dressers and Simon

Pearce glass lamps. I could kill Andrea. I only need to pee, but I'm tempted to take a shit in the toilet just to make a point.

Instead, I go down the long hallway to where it dead-ends at the Jack and Jill bathroom. I am locking the door behind me when the dorm-side door opens and Gina steps inside.

"Hey," she says, as if meeting in a bathroom is perfectly normal. She pulls down her jeans and sits on the toilet.

I stand there, mute. *He is here* is all I can think, heart racing, breathless.

Gina grabs a wodge of toilet paper and wipes herself. "When did you guys get here?"

"Maybe half an hour," I manage to say. "We walked."

"We weren't planning to come, but his mother was threatening to make a tofu stir-fry." She flushes the toilet and stands up to zip her jeans. She has a full Brazilian. A sudden self-conscious worry blazes through me as I picture my own old-fashioned pubic hair. Did it bother Jonas? Turn him off? He is used to something else. Smooth, childlike.

"Your turn," Gina says.

I cannot look at her. I cannot look away.

She opens the medicine cabinet and finds a tube of Neosporin, squeezes some on the tip of her finger, takes a Band-Aid out of a box. "I did something to my foot earlier," she says. "Just a little scratch, but it hurts like hell, and now there's a blood blister. Jonas thinks I stepped on a crab."

I watch her rub ointment on the wound in a tidy circular motion. She peels the little strips off the back of the Band-Aid, stretches it over what is clearly a *nothing* scratch, smooths both ends over her skin just so—lovingly. I'm fascinated by the care she gives herself, the importance of every gesture. It's like watching one of those women who actually brush their teeth for the full two minutes. I wait for her to leave, but she takes a lip gloss out of her back pocket, leans in to the mirror. I have no choice but to sit down and pee with Gina two feet away, underpants around my ankles, the barest weight of Jonas's ring nudging me through my dress pocket.

"I forced Jonas to drive here," Gina says, making a pout, checking that her lips are perfect. "By the time he got home, it was the total witching hour for mosquitoes at our place. God knows where that man disappears to."

My pee stops midstream in a tiny gasp, before starting again. Gina turns, looks at me, at if she is considering something. I still myself, like a deer sensing a hunter in the blind.

But she smiles. "You won't believe this, and I probably shouldn't tell you, but I used to think it was *you*." She dries her hands on a guest towel. "It seems so ludicrous now. I actually followed him once. Turned out he'd been trying to find some osprey nest all summer." She laughs.

"He loves these woods," I say, and reach for the toilet paper.

Crossing the dorm on our way back downstairs, Gina says, "Have you seen the new master? Andrea did an amazing reno. She finally convinced Dixon to get rid of that hideous wallpaper. They're gutting the kitchen next."

"I grew up in that kitchen."

"Yeah. But have you seen it?"

She will never know how close she came to losing him.

"This room must have been the ultimate teenage crash pad." She gestures to the wall of bunk beds. "Jonas probably made out with some girl on one of those."

"He was much younger than us."

I follow her down the narrow staircase.

"But you must know if he had girlfriends or whatever," Gina says over her shoulder.

My hair still smells of pond water.

My mother is exactly where I left her, Peter still perched on the arm of her chair. Citronella tiki lamps cut circles of light into the dusk.

"I'm getting a burger," Gina says. "Want one?"

I scan the lawn for Jonas, feel a queasy tightening. I find him in the shadows beyond the grill. He is staring at me. He's been waiting for me. I reach into my skirt pocket, close my fingers around the green glass ring, steady myself. "I think I'll wait a bit."

Gina crosses the lawn to him, wraps her arms around his waist, shoves her hands into his back pockets. Ownership. She must sense my stare, because she turns her head quickly, like a puma picking up a scent, looks out into the dark. Jonas whispers something in her ear and she smiles, turns back to him.

"Hey, wife," Peter says. "Where've you been?"

"With Gina. Peeing."

"Have some peanuts." My mother passes me the can.

"I was upstairs in the kid's bathroom. Gina opened the door from the dorm side without knocking and came in. Sat down and took a pee in front of me."

"She's vulgar," my mother says.

"Your mother is on the warpath tonight."

"I'm not on any *war* or any *path*," Mum says. "I simply told Andrea that none of us likes the new landscaping she's had done. It isn't 'woods.'"

"That was very politic of you, Mum."

"If she didn't want my opinion, she shouldn't have asked me what I thought of her improvements in the first place."

"Your mother told her it looks *bourgeois*." Peter laughs.

"If she's going to lecture us all about native plants, she shouldn't do an herbaceous border."

Across the lawn, the younger kids are playing horseshoes in the dusk. Jonas and Gina come toward us, balancing paper plates and drinks.

"Maddy should put on more bug spray. The mosquitoes love her," I say.

Jonas pulls up a chair beside me, puts his hand on my arm. "Mind if we join you?" he says to everyone, but only to me.

I stand up. "I left my wine upstairs."

This time I lock the bathroom door from both sides, leave the lights turned off. I lean against the windowsill, listen to the sweep and rustle of the trees, the wafting murmur, the tinkle of glass and conversation. Ever since I was old enough to question my own instincts, my mother has given me the same piece of advice: "Flip a coin, Eleanor. If the answer you get disappoints you, do the opposite." We already know the right answer, even when we don't—or we think we don't. But what if it's a trick coin? What if both sides are the same? If both are right, then both are wrong.

My wineglass is on the bathroom windowsill where I left it. Downstairs on the deck, Peter and Jonas are talking. Peter says something, and Gina laughs, throws back her head. Both men smile. It's surreal, unfathomable. Only hours ago, it felt like the world was daydreaming, suspended in the sky. I stare into the dusk, picturing the old abandoned ruin, the quiet of the woods, Jonas's frank, open-eyed stare. I slide down the wall, pull my knees to my chest, cocoon myself, suckerpunched. I have made my choice: to give up this love that pulses, aches—for a different kind of love. A patient love. A *love* love. But the anguish is raw. Outside, I hear my mother calling out across the lawn to where Dixon stands at the grill, demanding a hamburger. "Bloody," she shouts. "So I can hear it moo. And please do not lecture me about salmonella. I'd far rather die from diarrhea and dehydration than eat gray cardboard meat." I hear Peter's full-throated, easy laugh. "I swear, Wallace. One of these days I really *am* going to have you committed."

When I come downstairs, Jonas is at the kitchen sink running his hand under cold water.

"There you are." He takes his hand out of the water and holds it up. There's a red scalding, a sear mark, running diagonally across his palm. "I was getting your mother a hamburger. I grabbed a metal spatula that was lying on the hot grill." He leans back against the butcher block counter. I want to eat him, his lazy, languid confidence. Ingest him, absorb him.

"Come over here," he says softly.

"You need butter." I go to the fridge, find a stick of butter, peel back the waxy wrapper. Jonas puts out his hand and I rub butter over the sizzled skin. His fingers close over mine. I pull away, put the butter back in the fridge.

"Elle?"

"What?" I say, my back to him. Whatever he has to say, it will be unbearable.

"I doubt Dixon wants a smear of my burnt skin on his toast tomorrow morning."

"Right." I take the butter back out of the fridge, break a chunk off the top, throw it in the trash, find a clean dish towel and toss it to him. Contain myself. "Wrap it in this for now."

"I left you something at the camp," Jonas says. "In your cabin. Look for it when you get home."

"I found it," I say. "I went back for an onion." I reach into my pocket and pull out the ring. "I didn't know you still had it."

He takes the ring from me, holds it up to the light. The little piece of green glass glows like kryptonite. "My New Year's resolution that year was to forget you for good. And suddenly there you were, shrieking at some poor asshole in a coffee shop." He slides the ring onto my finger, over my wedding band.

All I want is to tell him I'm his. That I always have been, always will be. Instead, I take the ring off, put it on the counter. "I can't."

"It belongs to you."

I fight to keep my voice cool. "I'm going to join Peter and the kids. I'll send Gina in to bandage that hand up properly."

Jonas looks pale, unnerved, as if he has felt a ghost go by, been touched, ever so lightly by the frost of a passing sleeve. "Put it back on." His voice is hard.

I take his hand and kiss his burnt palm, try to hold it together.

"There," I say as I would to Finn. "All better now."

I move to leave, but he pins my hand hard to the counter, staring at me like a drowning man.

"Let me go," I say, my voice no more than a whisper. "Please."

Behind us I hear a creak. Peter is standing in the doorway on the far side of the room.

"Oh, hey," I say. "Jonas burned his hand."

33

9:30 P.M.

When we leave Dixon's, I don't look back. My chest is full of a hollow pressure, a balloon blown up to bursting with the empty weight of dead air. The nothingness. Darkness stretches ahead. All around me, the high-pitched trill of cicadas blends into the night air. Peter walks in front, his flashlight illuminating a narrow patch of road, the center strip of tall grasses, pale sandy tracks on either side. His light casts a halo into the trees. Moths fly out of the forest, drawn by the light—dust-brown flickers, desperate for wattage. I've never understood that suicidal draw. The kids trail behind Peter, complaining that their legs hurt; tired, spooked, staying close to the light. Maybe moths are terrified of the dark. Maybe it's as simple as that.

"There's no such thing as werewolves," Peter is telling Finn, reassuring him.

"But what about vampires?" Finn asks.

"No vampires, bunny," I say.

"But wouldn't it be great if there *were* such a thing as monsters," Peter says. "Think about it: if werewolves and vampires exist, then magic exists. Life after death exists. That's a *good* thing, right?"

"I guess," Finn says. "And ghosts?"

"Exactly," Peter says.

"What about serial killers?" Maddy says. "What if someone is hiding in the woods? What if he wants to hurt us? What if he has an axe?"

"Or *she*," Peter says.

"Did you guys have fun?" I say, mentally kicking Peter in the shins. Now Maddy will be awake all night, worrying. "I thought it was a nice gathering."

"We played freeze tag," Finn says. "Can we have ice cream when we get home?"

Jack walks beside me, carrying my straw bag. At some point, he slips his arm through mine and we walk like that, linked together, along the dark, sandy road, each thinking our own thoughts. Off on a high ridge a coyote barks, nips at the night. Far away, the pack howls back. I listen to their call-and-response, the empty hunger of it. They are coming in for the kill, their dinner of field mice and small dogs.

One of our garbage cans is lying on its side at the bottom of the driveway, two raccoons astride it. They freeze in place when the beam of Peter's flashlight hits them, little fur statues, bobsledders, eyes lit red in the glare. Corncobs and lettuce leaves and coffee grains and bits of shredded paper towel are strewn around in the dirt.

My mother shouts in annoyance, runs at them waving a stick. "Get out of here! Out! Out!"

We watch them slink-run into the tree line.

"Vermin," she says, giving the garbage can a sharp kick. "Which of you morons forgot to put the bungee cord back on?" She storms down the path to the house without waiting for a response.

"Imagine if she'd just discovered the Wreck of the Rhone," Peter says.

"You guys go inside," I say. "I'll deal with this mess. Don't eat all the pistachio. Save some for me. Jack, turn on the outside light, would you?"

I wait until I'm alone. Up above me in the trees I hear the whisper of guarded movements, feel pairs of watchful eyes. *What if someone is hiding in the dark? What if he wants to hurt us?* For so many years I have put that terrible night away. But now, in this flash flood of love and panic and sorrow, I let my skin go cold. I wonder how long raccoons live. Could these same raccoons have witnessed Conrad raping me? Were they those babies, peering in through the skylight at my moonlit bed? Did my tears scare them? My muffled screams? Or were they bored, waiting for a safe moment to go back to the pond for a few more minnows? Did Conrad's mother hear Rosemary's pounding heart in her dreams? *What if he has an axe?* I imagine Maddy alone, terrified, begging for mercy, Peter and I asleep in our cabin, unaware. I want to promise her that nothing bad will ever happen, that no one will hurt her. But I can't.

I sit down on the ground, amid the old salad and damp cigarette butts and tea bags. An empty box of Bisquick ripped to shreds by sharp little claws. Last night Jonas came at me in the dark, shoving himself into me, my head pressed hard against cold cinder block, unearthly, gasping, a beautiful pain, dress pushed up around my waist, and I felt my entire life coming together inside of me.

A bullfrog croaks in the pond. Somewhere, deep in the mud, a giant snapping turtle is lurking. Through the window, I see Peter in the pantry, dishing chocolate ice cream into mismatched bowls. He hands them out to the kids, then picks up the container of pistachio ice cream and considers it for a moment, before emptying the whole thing into his bowl.

10:00 P.M.

I've made a pile of corncobs and husks. The back door opens and Peter comes out with a big black garbage bag. He looks into the dark for me.

"Here," I say, stepping into the light. "It's a disaster area."

Peter opens the maw of the bag, and I dump everything in.

"I saw you," Peter says, his voice withheld, odd. "With Jonas."

"Saw me?"

"I *know*."

My skin goes blush-hot, an adrenaline rush quickening through me. I force away the rising panic, concentrate on picking up damp cigarette butts. "These fucking raccoons." I move out of the light, pick up a torn egg carton, hold my breath, wait for what's coming.

"You kissed him."

My heart releases a millibeat. There was no kiss. I didn't kiss Jonas last night. He came out of the dark, took me from behind. I breathe a sigh of relief without breathing. "I have no idea what you're talking about, Pete."

"Don't lie." His face is hard as river stones, sure in its rage.

"I'm not lying. What do you mean, saw me? Where?" A hideous thought creeps in: did Peter follow us to the old ruin? Did he watch us from the trees? See our raw, open sex?

Peter shakes his head in disgust. "Just now. In the kitchen. At Dixon's."

The sea changes in my body, the pure-water rush of *Thank God*. "You mean when I kissed the burn on his hand? Jesus."

"It wasn't just the kiss. I saw the way he was looking at you," Peter says. "Like he wanted you."

"Well, yeah," I say, my voice heavy with forced sarcasm. "How could he not? I'm irresistible."

"I saw the way you looked back at him," Peter says.

"I put butter on his hand. I handed him a dish towel."

Peter takes the egg carton from me. "You know what, Elle? I'm done here. I'm going to bed." He shoves the bag in the trash can, slams the lid, secures it with the bungee cord.

"For Christ's sake, Pete. It's Jonas. He's our oldest friend."

"He's *your* oldest friend."

"I 'kissed it better' like he was a little kid. You were right there."

"I was," Peter says, and walks away from me.

"Wait," I say, going after him. "Are you seriously upset with me because I kissed Jonas's burnt hand?"

Peter stares me down. His eyes are cold silver, a mercury streak.

"Fuck it. Think whatever you want," I say, covering my nerves with self-righteous anger. "Jonas is my oldest friend. Of course he loves me. But not that way. It would be like incest."

A pause flickers across his face—hope and doubt combined.

We stand there at an impasse, Peter desperately wanting to resolve his suspicions, uncertain; me, terrified, crossing my fingers behind my back, holding my ground, *willing* Peter to believe me, pretending defiance. I have given up Jonas. I have chosen Peter. I have died for him. I say a prayer to the God I know does not exist. After this, I swear, there will be no more lies.

"Okay," he says finally, his face giving a little. "But if you're lying . . ."

I keep my voice level and steady. "Good. Because there's nothing going on with Jonas, or anyone else for that matter. You're the only man I love. I promise you."

"Good," he says. He comes over and kisses me hard. "But no more kissing other men. You're mine."

"I am," I say.

"Now come to bed so I can make love to my wife."

"The kids are still awake and Mum is prowling around somewhere."

"Hush." He takes my hand, leads me down the dark path to our cabin door. He pushes me up the steps in front of him. "Turn around," he growls.

I face my body to him, brace myself inside the doorway. He puts his hands up my dress, pulls down my underpants, leans in and licks me slowly with the rough flat of his tongue.

"You taste like the sea," he whispers.

I close my eyes and imagine the ocean, the beach today, the tent, Jonas. I cum in his mouth, thinking of the other man I love. When the tears come, they are not for what I have lost, but for the truth about Jonas I cannot seem to shed.

10:30 P.M.

We lie together, Peter crashed out in his postcoital slump, sheets squashed down around our ankles, our akimbo parts. I turn my pillow over, press my cheek against the cold side, listen to the rise and fall of Peter's chest, the rasp of his soft snores, the sweet exhale of his cigarette breath. I am restless, nervous. I need him to come back to me. But I know that nothing will wake him from this particular sleep. Men fall asleep immediately after orgasm. Women wake up. It's curious, that off-rhythm. Perhaps, after the exhaustion of trying to impregnate us, they need their rest. It's our job to get back up on our feet, sweep the cave, tuck the children into their bed of rushes, nitpick their head lice, tell them stories that someday they will tell their own children: about fire, stone wheels, a cave dripping with stalactites—luminous color, frozen in time; the boy who chased a great bird through the sky; how to cross the open sea. I put my clothes back on, let myself out of the cabin. It's late, but I need to kiss my children.

Their light is still on.

"Where were you?" Maddy says. "You were supposed to come back for ice cream."

"Daddy wasn't feeling well. I had to find him some aspirin and get him into bed."

"Right," Jack says without raising his eyes from the bare-bulb glow of his computer screen.

Maddy has been reading aloud to Finn. They are snuggled up together on her bed. She's holding a heavy, tattered book, its olive-green cover mildewed and time-stained.

"What are you reading?"

"I found it on the bathroom bookshelf," Maddy says, and holds it up for me to see.

"That book has been on the bathroom shelf since before I was born. I don't think anyone has ever read it." I sit down on the edge of the bed. "Make room for me."

Maddy moves closer to the wall. Finn makes a space, rests his head against my arm. "It's about a crow named Johnny," he says.

"I know," I say. "That's why no one's ever read it."

"There are spiders in here." He points to a web in a high corner. Next to it, peeking out above the edge of the beam, I notice a small ragged mouse hole in the cardboard ceiling. I'll have to get Peter to patch it. A fine-legged spider fusses around her web, preparing a dead fly. Five heavy brown eggs are suspended below her, held in a hammock of filament.

"Can you kill it?" Finn says.

"Spiders are good," I say. "We like spiders. They catch mosquitoes."

"I don't like them," he says.

"Don't be a pussy," Jack says.

"That's not nice, Jack." Another night I would get into it with him, but not tonight. Tonight I want to be here with my beautiful children—warm and happy, believing this will last forever. "You were terrified of spiders when you were Finn's age."

"Whatever."

"Not whatever. Apologize to your brother and then come over here and snuggle with us, please. I need a massive cuddle right this second. Non-negotiable."

Jack sighs, puts his computer down, comes over, and lies down in the narrow bit of space that's left.

I wrap my arm around him, pull him close to me. "That's better." The four of us lie there, squished like sardines.

"Now what?" Jack says.

"You guys are suffocating me," Maddy moans. "I can't breathe."

"Did I ever tell you the story about the hamster my sister Anna squashed between the bed and the wall?"

"On purpose?" Finn asks.

"I'm not sure," I say. "It's possible. Anna could be hard to read. But I don't think she meant to kill it."

"Well, either she did or she didn't," Jack says.

"Right. Lights out." I take the book from Maddy. "*Johnny Crow* will still be here tomorrow." I scoop Finn up off Maddy's bed, tuck him under his covers, and kiss him all over his beautiful sweet face until he pushes me away.

Maddy puts her arms up for a final hug. "Me," she says.

I hold her tight in my arms. "You didn't brush your teeth. Your breath smells like creamed corn."

"I did," she says, but we both know she's not telling the truth. "I did!" she says again.

"Corn is delicious," I whisper in her ear, and she smiles.

"Okay, fine. I didn't. But I'll brush double in the morning."

"I'm coming for you next," I say to Jack.

"Whatever," he says, but he's smiling.

11:00 P.M.

Mum is sitting on the porch sofa in the dark.

"You're still up," I say.

"All those peanuts I ate at Dixon's are repeating on me."

"I'm getting a glass of wine. Do you want anything?"

"I'm headed for bed in a minute. There's an open rosé."

I pour myself a glass of wine and sit down beside her. "I'm exhausted."

"I don't know how you do it. All these people you take care of."

"My husband and children?" I laugh.

"You coddle them far too much. I barely paid attention to you and Anna, and look how well you turned out."

In a way, her blindness—her total lack of self-examination—is a gift.

"They can't even put their own dishes in the sink. I barely survived while you and Peter were in Memphis. Though Finn *did* give me a nice foot rub."

"You asked Finn to rub your feet?"

"His hands seem a bit small for his age."

I shake my head in despair. My mother is who she is. But a piece of her has been in the wrong place for far too long and I have to set it right.

"You know how I was trying to tell you this afternoon? About Leo?"

My mother yawns. "You told me. He went back to his first wife, God help her. I should have written to her—told her what he did to you."

"Mum." My heart starts beating so fast I can see its tremoring on the surface of my chest. "It wasn't Leo."

"What wasn't?"

"It wasn't Leo," I say again, my voice barely more than a whisper. "It happened, but it wasn't Leo."

She looks utterly confused. I watch her puzzling out what I've said, putting the pieces together. I recognize the exact second it comes clear to her: a twitch, an imperceptible shift, the nervous dilating of pupils.

"Conrad?" she says at last.

"Yes."

"All of it?"

"Yes."

"Not Leo."

"Not Leo. It was Conrad. Conrad raped me."

For a long time, my mother says nothing. In the darkness, I feel her energy slipping, dimming. She sighs, a heaviness upon her.

"I'm sorry I let you blame Leo."

"Leo left me. Our baby died."

I can see from her face that she is preparing for the worst as she asks me the next question.

"And Conrad drowning?"

"The boom hit him. He fell in."

Her look of relief is palpable, and I so wish I could leave it there.

"But we both knew he wasn't a strong swimmer. We didn't throw him the life preserver."

"We . . ." There's a flicker of confusion. "Of course, Jonas was with you. I'd forgotten."

"He knew everything," I say. "He's the only one."

She nods. "You two were inseparable. He had such a crush on you back then. I think you broke his heart when you married Peter."

"I did."

An image of Jonas comes to me. Not the man I have loved, eaten, wanted, ached for today, but a small, green-eyed, dark-haired boy, lying beside me in the woods on a bed of velvet moss. I do not know him yet. But we are there together, lying by the spring, two strangers with one heart.

"I loved him, too."

My mother is not one for warmth, but she puts her arms around me, cradles my head against her neck, strokes my hair the way she did when I was a little girl. I feel a thousand years of bile and bitter and silt seeping out of my veins, my muscles and tendons, the darkest places, pouring into the pocket of her lap.

"I'm sorry, Mum. I meant to be good."

"No," she says. "I'm the one who let Conrad in the door." She pushes herself up off the sofa with a heavy creak. "My bones are not what they once were. I'm going to find a Maalox and hit the hay."

On her way past the big picnic table she clears the children's ice cream bowls, takes them inside to the sink, spoons clinking. "These can wait until morning."

She pauses at the screen door, an odd expression on her face, as if she's tasting something, digesting it, trying to decide whether or not it's good. When at last she speaks, her voice is decisive, the way it's always been when she's given me serious advice.

"There are some swims you *do* regret, Eleanor. The problem is, you never know until you take them. Don't stay up too late. And remember to close your skylight. They say we may get two inches of rain."

I wait until I hear her cabin door click shut before following her down the path. There's a ring around the moon. The rains we hoped for are finally coming. I can feel it in the brooding air, the impatient sky. Outside Anna's and my old cabin, where my children sleep, I pause. All their lights are off—even the dim glow of Jack's computer. I listen to the silence, imagine I can hear their soft, safe breathing. No demons, no monsters. If I could protect them from every terror, every loss, every heartbreak, I would.

A swath of moonlight stretches toward me from the center of the pond, widening as it approaches. I push my way through the bushes to the water's edge. The pond is low. In the wet, sandy shoreline, raccoons have left a trail of sharp footprints. I take off all my clothes, hang my dress over a tree branch, and wade naked into the silk water, the pond obsidian clear, the croaking of bullfrogs, the whisper of moths. I can feel the molecules Jonas has left behind him all around me in the water. I cup my hands in the pond, put them to my mouth, and drink him. In the distance, lightning fractures the sky.

I stop on the path outside our cabin, count the seconds, listen for the faraway rumble of thunder, watch as the acid strobe fades away, watch as darkness takes itself back. My body feels like a sigh—relief and regret. But for which swim? I climb the steps of our cabin, knowing the answer. For either. For both.

Peter is still in his deep, satisfied sleep. I unhook the skylight, lower it softly into place. I climb into our bed beside him, spoon him, latch on to him the familiar warmth of his body, the comfort of his calming breath—and wait for the storm to make its way inland from the sea.

4:00 A.M.

At four in the morning, when the winds come up, it's the cabin door rattling against its hinges that startles me awake. Outside, pine trees are bent sideways, limbs howling in rage. I climb out of bed and go to the door. A beach towel has flown off the laundry line and landed on the roof of my mother's cabin. Birds tumble through the stormy sky like fall leaves wheeling through the air, helpless in the wind, the relentless, circular current. Wrens and finches, skylarks—airborne, but not in flight. I stare out into the dreamlike predawn light. A few inches beyond the screen, a ruby-throated hummingbird is thrumming, fighting to hold its ground in the air, trilling against the tide, its iridescent wings beating invisibly fast, a flash of gemstone in the gray sky. It is flying backward. Not pushed by the wind, but deliberate, frantic with purpose, pressing for shelter in a thicket of white-blooming clethra outside our cabin. Its wings, attached with minuscule wrists, make figure eights—infinity symbols.

I call over to Peter. "Wake up."

He stirs, but doesn't wake.

"Peter," I say, louder this time. "Wake up. I want you to see this." But he is dead to the world.

I go over to his side of the bed, nudge him.

"What?" he says, voice groggy with sleep. "Jesus. What time is it?"

"I don't know. Early. But wake up. You have to see this. It's insane out there—like some sort of bird maelstrom."

"It's the middle of the night."

"I think we might be in the eye of a hurricane."

"There wouldn't be all this wind—only dead air. It's just a big storm coming. Nothing to worry about. Now fuck off and let me sleep," he grumbles sweetly.

A few years after Maddy and Finn were born, long after our lives had meshed into a different song, Jonas and I were walking in the woods one afternoon and passed an oak tree entwined in honeysuckle. There were what seemed like a hundred hummingbirds drinking flower nectar with their needle-beaks.

"Hummingbirds are the only birds that can fly backward," Jonas said. "It's one of those facts that's always astonished me. They can fly backward and forward at equal speed. Thirty miles an hour."

"If I could fly backward, I would," I said. To the safety of branches, to the time when my heart raced for him like a hummingbird's, 1,200 beats per minute.

And he said, as he always did, "I know."

6:30 A.M.

When I wake again, the heavy rains have passed. Water has pooled on the floorboards next to our bed, soaking the stack of books I keep planning to read. Peter is dreaming. I can tell by the way his eyelids twitch, by the length of his rough-saw breaths. I brush the hair off his forehead, kiss his cheek, his brow.

He stirs, shifts, his eyes crack open.

"Hey," I whisper. "You're here," and cover his face in butterfly kisses.

"Morning, baby," he says, swatting me away. "You going for your swim?"

"Why don't you come with me? The pond will be warm after the rain." I hold my breath, wait. *Come with me. End this.*

He rolls over, his back to me. "I promised Jack I'd take him into town at nine. Wake me up if I oversleep."

I press my hand flat against the curve of his shoulder, splay my fingers wide. I like the way his freckles look inside the Vs my fingers make, like constellations of stars. I trace a heart with the tip of my finger across the wide plane of his back.

"I love you, too," he mumbles from the tangle of sheets.

The early morning air is clammy. I wrap my mother's old lavender bathrobe tight around me, stand in the doorway looking out. The surface of the pond is motionless, sheet glass, as if the storm never happened, the water lilies shuttered in their circadian sleep. A stillness, the world bathed in a blush of watermelon-pink. On the steps of our cabin I spy a single iridescent feather. I pick it up. Twirl it in my fingers by its sharp bony stem. Across the pond a figure stands. Waiting. Hoping. I can just make out his blue shirt.

The cabin step sags beneath me with a sigh, then springs back with a quiet thwang I've heard a thousand times before. This place—every wheeze, every grunt—is in my bones. The soft crunch of pine needles under my bare feet, the waft of minnows, the musk-fishy smell of wet sand and pond water. This house, built out of paper—tiny bits of shredded cardboard pressed together into something strong enough to withstand time, the difficult, lonely winters; always threatening to fall into ruin, yet still standing, year after year, when we return. This house, this place, knows all my secrets. I am in its bones, too.

I close my eyes and breathe in the everything-ness of it all. Jonas. Peter. Me. What it all could have been. What it could be. I take off my wedding ring, hold it in the palm of my hand, considering it, feeling the weight of it—its worn, eternal shape, its gold-ness. I squeeze it tight against my life line one final time before leaving it behind me on the top step and heading down the path to take my swim.

On the far side of the pond, an egg-yolk sun rises out of the dense tree line like a hot air balloon, slow, graceful. It hovers, suspended for a moment, before breaking free of its tethers—the break of dawn. In that instant, the smallest breeze shirrs the water, waking the pond for another day.

ACKNOWLEDGMENTS

When I was in my teens and first attempting to write fiction, my grandfather Malcolm Cowley gave me a piece of advice that I have carried with me: the only thing you need to know, he said, is that every good story must have a beginning, a middle, and an end, with the end foreshadowed in the beginning.

It took me a lifetime to get there, but I have followed his advice to a T.

There are so many people I am grateful to for pushing, shoving, supporting, and propping me up on this journey—most especially my extraordinary mother, Blair Resika, who taught me how to set a table and raised us in uncompromising beauty. My beloved sisters, Lizzie and Sonia—you are my rocks and my soul.

My father, Robert Cowley, editor and historian extraordinaire, told me when I was eleven years old that the best writing is always the shortest distance between two points. I thank him for that, but even more so for giving me the dazzling whirlwinds that are my younger sisters, Olivia and Savannah.

Thank you to my grandfather, Jack Phillips, for giving us the landscape. My wonderful stepfather, Paul Resika, for immortalizing it. My godmother, Florence Phillips, for a magical can of corn that changed the course of a little girl's life.

Boundless thanks to my brilliant, thought-provoking editor, Sarah McGrath, whose keen eye never misses. Huge thanks, too, to the entire Riverhead team, and to the Valkyries of Viking, Venetia Butterfield and Mary Mount.

Thank you, Anna Stein, my gorgeous, kick-ass agent, for making my dreams come true, and for choosing me. I am beyond lucky to have Will Watkins at ICM, Susan Armstrong at C&W, Claire Nozieres at Curtis Brown, and Jason Hendler at HJTH on my team.

Mark Sarvas. Mentor and friend for life. You held me steady every step of the way. Words will never be enough, but I won't stop trying. Thank you, Adam Cushman, for believing in this book before I even knew it was a book. Jack Grapes, for teaching me that fiction is poetry. Thank you to all the writers in the *Novel Writers Group* who workshopped *The Paper Palace* with me. Among them, Andrea Custer, Samuel Stackhouse, Ondrea Harr, Victoria Pynchon, Catherine Ellsworth, and Joel Villaseñor, a wordsmith extraordinaire, who caught the Metrecal. My compadres at PEN America. My fellow board members at the Fine Arts Work Center.

Stepha, for anything and everything. Faran, for the trees. Estelle, for her wisdom and heart. Jimmy, for bringing the light. Tanya, for keeping it lit. Nick, for the joy you brought me from Day One. Christina and Olivia, for keeping my world spinning on its axis. Lily and Nell, for making sure it can still spin out of control. August, whose fine, strong drumbeat we all hope to follow. Lasher, Calder, and Sebastian— tiny scrumptious beings. And Georgia, oh Georgia, my woodland sprite, for inspiring the dreaminess.

I was raised in a world of strong women with strong voices and constant hearts. I thank each and every one of you for your remarkable friendship. It has been the greatest blessing. Thank you, Margot, Angela, Laura, Nonny, Tory, Busby—my Girls for life; Charlotte, who read it first and said "yes";

Nina, who sat beside me day after day, both of us typing away; Kate, for your boundless optimism; Nicky and Louise for your sweet support; Laura B., Evgenia, Katie, and Elizabeth—whip-smart friends and early readers; Libby, who made me get off my bum and finish the damn thing; Zoe, Lucy, and Emily; the magnificent women in my family—Antonia, Susannah, Hayden, Saskia, Cosima, Rachel, Frankie, Lula, Lotte, Grace, Louisa, Millie. Each of you shapes the path.

My sons, Lukas and Felix—I love you to the moon. But you know that.

Lastly, and above all, thank you, Bruno, for the roads we walked together, and for the amazing journey.